The Baraboo Guards

A Novel of the American Civil War

John K. Driscoll

FIRESIDE FICTION
2006

FIRESIDE FICTION
AN IMPRINT OF HERITAGE BOOKS, INC.

Books, CDs, and more—Worldwide

For our listing of thousands of titles see our website
at
www.HeritageBooks.com

Published 2006 by
HERITAGE BOOKS, INC.
Publishing Division
65 East Main Street
Westminster, Maryland 21157-5026

International Standard Book Number: 978-0-7884-4122-1

THE BARABOO GUARDS

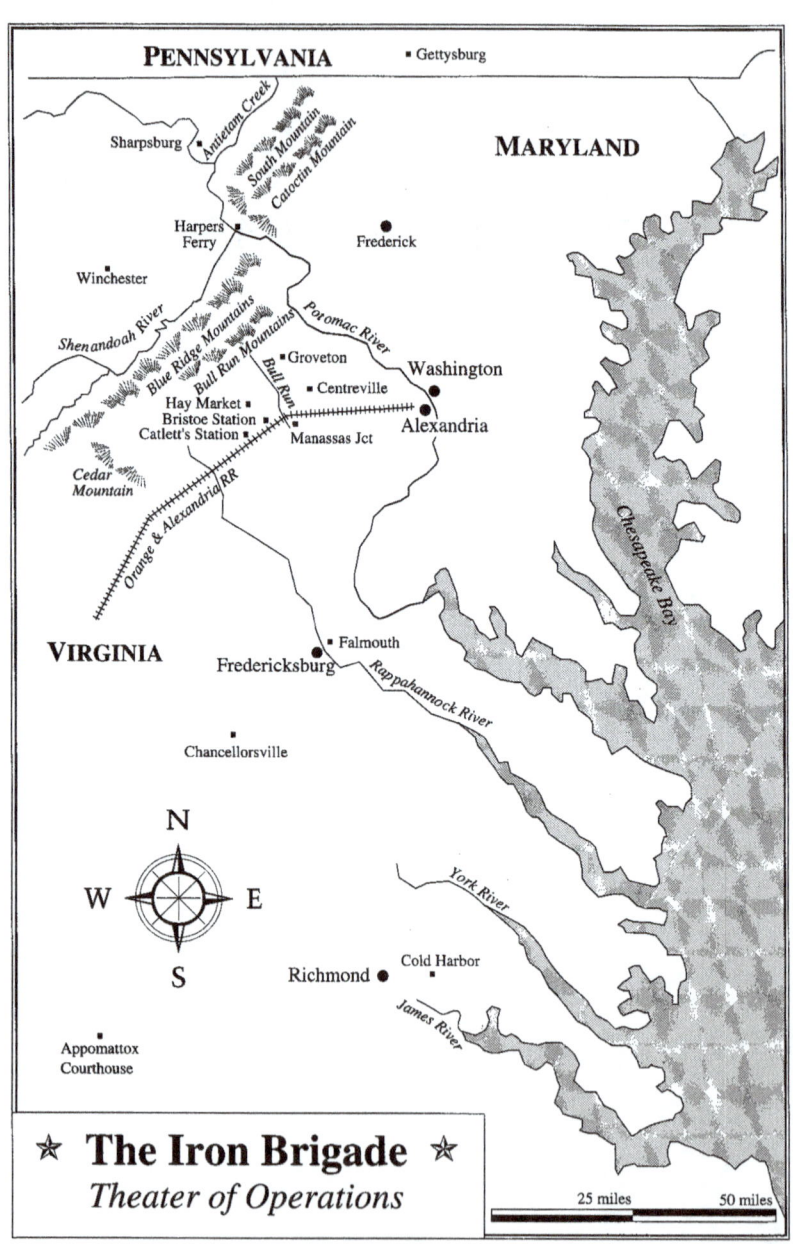

PENNSYLVANIA   ▪ Gettysburg

Sharpsburg ▪   *Antietam Creek*   *South Mountain*   *Catoctin Mountain*   MARYLAND

Harpers ▪   Frederick ●
Ferry

▪ Winchester

Shenandoah River   *Blue Ridge Mountains*   *Bull Run Mountains*   *Potomac River*   ▪ Groveton

▪ Centreville   Washington ●

Hay Market ▪
Bristoe Station ▪   Alexandria ●
Catlett's Station ▪   ▪ Manassas Jct

Cedar Mountain

Orange & Alexandria RR

VIRGINIA   ▪ Falmouth
Fredericksburg ▪   *Rappahannock River*

▪ Chancellorsville

N
W — E
S

Chesapeake Bay

York River

Cold Harbor ▪
Richmond ●

James River

▪ Appomattox
Courthouse

☆ The Iron Brigade ☆
Theater of Operations

25 miles   50 miles

1

I n the basement of the Sauk County Courthouse, the door to the jailer's office stood open. The dim glow from an oil lamp there provided a faint light in the bitterly cold cells.

In one of the barred cages the little man who called himself Murphy wrapped a wool blanket around his shoulders. His narrow face, pointed nose, and small green eyes gave him the visage of a rat. Stringy, dusty brown hair tinged with gray fell over his jacket collar. His clothing was too large for his frame and his boots were too big for his feet.

The Irishman cradled a bottle of local brandy between his knees, a bottle bought after lengthy negotiations and a bribe that earned for the jailer a tidy profit. Murphy puffed on a briar pipe and cursed his evil luck.

The bleeding folly of it! To be stealing a matched team of bay horses and then be caught trying to sell them off in the same county! Now, he asked himself, had not that been a foolish thing for an experienced trader in horse-flesh to be doing?

Ah, he conceded, he'd deserved what had come upon him. There was naught to be gained by complaining about it when he was more than halfway through his sentence. The Sauk County jail was dry and life was comfortable enough for a man in his condition. There was food every day. Were it not for the other matter, he considered, he'd be finding contentment in the place for the rest of his term, harsh though he thought the sentence to be. It was the rotting injustice of the other matter that had him sitting and cursing in the cold darkness of the cell. It could only be the working of that evil luck which followed him through life. It was enough to bring the haunts to the soul of a lonely man.

Murphy dreaded the haunts, the dark moods and the feelings of loss and loneliness, of wrong and hopelessness and guilt. They'd pursued his soul since he'd run off, leaving his widowed mother and the brood in County Tyrone, back these forty years.

He shifted his backside on the straw mattress of the cot and took a pull on the bottle. He'd never had the good fortune of other men, always having to do more in the struggle to keep body and soul together.

Murphy had shaken the dirt of Ireland from his bare feet on the wooden deck of an English man-o'-war. He'd determined to seek his fortune upon the sea but he'd not found it there. What that rough crew taught an Irish lad of twelve in the dark corners of the 'tween decks were not attributes that lad would be using in the pursuit of his fortune. He'd jumped ship in Halifax and wandered the coasts of Canada and New England, using his wits and learning life's ways. His fortune eluded him but his basic wants were filled. The saints who set things so had not given him the body nor the grace and style to help in the search for his fortune. He'd made do with quick hands, fast feet, hard muscles and bones that took and gave back the batterings that came his way.

He'd enlisted into the American army in the late 'Forties and marched into Mexico. He still carried in his memory visions of warm climates, high mountains, and dark-skinned lovelies who'd overlook his runtiness for a few coins.

After the army, Murphy worked the river ports along the Mississippi doing some stevedoring, a little pimping, some theft. He'd traveled the towns along the Ohio doing the same, heading eastward. Taking his knocks, keeping one step ahead of the devil but a league behind his fortune, he'd come to the city of Boston in Massachusetts. He'd married into the Irish population there, a large woman with a past that would stand no looking into. There was work, he being one of her family, a bit of political running to be done, a beating to be given, a coffin to be borne.

It had been such that brought him to his downfall. They'd given him a package to carry across the city to a committee chairman and hadn't it it tinkled and clinked with the exciting sound of heavy coin? He'd helped himself to a mere handful, not anywhere enough to be missed from the whole.

He didn't remember her brothers catching him. He did remember waking to the agony of the beating they'd given him and to the pitch and roll of a wooden deck. Hadn't they gone and abused him sorely for his theft and then, as he lay unconsious, signed him into the Corps of Marines, and for the full term of five years! Himself, who'd done time before the mast in one navy and in the ranks of another army, and into the Corps of Marines which was the worse of both bad worlds!

Ah, the little man reminisced, hadn't he been the one to adjust to the flow, once he'd seen there was nothing else to do? With the bleeding frigate outward bound on a two-year cruise, what had there been for a soul to do but adjust? He'd scrubbed his white cross-belts and polished his brass buttons. He'd brushed his blue uniform and burnished his musket. He'd stood his watches and stayed out of harm's way for the whole of the cruise.

It was when the frigate returned, coming into the navy yard at Norfolk, that his evil luck turned upon him again. The second day in port, while slipping below to stow a couple of bottles into a hidden corner, against the time to come at sea when a man would be wanting a drop from his own supply, he'd come upon them. In a dark corner of the cargo hold he found Mister Haynes, the midshipman newly assigned to the frigate, and Jeremy, the pretty ship's boy, and weren't the two of them grunting and grinning and straining and embracing, smiling and whispering and enjoying pleasures God never had in mind when He put men together at the start.

Not one to intrude where he wasn't wanted, Murphy tried to back away and out of sight. Jeremy saw him and squealed his alarm, for what the two were doing was sure to bring hanging for the boy and disgrace for the midshipman. Mister Haynes snatched out his dirk and, in his panic, managed to slash the throat of the boy. He'd then pointed his blade into Murphy's face, who was only wanting to be far from where he was and what he was seeing.

Murphy never clearly remembered what followed. He did remember hiding the two bodies under rolls of sail canvas after taking forty dollars from the midshipman's purse. In darkness topside he slipped over the rail and made a hasty farewell to the Corps of Marines. In months, he was in the states to the northwest trading horses when he could buy them, stealing them when he had the chance, and doing well.

Ah, the little man sighed. Just when he'd thought he'd finally found the trail to his fortune, hadn't this other thing happened? There was naught of justice in that, for hadn't the sheriff of Sauk County come and announced he would be taking Murphy along with the company of volunteers that was forming and preparing to march off to the war that was sweeping onto the land!

There was no fear of war in the turmoil that tortured the Irishman's soul this dark, cold evening. He'd seen war for what it was. It was the dread, in the course of that war, of meeting up with the white cross-belts and blue frock coats and red-topped shakoes of the Corps of Marines. There'd be no mercy for himself, should those jollies get their hard hands on his humble person.

Mercy? There'd be a flogging on his naked back for robbing the midshipman's purse. There'd be a branding with a hot iron on the cheek of his arse for deserting. There'd be a hanging by the neck until dead for the two killings, though he'd done but one of them. That much he could count on, should he find himself in the company of the Corps of Marines for any time. And, he thought, weren't those all things of no use to a man who wanted only to be finding his fortune?

Murphy took a long pull on the bottle of brandy. There was naught to be gained by struggling against the goad. He'd wait his time. He'd take it when it came. One night on sentry duty, alone in the darkness, and it would be off and away for the California coasts for this one.

And, he cautioned himself, taking a puff on his briar pipe, there was naught to be gained by any reference to his past military experiences, interesting though he thought them to have been.

Murphy took a pull on the bottle and a puff on his pipe. Tum-tiddley-tum-tee-day, he crooned silently. Tum-tum-tiddley-tum-tee-day.

2

That evening, the first Friday in May, Elsasser's Tavern was crowded with men from Baraboo and the settlements out in Sauk County. Oil lamps guttered and smoked in glass chimneys. Two iron stoves glowed. Tobacco fumes mixed with the odors of many men in winter clothing.

Carl Elsasser tended behind the oak planks of his bar, a tall man, broad at the shoulders, grim, going bald, his eyes set close over the bridge of a large nose. He tapped beer into schooners from kegs set behind the bar and poured brandy from bottles into glasses he took from a pan on the back shelf. He worked steadily, saying little. The evening would be profitable. Twice he'd emptied the wooden cash box under the bar and he'd empty it again as his customers bought drinks for themselves and for each other.

Carl knew the men in his place. He'd known many of them for years. They were typical men of Sauk County, farmers and farmhands, tanners and loggers and sawyers, draymen and clerks and mechanics. Most were young, within a year or two of their twentieth birthdays. Few were married and few were educated beyond simple reading, writing and ciphering. They mixed and moved and drank, talking, greeting relatives and friends they hadn't seen since Wisconsin's winter swept down from the north, freezing the rivers and blocking the roads, isolating people in the villages, at the settlements, on the farms.

The volunteers among Carl's patrons, the Baraboo Guards as they'd named themselves, would muster on the lawn of the courthouse at noon the following day. Contingents of families and neighbors would gather to witness the doings. After the speeches were spoken, Captain Nathaniel Bachmann's company of volunteers would leave Baraboo for the state capitol at Madison, forty miles to the southeast.

Carl was a well-read man. He studied the Milwaukee and Madison newspapers that were delivered to his tavern every week. He was aware of the issues of the times.

When South Carolina state batteries fired on the Federal fort in the harbor at Charleston four weeks earlier, Carl hadn't joined in the cry of patriotism or the clamor for revenge that swept through Sauk County, through Wisconsin, through the states of the North. He'd been appalled when President Lincoln called on the governors of the loyal states for seventy-five thousand volunteers to put down the southern rebellion. Carl thought Lincoln was reacting to an incident, taking his nation into civil war in the cause of partisan politics. He thought Wisconsin's governor, Alexander Randall, was seeking political gain by authorizing citizens like Nathaniel Bachmann to organize and enlist volunteer companies from the counties in the state. He thought the men of the Baraboo Guards who talked and laughed and bought his brandy and beer this night were wrong to follow the likes of Nathaniel Bachmann off to war.

The grim tavern keeper doubted that many of his patrons were concerned or knowledgeable about national issues. The secession of the Southern states and the rending of the Federal Union might be matters for political speeches and editorial bombast but, Carl felt, they were not matters for which Wisconsin farmers should march off to war. Even, he considered, the underlying issue of human slavery was not justification for a farmhand from Sauk County who had never seen a black man to go rushing away from hearth and homestead to answer the roll of an army drum.

Carl thought that the volunteers were interested more in adventure then in the preservation of Abraham Lincoln's Union. They were attracted by the promise of excitement and travel and the escape from plowing furrows in wheat fields. He considered them fools for thinking their government would keep them only the ninety days for which they had signed on. Carl poured glasses of brandy for two farmhands who had walked fifteen miles from Reedsburg to be with their comrades in the Baraboo Guards this night. He worked steadily behind his bar, keeping his own counsel, saying little.

Adolph Zimmerman, Sauk County's sheriff, strode into the tavern. Adolph, a heavy man in his late thirties, wore a brown woolen jacket with the county's six-pointed star of office pinned to its breast. With him was Judge Blane's law clerk, James Peck, a lean man in his early twenties.

Carl returned the sheriff's inquiring glance with a short nod. In spite of the drinking, the men were behaving reasonably well. Carl kept an orderly place. He was big enough to throw any drunken rowdy into the street and he was known to have done it.

Satisfied that the peace was being kept in this part of Sauk County, Adolph led James to the corner where the bar met the wall. Men moved to make room for the sheriff and the law clerk. Carl served Adolph a schooner of beer. James hesitated, then pointed to a glass. The tavern keeper poured brandy. He stood, waiting.

"Pay the man," Adolph urged, drinking from the schooner.

James put a ten dollar bank note on the bar. "Captain Bachmann is buying drinks tonight for the men of the Baraboo Guards, as far as ten dollars goes," he told Carl. Adolph quickly drained his schooner and set it on the bar. "Here, Carl! Bring me a schooner of Nate Bachmann's beer!"

The men in Elsasser's Tavern roared their approval when they learned of their captain's generosity. Carl shouted for his wife and son to come from the back room to help with the rush of orders for free drinks.

Ethan Evans stepped into the tavern. He loosened his muffler and tucked his gloves into the pockets of his tailored coat, nodding to Adolph and James as he passed them. Ethan, a stocky man with a dark beard and sad eyes, was Baraboo's leading merchant, the owner of a large dry goods store on the square. He also owned the building Elsasser's Tavern occupied. Ethan was dressed in a dark suit under his heavy coat. He wore a low-crowned hat set squarely on his head. He moved through the crowd, nodding when greeted. At the bar, he put his hands on the planks and waited patiently as Carl worked his way to where he stood.

The tavern keeper was surprised to see him. "'Evening, Ethan," he said, wiping the bar with his towel.

"'Evening, Carl," Ethan murmured.

"You here for the rent?" Carl wondered.

Ethan shook his head. Standing shorter than the tavern keeper, the merchant's eyes were hidden under the brim of his hat. "I came to have a drink."

Carl raised an eyebrow. "You don't drink. You haven't for three, maybe four years."

"I'd like to have a drink, Carl," Ethan said. "Whiskey."

Carl shrugged. It wasn't his concern if the merchant wanted to start drinking. He reached under the bar and brought up a dusty bottle. Carl's customers usually drank beer or brandy, seldom whiskey. The tavern keeper wiped the bottle with his towel and pulled its cork. He took a glass from the back shelf and poured it half full. He raised the bottle, questioning.

"You might want to leave it," Ethan suggested.

Carl set the bottle next to the glass on the bar.

Ethan reached into his pocket and brought out coins in the palm of his hand. "Still five cents the drink?"

"Still five cents," Carl said, watching the merchant. "Listen, Ethan," he offered, "Nathaniel Bachmann is buying drinks for the boys tonight. He can pay for yours."

"I'll pay." Ethan placed coins on the bar. He took the glass and swirled liquor around its sides. He raised the glass and sipped. He swallowed, grimaced, shook slightly. "Ah," he sighed, "that's good whiskey."

Carl nodded.

"Gus is here?" the merchant asked.

Carl pointed with his chin to where Gus Gaard sat at a table with his circle of cronies. "Since noon."

"Any trouble?" Ethan asked, swirling liquor inside his glass.

"Not yet," Carl said. He didn't understand the relationship between the brothers-in-law. Ethan Evans was a successful merchant, honest, established, a man of substance. He'd married well. His wife, Lily Gaard Evans, was the daughter of the Milwaukee merchant, Amos Augustus Gaard. Ethan brought his bride to Baraboo in 1857. The merchant worked hard at his business and prospered. His wife became active in the village library society, the Methodist church choir, and several charities.

Prior to his marriage, Carl knew, Ethan had taken a drink or two with the boys. After his marriage, Ethan changed, swore off liquor, joined the temperance society. He kept to himself, to his business. He matured, became dignified, became sad.

Sixty days after Ethan installed himself and his bride in the house on Oak Street, Gus Gaard, Lily's younger brother, arrived in Baraboo, exiled from his father's home in Milwaukee for some series of sins. Gus took to Baraboo, to the despair of the decent citizens of Sauk County. He lived in the house on Oak Street with Ethan and Lily when his adventures brought him home. He ran a wagon circuit for Ethan to the settlements and farms north and west of Baraboo, which gave Gus a claim to employment although he had access to unlimited spending money from his father's account in a Milwaukee bank. Every boy in Baraboo knew it was worth ten cents to run to the house on Oak Street to tell Ethan that Gus was drunk in some tavern.

Carl returned to his work behind the bar, filling schooners with beer and glasses with brandy. He kept a running tally in his head of how much of Nathaniel Bachmann's ten dollars remained. He'd make money on the balance. The Baraboo Guards couldn't drink up what was left of the sum in the few hours before closing time.

"Is our captain going to be here with the men the night before we leave town?" the sheriff asked the law clerk.

"Captain Bachmann is in Madison on business for the governor," James told Adolph. "He'll be here for the muster tomorrow."

"He damned well better be here! Lots of people are going to be coming to see the likes of Nate Bachmann! They're not coming to see the likes of me and you!"

"He'll be here!" James argued. "Sheriff, why don't you like the man? We're going to be his lieutenants. We have to try to help him."

"He'll earn his way to sainthood before I kneel at the shrine of Nate Bachmann!" Adolph declared.

"If that's how you feel," James asked, "why did you agree to go with him?"

Adolph shrugged. "He was the one who came through with the governor's warrant to enlist Sauk County's company of volunteers. Hell, we'd have gone with anyone. Here, Carl! I need another beer!"

"Do you know Captain Bachmann well?" James asked.

Adolph shook his head. "Hardly know the man at all. He's not from around here. Somewhere down in Illinois, I've heard. Graduated from West Point. Served in the war with Mexico and against the Indians out West. Been spending most of his time lately lobbying the governor with the people who want to build the railroad. He might know something that'll be of use to me and you."

"He appointed me first lieutenant of the company," James said, carefully, concerned that this might be a sore point to the lawman. "Why did you agree to be the second lieutenant? You know more about all of this than I do."

"I told him I didn't want your job when he offered it. You can play soldier to Nate Bachmann in front of me. I come with the boys from Sauk County. That's how I fit into this."

James blushed. He hadn't known about that earlier offer. "Captain Bachmann made a mistake when he appointed me his first lieutenant," he said. "I don't know anything about being an army officer."

Adolph looked at the law clerk. "Can't be much to it," the heavy man said. "No soldier I met ever showed me any great amount of smarts. Why did you agree to go with him?"

James shrugged. "Judge Blane told me to help Captain Bachmann recruit the company. I set up meetings around the county for him and signed on men as they enlisted. At the meeting in Delton, he introduced me as the company's first lieutenant. The men seemed to look up to me after that. I liked it. I guess it just happened."

Adolph grunted. "Sounds like Nate Bachmann made it just happen. Tell me, have you signed up all the men we need?"

"Eighty-eight have signed up," James answered, touching the leather portfolio in which he carried the company's enlistment records. "We still have eight vacancies. I'm sure more men will sign up when Captain Bachmann speaks tomorrow at the muster."

"You save me one place," Adolph said, drinking from his schooner. "I've got a patriot over in the jail who'll be coming along with us."

"A prisoner?

"Horse thief. An Irishman, doing his time. I won't leave him behind while me and you and most of the able-bodied men of Sauk County march off to war behind Nate Bachmann."

James frowned. "Will Captain Bachmann agree to a prisoner enlisting in the company?

"There's no need for Nate Bachmann to concern himself about this one man!" Adolph stated, his voice rising. "We'll keep this matter to ourselves."

James didn't like the idea of being part of a conspiracy against their commanding officer. To change the subject, he asked, "Did the tailor deliver your uniform this afternoon?"

"He did," Adolph growled, "with a bill for me to pay!"

"Officers have to buy our uniforms. I read that somewhere."

"Shouldn't cost a man money to go to war," the lawman grumbled.

"We're to wear the uniforms to the muster tomorrow. Captain Bachmann wants us to do that, to inspire the men."

"The hell with what he wants!"

James sipped slowly at his glass of brandy. He knew better than to argue when Adolph Zimmerman had set a thing in his mind.

Carl was bothered by the sight of Ethan Evans standing and drinking at his bar on this of all nights. The bother gave rise to an annoying question in his mind that grew, as he worked and worried at it, into a supposition. Ignoring orders for drinks, Carl strode the length of his bar and stood across from the merchant. "You signed on to go with Bachmann!" he accused.

Ethan didn't raise his head to meet the tavern keeper's eyes. He nodded.

"My God," Carl groaned.

The merchant stood silently, staring into his glass of whiskey.

"That's not like you, Ethan," Carl said. "To do a thing like that."

"Not like me," the merchant agreed quietly.

"Hell!" the tavern keeper cried, waving his towel toward the men who lined his bar. "The likes of these can go and be damned! They just want to get away from the fields for the summer! But Ethan, you're a man with position! You've a business! A wife! Why would you do this?"

Ethan shook his head slowly. He kept his eyes down on the glass of whiskey.

Carl felt stunned. He liked the stocky merchant. He respected the man. He nodded his head sorrowfully, staring at Ethan. "You must have your reasons."

Ethan didn't respond.

"You can back out," Carl encouraged. "You haven't given your oath. Tell Bachmann you've had to change your mind. Tell him your business won't let you be away for ninety days. Tell him your wife doesn't want you to go. This isn't for you to do."

The merchant shook his head.

Carl felt desperate, angry. "Are you going as one of Bachmann's officers?"

Again, the merchant shook his head.

"You're going to tote a musket and tramp in the ranks with the likes of these?" Carl challenged, jerking his head at the men who lined his bar.

Ethan nodded.

Carl sagged. He didn't know why he felt strongly about what Ethan did with his life. The tavern keeper pointed a finger forward and touched the merchant's coins on the bar. He pushed them toward Ethan. "Your captain's buying the drinks for his men," Carl said. "You drink on him tonight."

Ethan flinched. He finished the whiskey in his glass and poured more from the bottle.

Carl busied himself with orders called across his bar. The anger he felt at what Ethan had done changed as he worked. In the tavern keeper's mind was the beginning of something that he didn't try to define but that seemed to include portions of guilt and fear.

James sipped lightly at his glass of brandy. He wasn't one to drink much. "You know the men, Sheriff," he said to make conversation. "You told me once there were good ones and bad ones among them. How will I know who are which?"

"Something you've got to learn!" the lawman snorted. "I can't line them up and put tags on them for you."

"I guess not," James admitted, regretting having asked.

"I'll tell you one man we'll be able to count on," Adolph continued. "Ethan Evans, down the bar."

"I know Ethan."

"He could have been one of the officers. Wouldn't let Nate Bachmann appoint him. Could have been one of the sergeants or corporals, for that matter. Wouldn't let the men elect him. Still, he better stay on his toes!"

"Why is that?"

"Why? That damned brother-in-law of his is why! Gus Gaard, the big blond over there at that table of drunks. Gus isn't going to be one of the good ones, I can tell you! That man lives for fighting, fornicating and mischief. He must service half the widows and most of the wayward wives in Sauk County. He'll be trouble and that gang of his isn't going to be worth much either. Ah, hell, like I said, there're good ones and there're other ones.

Most of the good ones aren't here tonight. They're at home where they ought to be the night before we leave town."

"What about your prisoner?" James asked. "Will he be a problem?"

"You leave that man to me!" the sheriff cautioned. "Here, Carl! I need another schooner of Nate Bachmann's beer!"

Gus Gaard pushed himself to his feet. The husky blond had tired of his companions who listened and laughed as long as he paid for their drinks. Nathaniel Bachmann's free drinks interfered with Gus's ability to hold their interest and they'd begun wandering off into the crowd. Gus glanced along the bar. Grinning, he lurched drunkenly through the crowd toward Ethan. He threw a heavy arm across the merchant's shoulders. "Well, hell!" he shouted into his brother-in-law's face. "Look who threw off the traces and took himself out for a night on the town!"

Ethan grimaced at Gus' brandy-sour breath. He sipped whiskey, his head down.

"Elsasser!" Gus called, spit flying from his lips. "A glass! I intend to join my sober-sided brother-in-law as he falls off the temperance wagon!"

Carl glanced at Ethan. The merchant nodded. Carl slid a clean glass several yards along the bar. Gus grabbed it and sloshed whiskey from Ethan's bottle into the glass, spilling liquor onto the bar. "Hey!" he shouted, grinning at the men along the bar who watched him. "The Baraboo Guards!" he toasted.

Few of the men responded.

"Go to hell!" Gus bellowed at them, drinking what was in his glass and refilling, spilling more onto the bar. "God damn, Ethan!" he sang out. "Great to have you along! We got great times coming. Do us both a lot of good to get away from Baraboo for the summer."

Ethan drank silently.

"Do you good, too, my brother-in-law," Gus confided, speaking close to Ethan, slurring his words, "to put some distance between you and that sister of mine. Beautiful girl, Ethan. No disrespect. Love her as much as you do. But, Ethan, she's a possessive woman. Possessive! Threw the hook into you when she married you and she hasn't let you shake the barb yet."

The merchant didn't respond.

"By God!" Gus shouted, slapping the bar. "We're going to have great times! This village was starting to draw on me, Ethan. Know what I mean? Baraboo's a nice place but a man has to make his own excitement here."

"You seldom lack excitement," Ethan noted.

"Well, hell! Excitement's what makes a man's blood run. Hey, we're off to Madison city tomorrow, right?"

"Right."

"How long do you think they'll keep us there, Ethan? Before they send us down South?"

The merchant shrugged.

"Probably long enough for me to diddle my way through half the ladies of Madison. Figure I can do that in about two weeks. What do you think, Ethan?"

"Two weeks should suffice."

"Damn, Ethan! You're all right. Drink up. I'd carry you home for a change, but I sure don't like the idea of facing that sister of mine with you over my shoulder. She's a mouth like an adder snake when she gets a mad on. Don't suppose she's much in favor of you cutting out and marching off with the boys from Sauk County?"

"I wouldn't say Lily is in favor of the idea," Ethan admitted.

Carl came and stood across the bar from the brothers-in-law. "Are you talking him out of this foolishness?" he demanded of Gus.

"Hell, no!" the blond flared. "Me and Ethan, we've got great times coming."

"What about your business?" Carl asked, still trying.

"Taken care of," the merchant explained quietly. "Herman Priecz will look after things until I get back."

"You don't have to go!" Carl insisted.

"None of us has to go," Gus sneered. "We're going because we want to go, Elsasser! We're volunteers, man. Patriots!"

"Patriots!" Carl cursed. "Adventurers! That's what you are. Adventure's your cause. What have any of you to do with this fool Lincoln? With his war? You should stay in Sauk County and tend to your farms and your businesses."

"You can speak about tending to business!" Gus taunted. "You're doing good business tonight, making money off men who've answered their nation's call."

"I make an honest living! What of you?"

"What of me?" Gus challenged, stepping back from the bar and raising his fists.

Men along the bar craned their necks to watch. There'd been speculation in Sauk County for years on who would win when Carl Elsasser finally went for Gus Gaard.

"Gus," Ethan cautioned. "Sheriff Zimmerman is watching."

"God!" Gus spat, lowering his fists but keeping his eyes on the grim tavern keeper. "To think that fat Adolph is going to be an officer over the likes of me and Ethan!" Gus picked up his glass and drank noisily.

Carl slapped the bar with his hand and turned away from the brothers-in-law. He busied himself with his customers, his mind working furiously. It was wrong for them to go! He believed that in his soul! It was wrong for President Lincoln to call the men to war and wrong for Governor Randall to support the call. Yet, they were going, the men from Sauk County, Ethan Evans and his loud-mouthed brother-in-law, Adolph Zimmerman, James Peck, almost a hundred others. And, Carl realized, he too was a man from Sauk County. Could he stay behind? Were he not to go with them, would he be able to live with himself while they were away? Would he be able to stand among them when they came back? As strongly as he felt against the war, he was still one of the men from Sauk County. He filled a schooner with beer and poured a glass of brandy. He carried the drinks to where the sheriff and the law clerk stood near the wall. The tavern keeper glared at the sheriff.

"Something I can do for you, Carl?" Adolph asked.

Carl glanced at the leather portfolio on the bar. "Have you a place for another name?" he demanded, his teeth clenched.

James nodded.

"Give me the paper."

James looked at the sheriff. Adolph nodded.

James drew a blank enlistment form from the portfolio and set a glass inkwell and a steel pen beside the document on the bar.

Carl dipped the pen. Carefully, he wrote his name at the top of the document. He threw the pen down and stared along the bar at Ethan and Gus.

"Are you sure you want to do that?" Adolph asked.

Carl turned his eyes to the sheriff. "I've done it."

"I'll need some more information," James said, taking up the pen.

"Later!" Carl snapped. He glanced the length of his bar and saw the shock reflected in the faces of his wife and his son. Carl went to them, taking his wife in his arms, pulling his son close to his side. "I'm one of them," he told his wife. "I can't stay behind, not with them going. I've got to go with them. Can you understand that?"

His wife nodded, but she could not understand.

3

By mid-morning on Saturday the courthouse square in Baraboo was jammed with people from farms and settlements throughout Sauk County. Wagons and teams were parked in front of stores on the square and crowded into the side streets.

Families gathered on the dead grass of the courthouse lawn under low-ering clouds and chill winds. They spread huge farm dinners on blankets, anchoring the corners against the wind with crocks of preserves and pots of cheese. Children ran about screaming and playing.

To witness the muster of Nathaniel Bachmann's hundred volunteers Sauk County turned out a thousand fathers and mothers, brothers and sis-ters, wives and aunts and uncles and neighbors. Young men going with Bachmann walked with long faces beside young ladies with reddened eyes, hand in hand, among the picnicking groups. Husbands going with Bach-mann stood silently with wives, parents, children.

Gus Gaard sent the Shoate brothers out from Elsasser's Tavern to put a fire-cracker under the tail of a deputy sheriff's horse. The big blond led the laughter when the startled mare bolted and tumbled over two matrons caught crossing the street.

On time, the Madison-Baraboo Stage pulled into the depot a half block from the square. Nathaniel Bachmann, wearing a gray uniform and side arms, alighted and strode quickly to the courthouse.

James and Adolph waited out of the cold in the hall of the courthouse. The law clerk carried his overcoat on his arm, not sure it would be appro-priate to wear the civilian garment over his new uniform, which consisted of a gray coat trimmed with a blue collar and cuffs, and gray trousers bear-ing a gold stripe down each outer seam. He wore the small French-style kepi that came with the uniform, taller at the rear than the front, with a leather visor beneath a brass wreath around the word "Wisconsin." Sher-iff Zimmerman wore his uniform with Sauk County's six-pointed star of office pinned to the breast of his coat. The sheriff carried his revolver in an old leather holster hung from a worn leather belt.

Nathaniel Bachmann entered the hall, pulling on leather gauntlets as he walked.

"Captain Bachmann," James greeted the officer, thankful the man had arrived, still wondering what he should do with his overcoat.

"Mister Peck," Bachmann returned the greeting.

Adolph faced the officer, chewing seriously on his tobacco. "Your ass must be sore after twelve hours pounding on the stage," he grinned.

Bachmann worked the fingers of his left hand inside the gauntlet, ignor-ing the lawman's rudeness. "The company is ready to muster?" he asked.

"More or less," Adolph offered.

James flushed, embarrassed at the sheriff's contentious manner. He was sure he should have been doing something to prepare the company for its commander's arrival. He had no idea what that was.

"There will be ceremonies?" the captain asked, facing the lawman.

Adolph laughed. "If you think those farmers are going to let you get the men out of town without a lot of speech-making and praying and singing and calling down the wrath of the Almighty on the heads of the Confederates, you've got another think coming, Nate. You try that, you'll have your own rebellion right here in Sauk County."

Bachmann stared at the lawman. "What have you arranged, Lieutenant Zimmerman?" he asked coldly.

"You can call me Adolph, Nate," the sheriff said, taking the captain's measure. "We haven't left town yet." He frowned, pretending seriousness. "Let me see now. The mayor of Baraboo wants to enthuse us. Minister of the Methodist church wants to pray over us. County supervisor wants to inspire us. Ladies' choir wants to sing some songs. I figure, by the time that gets done, they'll be ready for you to wrap it up with words of encouragement for them who're going with us and words of consolation for them who're staying at home. Figure a couple of hours, at least."

"See that it takes less time than that!" Bachmann snapped. "I want this company on the road in an hour. The men are to be in Madison city before noon tomorrow. Transportation is arranged?"

"Ten wagons," Adolph answered, not changing his manner. "Teams and drivers paid for by the county board. Ready to roll when you say, after I drag the drivers out of the taverns."

"The local dignitaries are here?" the captain asked.

"Tucked away with a bottle of brandy in Judge Blane's chambers," Adolph replied. "The judge, he wanted to make a speech but the brandy got to him. He's asleep on the table in the court room. I'll round up the rest of them and bring them out right behind you."

"Have them precede me," Bachmann told the sheriff, putting the lawman in his place. He turned. "Lieutenant Peck, have the men fall in on the lawn in front of the steps."

"Yes, sir!" James blurted. He hesitated. "Captain Bachmann, how do I have the men fall in?"

"I suggest, Mister Peck, that you step out the door and call the men to attention. Have them form two lines facing the steps. Have you a roll book?"

James held up the bound book in which he'd drawn up an alphabetical listing of the men's names.

"Take your book with you and call the roll. Have each man answer to muster when his name is called. Can you do that?"

"Yes, sir!" James promised.

"Then, do it!" the captain ordered.

The law clerk stepped through the door and stood on the top step. Farmers and townspeople milled randomly on the lawn. Standing in the cold wind, James wished he'd left his overcoat back in the hall instead of carrying it out the door on his arm. He hadn't thought to ask Captain Bachmann how to call the men to attention.

Adolph ushered the dignitaries through the door, forming them into a line along the wall. "You don't have them ready!" he charged, speaking to James, his breath strong from the last of the brandy in the bottle in Judge Blane's chambers.

"They seem to want to visit and talk," James explained.

"Damn it!" the sheriff exploded. "They'll do that for a week!"

"What should I do?" James pleaded.

Adolph scratched his belly, considering. He scratched one more time and pulled his revolver from its holster. He fired the weapon three times into the air. Conversations ceased. Heads turned in the direction of the two uniformed men and the party of dignitaries standing on the top step.

"That got their attention," Adolph growled, holstering the revolver. He raised his arms. "Now, you people!" he shouted. "Listen to me! You can do your hugging and kissing and saying good-bye after the speeches are said. You boys of the Baraboo Guards, come and form two lines right here in front of me. John Barks," he called to the carpenter the men had elected to be one of the sergeants, "stand over there and have the men form on you. Castle Newton," he told the tanner's son, another new sergeant, "stand behind John so some of the men can make a line on you. Ethan, send a boy off to get Gus out of Carl's tavern. Have him bring his gang with him. And Ethan! You keep an eye on him!"

James was grateful the sheriff had come to his aid but he felt useless as the men from Sauk County responded to the lawman's orders and ignored him completely. James wished he had a revolver.

"All right!" Adolph called out. "Quiet down! Lieutenant Peck, now, he's going to call your names. When he does, you answer 'here'!"

"Here!" Gus and his cronies shouted as they trotted from Elsasser's Tavern to take places in the two lines. People in the crowd laughed at the blond and his gang.

"Wait till I call your names!" James ordered, stepping forward.

"Why wait, General?" Jack Black asked. "I'm here."

"You're not here until I call your name," James told the dark man.

"Just where the hell might I be until you do call my name, General?" Jack challenged.

James blushed at the laughter this produced.

"You're in my sight, Jack!" Adolph threatened. The laughter died. "Go ahead," the lawman said. "Call your roll. Do the best you can."

James wondered if Sheriff Zimmerman was siding with the men against him. He fumbled with his book and overcoat until Adolph reached and took the heavy garment from him. He opened the book. Cold wind ruffled its pages. James drew a breath and called the first name. "Auchter, Herbert!"

"You got it backwards, Mister!" the farmer corrected. "I'm Herby Auchter, from over west of Reedsburg."

"They do it backwards in the army, Herby," Jack snickered.

"Just answer 'here,' all right?" James asked.

"Sure," Herby agreed, grinning at Jack. "Here! All right!"

"Auerbach, Frederick!"

"Here! All right!" the cobbler from Merrimac laughed.

"Aussman, John!"

"Hey, General?" Dewey Shoate called. "When do we get paid?"

"Hey, General?" Andy Shoate, Dewey's twin, echoed. "When do we get laid?"

"Watch what you say!" Castle Newton hissed. "My mother is standing over there!"

"Aussman, are you here?" James demanded. He turned to the sheriff. "This isn't working."

"You're doing fine," the lawman told him, chuckling. "They don't know any better. Not yet. Let them have their fun. They might have hard times coming."

"They're mocking me!"

"Not you. They're all wound up with the folks here and watching. Get on with your roll call." Adolph was hoping the frivolity could somehow be turned against Nate Bachmann. He nodded to the law clerk.

"Aussman!" James shouted angrily. "Are you here?"

"I'm here," the surveyor answered.

"Answer when I call your name! Axt, Ludwig!"

"Here!" the teamster responded.

James felt some confidence. The men were responding to the authority he represented. "Ball, George!"

"He's here," Johnny Makepeace said.

"Where?"

"Here," the student nodded. "Beside me. On the ground."

"What's he doing on the ground?" James wanted to know.

"He can't stand up."

"Why not?"

"He's too drunk."

"Stand him up!" James ordered. "He can't answer to muster laying on his belly!"

"I don't know why not, Mister," the student said. "Old George does some of his best work on his belly."

Gus and his friends roared. Johnny Makepeace grinned at his own group of friends. James sighed and marked the page next to George Ball's name. "Barks, John!"

"I'm here," the big carpenter said, his eyes fixed on the form of his wife, Peggy, standing next to her father, wrapped in her shawl and weeping silently. Peggy had pleaded through the night for John to stay home.

"Black, Jack!"

"Hey, deal me in!" Edgar Pendar called out.

"I'm here," Jack sneered, digging an elbow into Edgar's ribs.

"Bland, Wilfred!"

"Yo!"

"Write to me, Wilfie!" Alice Himmelsbach called to the farmer from Prairie du Sac.

"We all will!" Gus' gang sang out.

"Blumenfeld, Ottis!"

"Here!"

"Calef, Henry!"

"Yea."

"Christensen, Preston!"

"Over here!"

"Dean, Wallace!"

"Here!" the farmer called.

"What do you think?" Jack asked Gus. "Should we send someone for a bottle of brandy? The damned speeches will go on forever."

"We better," Gus decided. "Here, sonny!" he called to a lad. "Take this money to that tavern. Bring me a bottle of brandy. You can keep five cents of the change."

"Elsasser, Carl!"

"Here!" Carl had second thoughts about signing his name on the enlistment form the night before. He still thought the men in the formation were fools. He accepted the fact that he was now a fool among them.

"Evans, Ethan!"

"I'm here," the merchant said. Ethan's eyes burned and his head ached from the whiskey he'd drunk at Carl's tavern the night before. His mouth was dry and his throat was tight. He thought of Lily, who'd refused to come to the muster with him.

"Everett, Peter!"

The farmhand from Sauk City answered.

"Ewart, Frank!"

"Yea!" the Baraboo mechanic called.

"Fedkenheuer, Stepan!"

"Hey, Step!" Jack goaded the farmer. "The general called your name."

"I'm here!" Stepan told Jack.

"Gaard, Amos Augustus! Junior!"

The name brought looks and grins from men in the ranks. "Amos!" one voice shrieked. "Amos! Augustus! Junior!"

Gus scowled. He searched for the source of that voice.

"Amos!" the voice trilled. Johnny Makepeace waved his hands to get men near him to join in a chant. "Amos! Augustus! Junior!"

"What man mocks my name?" Gus roared. He searched the faces in the rank behind him.

"Amos! Augustus! Junior!" Johnny Makepeace chanted with several men joining him.

"I'll do harm to the man who mocks my name!" Gus screeched.

"Ethan, hold him down!" Adolph warned. The merchant put a restraining hand on his brother-in-law's arm.

"He didn't have to use my full name!" Gus argued.

"Get on with it," the sheriff told James, grinning, enjoying Gus's discomfort. "You're doing fine."

James wasn't sure he was doing fine. He wasn't sure the sheriff was his friend. "Larson, Hans!"

"Here," Olaf answered for his brother.

"Larson, Olaf!"

"Here," Olaf answered for himself. He didn't think Lieutenant Peck would be angry if he answered for himself and Hans. Hans couldn't answer. Hans was simple. He stood beside Olaf, staring at the ladies in the crowd, rubbing the front of his work trousers.

"Makepeace, Johnny!"

"Here!" the student called. He'd been tempted to respond in the falsetto voice, but seeing Gus still searching for the source of his embarrassment, thought better of the idea.

"Murphy, Michael Patrick!"

"He's here," the sheriff said.

"Isn't he supposed to answer for himself?" James asked.

"Take my word for it. He's here."

James made a mark in the book next to the Irishman's name, remembering the prisoner in the jail. He felt that a man should answer to muster for himself, but he didn't want to antagonize the lawman. "Newton, Castle!"

"Here," the tanner's son responded.

"Oostendorp, Hollis!"

"Over here."

"Pendar, Edgar!"

"Yea."

"Roohr, Wayne!"

"Yo!" the cross-eyed stage clerk called. Wayne held his left eyelid closed, his right eye focused on Veronica Koch, who stood among the spectators and smiled her love to Wayne.

"Schoming, Willy!"

"Here," the brewer from Prairie du Sac answered.

"Shoate, Andy!"

"The Shoates can't be far behind if Amos Augustus is here," Henry Calef laughed.

Gus glared at the farmhand.

"I'm here," Andy answered.

"Shoate, Dewey!"

"Right here!"

"Swartz, Alois!"

"Over here."

"Wright, Robert!"

"Yes," the farmer from south of Baraboo called.

"Wright, Willis!"

"You better show Willis where he is, Bob," Jack Black called out, taking a drink from the bottle he shared with Gus. "Willis tends to get lost when he isn't following the ass-end of an ox down a furrow."

"I'm here!" Willis argued, as if that took care of Jack Black.

James snapped the book shut. The men had shown no regard for the seriousness of the muster. They'd laughed at him and at each other as if the whole process were some gross carnival. James was thankful that Captain Bachmann had remained inside the courthouse and hadn't witnessed the farce the men had made of the roll call. The law clerk stepped behind the line of dignitaries, wondering why he'd ever let Judge Blane talk him into helping Captain Bachmann in the first place.

The speeches started.

The speeches dragged on.

A line of boys worked from the rear of the formation to the taverns and back, returning with bottles of brandy tucked under their jackets. Adolph sent a deputy sheriff to close the taverns but the line of boys moved the business to the back doors and the supply of brandy to the men in the formation continued.

When the last of the speakers had spoken and the ladies of the choir had sung, the volunteers and the people of Sauk County prepared themselves for what they expected to be the main part of the occasion. Even the drunks in the formation tried to pay attention.

Nathaniel Bachmann stepped through the door of the courthouse and stood on the top step, facing the men of the Baraboo Guards, ignoring the people in the crowd.

Bachmann was a short man, compact and dark with a closely trimmed beard. His stance was stiff and straight, feet apart, military, commanding. He stood with his gauntleted right hand in the open breast of his gray uniform coat, his left hand resting lightly on the hilt of his officer's sword. He gazed along the lines of faces in the two ranks, left to right.

The captain withdrew his hand from his coat and raised the fingers to touch the leather visor of his cap. He turned, again left to right. "Men of the Baraboo Guards!" he called out in a deep voice. "I salute you!" He lowered his right hand to rest on the pistol holster on his belt.

"Men of the Baraboo Guards," he addressed the volunteers, repeating his words. "You've heard your nation's call! You yeomen of the American Northwest have heard and have answered that call!"

The captain paused, taking a step to the right, the men in the ranks closely watching as he moved.

"Foul treason has infected our brothers in the states to the south," he went on, his voice clear. "They've listened to the words of evil men. They've fallen under the spell of those who would tear apart our Federal Union. They've allowed themselves to be seduced into taking up arms to attack those institutions that we hold sacred."

Bachmann took a step to the left. He studied them, their faces, their eyes.

"Our president and our governor have called on you, on your stout hearts and your strong arms, to bring our wayward brothers back to the fold of liberty, freedom, and union. You loyal men have offered to carry the bayonet to the throat of secession! It will be you who will restore what they have so treacherously betrayed!"

Ethan, standing in the front rank, swallowed and licked his lips. Through his hangover, he gave Bachmann credit for being a powerful speaker.

"I have led regular infantry into battle against the foes of this nation on many fields," Bachmann continued. "Yet, I stand here, awed and impressed at the might and the determination and the power that you men represent. No officer could seek a more gallant command. No warrior could ask for more formidable a force. No soldier could want for better comrades in arms!" The captain paused, dropping his gaze as if searching for thoughts. He raised his eyes, gathering those thoughts, scanning the faces before him. "I didn't come here to make a speech," he told the men. "I won't lead you with words or phrases. Follow me!" he shouted. "Carry your steel to the heart of the rebellion!"

The Baraboo Guards had been waiting, listening to other men speak for two hours. Now was the time for them to make their own voices heard, to cheer, to shout, to cry out their pride and their enthusiasm. They roared. They hollered. They broke out in wild Indian yells and in the deep-throated bellows of the northwest woods. They pounded each other on the shoulders and some of them jumped into the air.

"Now!" Bachmann called after a minute of watching the exuberant men. "Give me your attention!"

The volunteers became orderly, after their fashion and their levels of sobriety.

"I want to tell you about your entry into Wisconsin state service. As soon as you are dismissed, you will load into the wagons your Sauk County Board has provided. You'll be carried in them to the state capitol at Madison. There, tomorrow, you'll go into the camp of instruction were you'll train, where you'll be issued your uniforms and your weapons. You'll join the Second Wisconsin Volunteer Infantry Regiment as its Company K!"

This was news to the men. It was reason enough for some of them to break out in more cheers and shouts and Indian yells.

Bachmann nodded, giving them time. He was about to continue when a brandy-blurred voice called out, "Hold on there, Cap! Just hold on there a God-damned minute!"

Bachmann sought out the speaker. Sheriff Zimmerman had pointed the man out when he enlisted. Gus Gaard, a trouble-maker.

The blond swaggered from his place in the ranks.

"Yes, Private Gaard?" Bachmann asked.

Gus was smarting from the mockery of his given name during the roll call. He'd been waiting for a chance to take back some of what he'd lost. The eyes of the men in the formation were on him as was the attention of the people in the crowd. He hooked his thumbs into his belt. "What's this you're telling us about being some Company K?" he demanded. "In case you don't recall, Cap, we are the Baraboo Guards. We intend to fight this war of yours as the Baraboo Guards. What's this Company K stuff?"

There were murmurs of agreement from the men. Now that Gus had brought the issue up, the designation as Company K was news to them and they were interested in what the captain would tell them about that.

Bachmann felt a rush of anger. He worked to control himself. "I'm sure your comrades have the same concern, Private Gaard," he conceded patiently, looking at the men in the ranks and addressing his response to them, taking away some of Gaard's insolence. "This company, men, will always be the Baraboo Guards out of Sauk County. That will never change. However, when we get to Madison, we'll join nine other companies to form our regiment. These companies, as we've done, have taken local names. Many call themselves Guards. Among them, we'll want to preserve our identity. After all, Private Gaard, here, wouldn't want any tender letters of a personal nature to go astray and be delivered to the wrong Private Gaard in the wrong company of Guards, would he?"

Hearty laughs came from the men in the formation and blushes brightened the cheeks of a few ladies in the crowd.

Gus leered over his shoulder at his gang. "Damned considerate of you, Cap," he admitted, turning back to the officer. "Damned considerate."

"Will any of you men want to share the glory this company will earn with the Citizens' Guards, out of Dodge County?" Bachmann asked.

"No!" the Baraboo Guards responded.

"The La Crosse Guards, out of La Crosse County?"

"No!" they cried.

"The Portage City Guards, out of Columbia County?"

"No! No!"

"The Randall Guards, out of Dane County?"

"No! No! Hell, no!"

"So, Private Gaard," Bachmann said, "do you understand why we'll be known as Company K?"

"You make your point, Cap," Gus admitted. "We'll go as your Company K." He wasn't finished. He wrinkled his forehead. "I think I've got this army thing figured out," he admitted. "From what you've just told me."

"I'm grateful for that, Gaard," the officer said, dismissing the drunk from his mind.

"We're the Baraboo Guards, but we aren't the Baraboo Guards," Gus insisted. "Yet, we'll always be the Baraboo Guards. That's what you said, isn't it?"

"Well, in a way, Private Gaard, that's correct."

"Right, Cap. Like I said, I've got this army thing figured out," Gus drawled, looking back at his grinning gang. "We take what makes sense, then we turn it around so it doesn't make sense. Then, we say it still makes sense anyway! That about it, Cap?"

The men in the formation and the people of Sauk County howled at Gus' convoluted logic and at the captain's obvious embarrassment.

Bachmann struggled to control himself. He could easily have shot the grinning drunk standing before him. "Mister Peck!" he hissed through clenched teeth.

"Sir?" James responded, trying to conceal the grin on his face.

"Take this company to Madison city!" Bachmann snapped, loud enough for the men to hear. He turned and glared at the law clerk. "I'll precede you, traveling on horseback. I assume, Mister Peck, that you can move this company from Baraboo to Madison?"

"I intend to try, Captain Bachmann," James insisted, angry that the company commander was taking his rage at Gus Gaard out on him.

"Do that! Lieutenant Zimmerman will assist you. I expect you to report to me with the company at the state fairground in Madison before noon, tomorrow!"

"Yes, sir," James said.

Bachmann glared at the law clerk and at the sheriff. He slapped a thigh with a leather gauntlet and marched into the courthouse.

James swallowed. He stared down from the top step into the faces of the Baraboo Guards without the slightest idea what to do next. The men stared back. They waited.

"All right!" Adolph called, stepping forward. "You heard what the man said. You've got time for one kiss and one hug and one pat on the backside. Then, pick up your bundles and head down Oak Street to those county wagons. Pile in, ten men to the load. Carl, send a man to get the drivers from your tavern. If they're drunk, prop'em up in the seats. Now, move! The Baraboo Guards are going to war!"

4

MADISON, WISCONSIN—May, 1861.

James woke to the jolt and roll of the wagon. He lay for a few minutes, listening to the soft shuffle of hooves, the tink of trace chains, the steady turn of iron-bound wheels on the dirt of the road as the column of Sauk County wagons moved through darkness toward Madison.

He pulled himself up in the corner of the wagon box. His mouth was sour. He was cold. He pulled the collar of his overcoat up around his ears and worked his hips to find a confortable position in the thin layer of straw that lined the wagon bed.

He didn't know how long he'd slept. It had to be close to dawn. The column of wagons hadn't started from the ferry crossing over the Wisconsin River at Merrimac until after midnight.

Adolph Zimmerman and the other men in the wagon were asleep, save one. James smelled smoke from the briar pipe where Murphy the Irishman sat forward in the wagon, manacled to an iron brace of the wagon box.

James recalled with despair the company's departure from Baraboo. Many of the men were drunk when they loaded into the wagons. The drinking continued. Horsemen rode with the column for miles and replenished their friends' brandy supplies from roadside taverns. Drunk volunteers fell from the wagons along the route. Men jumped from the wagons into thickets to take care of calls of nature, crowding into the following wagons when they finished. James stopped the column twice to redistribute riders forward into the emptied wagons.

At the ferry the ten wagons should have made the crossing of the broad Wisconsin River in an hour. Instead, the column halted for four hours while the men ate and drank at the tavern, flirted with the daughters of the ferry master, wrestled and argued and bragged. Adolph got drunk. Sober men helped James shove drunk men into the wagons on the eastern bank of the river for the remainder of the journey to Madison.

James hadn't thought to take a roll call after the ferry crossing. He didn't know if all the men who left Baraboo were in the ten wagons. Some of them could have been left on the western bank of the river for all he knew. He wondered if he should climb down and count the men as the following wagons passed. That would do no good, he decided. He had no lantern and he wasn't sure how many men were now on the company's roster. Several of the original volunteers had opted not to come at the last minute. Several new men had enlisted after Captain Bachmann's speech. James had written the names of the new men in his book but he wasn't sure he had made note of the men who had dropped out. There'd been a lot of confusion. James had given the roll book to Carl Elsasser, whom the men had elected to be their first sergeant. James didn't know where in the column of wagons the tavern keeper rode. There was so much to the whole business that he didn't understand. He wrapped himself close into the folds of his overcoat, cold, tired, miserable.

He had no business being where he was, he thought. He was a clerk, a person of papers and files and schedules and court documents. He wasn't a leader of men, not an army officer, not a soldier.

James believed in what the Federal government was doing to preserve the union of the states but he'd never considered that helping Captain Bachmann with the company's papers would bring him to this night in a wagon on the road to Madison. He wished he were back in his clerk's office in the Sauk County courthouse in Baraboo.

In waning darkness James made out a building beside the road, a store, a few houses. A man with a lantern stepped from a doorway and watched the wagons approach.

"Where are we?" James asked.

"Lodi village," the man yawned. "Who are you?"

"The Baraboo Guards," James answered. "Out of Sauk County."

"Bound on to Madison city?"

"How far is that from here?"

"You'll be there by noon. Outfit from La Crosse County came through earlier this night. Heading for the same place. How many of you?"

"A hundred and four," James told the citizen of Lodi, guessing at the number. There was no purpose in letting the man know of his uncertainty.

"Sell you a jar to make the trip easy?" the man offered.

"I don't think so," James told him.

A bout of suggestive coughing broke out where the manacled Irishman sat forward in the wagon.

"Well, yes!" James called to the man. "I'll buy a jar from you." Buying a jar of brandy and sharing it with the Irishman was something he could do with some degree of confidence. He needed to do something with some degree of confidence. "How much will it be?"

"Have to ask you a dollar for the jar, friend," the man said. "Everything here is closed up for the night. I'll have to dig into my own supply for you. A dollar will get you to Madison city with a glow on."

James dug his leather purse from a pocket of his overcoat. A dollar was a lot of money for a jar of local brandy.

As the column of Sauk County wagons passed out of the village, James opened the jar and took a sip. He choked, grimaced, then spat the liquor over the side of the wagon box. He wasn't much of a drinker and the single sip of the contents of the jar confirmed his reluctance to become one. He crawled forward over the sleeping bodies and gave the jar to the chained Irishman.

Murphy took the jar without speaking. He tapped the coals from his briar pipe and slipped it into his pocket. He crooned to himself as he tasted the unexpected pleasure of strong drink, tum-tum-tiddley-tum-tee-day. Tum-tum-tiddley-tum-tee-day.

Dawn broke and day came and the column of Sauk County wagons rolled through the villages of Dane and Waunakee. Morning brought low gray clouds, the wind and the cold of the day before.

Two hours after noon the wagons rolled into Madison from the north. On the right of the road was Lake Mendota, its dark waters whipped into white-caps by the harsh wind.

The streets of Madison were wide, muddy, rutted. Bare, unbudded limbs of trees reached into the gray sky. Board walks lined the streets. White plank fences separated gardens and dooryards. Men and women stood and watched the ten wagons. Pretty girls, muffled and wrapped against the cold wind, waved and called bright greetings.

Few of the Sauk County volunteers returned the courtesies. Many were sleeping. Some were hung over. A few were still drunk.

The wagons rolled through and out of the city, passing small farms to the west. Close under the hill that held the few buildings of the state university the column came to the fairground that had been turned over to the governor for use as the camp of instruction for the Second Wisconsin Regiment.

Outside a guarded gate in the plank fence that surrounded the fairground a boy in Wisconsin gray met the column. He held up a hand to halt the wagons. "Lieutenant Peck!" he called.

James pulled himself up from the box of the lead wagon, brushing straw from the skirts of his overcoat. He leaned on the back of the driver's seat. "Here," he said, stiff, sore, half-asleep. "I'm Lieutenant Peck."

"I'm Second Lieutenant Thad Able," the boy introduced himself, grinning up at James through cheeks covered with freckles. "I'm with the Citizens' Guards. We're from Dodge County. I'm from Beaver Dam. I'm supposed to show you where you'll be quartered."

James nodded, brushing the last of the straw from his overcoat. He climbed down from the wagon over its off wheel.

"You're late, Lieutenant Peck," the boy chided.

"Late," James echoed. "Yes. Have you been waiting long, Lieutenant . . ."

"Able. Thad Able. You can call me Thad. I'm just learning to be a lieutenant. What's the rest of your name, Lieutenant Peck?"

"It's James. As I asked, have you been waiting long?"

"Since noon. It's all right. I didn't have anything else to do. Come on. Walk with me. I'll show you where you're going to have to live. I've messages for you from your Captain Bachmann."

James had expected Nathaniel Bachmann to meet the company in person. He tugged his cap tightly onto his head and followed Thad Able through the gate, passing the uniformed guards and waving for the column of wagons to follow him.

The fairground was a fenced plot of thirty muddy acres. James saw a race track and wooden grandstand, several buildings for displaying livestock, produce, machinery. Volunteers, most still wearing their civilian clothing, moved about under the loose direction of newly-elected sergeants. Carriages and wagons crowded the streets.

"You said you had messages for me from Captain Bachmann?" James asked the boy from Beaver Dam.

"He said to tell you he's here. Busy at headquarters. That building over there is headquarters. He said to tell you to get your men settled into their quarters and to keep them there. He'll see you and the other lieutenant in the morning."

"That's all?" James asked.

"That's all," the freckled boy confirmed. "Did you expect more?"

"No," James murmured. He had expected more. He'd expected Captain Bachmann to meet the column of wagons and assume command of the Baraboo Guards.

"Your building is at the end of this street," Thad said. "Too bad you got here late. You're the last company in."

"Why is that bad?" James asked.

"We got to pick our buildings in order of arrival. We got here yesterday, the Citizens' Guards. We picked Harness Shed. It isn't bad. Never had livestock living in it. By the way, we aren't supposed to call ourselves the Citizen's Guards. We're Company A. Did they hang a letter on the Baraboo Guards?"

"We're Company K."

"Last in letter order, last into camp," Thad chuckled.

James remembered Nathaniel Bachmann promising the Baraboo Guards they would be second to none. "I take it, being last in, we don't have much choice of where we'll live?"

"No choice at all. There's only one building left. You'll have to take it or camp in the mud."

"I'm sure it will do," James said. "Have we missed anything, being last in?"

"Nope. All we've done since we got here has been to move into our building and try to keep warm and dry. You can see," the boy from Beaver Dam said, pointing to a gang of carpenters working on the roof of one building, "they aren't ready for us."

"There seem to be a lot of carpenters," James noted. Sounds of pounding, sawing, hammering, chopping came from all sides. Stacks of boards were piled in the narrow streets.

"The buildings were made to house the exhibits of the state fair," Thad told him. "They weren't intended to serve as barracks. The carpenters are getting to each building in turn."

"Being last in, will we be last on the carpenters' list?"

"Count on it. By the way, I'm supposed to tell you the colonel has issued an order that the men aren't allowed to go into Madison city until a system of passes is worked out."

"I see. Who is the colonel?"

"He was the state's attorney general until yesterday."

"Mister Coon?"

"The same. Today, he's the boss man around here. He commands the regiment."

James nodded. He felt depressed, alone. Nathaniel Bachmann should have been at the gate to tell the men what to do. The law clerk had no idea what was expected of him next.

"I have to leave," Thad said. "I have to go to a meeting of the officers in our company. We have a lot of meetings. There's your building, the one at the end of the street. Good luck, James."

"I'm sure the Baraboo Guards will get along fine, Thad," James said, "Thanks for your help."

The boy from Beaver Dam saluted.

James didn't know what to do about that so he nodded.

Adolph woke when the wagons came to a halt. He sat up in the wagon box, blinking, suffering from a thick tongue and a pounding head. He was sorely hung over. He pulled himself to his feet, groaning and grunting. Giving himself a good shake to put his miseries out of his mind for the while, he belched and climbed over the wheel, joining the law clerk. "Ach!" he spat. "Well, are we here?"

"We're here."

"Where're we going to live?"

James nodded toward the low building at the end of the street.

Adolph walked to the whitewashed structure, bending to read the sign hung under the eaves. "Swine!" he bellowed. "A swine shed! You brought us all the way from Baraboo to live in a swine shed!"

"This is where the officer who met us at the gate brought us," James explained.

"For Christ's sake!" Adolph swore. "A pig pen! A God-damned pig pen!" He rubbed his throbbing temples. There was no sense in taking his hang-over out on the law clerk. "Well, hell," he conceded. "I've lived in worse. I'll see what shape it's in." He hitched up his gray trousers and walked into the building. He was back in less than a minute. "It's bad in there," he stated. "Side walls open to the weather. Roof leaks. Place is damp. Pig shit a foot thick in some places. Nothing built up but some stalls."

"We're the last company into camp," James told him. "I gather, from what that officer told me, we take this or we sleep in the open."

"It's going to rain," the fat man said, looking into the overcast sky. "Rain, then maybe some snow. We better get the boys busy and make what we can out of what we've got. Them carpenters I hear chopping and hammering, they going to do work for us?"

"Not soon. They're taking each company's building in the order of arrival. We're last."

The sheriff rolled tobacco from his pouch and fingered a ball into his mouth. He chewed.

"What are you thinking?" James asked.

"I'm thinking I'm not going to have a hundred boys from Sauk County sleeping in pig shit with the rain falling through the roof on their heads!"

"I don't want that either," James agreed. "What can we do? They aren't ready for us. Captain Bachmann should be here. We haven't held a roll call. We don't know if all the men are with us. This is all wrong!"

"Where is our captain?" the lawman asked, pursing his lips and sluicing tobacco juice into the mud.

"He's at headquarters. He left word he'll see you and me in the morning."

Adolph chewed, thinking. "We'll get the boys a place to sleep," he decided. "Carl Elsasser!"

The tavern keeper was asleep in the fourth wagon. Jack Black gave him a vicious kick. Carl sat up, rubbing his face. Jack pointed over the side of the wagon box. "What do you want?" Carl demanded.

"Climb down," Adolph told him. "Count off twenty men and get them started cleaning the pig shit out of there. Find shovels or something."

"Adolph?" Carl asked, trying to be reasonable. He was confused, not yet fully awake. "Are you talking to me about pig shit?"

"I am."

"What pig shit?"

"In there. The building we've got to live in."

The tavern keeper shook his head. He hoped what he was hearing wasn't so. He blinked his eyes and looked over the side of the wagon at the lawman, who looked back at him. "Pig shit?"

"Get twenty men and start cleaning it out."

"What'll I have them do with it?" the tavern keeper asked, accepting the fact that the sheriff was talking about pig shit and that he was going to have to do something about it. He climbed down from the wagon and walked toward the low building.

"You figure out what to do with it," Adolph shouted after him. "You're the first sergeant. Hell, load it into the wagons! Have the drivers haul it back to Sauk County!"

"Here!" one of the drivers objected. "Hold on, Adolph! We didn't contract with the county to haul pig shit!"

"Are you going to argue with me, Harold Calef?" the sheriff demanded, facing the nine other drivers who were gathering behind the farmer. "Are the rest of you going to argue with me?"

"Well, no," Harold gave in. "We know better than to argue with you. But, pig shit? Hell! Well, hell! Just plain, damned hell!"

"Your boy, Henry, is with this company. Do you want him sleeping in pig shit?"

"I don't want him sleeping in pig shit, Adolph. All right, we'll haul it."

"You'll help Carl and the boys load it, too!"

"We'll help load it. We're going to remember this when you come up for election, Adolph. Count on that!"

"Where's John Barks?" the lawman demanded, dismissing the confrontation with the drivers from his mind.

"Here," the carpenter answered.

"Go inside there and take a look at the place, John. We're going to live here for a while. Figure out what you'll need to keep the rain off the boys' heads. Figure out what else you'll need to make the place fit for habitation, then come back here and tell me."

John took a pencil and notebook from his jacket pocket. He studied the shed from the outside, shaking his head, making quick notes.

"The rest of you men!" Adolph called. "Unload from the wagons and form two lines, right here in front of me!"

The Sauk County volunteers stood and stretched, complaining, working at sore muscles and bones. They climbed down from the wagons, tired, cold, hungry. Carl returned and counted off twenty men. He led them into the swine shed. The drivers followed, grumbling, carrying shovels from the wagons' tool boxes.

"Bob Wright!"

"Here, Adolph."

"Take this key and go unlock that Irishman from the brace of the first wagon. I want him here."

"Sheriff?" the farmer asked. "Is that man dangerous?"

"Only to himself, Bob. Take your brother with you if you want company."

Robert motioned for Willis to follow him. He cautiously approached the lead wagon and the manacled Irishman.

"Where's Wayne Roohr?

"Yo!" the cross-eyed stage clerk spoke up. He stood in front of Adolph, his left eyelid held closed.

"Take three or four of the boys, Wayne, and scout this place out. Talk to people. Find out what's happening. Ask around. Check on where we eat and where we get water. You get that figured out and come back and tell me."

"Sure," the stage clerk said. He motioned to three friends and the four sauntered away into the bustle of the fairground.

John Barks came from the shed scribbling in his notebook.

"Well?" the fat man asked.

"It's bad, Adolph," the carpenter reported. "Needs a whole new roof. Lumber to do a floor. Boards to make bunks and close up the holes in the sides. I'll need tools, hammers, saws, nails. Lot of work in there."

"You'll have to do it, John."

The carpenter gazed at the lawman. "How?"

"Get what you need and do it."

"Hell, Adolph, for a start, I need a whole lot of lumber."

Robert and Willis Wright came up with the Irishman between them. Murphy's wrists were still manacled.

Adolph took the brass key from Robert and unlocked the manacles, pulling the little man close to him. "John Barks, here, tells me he needs lumber to make us a place fit to live in."

The Irishman blinked. He was sadly hung-over from the jar of brandy James had given him in Lodi. He blinked again. He didn't know who John Barks was and he had no idea what was happening about him.

"I see piles of boards that belong to the carpenters from where I'm standing," the sheriff said, speaking close into the Irishman's face.

Murphy squinted. "Ah, well, now . . ." he began, wiping his pointed red nose on the sleeve of his jacket.

"Don't try to finagle me, you Irish horse thief!" Adolph threatened, shaking the little man.

"As you're saying it," Murphy quickly agreed. "You're seeing piles of boards from where you're standing." Murphy looked at the men around him. Other than the fat sheriff, they were strangers to him.

"That's better!" the lawman said, spitting tobacco juice. "You talk with John, here. He'll figure out what he wants from those piles of lumber. Pick some of the boys and go get him what he needs. Do you hear me?"

"I hear you," the little man acknowledged. He assumed the big one with the notebook would be John. The man had the look of a carpenter about him.

"I'll have my eye on you!" the lawman threatened.

"Aye."

"It'll take more than just lumber, Adolph," John said. "I need tools. Hammers and saws, a plane. Keg of nails. Couple of hatchets and a level."

The sheriff chewed and thought.

"Adolph," Ethan Evans spoke quietly.

"What'll you have?"

"I know merchants in Madison who'll give me what John needs. They'll extend me credit."

"Go get what we need, Ethan. We'll figure out how to pay for it later."

"Sheriff," James spoke up. He'd been standing beside Adolph as the lawman took charge and issued orders.

"What is it?"

"There are guards at the gate. The officer who met me when we came in said the men won't be allowed to go into Madison until a system of passes is worked out."

"When will that be?"

"The officer didn't say."

"That figures," the sheriff said, rubbing his temples. His head ached from the load of brandy he'd taken on at the ferry crossing the night before. "Ethan, get that brother-in-law of yours and some of his gang. Have Gus figure out how to get through the board fence that surrounds this place. Go with him, Ethan."

"Get us some shovels and brooms!" Carl called from the door of the shed. "That shit is pretty thick in here."

Wilfred Bland and Stepan Fedkenheuer returned to the building and dropped a load of boards from their shoulders. They turned to walk away.

"Where the hell do you two think you're going?" Adolph shouted at the farmers from Prairie du Sac.

"That Irishman told us not to steal boards from the same pile two times in a row, Sheriff," Wilfred explained. "We thought we'd steal some off a pile over that way next."

"Damn!" Adolph chuckled to the law clerk. "We're doing all right."

James shook his head.

"What's the matter with you?" the sheriff demanded.

"This is wrong!" James blurted. He was angry, tired, frustrated. He felt inadequate. The sheriff had taken charge of the men and James had been able to add nothing. "They aren't ready for us!" he cried. "Captain Bachmann should be here! We're sending men out to steal! We're breaking the law! This is wrong!"

"Steal, huh?" Adolph said, chewing and glaring. "You might be right about what ought to be! You better start looking at what isn't, not what ought to be, and you better start doing that fast! They aren't ready for us. There aren't places for us to sleep. And, let me tell you, Nate Bachmann hasn't been a hell of a lot of help to us since yesterday noon, back in Baraboo. You better start looking at what has to be, not what ought to be. And," Adolph added ominously, "I sure hope you don't get caught!"

"What do you mean, you hope I don't get caught?" James asked, suddenly apprehensive.

"Well," the sheriff said casually, spitting tobacco juice, "you're the first lieutenant. You're the one in command around here. You're the one responsible."

"You did all this!" James protested.

"Sure as hell did. Didn't notice you taking much of a hand in things. But, like I said, you're the one in command. They only hang the one in command."

"Hang?" James whispered.

"So I hear," Adolph confirmed.

"But . . ."

"Hey!" the sheriff shouted, grabbing James by the arm. "Have we any choice? Look around you. We're doing what we have to do. The men are busy. We'll have a place to sleep the night. We're following the first rule of war."

"The first rule of war?" James asked. He was confused. He didn't want to be hanged. He was sure the sheriff was not his friend. "What's the first rule of war?"

"Have a place to sleep the night."

"Sheriff," James asked, doubting. "Is that really the first rule of war?"

"Damned if I know," the lawman admitted. "I just made that up."

"Do they really hang the one in command?"

"Not if you follow the second rule of war."

"What's that?"

"Don't get caught!"

5

Governor Alexander Randall had, as Thad Able informed James, appointed the state's attorney general to the colonelcy of the Second Wisconsin Infantry Regiment. In return, the new colonel named the fairground where the regiment gathered to train Camp Randall in honor of the state executive.

The second day in Madison James stood in the door of the swine shed that housed the Baraboo Guards and looked out into a steady fall of cold rain drumming onto Camp Randall. He watched the white buns of Hans Larson as the simple boy squatted with his trousers at his ankles and dribbled strings of feces into the mud of the street. Olaf held his coat over Hans' head to protect his brother from the rain.

"God damn you, Larson!" Adolph shouted, trotting up the street from the row of privies that had been built along the board fence. "Don't let your brother shit in the street! What the hell's the matter with you?"

"Rain," Olaf explained. "He'll get wet walking to the privies. Besides, they stink."

"Stink!" the fat man screamed. "What in Christ's name do you think this street is going to smell like with every man in the Baraboo Guards taking his dump in it?"

Olaf shrugged. He hadn't thought about that.

"Get a board!" the sheriff roared. "Scrape that up and dump it down the privy!"

"Rain'll wash it away," Olaf suggested, trying to reason with the lawman. No one had told him Hans shouldn't take his dump in the mud of the street. It was all right to take a dump in the mud of a farm road back in Sauk County.

"Scrape that up!" Adolph insisted, pointing a thick finger into the farmhand's face.

Olaf wandered off to find a board.

Adolph shoved past James, storming into the swine shed. He whipped off his wet cap, sending a spray of water across the small room the officers shared. "Shitting in the middle of the street!" he shouted, turning on the law clerk. "And, boy, I'm going to tell you! I'm damned mad at you! You should have been all over him!" The fat man wiped his face with his hand and flung water from his fingers. "I don't know army regulations, damn it! They may permit a man to take a dump wherever he gets caught short but I'll tell you this! No man is going to shit on the sill of the swine shed I've got to live in and army regulations can be damned!"

James knew he should have stopped Hans. "Next time, Sheriff . . ." he began.

The lawman glared at him. He shook his head, then relaxed. "Oh, hell," he sighed. "Let it go. What are the rest of the men doing?"

James nodded over his shoulder toward the large room where the men lived.

Adolph looked through the doorway. John Barks and his gang of carpenters had repaired the roof and were now building bunks two-high along the sides of the shed. The rest of the men were idle. Some gathered, huddled and wet, talking in low voices. Some slept. Gus and his friends sat in a corner and shared a bottle of brandy the blond had brought back from his foray into Madison city. Castle Newton and Hollis Oostendorp read their Testaments. Ethan Evans read a Madison newspaper. Many of the men simply stood and stared at the rough boards of the walls. "This isn't good," the lawman said.

"They have nothing to do," James explained. "There's no place for them to go in the rain."

The sheriff didn't need an explanation. "We've got to get them busy."

"Yes, but doing what?"

"You got any ideas?"

"No. Captain Bachmann should be here, Sheriff."

"That son of a bitch hasn't been around much."

"I think we ought to go and find him," James decided.

Adolph nodded.

"I feel that Captain Bachmann has let us down."

"You're right about that."

"He should have met us when we got here. He should have left instructions for us if he couldn't meet us."

"Are you getting mad?" Adolph asked hopefully.

"I think Captain Bachmann's conduct so far as our commanding officer has been inconsiderate, to say the least," James added with conviction.

"You're getting there," the lawman encouraged.

"Sheriff?" James asked, his voice falling.

"Well?"

"We haven't held a roll call. What if he asks me if all the men are here? What if he's learned about the lumber we've had the men steal from the carpenters? What if he knows we've sent men through the fence into Madison?"

"You're coming off your mad real fast!"

"I just don't know about all this, Sheriff!"

Adolph shook his head. He was annoyed that James had given in to his fears so readily. "Well, hell, let's see if we can fix some of it. Carl Elsasser!"

"What'll you have?" the tavern keeper asked, coming to the door of the small room.

"Did you hold a roll call when we got here?"

"You had me shoveling pig shit, remember?"

"Get your book and hold a roll call. You're supposed to do that every morning, noon and night."

"How was I supposed to know that?"

"You know it now!"

"I know it now," the tavern keeper countered, not backing down. "I'm not sure I like finding out what I know. I'm having second thoughts about this whole business, Adolph. I wouldn't be wet and cold and staring at a board wall if I'd stayed behind my bar in Baraboo."

"You're a couple days late to be thinking like that!"

"I don't know that I am, Adolph."

"Listen, Carl," the sheriff said, wiping his face with one hand. "None of us likes this. We've got to make do with what we have. Me and Lieutenant

Peck, here, we're going to hunt up Nate Bachmann. While we're doing that, I've got to count on you. Help me with this, Carl. Get the men to line up in the middle of the shed and call the roll. Make sure all the men are here."

The tavern keeper considered this for several moments. "I'll do it, Adolph," he decided. "I don't like it."

"I'm not asking you to like it!"

"I said I'd do it! I just don't like having to be in charge."

"We'll be back as soon as we can, Carl. Keep the men busy until then."

The sheriff and the law clerk left the swine shed and headed across the camp through heavy, cold rain. Their gray uniforms were soaked by the time they arrived at the wooden building that Thad Able had pointed out to James as headquarters. Inside, James asked directions from a clerk and was directed down a long corridor to a closed door. He knocked.

"Yes?" Nathaniel Bachmann asked. The captain looked up from a field desk behind which he sat on a canvas stool. The front of the desk was let down to make a working surface. Papers were piled on the surface and more papers were stuck into pigeon holes in the upright back. The small room was crowded with the desk, a cot and wooden trunk. A window let Bachmanan look out onto the mud of Camp Randall. "James! Adolph! Come in!" Bachmann greeted his lieutenants. "I was about to have you sent for. Make yourselves at ease, gentlemen," the captain said, glancing around the room. "Not much comfort in Spartan quarters, right?"

James opened his sodden coat and sat on the trunk. Adolph glanced at the cot, its gray blanket tightly stretched and tucked. The sheriff decided to stand. He pushed his cap onto the back of his head and wiped rain water from his face.

"Paper," Bachmann said, waving a hand at the documents on his desk. "The curse of organization. What this army could accomplish were it not loaded down with paper! But, without the paper, we wouldn't have the organization, would we? And, without the organization, we wouldn't have the army. Even our humble Wisconsin militia must have its fodder of ration returns, daily reports, requisitions. In triplicate, of course. We few who have regular army experience are doing all we can to assist the governor. Doing our best. Twenty hours a day. But," the captain said, waving again at the piles of documents, "it's barely enough. I'm grateful that I can count on the two of you to see to the company while I do what I can here. God, for half a dozen regular army orderly sergeants!"

James felt remiss that he wasn't a regular army orderly sergeant.

"Well, gentlemen," Bachmann said, his eyes on a paper on the working surface of the desk. "Tell me about Company K. Give me your report. All here? All in fine shape? Settled into quarters, warm and dry? Hate to think of the men having to live in tents in this weather. Plenty to eat? First duty of the officer, gentlemen. See to the welfare of the men."

James recalled Adolph's first rule of war. He wondered if Captain Bachmann had just made up the first duty of the officer.

"Counting heavily on you, gentlemen," the captain went on, his gaze not leaving the documents on the working surface of the field desk. "Both of you in adequate quarters?" he asked. "No need to be with the men any more than your duties require. Familiarity breeds contempt, they say, and with good reason, Right?"

James studied the captain. He didn't know what he'd expected from this first meeting with Nathaniel Bachmann since the muster at Baraboo but he had not expected the distracted man who sat before him. James wondered what had become of the proud, competent officer who had saluted the Baraboo Guards two days earlier.

"Right?" Bachmann repeated, looking at James.

"Ah, right, sir," James caught himself.

Bachmann stared at the law clerk.

"Captain," James blurted, uncomfortable under the officer's silent gaze, "the men are in quarters, sir. Actually, they're in a swine shed. The roof leaks. The sides are open in some places to the rain. The floor is still covered with manure where our carpenter hasn't had time to lay new boards. We've had to do the work ourselves. We've had to buy tools and nails on our own. Some of the men brought no blankets with them. We're trying to make do, Captain, but . . ." James stopped. He glanced at the sheriff, who frowned at him. James wondered if he'd said too much.

"Good!" Bachmann said. "Initiative! Mark of the competent officer! The officer uses initiative and the hearts of the men follow. I'm sure you'll continue to solve your problems with initiative. Now, let me see. Somewhere in all this paper I have orders for company commanders. Let me see which of them apply to you. Here. The men aren't to be permitted into Madison city without a pass signed by one of you in my name," Bachmann read. "Makes sense, that. Don't want to wear thin our welcome from the citizens of Madison, do we? Men tend to get loose when first away from home before order and discipline take hold. What else? The men are to march to and from meals in formation. Good, that! Won't realize they're getting a little extra close order drill, will they?"

James looked confusedly at the officer sitting at the field desk.

"Will they?" Bachmann repeated.

"Captain Bachmann?" the law clerk asked.

"What is it?"

"You said the men are to march to meals in formation. The men don't know how to do that. To march in formation. They haven't been fed the first of those meals yet."

"Patience, young man," the captain counseled. "It takes time. It will come. Can't learn all there is about army life in a few days. That's why you're here in a camp of instruction."

"Yes, sir," James admitted. He glanced at the sheriff.

Adolph studied his fingernails intently.

"Let me see," Bachmann continued, turning his eyes to the document. "Thefts have been reported from the contract carpenters' lumber supplies. Can't permit that."

"No, sir," James concurred, looking at the sheriff.

The fat man grinned.

"Now, here, the order of the day. Reveille at five o'clock."

"Reveille, sir?"

"Wake-up call. French word, as are many of our military terms. Our debt to the excellent bequest our profession received from Napoleon, the greatest general of all time. Roll call at five-thirty. Breakfast at six. Company drill from eight to eleven. Dinner and roll call at noon. Company drill, again, from one to three. Supper at five. Roll call at seven. Retreat at nine. Can you remember all of that, Mister Peck?"

"Retreat, sir?"

"Go-to-bed call. Oho!" the captain beamed. "No, not the fall-back call by the same name. Some unit pride developing in Company K already? No retreat for the brave men from Sauk County, right?"

"Right, sir," James agreed, looking at the wet lawman.

Adolph shrugged.

"Now, for you two. Company officers instruction each evening. You'll learn what you're to teach the men the following day. Keep yourselves one day ahead of them, right?"

James nodded.

"Well, gentlemen," Bachmann said, tucking the paper into one of the field desk's pigeon holes. "That should do it. Questions? Problems? Anything I can help you with?"

James stood and put on his wet cap. "I don't think there's anything you can help us with, Captain."

"Good. Shows capability, that, James. Knew you had the basics for command when I first met you. Well, gentlemen, don't let me keep you from your duties. I'm sure you have much to do. God knows, I have."

"Will you be speaking to the men, sir?" James asked.

"Certainly! But," the company commander said, waving at the papers on the working surface of the field desk, "first things first. That's the army way. The men will understand. See that they do."

Adolph led the way down the long corridor from the captain's room. He held the door to the outside open for James, chuckling so heartily that his belly shook.

James was unable to speak. He shoved past the lawman and strode into the falling rain. He'd never experienced the fury that surged through his body. He kicked at mud in the street as he walked.

A man squatted beside a building, trousers at his knees.

James ran at the man, grabbing him by the collar of his jacket and pulling him upright. The man's trousers fell to the mud. His head cleared James' by a good six inches.

"You're shitting in the street!" the law clerk screamed up into the startled man's face.

"Hey, mister!" the man objected. "Hey, leave off!"

"Leave off?" James screeched. "Leave off? What's your name and your company?"

"Hey, I'm Kramer, Felix Kramer. Company D, the Janesville Volunteers. Who're you, to get all over a man?"

"I'm an officer in this regiment, Kramer!" James cried. "I will not have any man shitting in the street of this camp! Do you hear me?"

"Hell, I hear you. I got caught short and it's raining like hell. The privies are way the hell and gone over there. I didn't mean to offend."

"The next time you get caught short," James shouted, "you cross your legs and you hop to the privies!"

Felix Kramer shook himself from the law clerk's grip. He pulled up his trousers."No need to get wrought," he mumbled, edging away from the furious lieutenant.

James glared as the man from Company D hurried off into the falling rain.

"Damn!" the sheriff laughed. "Never heard you talk like that."

"I never have talked like that," James admitted, breathing deeply, bringing his emotions under control.

"If that was the first time, you got the words and the music right without any practice."

James felt depressed. "I shouldn't have done that."

"Did you a world of good."

"That man. He didn't know any better."

"Next time, maybe he'll use the privies."

"It's not that," James said, walking with the fat man in the falling rain. "I was angry at Captain Bachmann. That man just happened along and I took my anger out on him."

"He was a big one, once you got him stood up."

"If I'd known how big he was going to be, Sheriff, I think I'd have held my tongue and my temper."

"I don't think so. You're doing all right," the lawman declared, slapping the younger man on the soaked shoulders of his gray coat.

"Did you hear Captain Bachmann?" James asked as they plodded through the rain and the mud. "He talked like a clerk. All he was interested in were his papers. He didn't want to hear about the Baraboo Guards. He just wanted to dig around in that pile of papers. At the muster at Baraboo, he acted like a soldier. He acted like one of his regular army orderly sergeants this morning."

"I was there with you."

"He didn't listen to anything I said to him. He was so involved in being a help to the governor. We're living in a leaking swine shed and he was talking about tricking the men into some extra drill by making them march in formation to their meals. Who's going to teach them to do that, Sheriff?"

"I'm with you, boy."

"He said his paperwork was more important than coming to speak to the men."

"First things first is what he said."

"I still don't know what relivee is."

"Reveille," the sheriff corrected.

James stopped and stood in the falling rain. Water ran down the side of his face and dripped from his chin. He looked at Adolph. "What are we going to do?" he pleaded.

"Without Nate Bachmann?"

"Without Nate Bachmann."

"We're going to do what we can," Adolph said. "Me and you."

"I didn't think it would be like this."

"None of us did," the sheriff said. "None of us did."

6

"Left! Right! Left! Right!" Carl Elsasser chanted.

A hundred pairs of feet shuffle-shuffle-shuffled in the mud of Camp Randall.

"Left! Right! Left! Right!"

Shuffle-shuffle-shuffle.

The gray Wisconsin uniforms hadn't been issued to the men. The Baraboo Guards tried to learn to march wearing the civilian clothing they'd worn since leaving Sauk County.

"Left! Right! Left! Right!"

Shuffle-shuffle-shuffle.

"Get off my God-damned heels, Jack!" Gus snarled.

"Left! Right! Left! Right!"

"I haven't felt this dumb since my sister tried to teach me how to dance," Castle Newton told Hollis Oostendorp.

"I didn't feel dumb when she taught me how to dance," Dewey Shoate snickered.

"Who said that about my sister?" the tanner's son demanded.

"We all did!" Gus' gang sang out.

"Left! Right! Left! Right!"

"What do I yell at them to make them stop?" Carl asked as the company wandered past the two lieutenants.

"Halt," James answered. "I think."

"Tell them whoa," Adolph advised. "They'll understand whoa."

"Company!" Carl shouted. "Whoa!"

The Baraboo Guards stumbled to a stop, pushing and shoving.

Carl spat into the mud. He glared at the men. The men glared back at him. Some of them stared off into the distance where other companies of volunteers in civilian clothing tramped in the mud of Camp Randall as they tried to learn to march in step.

"This isn't working," James said to Adolph.

The sheriff grunted, chewing tobacco, his eyes working back and forth on the faces of the men in the formation.

"Turn around," the tavern keeper called. "We'll go back the other way."

"Already been there, Carl," Johnny Makepeace said.

"Turn around!" the tavern keeper shouted.

"Come on, you men!" Carl pleaded. "Get turned around. Larson, haul your brother back into his place in line. We've got to try it again."

"There's a man by the gate selling beer," Herby Auchter told Alois Swartz. "Want to get some beer?"

"Stay here!" Carl shouted. "We're going to learn to march!"

"Teach us after you learn it, Carl," Peter Everett called out.

"Do you think I like this?" Carl demanded of the men.

"You don't have Jack Black treading on your heels, Carl!" Gus Gaard argued.

"Hey, men!" James shouted. The men paid no attention to the law clerk.

"This is dumb," Willis Wright told his brother Robert.

"I already know how to walk, Carl," Willy Schoming said.

"Tired of sleeping in pig shit."

"Ate better at home."

"This isn't what I left Prairie du Sac for."

"Where the hell is Nate Bachmann?"

"All right!" the tavern keeper screamed, turning on the two lieutenants. "That does it! Get yourself another first sergeant! I quit! I don't have to take this! Dumb army! Dumb men! Pig shit! Rain! Mud! I haven't changed my clothes in five days! I'm going back to Baraboo, Adolph, and don't you stand in my way!"

"Now, Carl," the sheriff cautioned.

"Let's all go back to Baraboo!" Dewey Shoate shouted.

"Hey, men!" James called.

Adolph tugged his holstered revolver around to the front of his fat belly.

Murphy the Irishman stepped from the formation to a pile of lumber scraps left over from John Barks' repair work.

"Let's go to the store!"

"Let's get some beer!"

"Let's go back to Baraboo!"

"Let's get laid!"

"Men!" James called out, raising his arms and stepping forward. Adolph put a hand on the law clerk's arm and held him back.

Murphy picked up a small piece of plank and a short stick.

Adolpf's gaze moved from the florid face of the furious tavern keeper to the challenging face of Gus Gaard, to the taunting face of Jack Black. The lawman didn't want to draw his revolver on men from Sauk County but he was determined they would not leave Camp Randall. He was at a loss.

Murphy strode with his stick and plank to the center of the formation of shouting men.

Adolph shifted his eyes to the face of the Irishman. The horse thief had been no trouble since the company's arrival at Camp Randall.

Men who were not shouting watched the little man.

Murphy squared his shoulders and snapped the heels of his over-sized boots together.

"What's this?" James asked the sheriff.

"Damned if I know."

Murphy stared ahead into the faces of the men in the front rank. Some of the shouting died away.

"First Sergeant!" the little man called out. "Will you be counting the cadence? For me, and for me alone?"

"What the hell does he want?" Carl demanded of Adolph.

"How the hell do I know?" the sheriff shouted. "Why not do what the man asks and find out?" Adolph didn't know what the Irishman was up to but he did know that most of the shouting had died down.

"Will you just be singing the words of the heel-and-toe polka, First Sergeant?" Murphy asked. "Like a good man? Left and right, and left and right again?"

"I quit," the tavern keeper declared.

"Go on, Carl," James suggested.

"I don't think I will," the tavern keeper pouted.

"Won't hurt to try," Adolph urged.

"Even if I do, it doesn't mean I'm not going back to Baraboo."

"God damn you, Carl!" the sheriff exploded, angry at the tavern keeper's obstinancy but relieved that the men had quieted down. "Do it!"

"I don't like this, Adolph!"

"Just do it!" the sheriff screamed.

"There's no need to shout at me!" Carl shouted back at Adolph. "All right! Left! Right! Left! Right!"

Murphy nodded his head fiercely at each call.

"Left! Right! Left! Right!"

Nod! Nod! Nod! Nod!

"Jesus Christ!" the tavern keeper screeched at the little man. "Is that all you're going to do? Stand there and nod your head the whole damned day?"

"Seeing as you're asking, First Sergeant," the little man advised, "would you mind calling the cadence a little more regular and even? As if you were singing a sweet lullaby to a sleeping babe?"

"A sleeping babe!" Carl shrieked, turning on the sheriff. "God damn you, Adolph Zimmerman! I'll sing no God-damned lullaby to no God-damned Irishman!"

"Carl!" the fat man threatened.

"God damn you, Adolph! God damn you! I won't forget this! Left! Right! Left! Right!"

Murphy tapped his stick against the piece of plank.

"Left! Right! Left! Right!"

Tap! Tap! Tap! Tap!

Murphy began to lift a foot with each call.

"Left! Right! Left! Right!"

Tap! Tap! Tap! Tap!

Lift! Lift! Lift! Lift!

Jack Black laughed at the ludicrous sight of the furious tavern keeper chanting nonsense and the ridiculous little Irishman beating on a piece of plank, marching in place and going nowhere. Others in the formation laughed.

Murphy turned sharply and stepped off. The laughter ceased. Murphy marched, striding in time to the call of the cadence and the tap of his stick.

"Left! Right! Left! Right!"

Tap! Tap! Tap! Tap!

Murphy marched. Murphy strode. Murphy strutted. Murphy paced the length of the company front, halted, did a sharp about-face and marched back the length of the company again. All eyes were on him now.

"Left! Right! Left! Right!" Carl chanted, matching the rhythm of the Irishman's stick as it beat on the piece of plank.

"I'll be damned," Adolph whispered to James.

"Whooo!" Johnny Makepeace warbled. "Strut, you rooster!"

"He's prancing like a whore on Main Street," Jack Black sneered.

"Look at him," Willis Wright said to Robert.

Hans and Olaf Larson watched the little man in wonder.

Murphy slammed to a halt at the center of the formation. He executed a sharp left-face and stood at attention, looking at the men.

"I'll thank you, First Sergeant, darling," Murphy said.

"Don't you call me your darling, you unnatural Irish bastard!" Carl screeched.

"'Twas but a term of respect, First Sergeant," Murphy assured the furious tavern keeper. "A term of respect. Now," he said, addressing the men, "you'll be listening to your first sergeant's manly voice as he's calling out the count of the cadence. You'll want to have the heel of that foot come down into the mud of the earth as he's calling out that foot's name. Left, and that heel hits the mud. Right, and that heel. And, so on."

"What's he saying?" Ottis Blumenfeld asked.

"I think he's talking in Irish," Johnny Makepeace decided.

"Hey, Murphy!" Jack Black called out. "Say that in German so these farmers can understand it!"

Murphy moved to stand in front of Jack. He squinted up into the taller man's face. "Will you step out here, Mister Black, and flap your yap like that one more time when I'm speaking?"

Jack hesitated. "Well, hell, I didn't mean . . ."

"Then don't be saying!" the little man snapped.

Jack looked over his shoulder for support from the men of Sauk County. There was none. The men were interested in what the Irishman had shown them about marching and, moreso, they wanted to see how Murphy, the stranger among them, would handle the dark, dangerous man they did know.

Murphy stared up into Jack's face. Jack dropped his gaze and spat into the mud at his feet.

Murphy nodded. "Now, for the rest of you," he went on. "Pay attention to what you're doing. Listen to my own sweet patter as I'm tapping on this piece of kindling. Hear the call of your first sergeant as he sings the cadence. Find the music in it and take it into your souls! Ah, you'll be marching for hundreds of miles and not even thinking about it!"

"What's he saying?" Willis Wright wanted to know.

"He's talking that Irish again," Johnny Makepeace whispered, not wanting to speak loud and risk being faced down by the little man.

"First Sergeant!" Murphy called. "Will you be drilling your company?"

"I don't know if I will," Carl said, still pouting.

"No? And, with the high sheriff of Sauk County promising to buy beer for the whole of the company after one good hour's drilling?" the little man shouted for all to hear.

"Hey!" Adolph objected. "I didn't promise to buy any beer!"

"Beer! Beer!" the chant began.

"I didn't promise to buy any beer!" Adolph protested to James.

"Mighty generous of you," James grinned.

"Beer! Beer!"

"Let's get it over with, Elsasser," Gus called out.

"Beer! Beer!"

"That Irish horse thief!" Adolph growled. "I'll get even with him!"

"I think he just got even with you," James said. "You brought him along in chains, remember?"

"I'll send him back to Sauk County in those same chains!"

"This might work for us," James objected. "The men were close to mutiny. Now, they want to learn how to drill."

"Beer! Beer!" the men around Johnny Makepeace chanted.

Carl chewed his lip. He'd lost place to the Irishman and he didn't like that. He wasn't ready to go back to Baraboo as he'd threatened. He thought what the Irishman had shown might help the men learn to march but he didn't care for the little man's taking over his own place of command. The men were calling for him to get on with the drilling. They were willing to give it another try. "All right!" he shouted at them. "But, you listen to me! You do what I tell you! I'm the one in charge around here! That Irishman is just a drummer! That's all he is. A drummer!"

"Murphy, drummer!" simple Hans Larson repeated the words he'd heard the tavern keeper use.

"Murphy the Drummer!" Johnny Makepeace shouted.

"Murphy the Drummer!" the men confirmed.

"Attention!" Carl Elsasser ordered. "Right face! Forward, march! Left! Right! Left! Right!"

Tap! Tap! Tap! Tap! Murphy the Drummer beat on his piece of kindling. The men tried to march to the cadence.

"Small steps, now," the little man called to them. "You aren't striding the miles from here to Baraboo. Small steps. You'll have more small steps in you than long ones."

"Left! Right! Left! Right!" Carl called to the rhythm.

Tap! Tap! Tap! Tap!

"I'll be God-damned," the sheriff admitted. The men were doing better at marching with the help of the Irishman's tapping of the stick on his piece of plank.

"Something seems to be working," James said.

"I don't like this," the lawman declared.

"It'll be worth the beer you have to buy if the men learn to march in step, Adolph."

The lawman didn't answer. He watched the striding, strutting Irishman. He made up his mind. "Murphy the Drummer, there, he's been in the army."

"Do you think so?"

"You're damned right I think so! He didn't learn this stealing horses in Sauk County."

"Isn't this good for us?" James asked. "If he can help the men learn to march? Neither of us knows anything about it. I take this as a pleasant surprise."

"I don't like surprises from the likes of him."

"I consider this to be our good fortune," James declared, taking his position.

"Why didn't he tell me he'd been in the army?"

"You never gave him the chance."

Adolph glared at James.

James returned the lawman's glare.

"Look at him!" Adolph shouted, turning away and pointing. "He's enjoying this!"

"He's teaching the men to march in step."

"I'll bet he's a deserter."

"From the army?"

"I'll put money on it."

"Does that matter?"

"If he's a deserter from the army, we'll have to keep a close eye on him. He won't want to get close to the regulars."

"Will they put him in jail?"

"They'll brand him. With a hot iron. A big letter D. Right on the hip."

"That's inhuman," James said, shuddering.

"They'll do it. I've seen the brand on men. I don't think your Murphy the Drummer will wait around for them to take him."

"He's not my Murphy the Drummer, Sheriff," James said. "You're the one who brought him along in chains."

"All the more reason to keep those chains handy."

The lieutenants watched the Baraboo Guards march past them, the Irishman strutting, the tavern keeper chanting. The men tried, intent on keeping in step.

"We'll let things work themselves out," the sheriff decided. "We'll see how things go for now."

"I think that's best," James concurred. "Sheriff?"

The lawman looked at the law clerk.

"Is that true? Does the army brand deserters when it catches them?"

"It does."

"I can't believe that. Captain Bachmann was in the army. I can't see him branding a man's flesh with a hot iron."

"Nate Bachmann wouldn't do a thing like that."

"I'm relieved to hear so."

"Nate Bachmann was an officer in the army. He'd order a sergeant to brand the man."

7

The gray Wisconsin uniforms were issued the seventh day the men from Sauk County were at Camp Randall. Each of the Baraboo Guards received a gray wool jacket that came to his hip and was trimmed at collar and cuff in dark blue. Each man was issued a pair of gray wool trousers with deep pockets, three suits of long underwear, two flannel shirts, four pairs of thick wool stockings and one pair of heavy army shoes. The cap, unlike the small kepi worn by the officers, was a stiff, high affair made of felt and leather and called a shako.

Each man was issued a black leather belt with a brass buckle, a white canvas haversack for carrying rations, a flannel-covered tin canteen, and a heavy knapsack that had an array of straps and buckles to it. Wool blankets and canvas shelter-halves, ordered from a firm in New York, had not arrived. There were no weapons to issue to the men.

As the men were trying on their new uniforms and fumbling with their new equipment, word passed through the camp that the War Department in Washington had ordered that no further state militia regiments would be accepted into Federal service for terms of ninety days. Regiments willing to sign on for three years, or for the duration of the war if shorter, were to be retained by the states and forwarded to the Federal government as called for. All others were to be disbanded and sent home. Colonel Coon gave the men of the Second Wisconsin the rest of the day to discuss what they wanted to do.

Nine of the companies of the Second Wisconsin signed on for three years. One company, composed of students from the college at Beloit, decided their return to classes after the summer took precedence over their quest for glory. The students disbanded and left, hooted from Camp Randall by the men who had opted to stay. The boys from Beloit were replaced in a day by a company of Green County volunteers who were elated at the unforeseen opportunity of joining the Second Regiment.

The following day the drilling went on.

The drill consisted of learning to march in a column of fours, four men wide and twenty-five men deep, the formation the companies would use to march from one place to another, as in marching down a road. From the column of fours the men had to learn to move into line of battle, a formation fifty men wide and two men deep, the formation from which they would fight. From these two basic formations there were countless variations and angulations and combinations that had to be paced out, practiced, learned. Once mastered, the drill provided an ideal means for moving large bodies of men from one place to another without losing cohesiveness even when under fire.

For army regulars with years to spend on parade grounds the drill was a pastime. For volunteers left to teach themselves from a few tactics manuals in the hands of amateur officers the drill was difficult in the extreme.

Four weeks passed slowly at Camp Randall. The drilling went on.

Ethan read in the newspapers of fighting late in May in St. Louis, Missouri, and of Federal troops occupying Baltimore, Maryland. He read that North Carolina had seceded and joined South Carolina, Mississippi, Florida, Alabama, Georgia, Louisiana, Texas, Tennessee, Virginia and Arkansas to form the Southern Confederacy.

He read that Federal troops had invaded Virginia and occupied the city of Alexandria across the Potomac River from Washington, D. C.

Ethan shared the impatience of the men who drilled at Camp Randall, day after day, while Federal soldiers from other Northern states took the fight to the throat of secession, as Nathaniel Bachmann had promised the Baraboo Guards they would do.

The drilling went on.

Sickness came to Camp Randall as May gave way to June and the weather warmed. Camp fever, diarrhea and measles appeared. Ethan found himself suffering from the heaviness and tightness of chronic constipation.

And still the drilling went on.

"Left! Right! Left! Right!"

"Column, left!" Carl shouted. "March!"

"Hold your pivot!" James called, pacing backwards and watching closely as the men made the turn.

"Left! Right! Left! Right!"

"Get off my God-damned heels, Jack!" Gus growled.

"Left! Right! Left! Right!"

Murphy no longer marched at the side of the company with his plank and stick. The men had picked up the simple rhythm of the cadence. They didn't need his tapping. But the name Murphy the Drummer stuck.

"Left! Right! Left! Right!"

Ethan marched beside his brother-in-law in the second rank of four at the head of the column. The merchant had mastered the requirements of the drill. He let his mind wander as he paced along.

He'd received a letter from his wife the evening before. Lily lamented his decision to enlist into the ranks when he could have been an officer, which would befit his place in Baraboo society. Lily wrote that his being an officer would help make her time in Baraboo while he was gone less embarrassing for her.

"Left! Right! Left! Right!"

As a young man trying to make his way in the world of commerce Ethan had never dreamed of a bride with the wealth and the beauty of his Lily. He had never imagined, on the other hand, the strictures, the conformities, the adherences Lily would bring into his life when they married.

"Left! Right! Left! Right!"

Ethan thought back to their marriage in Milwaukee, to their wedding trip to New York City. It started in innocence there in New York. Ethan ordered a bottle of whiskey for their hotel room. On a chance he mixed Lily a drink of a little whiskey and a lot of water.

With the whiskey, Lily had shed her inhibitions as she shed her clothing under Ethan's gaze. She led Ethan to wonders that pleased, attracted, and even frightened him. She was a wild thing without limit to her demands, her delights, her discoveries. The couple didn't leave the hotel room for three days, barely leaving their bed but to admit room service.

The passion continued until Lily and Ethan came home to Baraboo. There Lily let Ethan know that things connected with whiskey were not things on which Christian marriage was founded. Whiskey, she let him know, took men to a level below that of the creatures of the fields. Lily gave as evidence the witness of her father's behavior when drunk, the witness of her brother's deportment most of the time, the witness of their own sinfulness when whiskey entered their honeymoon. Such things Lily let Ethan know might be things of a wedding trip, possibly, but not things to be continued, remembered, talked about or repeated.

"Left! Right! Left! Right!"

Ethan had worked to understand her. He tried to change his own attitude, tried to accept hers. He was patient, gentle, kind. Early on, Lily had been passive when he pressed for his right with her, waiting for him to finish and then rising to wash herself. A year ago, Lily had taken to placing a lace doily over her face when her husband rutted on her. At that, Ethan gave up.

When he heard that Nathaniel Bachmann was raising the company of militia, he enlisted. He loved Lily. He would not divorce her. He would not break his vows to her. He would not go on living with her. He would run off to march in the mud of Camp Randall with the men from Sauk County.

The stocky merchant wondered if his chronic constipation had anything to do with the feeling of guilt he carried after leaving her.

"Left! Right! Left! Right!"

Yet, he considered, there was another side to Lily. That last night in Baraboo, Ethan had stumbled when stepping up to the porch of the house on Oak Street. The merchant had stood before his door, unsteady from the load of whiskey he'd taken on at Elsasser's Tavern, burdened by the weight of Gus' drunk form hanging from his shoulder.

Lily heard and threw open the door, standing with her back to the lamp light, staring at Ethan, who stood ready for her condemnation.

Instead, Lily led him through the house to the room behind the kitchen where Gus slept. After Ethan dropped the unconscious form of his brother-in-law onto the cot, Lily took his hand and led him to their room at the top of the stairs. He recalled she wore the wine-red robe he'd brought her from Chicago. Her blond hair was piled on her head as it had been on their wedding trip to New York. Her flesh glowed, he remembered, from her bath. She undressed him, helped him into the copper tub set on the carpet in the bedroom, and gently bathed him.

When Ethan stepped from the tub to dry himself, somewhat sobered and much refreshed, he saw the bottle of whiskey on the table next to the bed. As he patted himself with a large towel, Lily, watching him, poured two drinks from the bottle, one straight for him, one mixed with water for herself. Smiling at him, determined, somewhat unsure of herself, Lily lay back on the coverlet, arranging the folds of her gown at her sides. Her long legs showed, white and perfect. Her flat stomach, her golden pubic hair, reflected the soft glimmer of the oil lamp. Ethan watched as Lily touched one long finger into her glass of whiskey and water and held a drop of the liquor on the tip of her finger for a moment. She opened her legs and touched the tip of that finger to herself, mixing whiskey and water into her own dampness.

"Company, halt!" Carl called.

Ethan marched into the back of the man in front of him. The merchant tripped. Both men fell into the mud.

"Aw, shit!" John Barks shouted at Ethan.

Ethan sat in the mud next to the carpenter. Wetness, heavy and cold, seeped into his gray trousers, touching and ending his tumescence. "Sorry," the merchant apologized. "I wasn't thinking."

"God damn!" the carpenter shouted back. "I hope to Christ you weren't thinking when you tromped into me. I'm all over mud!"

Ethan got to his feet. Men gathered around laughing. Carl ran at them. "March?" the tavern keeper screamed. "March? You can't walk without knocking each other down!"

Ethan put out his hand and helped the carpenter to his feet. "Sorry about the trousers," he said quietly. "I'll brush them out for you."

"Aw, hell," John said, flinging mud from his fingers. "Don't worry about it. We both have a night of brushing before us. Cost you a beer at the suttler's."

Late that night, after drinking several bottles of beer and then spending hours brushing the tenacious mud of Camp Randall from the fabric of their gray uniform trousers, John whispered from his bunk, "Hey, Ethan!"

"What?"

"Are you sleeping?"

"Not while I'm talking to you, John."

"Yea. Hey, Ethan? Today? Remember?"

"I can't forget. I'm sorry I marched into you."

"Never mind that. Hey, Ethan?"

"What?"

"When you marched into me, well, were you thinking?"

"Had I been thinking, John, I wouldn't have marched into you."

"That's not what I mean. What I mean is, were you thinking about fucking with your wife?"

Ethan considered the carpenter's question. He was not one to discuss this topic with other men. "Matter of fact," he admitted, "I was."

"Yeah, I know. That's what I mean. God, Ethan, I can't get Peggy off my mind. She didn't want me to come, you know? I wonder if I should have. Know what I mean?"

"I think I do."

"Yeah. Well, hell, good night, Ethan."

"Good night, John," the merchant said, his mind slipping back to thoughts of Lily.

8

The dining room of the Dorn House was lighted by a central chandelier and by oil lamps in glistening crystal and brass wall brackets. Waiters moved silently through the room, serving, removing settings, pouring wine.

James sat alone at a table and finished his coffee. He watched the diners around him eating and laughing. He didn't want to leave the warmth of the Dorn House dining room and walk the mile to the small room in the swine shed at Camp Randall.

He selected a cigar from the humidor his waiter offered and lit it from a candle, inhaling the aroma of good Havana leaf, sharp, biting and pleasant. He stood, brushed a few crumbs from his gray uniform trousers, and walked to the entrance of the room to pay. He took his change and strolled into the narrow bar to have a drink. He wanted to prolong the evening.

Men crowded the space between the bar and the wall. Noisy discussion filled the barroom, an antidote to the soft conversation of the dining room. Some of the men at the bar were officers from the Second Regiment, wearing uniforms of Wisconsin gray. A few wore the colorful uniforms of local volunteer companies, social organizations not yet called into state service. A half-dozen wore the dark blue of the regular army. There were men in civilian dress—politicians, legislators, contractors.

The law clerk found an opening at the bar between a heavy man in black and a tall major of Engineers.

"Cognac," James told the bartender. A man at the table next to him in the dining room had ordered cognac, a light amber liquor in a large, fragile glass. When the bartender served him, James raised the glass and inhaled the rich, sharp spirit that seemed to blend well with the aroma of his cigar. This, he decided, was much better than starting the long walk back to Camp Randall.

James wondered whether he should leave the company and return to Baraboo. He didn't think the men would miss him. Nathaniel Bachmann seldom dealt with him. Adolph didn't seem to like him. Carl spent his time with the men and ignored him. His commitment to help Nathaniel Bachmann enlist the volunteers from Sauk County had been fulfilled. He seemed to be serving no useful purpose living in the swine shed at Camp Randall and watching Sheriff Zimmerman tell the men what to do.

As he raised the glass to his lips and prepared to take a sip, a sharp jolt to his arm splashed cognac onto his coat. The glass slipped from his fingers and shattered on the floor.

"I'm sorry!" a young voice cried out.

James glanced up from brushing drops of cognac from his lapel. He recognized the officer standing behind him. "Please don't concern yourself, Lieutenant Able," he said.

"That was terribly clumsy of me, sir," the young man offered.

The heavy man next to James left the bar and Thad Able slipped into his place. "Two of whatever Lieutenant Peck was having," he told the bartender. "Sir, I am sorry."

"Please," James insisted, "forget it." He was grateful for the company of a familiar face. "How are you getting on?"

"If I told you Company A is getting on well, Lieutenant Peck, I wouldn't be telling you the truth. You, sir?"

James thought about the question. There was no reason to involve the young officer in his own uncertainties. "The same," he said. "Look, if we're going to stand here and drink together, why don't we use first names? You insisted on that when we met at Camp Randall. Call me James."

"Sir, since then, I've been learning military customs and courtesies. A second lieutenant addresses a first lieutenant by his rank."

"Not when off duty," James countered.

"Is that so?"

James recalled Adolph making up the first and second rules of war. "I really don't know," he admitted.

"All right, James," the lad from Beaver Dam grinned, pleased to be part of a conspiracy against an establishment he didn't understand. "Are you dining with Captain Bachmann?"

"I'm dining alone. Today is my birthday. The other lieutenant in the Baraboo Guards has the company this evening so I took myself into town to have dinner."

"Well, happy birthday!" the boy grinned, raising his glass. "We've all been noticing that the Baraboo Guards are drilling well. Your company is far ahead of the rest of us. Do you have men with prior military service?"

"I'm not sure," James hesitated. "We have an Irishman who seems to know something about all of this. He's been a help."

"And, of course, you have Captain Bachmann. You're fortunate to have a West Point graduate for your company commander."

James remembered making the same point to Sheriff Zimmerman the night before the muster in Baraboo. He nodded as if in agreement. He didn't want to talk about Nathaniel Bachmann's contribution to the training of the Baraboo Guards.

To change the subject, he asked, "Why are you in Wisconsin gray, Thad?"

"I was studying law here at the university and clerking for Judge Faircloth when the call for volunteers went out. I received a telegram from my father saying he'd secured the second lieutenancy in the Citizens' Guards for me."

"Was that all the telegram said?" James asked.

"He wished me well. He added something about the honor of the family name."

James frowned at what he considered a cold and distant thing for a father to do. Never having known his own father, he'd have expected more.

"It's not as bad as it sounds," Thad said, noticing the law clerk's expression. "Father and I have never been close. I'm sure he has my interests at heart. A good war record will be of value to a young lawyer after this is over."

"I'm sure he had that in mind," James agreed. "I read law. I clerk for Judge Blane in Baraboo."

"A well-known jurist!"

"Not as eminent as your Judge Faircloth, sitting on the bench of the Supreme Court of Wisconsin."

"I'm sure you got to work more closely with Judge Blane than I ever got to work with Judge Faircloth. All I ever did was busy myself in his library, filing briefs. He did insist, though, that we clerks attend his evenings at home where we got to eat, drink and mingle with Madison's legal fraternity. Food, wine and the devastating Miss Lucille."

"Miss Lucille?"

"Judge Faircloth's daughter. Every attorney and office holder in the city has set his cap for her. She destroys them, each in turn, with her flashing brown eyes."

"I take it," James said, smiling, "that you've set your own cap for the devastating Miss Faircloth?"

"Were I so brave! What chance has a lowly law student from Dodge County with every success story in Madison paying court to her? She's unassailable."

"Possibly, in your military career," James grinned, "you'll learn to storm and take breastworks as unassailable as you describe those of Miss Faircloth."

"That, in military terminology, James, is called a forlorn hope," the boy sighed. "And, speaking of Miss Faircloth, I have to excuse myself and be off in that direction. Again, James, I apologize for spilling cognac on you."

"Think nothing of it. I've enjoyed talking with you. I'll recall our conversation as I walk back to Camp Randall."

"You've no further plans for the evening?"

"No."

"Come with me. We'll attend Judge Faircloth's evening at home. That's where I'm going."

James shrugged. "I wasn't invited."

"No one is invited. If you're in the legal profession in Madison, you're expected to be there."

"I'm hardly a member of the legal profession of Madison," James protested without conviction. "I won't be intruding?"

"You'll give offense by not being there, I assure you."

"All right," James agreed. He didn't want to walk back to the swine shed at Camp Randall. He finished his cognac and followed the law student from the Dorn House.

The lieutenants strolled past the state capitol building, where lamps glowed as clerks and scribes worked through the evening with the documents on which the domestic affairs of the state and the military affairs of the nation depended. They walked up Wisconsin Avenue, a broad, rutted street that led to the ridge above Lake Mendota, the larger of the two lakes that edged the isthmus on which the city of Madison was built. They turned into a residential avenue lined with impressive houses.

The Faircloth home was three stories high, built of local stone, its main entrance a wide doorway set behind tall columns. A coach entrance was to one side at the end of a long drive. Through the tall windows James could see light and activity within.

The lieutenants stepped into the foyer and added their gray caps to the pile of hats on a high table.

"Follow me," Thad Able stated, taking charge. "You've eaten. I haven't. First, food. Then, wine. Later, the introductions."

"Mister Peck," Nathaniel Bachmann said. The officer stepped into the foyer.

Thad snapped to attention.

"Captain Bachmann," James returned the greeting.

"Good to see you, Mister Peck," Bachmann continued, ignoring the boy from Beaver Dam. "Good to see that you're getting out and making the social contacts that are so important to a young officer. Your timing is providential, also."

"Sir," James said, "I'd like to present Lieutenant Able, Company A."

Bachmann nodded curtly.

"Honored to make your acquaintance, sir!" the law student recited.

"Yes," Bachmann nodded, dismissing the lad. "James, I wish to speak with you. You will excuse us, Mister . . ."

"Able, sir! Company A!"

"Yes. James, step this way."

Thad made eating motions and pointed toward the main hall as Bachmann led James to a corner.

"There's a problem developing here," Bachmann said, "that I want you to take in hand and resolve."

"What is that, sir?"

"Young officer. Quite inebriated. About to make a scene. Hardly the place for that, I'd say."

"Hardly, sir," James agreed, not sure what he was being carried into.

"Want you to step in and prevent any unpleasantness. Take the man under control. Remove him. Use discretion. I have full confidence that I can count on you to do this."

"Is he an officer from our regiment, sir?"

"Of course not. One of the local companies. He's about to become quite obnoxious."

"Can I order a local officer to the guard house at Camp Randall, sir?"

"Doubt if it will come to that. Take him under your control and remove him. That should be all that is required."

"Sir!" James said. He felt he was being imposed on. "The officer's name, sir?"

"Faircloth."

"Sir?"

"Judge Faircloth's son."

"But, Captain, this is his home."

"Quite. I said this would require discretion on your part. Use your initiative. Do it. Then, mingle, mix, meet people. Do you good. For myself, unfortunately, it's back to the headquarters at Camp Randall and the midnight oil. No end to the paperwork, James. No end at all."

James watched in despair as the captain searched through the pile of hats on the table. Bachmann found his gray cap, tapped it onto his head at the proper angle, and smiling reassuringly at the law clerk, left.

James shook his head. He walked into the main hall and found Thad Able filling a plate with slices of cheese and cold meat. The law student offered a plate.

James waved it away, drawing the boy away from the people at the table. "I've a problem."

"From your discussion with Captain Bachmann?"

"Do you know young Faircloth? The judge's son?"

"Preston? Sure. We sat together in lectures at the university. Nice enough when he's sober, which is seldom. Loses every battle he fights with old demon rum. Is he part of your problem?"

"He is my problem. He's here and he's about to make some kind of scene. Captain Bachmann told me to get him away before he causes trouble."

"Away? This is his home. He lives here."

"I know that. Will you help me?"

"Sure. I remember one time he got so blasted . . ."

"Tell me about that later. Do you see him?"

Thad stood on his toes, shoving cheese into his mouth and scanning the room over the heads of the people nearby. "Over there."

"Where?"

"Across the room. Near the pantry door. Uniform of the Mendota Guards, scarlet and gray. Oh, he's got a bag on tonight! He's drooling! See him?"

"I see him."

"Captain Bachmann was right, James. He's going to make a scene. That's a justice of the supreme court he's got by the shirt and he's holding the dean of the law school by the coat. If he falls, he's going to take those two with him."

"You said that door leads to the pantry?"

"A long hall back to the kitchen."

"Can you get from here to there, Thad? Into the pantry?"

"Want me to come through the pantry and open the door behind him?"

"I'll get Faircloth. He can make his scene to the pots and pans in his father's kitchen. You close the door after us and take those two to the bar."

"Good plan, James. You can drag him into the pantry and hit him over the head with a skillet."

"I don't think I'll have to hit him. He's pretty far gone from what I see."

"Two minutes?"

"Eat up and we'll go."

"I'll come back for this," Thad said, putting his plate on the buffet and making his way through the people near the table, heading for the rear of the Faircloth home.

James walked into the crowd, keeping his eyes on Preston Faircloth, hoping the judge's son wouldn't fall before he got to him. As he approached, James heard the two men objecting. Preston was shaking the men, earnestly blabbering some drunken discourse into their faces, using his greater strength to overcome their efforts to free themselves from his grip. One of the men was becoming very red in the face, his mouth opening and closing as he gasped for air.

James stepped in front of Preston and took the boy's forearms in his hands. He held tightly, tugging downward. Preston released the two men, stepping unsteadily away, trying to focus his wandering vision on the gray-clad form that held him. James pulled the judge's son to him, pinning the boy's arms behind his back.

"James!" Thad whispered from the open pantry door.

Preston struggled in James' arms. Holding the boy with difficulty, the law clerk stepped backward into the dark hall. Thad closed the door after him.

A lamp glowed from the kitchen at the end of the hall. James felt his way with his feet. In the kitchen, the law clerk saw a wooden bench along one wall. He shuffled toward it, Preston's head angrily banging on his chest. James turned for the bench. Preston twisted back, then forward. He managed to work one arm loose and swung that fist wildly, landing a wild punch on the law clerk's nose. A flash of pain seared through his eyes. Blood spurted onto his lips and chin. James threw Preston toward the bench, where the boy collapsed. James stood swaying, his eyes closed, his stomach churning. He wanted to scream. Carefully, he touched his face. Nausea swept through him when bone and gristle moved under his exploring fingers.

"Here," a voice said. A hand touched his elbow, steadying him. Something was pressed into his hand, a towel. James wasn't sure he could stand. He touched the towel gently to his face. Bone moved. He shuddered. Pain flared outward from his broken nose into the bones of his cheeks. He tried to open his eyes. The eyelids stuck together.

"There's a chair behind you," a woman's voice said. "Sit, if you can. I'll help you."

The hand on his elbow guided him. He felt the chair behind his knees and sat. He bent forward. That hurt. He raised his head.

"This is another towel," the voice told him. "It's wet. I'm going to put it on the back of your neck."

Cool dampness there helped his nausea. He wasn't interested in the source of the voice. He was trying not to throw up his dinner. His eyelids wouldn't part.

"Some blood is congealing here," the voice told him. "Be still." A damp cloth and gentle fingers worked below his forehead, avoiding the source of the throbbing pain in his nose and cheeks. "There," she said.

James managed to open his eyes. He blinked. His eyes wouldn't focus.

"Is there pain?" she asked, her eyes intently studying his face.

James blinked again. He didn't want to nod.

"You're one of Nathaniel Bachmann's officers?" the woman asked, stepping back from him. She was tall, as tall as he.

James blinked. His upper lip was swelling rapidly.

"I saw Nathaniel speak to you when you entered," she explained, studying the features of his bruised face. "I saw him delegate this unsavory task to you and then leave. Retreat is the military word, isn't it?"

James nodded slowly, carefully. He didn't want to try to speak. His eyes followed hers.

"Well!" Thad Able called, coming through the door to the pantry. "You've met!"

James turned to face the law student. He wasn't sure what words would sound like spoken through swelling lips.

The boy from Beaver Dam gasped, pointing. "Did you do that?"

"I didn't do that," the woman said. "My brother, well, you can see."

"First blood shed in the regiment, James!" Thad grinned.

James silently cursed the law student. He didn't want levity.

"You could introduce us, Thad," the woman suggested.

"I thought you'd already done that, what with . . ."

James looked pleadingly at the boy.

"I see. Miss Lucille Faircloth, meet Lieutenant James Peck. James, Lucille. You're introduced."

"Thank you, Thad," Lucille Faircloth said, taking the law student by the arm and steering him toward the door to the pantry.

Thad hesitated, looking at the woman and the injured law clerk, wondering if he should leave. Lucille gave his arm a push. He closed the door behind himself.

Lucille smiled and shook her head. She glanced at James.

He tried to smile back, then grimaced with pain.

Lucille took the damp towel from the back of James' neck and rinsed it in a basin of water in the kitchen's dry sink. She folded the towel and handed it to him.

"Thank you, Miss Faircloth," he managed painfully.

"I'm the one to thank you, Lieutenant Peck," she said, standing before him and studying his face, his eyes. "My brother was about to embarrass my father. You stepped in to help. You were injured. Forgive us as a family, Lieutenant Peck. Accept our gratitude for what you did."

James wanted to speak. Instead, he nodded. Pain flared from his shattered nose.

"Can I do anything?" she asked.

"I'd like to leave," he whispered carefully. He glanced at the door to the pantry that led to the main hall of the Faircloth home.

"You'd like to do that without exposing your wounded face to most of Madison's society?" She smiled.

He carefully nodded.

"I understand," she said warmly. "You mustn't let your wound embarrass you. You received it in an act of kindness. You may leave this way when you're ready." She nodded to a door in the rear of the kitchen wall. "It leads to our garden. Your cap?"

He groaned. He'd forgotten about his cap. He wanted to put his fingers to his nose, to examine the damage there. He didn't do that. "The foyer," he whispered. "A high table there."

"How will I recognize it?"

"A gray Wisconsin kepi," he told her, careful with every word. "My name's stamped into the band."

Lucille leaned close to James, looking carefully at his face, his injury. "You'll be all right while I'm gone," she said. She rose and turned, leaving the kitchen.

James had never seen more alluring eyes. She was an entrancing creature. No, he corrected himself, she was as devastating as Thad Able had described her. James felt a sense of security, content that he was not a Madison suitor about to be destroyed by those eyes. He smiled at that, sending bolts of pain outward from his broken nose into his cheekbones, his jaws, his teeth. Nausea rolled within him. He prayed he wouldn't vomit.

Lucille Faircloth swept into the kitchen minutes later, a napkin on one hand, James' gray Wisconsin kepi perched on the dark curls of her head. "The napkin has ice," she told him. "Hold it to your face. It may help with the swelling. It's sure to help with the pain. Although . . ."

James looked at her.

"Lieutenant Peck," she said seriously, lightly touching the side of his head with soft fingers, "you're going to look a sight for several weeks."

James blinked. He hadn't thought of his appearance. He hadn't thought of anything beyond getting away from the Faircloth home, that and those eyes. He touched the napkin with ice to his cheek. The cold, damp fabric refreshed him until it touched broken bone. Pain made his mind spin. When he could open his eyes he had to brace himself firmly in the chair to keep from slipping to the floor.

"Are you all right?" Lucille asked, concerned.

James blinked.

"Will a walk in the night air help?"

He exhaled. "Possibly."

"Give me a moment to raise my brother's feet to the bench you almost got him laid out on so he doesn't roll off and do to his own face what he's done to yours."

James watched her bend and lift Preston's feet to the bench. She tugged at the boy's uniform coat, pulling an arm from under him. Her movements were sure, specific. Her manner seemed to James to indicate disdain for Preston's condition and yet concern for his well-being. Then she turned to James. "Can you stand if I help you?"

"I'll try."

She put an arm around his chest and took his left hand. James stood, wavering, leaning against her.

"We have a lovely garden, Lieutenant Peck," she told him, leading him slowly to the door. "We'll walk for a while. I've asked Thad Able to remain and take you back to Camp Randall in my father's carriage."

"I thank you for your concern, Miss Faircloth," he said thickly.

"Lean on me," she told him, holding him.

James leaned, stepping from the kitchen to the garden. He thrilled at the feel of the woman who helped him. She was, as Thad had told him, devastating.

9

The cottage of the widows Baumgarten was a poor, small place. Coals glowing in the hearth of its kitchen gave scant warmth and little light.

Murphy the Drummer stood in the dark. He was naked, a ragged quilt thrown over his shoulders. Somewhere before him in the shadows was a table. The little man squinted, trying to find the table without stumbling about in his bare feet on the cold stones of the floor. There was a bottle of whiskey on the table. He needed a drink.

Gus Gaard and the dark-haired widow Baumgarten had ceased their giggling and thumping in the loft over the room an hour ago. Murphy heard soft breathing from up there. The blond-haired widow Baumgarten snored fiercely in the trundle bed in the parlor from which Murphy had just risen. She'd be there, warm and fat, when he returned but, he prayed to the saints who had committed only small sins, she'd be well into the sleep her drinking and his passionate thrusting had taken her.

Murphy felt the cold fingers of the haunt touching the sides of his soul. He knew it. It would come to him often when he drank and when he fucked. He'd wake and he'd feel the touch of the haunt and he'd not be able to return to the comfort of sleep. He'd have to get up and away from the pallet of lust, wherever it might be at the time, to be off by himself lest the haunt touch the soul of the one with whom he'd coupled.

The little man shivered.

It was times such as this that brought it back to him. He'd see in his mind's eye the thatched roof of that rough cropper's cottage in Ireland and the whitewashed stones of its walls. In the hearth would be the dim glow of smouldering peat. There'd be the smells of cattle in the barn next to the kitchen and the soft sounds of many sleeping children. He'd be a boy again, wrapped in the horse's blanket because Patrick had taken his shirt from him to be more warm himself. His soul would be in Ireland and he'd be the boy, naked and cold in the one room of the cottage, wishing and wondering when and how he'd be getting away.

Murphy shook himself. It did a man no good to be dwelling on what had happened in the past, on what he'd done and on what had been done to himself in the course of it all. That only brought on the wishes and the doubts and the wonderings and those brought on the cold touch of the haunt.

He thought of his mother as he stood in the cold darkness of the cottage of the widows Baumgarten in Dane County, in Wisconsin, in America. She'd be gone, herself, now these many years.

How, he wondered, had she kept them going from one day to the next when it was herself who was the one condemned? There'd be no running off in search of fortune for her, whatever the hardship and the evil of life in County Tyrone. With her man, the father, gone off with the Irish Fusiliers to death or desertion in some foreign land and his offspring crawling in the dirt of the floor and tugging at the ragged edges of her skirt, to where was it ever she'd be getting away?

Murphy prayed there was some certain corner of heaven set aside for the likes of herself with a cozy of tea at hand and a good glow of peat working in the hearth.

He wiped tears from his red cheeks and sniffed at the run in his pointed nose. Ah, now, he thought, wasn't it his own lot he should be worrying about, even with herself there in heaven to be interceding with the Virgin on his own behalf?

He'd have to be making up his mind, and soon. His time with the lads of the Baraboo Guards hadn't been the worst of times when held up and compared to other times in his life but there had best be coming a moment in those times when he'd be granting himself a special discharge from the Wisconsin militia and be taking himself off in the direction of the California coasts. Were he to be staying too long with the farmers from Sauk County, wouldn't he be looking toward a day on the calendar of life that had a flogging, a branding and a hanging marked upon it?

He was safe, he considered, as long as the Baraboo Guards remained in Madison, for there were no American men-o'-war with their compliments of Marines sailing the lakes, Mendota and Monona, that flanked the city. He'd want to keep good space between himself and the Corps of Marines.

There were times in the nights when he would dream they were coming close upon him, their white cross-belts forming a fence about him as he sought to run, their cat-o'-nine-tails with its ends dipped into molten lead, their smoking iron for branding into his flesh, their rough hemp noose. When a man got to where the fears came upon him in his sleep, Murphy knew, it was time to be packing and leaving, going off to another place and hoping the fears wouldn't be following along too close behind.

Yet, the little man considered, wasn't there the other side of the coin?

He was coming to know some of the lads of the Baraboo Guards, he who had come among them the stranger, such as that great blond beast, Gus, sleeping in the loft over the room. Hadn't he been able to teach them some of the simple things of life such as the art and science of walking from one place to another to the rhythm of a counted cadence? He was pleased at having done that but it had been a wise thing to do when he'd dropped back into the ranks once the lads had learned.

His game with the stick and plank had brought the young Lieutenant Peck to ask him if he'd volunteer to be one of the regimental drummers, as if that were an honor to be bestowed. Wouldn't that be a compliment, now? And, with a huge drum to be hauled along on the march and making such a tempting target for the sharpshooters on the other side? Hadn't he seen the little drummer boys in Mexico with their faces all shot away and their intestines bulging out of hideous stomach wounds, and them still banging away on their drums as the infantry went forward like it would make something important happen? Even little drummer boys liked to die thinking they were part of something important.

No, that wouldn't do, Mister Peck, and thank you for the asking.

Murphy thought he might be staying on with the farmers from Sauk County for yet a short time. It wouldn't be wise to desert so close to the state capitol and to Baraboo. He'd stay for a while. He might be able to impart more of his hard-won wisdom to the lads, or he might not. Aye, but count on it, the moment the Baraboo Guards were coming into sighting distance of salt water and the chance of meeting up with the Corps of Marines, it'd be off and away for the California coasts for himself, and thank you for the time we've spent together.

It wasn't the fear of hanging that touched the little man's soul. He'd seen jack-tars hanged. A good step off the yardarm would give the body the fall to break the neck and bring the soul into the presence of the Creator quick and not too painful.

It was his dread of the flogging and the branding, the things they would be doing to his living body for the sake of the other men to see and take warning from, that touched his soul and brought on the cold hand of the haunt.

Murphy had seen men flogged and never seen one that didn't cry out for death or for mercy under the agony of the lead-tipped lashes of the cat-o'-nine-tails. He'd seen men branded and never seen a man that didn't faint at the stench of his own smoking flesh.

There it was, the little man saw, the bottle he sought. It was on the table in the darkness where he remembered it. Murphy grabbed the bottle and drank from it, sucking whiskey into his throat and down to his insides where it would quickly reach his tortured soul.

10

Mary Schmelzer, the serving girl, removed the course setting, replacing china plates with crystal cups of preserved fruit.

Judge Faircloth took a decanter of sherry and poured wine over his fruit. The judge, a spare man with full head of white hair and bright brown eyes, passed the decanter to James. "I learned this in Italy," the judge said. "My host served fruit and wine. I drank my wine. My host watched me and poured his wine over his serving of fruit. That made me feel like the bumpkin I was. It taught me a lesson."

"Sir?" James asked.

"When on foreign ground, Mister Peck, give the knowledgeable natives the lead. I suppose that could apply to you and to the men of your regiment at Camp Randall?"

"We're a little light on the knowledgeable natives there, sir, and a little heavy on the foreign ground."

"Well said!" the judge considered, spooning cherries and wine. "Don't I understand, though, that there are some half-dozen trained officers with the Second Regiment?"

"Governor Randall requires all the help the trained officers can give him, sir. They don't have much time for us. We do what we can on our own."

"Nathaniel Bachmann is West Point-trained."

"Captain Bachmann is heavily committed to the governor's needs, sir."

"As he was heavily committed to the governor's anteroom before he raised your company!"

"Father," Lucille Faircloth cautioned.

The judge looked at his daughter, then shrugged. "I shouldn't speak ill of Nathaniel Bachmann," he conceded. "He's doing his part in this as best he sees it. Finish your fruit and wine, young man. We'll have cognac and cigars. Do you drink cognac?"

"Yes, sir. Lately."

"Good. I see," the jurist said, nodding, "that you're recovering from your wound."

James blushed and his broken nose and bruised cheeks ached.

"I've embarrassed you," the judge apologized. "I'd no thought to do that. I'm in your debt, Mister Peck. My son was about to disgrace his home and my hospitality. You stepped in to help. I regret you have to bear the agony that caused you."

"My own fault for being clumsy, sir."

"My son was exhibiting inexcusable conduct! He was . . ."

"Father," Lucille interrupted, "Lieutenant Peck has accepted our apologies and our thanks. He's shown the graciousness of being our guest at dinner. I suggest we leave it at that."

Lucille brought glasses from a sideboard to the table. She took away the fruit cups and brought a decanter of cognac, pouring for each man. She let her father select two long cigars from a cedar humidor. The judge clipped the ends and offered one cigar to James. Lucille held a candle for the men to light.

"I'll leave you to your cigars, your cognac and your conversation," she said, addressing her father. "Try to be kind to Lieutenant Peck. He's a guest in our home. You have a few minutes." In a swirl of skirts she strode from the room.

"She hates to have to leave, Mister Peck," the judge said, exhaling a cloud of cigar smoke. "Hates to risk missing anything. Sits in on my meetings here. Can't keep her away. Charms my guests and my colleagues and takes their attention away from the topics at hand. She's insufferable."

The law clerk flushed, not knowing how to react to the rapidly changing levels of discourse he was experiencing at the Faircloth dinner table.

"Tell me," the judge asked, rolling his cigar in his fingers. "Will the war last the three years you've agreed to serve?"

James took a sip of cognac. "Most of the men in the regiment think it might last through this summer, sir. Possibly into next summer. Not more than that."

"I didn't ask what most of the men in the regiment think, Mister Peck."

"Ah, no, sir," James stammered. "You didn't. For myself, I don't know, sir. I don't think the states of the Confederacy can sustain a long war effort. They don't have the industry nor the wealth nor the manpower for that."

"Hm," the judge considered. "The South cannot sustain a long war?"

"No, sir."

"They started it. They must have something in mind."

"I think the Confederate government plans for its army to gain a quick victory over our army. If it can achieve that, the Confederacy will hold a position of power from which it will try to negotiate peace and independence."

"As simple as that?"

"They have only to defend themselves from us to win, sir."

"And, for us to win?"

"We'll have to conquer the Confederate army in the field. We'll have to invade the states of the South and put down their institutions by force of arms. Ours will be the harder task, sir."

Judge Faircloth blew cigar smoke, his brown eyes peering at the uncomfortable law clerk. "Tell me, Mister Peck," he pressed the lad, "have you contemplated what will happen if the Confederate army does win its quick victory over our army?"

James stared at his cigar. He hadn't considered a Confederate victory. "Sir, I don't know about that," he admitted. He thought for a moment. "I guess we'll have to pull ourselves together and go out and whip them the second time."

"I see. And, Mister Peck, what do you see as your role in this?"

"My role, sir?" The law clerk wondered if the jurist sensed his confusion and doubt as to what his role was.

"What is your role in what's happening to our state and our nation?"

"My role is to help Captain Bachmann command the Baraboo Guards," James answered, somewhat lamely.

"Not to preserve the Union of the states?" the judge demanded. "Not to put down the rebellion? Not to win glory for the arms of Wisconsin? Not any of the reasons the rest of your generation is making up to justify running off to an unnecessary war? Is your role so simple, Mister Peck? I find that hard to believe!"

James was uncomfortable that he was unable to better define his role in what had become his life. He understood the judge was pressing him. "My role, Judge Faircloth, is to help Captain Bachmann command the Baraboo Guards," he repeated.

"No dreams of glory, Lieutenant?"

"Sir, I . . ."

"Father!" Lucille cried, sweeping into the dining room. "You're intimidating our guest! I expect better of you! Lieutenant Peck," she said, glaring at her father, "walk with me to the band concert on the steps of the capitol. The fresh air will feel good and it may help me cool my anger at my parent!"

James looked from father to daughter, feeling out of place, wondering what to do, what to say.

"Go, Mister Peck," the judge told him. "Enjoy the concert. Perhaps, some day, you and I can continue our conversation." He glanced at his daughter. "Uninterrupted!"

Lucille bent and kissed her father on the forehead. The judge winked at James as the astonished law clerk escorted Lucille from the room.

With the couple gone, Judge Faircloth sat in his chair and poured himself another glass of cognac. Bright young man, he considered. Lack of experience and lack of exposure, but he'd gain experience and exposure following after Nathaniel Bachmann. That he would.

The judge compared the law clerk to his own son. If only he could find the way to make Preston become the son he needed and wanted. Were he not able to come to terms with Preston, the judge was prepared to look to his daughter's mate for the person who would carry on the work and manage the extensive holdings of the Faircloth estate.

And, the judge knew, he had little time.

11

On an evening later in the week, Lucille Faircloth stepped into the foyer and closed the door behind herself. She leaned against the frosted pane of the door gathering her thoughts. Lieutenant Peck had kissed her at the door. She'd let him go on thinking he'd initiated the kiss.

"Will you join me in a glass of sherry?" her father called.

Lucille walked into the judge's library, poured wine into a glass, and drank most of it. She refilled the glass and sat on a sofa across the room.

Judge Faircloth watched his daughter. The soft light from the oil lamp on his desk barely reached the girl. "Did you enjoy dining with Lieutenant Peck?"

She nodded, her eyes on the glass in her hand.

"You didn't ask the young man in?"

She shook her head.

"You parted friends?"

She looked at him.

"Lovers?" he asked gently.

"I don't know," she whispered.

Judge Faircloth watched her in silence for several moments. He stood and walked to the cabinet to refill his glass with sherry. He carried the decanter to the table beside her sofa. Behind his desk, he settled into his chair. "Well," he said, as if on his bench at court, "I'm prepared to hear pleadings."

"I don't want to plead anything," she whispered.

"Does Lieutenant Peck have any idea of this?"

She shrugged.

"I see," the judge said. He wanted to choose his next words with care. "'Cille," he spoke gently, "you've known Lieutenant Peck for only a few days. You've only a few more in which to come to know him better."

She nodded, sipping wine, holding back tears.

The judge leaned forward on his desk. "I won't act like a concerned parent. I haven't been one in the past and this isn't the time for me to begin. May I tell you what I see?"

"Please."

"He's a bright young man. Handsome in a poorly-fed way. Hasn't an ounce of fat on his body, which is more likely a lack of means rather than a lack of appetite. I doubt if he has thirty dollars to his name. He has little confidence in himself and he has no family. He's trying to make his way in life at law, which is good. He's trying to do that in Baraboo, which is not, although he has Judge Blane for a mentor. All in all, 'Cille, I take him to be a presentable young man, broken nose, bruised face, the rest. Does that help?"

She nodded, trying to smile.

The judge sipped sherry, letting moments pass. "'Cille," he eventually spoke. "I have to say some things that I want you to hear. You may have thought them out for yourself but hear me, will you?"

She looked at him, waiting.

"You'd never have met Lieutenant Peck were it not for this war. He's here in Madison because he's a soldier. He's not a real soldier, he's a law clerk in uniform, yet he's an officer in an infantry company. Infantry officers will fall like sparrows before the winter wind when our army comes up against the Southern army, girl. Your Lieutenant Peck's chances of living through the coming months are, simply, not good."

Tears rolled freely down Lucille's cheeks.

"I know men of the South," he went on, "colleagues on the bench in the courts of the Southern states. I know planters and and politicians down there. They're good people, much like us, although different in many ways. They're proud people. They'll fight us. They'll fight us until they're beaten and then they'll fight on. They'll fight with passion and without regard to danger, death or the odds against them. We'll win this war eventually, 'Cille, but only after we've fought them to where they haven't an arm left to wield a saber nor an eye left to aim a musket. It will be a terrible struggle. Its cost will be counted in the blood of young men like your Lieutenant Peck. He may never come back to you, 'Cille."

Lucille dropped her head into her hands.

The judge watched his daughter's shoulders shake with her sobbing. He wanted to tell her that he would do something to make everything right for her, that he would take care of things for her. He could only sit and watch the girl weep.

The judge thought as he watched that it was not like her to become so quickly enamored with a simple law clerk from Baraboo. The judge had been showing his daughter off since she'd become available and she'd steadfastly rejected every suitable swain out of hand. He wondered what attracted his daughter to Lieutenant Peck.

Lucille wiped her eyes and blew her nose into a small handkerchief. She tried to smile, bravely, to her father.

"When you decide what is to be, 'Cille," he said, committing himself to her decision, "then let nothing stand in your way. As much as I fear for your Lieutenant Peck, girl, I envy you. You have love."

"You had love," she said, "for Mother."

"To this day, and forever."

"You seldom talk about your love for Mother."

"I seldom can. After all these years, she's with me still, as if she never had been taken. I pray you'll not lose one so young and so dear, 'Cille. I pray the gods, whoever they are, will spare you that." Judge Faircloth stared into the soft light of the oil lamp on his desk. There were tears in his own eyes.

Lucille watched him. Her heart went out to him. "Did you know Mother long before you were married?"

He returned her gaze. He could tell her. He wanted to tell her. "Less than you've known your Lieutenant Peck, 'Cille. A day."

She smiled at him, intrigued.

"I should tell you," he went on, leaning back in his chair, "we were in bed with each other an hour after we met."

She was greatly intrigued. She forgot for the moment her own heartache.

Judge Faircloth reminisced. "I had, at the time, less than your Lieutenant Peck's presumed thirty dollars to my name and far less of his prospects as an attorney. I was a law clerk, as is he. In Baltimore. I was charged with carrying papers to her father's house on a Sunday morning. The family was at worship but the daughter, the only daughter, the woman who would be your mother, was ill. Too ill for services. She had a cold. She greeted me when I knocked at the door and she invited me in to wait for her family's return. She served me tea, all red-faced and watery at the eyes, clutching her gown about her and sneezing all over the serving tray. I was swept, 'Cille."

The judge sipped sherry, remembering.

Lucille waited, giving him time.

"What a scene did follow!" the judge went on, smiling, embarrassed at confessing to his daughter. "Her family returned from worship and found us in our guilt. You can imagine what had happened. I won't go into details. I was fully prepared to be murdered. Your mother was so calm. I always admired her ability to remain calm at the worst of times. She introduced me to her family as we dressed and she packed and sneezed. We got out of the house while her family thundered and roared and swore vengeance on the two of us. They were too stunned to do more than that, which was in our favor. We were on our way an hour in her father's carriage before they could get themselves together enough to set out in pursuit. They were very intent on avenging the wrong done to their family honor. We stopped in a village in western Maryland and convinced an elder of a German church there that our lives depended on a hasty marriage. As they did. They caught up with us, of course, later on the road, your grandfather and your uncles. They wailed and they moaned and they thrashed me, each in his turn. They disowned your mother on the spot. Threatened me with hanging from a tree after the removal of certain organs. Then, as they left, with me all bloody but unhung and ungelded, and with your mother sitting calmly in her father's carriage, which they did not think to claim, your uncle, Harry, threw me a purse with seventy dollars in it. I think I did like your uncle, Harry. Couldn't stand the rest of them. Your mother and I came west, Pittsburgh for a while. Cleveland. Indianapolis, where you were born. Finally, to Madison. Every day, 'Cille, was like the first day with her. I loved her. I even think she loved me."

The judge wiped his eyes. He removed his spectacles and blew his nose loudly in a large handkerchief.

"You've never told me this," Lucille said softly.

The judge shook his head. He couldn't speak.

"I'm happy for you," she told him. "For what you had."

The judge blinked. He replaced his spectacles. He cleared his throat and sipped some sherry. "I wish it all for you, girl," he said. "The love. The fulfillment. The heartbreak what comes with love. Take every day you're given. There will only be so many of them."

Lucille stood and crossed the room to her father's desk. The judge looked up to her. "Now I think I can understand why you hold back your love from Preston," she said.

"I don't hold back my love from your brother!" he replied angrily.

"You don't forgive him."

"He took her from me!"

"Mother died giving birth to Preston. He didn't take her from you. He's as much the child of your love for her as I am."

The judge closed his eyes.

"I pray, Father, that some day you two will find a way to each other. I won't take sides. You're very wrong. So is Preston. I thank you for sharing the love you have for Mother with me. I'm going to go to bed. I don't know if I'll be able to sleep."

"Good night, 'Cille."

She walked to the door, then stopped and turned, looking at her father.

"Yes?" Judge Faircloth asked.

"I know that you look to me to bring into the family the son that Preston never will be."

"I only look to your happiness."

"That isn't true," she said. "As you wish, and as I know I must, I'll marry a man who will carry on the Faircloth heritage and holdings. I don't know if James Peck is that man. I do know I haven't found another. I'll take your advice. When I'm sure, I'll let nothing stand in my way. Not even you. Good night, Father."

Judge Faircloth watched his daughter go. He'd wanted to tell her about her mother. He was sure his wife would have wanted him to tell. The judge settled back into his chair and picked up Cicero. He found comfort in translating the classical writings. His eyes moved along the lines of print on the page. He sensed her near him. After all these years, he could still sense her near him. He closed the book and sobbed silently into his hands.

12

James knocked on the door of the small room.

"Come!" Nathaniel Bachmann called.

James stepped into the room, standing at attention. "You've asked to see me, sir?"

"Yes. Find a place to sit," the captain said from his place at the field desk. "Not on those papers on the cot."

The law clerk removed his gray cap and sat on the captain's wooden trunk.

Bachmann looked up from the document he held in his hands. "I'm hearing good reports on the drill of Company K, Mister Peck. Credit to you."

"Thank you, sir." James enjoyed the praise. "Captain Bachmann," he asked, "will you be coming to inspect the men? They're proud of what they've learned and they want to show you."

"Certainly. I look forward to inspecting the company when the opportunity presents itself. You've no idea what the governor requires of my time."

"I was thinking what the Baraboo Guards require, sir. It would mean a great deal to them to have you come and compliment them."

"James," Bachmann said, stretching his arms over his head and working fingers that were stiff from writing, "you don't understand. Enlisted men are the same the world over. Regulars, volunteers, militia, they're children. They want to be coddled. Taken care of. Nursed. If we give in to their every want, we'll soon become their caretakers, not their commanders. We must make them grow, mature. They're here for a purpose, to prepare themselves to go into battle. When that time comes, I'll be there to command them. Until then, it's your responsibility to see that they develop into a trained, disciplined company of infantry, ready for me."

James was disappointed.

"Think of the men as a unit of a hundred muskets and bayonets, James. That's what they are, a hundred weapons bearers. If we could build a machine that could carry and fire a hundred muskets, we'd have no need of these farmers and townsmen. We could dispense with the caring for and the looking after, the housing and the feeding. Couldn't we?"

"They're a hundred men, sir," James objected. "They have needs, wants. Until you can build your fighting machine, Captain Bachmann, we've got to live with the fact that the Baraboo Guards are a hundred men who look to you for leadership."

"You've much to learn," Bachmann said, waving away James' concern. "And, Lieutenant Peck, I suggest you refer to the company by its proper designation."

"Sir?"

"Our command is Company K, James, of the Second Wisconsin Infantry Regiment. Let's leave the Baraboo Guards back in Sauk County where that name originated."

"Yes, sir."

"Don't become involved with these men. Keep your distance. It becomes very hard on officers who do get involved when the men start to fall as casualties."

"It must become very hard on the men themselves, sir, when they start to fall as casualties."

"As I said, you've much to learn. Officers strive to achieve their rank and their responsibilities. Men enlist to perform their duties. Officers are there to lead, to command. Men are there to follow, to obey, to fight and, unfortunately, to suffer wounds and to die if necessary. An officer cannot cross that line and become involved in the hardships and dangers the men have willingly agreed to bear. An officer must stand apart."

James stared at the captain, who studied the document he held in his hand. The law clerk shook his head. He had no response to the captain. "Sir," he said to change the subject, "you mentioned muskets and bayonets. The men haven't been issued their weapons. They've been drilling in pantomime, going through the loading and firing exercises with nothing in their hands. Can I tell them when they can expect to receive their arms?"

"Sorry. The few muskets the state possesses are being issued to provost guards and sentries. There are none for the companies of the regiment."

"Is there any word, sir, on when we'll leave Camp Randall or where we'll be sent?"

"All in good time."

"The men have been paid, Captain Bachmann. Some have asked permission to go back to Sauk County for the coming weekend. May I grant them leave?"

"Certainly not! The sooner they forget mama and papa and the girl down the lane, the sooner they'll concentrate on why they're here!"

"Yes, sir. Will there be anything else, Captain?"

"I'm sure you have much to apply yourself to," Bachmann said, turning to the papers on his desk. "I'll not keep you from your duties. Let's not have to speak of this again. I'll be gone from Camp Randall from this evening until mid-day, Tuesday. I expect I can leave the command of Company K in your hands during my absence?"

"You can, sir!"

"Carry on, then."

James marched from the headquarters building to the swine shed in a fit. He stormed into the room he shared with the sheriff.

"You've seen the company commander?" Adolph asked.

"I've seen more of the company commander than I care to comment about!"

"Got yourself a mad on?"

James glared at the lawman. He sighed, shrugged, and sat on his bunk. "I'm sorry I spoke to you like that," he apologized.

"Don't let that son of a bitch rile you."

James looked up at the fat man. He thought for several seconds. "First Sergeant Elsasser!"

The tavern keeper stepped into the room.

"Some of the men have asked permission to go to Sauk County this weekend, First Sergeant."

"Can they go, Lieutenant?" Carl asked. He was one of the men who'd asked.

"The company commander specifically denied permission for the men to go to Sauk County this weekend."

"They'll be disappointed, sir." Carl was disappointed.

"Have them back in time for roll call on Tuesday morning, First Sergeant."

"Thank you, sir. Will this get you into trouble?"

"I shall most likely be hanged. Make out whatever passes you need and I'll sign them."

The tavern keeper smiled and left the room.

"Signing passes will put you on record," the lawman said. "Nate Bachmann won't like that."

"He'd better like it. I intend to sign his name."

"You're turning into a real soldier," Adolph laughed. "Are you going to be seeing your Miss Faircloth tonight?"

James shook his head. "I have some things I want to think about."

"Why don't you stay with the company, those of it who aren't hauling off to Sauk County? I'll take myself into Madison city. Might have a drink or twelve. Might get my ashes hauled."

"Make out a pass. I'll sign it."

"Nah. I'll go through the fence with the boys. More fun that way. By the time I get back, you'll be ready to see your Miss Faircloth."

13

Six of the Baraboo Guards rode the stage on Saturday morning.

John Barks, the carpenter, and Ethan Evans, the merchant, sat on the forward seat, facing the rear. Castle Newton, the tanner's son, sat between them and tried to read his Testament against the roll of the coach as it rocked and swayed behind six bay horses.

Carl Elsasser, the tavern keeper, and Johnny Makepeace, the student, sat on the rear seat, facing forward.

Wayne Roohr, the cross-eyed stage clerk, sat up on the box beside the driver, his previous service with the stage line justifying his claim to that place.

Ethan nodded sleepily in the coach. He listened as John detailed his plans for the coming weekend with his Peggy. Ethan didn't share the carpenter's sense of anticipation. The merchant wished he hadn't let John and Carl talk him into making the trip to Baraboo with them.

Ethan did not look forward to seeing Lily. He'd thought of her during the boring days and long nights through five weeks at Camp Randall. She'd been constantly on his mind since the Baraboo Guards left Sauk County. There was the chance, he considered, that the woman he'd made love with the night before the muster would be waiting for him at the end of the twelve hour trip. There was more the chance, he supposed, that this would not be the case. It would have been better, Ethan decided, to have stayed at Camp Randall and gone off with his brother-in-law and his gang to get foul, falling down, stinking drunk. Now, as the coach rolled toward Baraboo, there was no way out for the troubled merchant. He'd have to see her. He couldn't ride the stage into Baraboo and not see her. She'd learn and that would hurt her and he had no wish to hurt her.

Ethan tucked his hands up under his arms. He let his head drop to his chest, let his body go loose to the movement of the coach. The other men might think him asleep and leave him alone.

He had to find a way to tell her. He should take her to their bedroom and close the door, have her stand before him and say to her calmly and gently that he loved her and needed her and wanted her to love and need him. That wouldn't work. She wouldn't understand. She wouldn't want to hear what he had to say. She wouldn't be able to admit that her revulsion to the physical side of marriage was wrong. She'd give in finally, he knew, but that was what he'd fled when he signed on to go with Bachmann and the Baraboo Guards. He didn't want her giving in, her submission, her lace doily over her face. He wanted her love, her soul, her company, her body. He wanted to give to her, to be one with her.

The stage pulled into the depot in Baraboo at eight-thirty in the evening.

"Hi-yup!" the driver shouted down from his seat high on the box. "Six o'clock Monday evening, gents! That's when I leave. Have you in Madison in time for breakfast at Camp Randall on Tuesday morning. If you aren't here when I'm ready to leave, you'll have to walk!"

The six volunteers climbed down from the coach and stood in the street, stretching sore muscles and rubbing stiff joints.

"I'll buy one drink for each of the Baraboo Guards at the finest tavern in Sauk County," Carl announced, leading off for his place. The volunteers followed.

Elsasser's Tavern was crowded with evening drinkers. Carl quickly counted heads. The place was doing well while he was gone. Carl's wife saw him and screeched, running to him, throwing her arms around his neck, kissing him and hugging him and calling at the same time for their son to come from the back room to greet his father.

The local men gathered around the volunteers and shook hands.

"Did you bring Gus back with you?" one of the locals asked Ethan. "It's been quiet here with him gone. We can hear the widows and the wandering wives crying on the night wind with him at the war."

"Ethan," the tavern keeper said, standing behind his bar across from the merchant. "I still have some of that whiskey."

"I'll take a drink of that," Ethan told him, reaching into his pocket for coins.

"I said I'd buy the first one."

Ethan put his coins on the bar. "These will go for the next."

It was after midnight when Ethan left the tavern and walked unsteadily along the courthouse square and up Oak Street. In front of his own house, Ethan stood on the dirt path before his gate. A soft light glowed in the kitchen at the end of the long wing. The porch, along the short wing, was in deep shadow. Ethan pushed open the gate and held it so it wouldn't slam. He didn't want to startle Lily. She might be in the kitchen or she might be upstairs in their bedroom.

"You look dashing in your uniform, Ethan," her voice said to him from the shadow of the porch. She was sitting on the wooden swing he'd hung there for her. "Are you hungry?"

"No," he answered, relieved she knew he was home. He released the gate and walked to the porch, toward the sound of her voice.

"There's cold ham and I can make up some eggs for you."

"Thank you, no. I didn't think you'd be awake."

"Mister Cowles came by this afternoon and told me that some of the men from Camp Randall were coming in on the stage. I waited up to see if you were one of them."

"We got in some time ago," he offered.

"I know that."

"I've been drinking. Carl offered to buy the first one at his place. I've had more than that first one."

"Would you like another drink?"

"Here?" He was surprised at the question. "Yes, I would." Ethan walked the rest of the way to the porch and climbed up the two stone steps, wondering which of the versions of Lily sat on the swing. He could see her now. She wore something dark that helped hide her in the shadow. Ethan sat on the wicker chair and took off his shako. He listened to Lily move, to the rustle of her garments, to the ringing sound of a bottle touching a glass. Her presence, her sound, excited him.

"Will you have water with your whiskey?"

"No, thank you."

"Here," she said, handing him the glass.

"Thank you."

"How long will you be able to stay?"

"We leave Baraboo on the evening stage, Monday."

"After that?"

"We'll stay at Camp Randall until they decide to send us somewhere. We think it will be to Washington, to the army that's forming there."

"Are you content, Ethan?"

"Marching up and down in the mud with common men?"

"Yes."

He sipped whiskey. The conversation was stiff, formal. It was hardly the conversation he'd hoped for. "I wish I could tell you I am content, Lily. I don't like marching in the mud. I don't find the men to be common."

"Farmers and drovers and mechanics?"

"Privates and corporals and sergeants."

"You could be an officer, Ethan."

"I think not. I'm no better, no different, than the others. We lose much of our individuality when we don Wisconsin gray. I find that hard to explain, but it's so."

"Does my brother lose any of his individuality?"

"Gus is Gus."

"Is it what you wanted when you left me, Ethan?"

"I don't know what I wanted when I left," he answered, avoiding the pronoun. "As I've written you, we live in a swine shed. The dining hall has no sides and the rain sometimes blows in and mixes with the bread and potatoes. There are only three large privies for the thousand men of the regiment."

"Do you find Nathaniel Bachmann the inspiring leader you thought him to be?"

"I don't find Nathaniel Bachmann to be anything. We haven't seen him. James Peck, the law clerk from Judge Blane's office, is the commander we have. Adolph Zimmerman is the second in command. They try to be officers. We try to be soldiers."

"You make it sound like an amateur theatrical group, Ethan."

"That would describe us fairly well if we were practicing to put on a play. We aren't."

Lily didn't respond.

Ethan sipped his whiskey. He wondered whether the whiskey came from the same bottle from which he had drunk that last night in Baraboo, when he'd tasted whiskey from the glass, when he'd tasted Lily.

"I'm pleased you came back to me for the weekend," Lily said after a while.

Ethan wondered if she were reciting something she'd rehearsed.

"I've thought and I've prayed while you've been gone."

Ethan didn't answer.

"I didn't mean to drive you from me, into the army."

"Lily . . ."

"No, hear me," she insisted. "I thought, when we married, that I'd find the life I wanted here in Baraboo with you. I didn't understand there would be so much of you in that life, Ethan. I'd never lived with a husband before. When I was a little girl in my father's house in Milwaukee, I was happy. I've thought of going back there. I haven't gone because I knew I'd lose you forever if I did. I don't want to lose you. I want to be your wife. I just don't know how to live all the time with you."

Ethan didn't know what to say. He sipped whiskey.

"I've thought of the night before you left with the men, Ethan," she said softly.

He wanted to tell her how he'd thought of that night, how he'd knocked big John Barks into the mud of Camp Randall thinking of that night.

"I'm wearing the gown I wore for you then," she whispered. "When we did those things you like to do. I put the gown on when I thought you might be one of the men coming in on the stage."

Ethan tried to see her face in the shadows of the porch.

"We'll do that tonight if you want to."

Ethan closed his eyes and shook his head.

"We'll do those things."

Ethan set his glass on the boards of the porch and buried his head in his hands.

"Will you have more whiskey?"

"No," he said softly. "I'm very tired. The trip on the stage was exhausting. I want to go to bed and go to sleep. This has been a very long day for me, Lily."

"I didn't think how tired you must be. Forgive me for talking about those other things."

"I forgive you," Ethan sighed.

"May I draw you a bath?"

"Thank you, no. I'll go right to sleep. I will have another drink."

Lily stood and padded on bare feet to where he sat, bringing the bottle of whiskey with her. "It's all right," she assured him. "If you have to drink, I understand."

Ethan drank the glass of whiskey in one swallow and made his way up the stairs to their bedroom.

14

Lucille Faircloth entered the governor's residence, a gloved hand resting lightly on her father's arm.

"Do you see your Lieutenant Peck?" the judge asked.

"No, I don't," Lucille answered, glancing through the gathering of political and social personages at the reception. "I do see someone with whom you can leave me while you go and argue with Alexander Randall, however."

"Who will that be?"

"Over there. In front of the buffet."

The judge smiled. "Should I forewarn Captain Bachmann that any gallant efforts on his part will be a waste of time?"

"I'm not sure that's totally the case," Lucille smiled. "If it is, let's permit him to come to the realization on his own." She squeezed her father's arm.

Nathaniel Bachmann drew himself to attention as the jurist and his daughter approached. "Judge Faircloth," he greeted formally. "Miss Lucille," he added, bowing slightly.

"Captain Bachmann," the judge returned the greeting. "It's good you are able to take yourself away from your duties at Camp Randall for a while."

"Quite the contrary, sir," the officer said. "I'm on duty at this very minute. Governor Randall will be calling his military staff to a meeting upstairs as soon as he can greet his guests and then politely excuse himself. I'm waiting his pleasure."

"Alexander Randall demands too much of his trained officers, Captain. You should have more time to spend with your company. I'll try to remedy that some. I'll be seeing him before he calls you away and I'll make it a point to keep him as busy as I can while you relax and recruit your strength for a short while. Will you do me the favor of entertaining Miss Lucille while I'm so engaged?"

"Sir!" Bachmann said, coming to attention and clicking his heels.

Judge Faircloth took two cups of punch from a waiter's tray. He handed one to his daughter. He saluted the officer with the other and walked to the rear of the executive residence where Alexander Randall stood in close conversation with several men.

"All is well with your command, Nathaniel?" Lucille asked, smiling. She was thinking of James and comparing the taller, thinner law clerk with the short, compact officer.

"Quite well, Lucille," Bachmann responded. "So good of you to inquire."

"I don't see your lieutenants," she said, sipping at the cup of punch, enjoying herself. It came to her, standing beside Nathaniel Bachmann, that she was taller than him.

"My junior officers are at Camp Randall," Bachmann said, turning toward Lucille. "Lieutenant Peck is regimental officer of the day. Lieutenant Zimmerman, interim, has command of Company K."

"Lieutenant Peck is the regimental officer of the day?" she asked, smiling brightly. "Is that a boon for Lieutenant Peck?"

"Punishment would be the more appropriate word," Bachmann said. "Extra duty that I was able to arrange. Lieutenant Peck foolishly signed my name to some passes, quite against my specific orders, last weekend while I was away from Camp Randall. He is paying for that by spending the day in command of the guard house."

Lucille sipped from her cup, watching the captain's face. "Are you a harsh disciplinarian, Nathaniel?"

"I am a soldier."

Lucille twirled the skirt of her gown slightly, still smiling, still studying his face. "I've known you for a little more than a year, Nathaniel. I tend to think of you more as an entrepreneur than as a soldier. Have you changed?"

"I've not changed."

"You exhibit qualities that I haven't seen before."

"Call those qualities discipline, Lucille. Once instilled in the cadet at West Point, discipline never leaves the soul of the professional soldier. Discipline, and the sure sense of one's duty. Never."

Lucille watched the man. He spoke of discipline and the sure sense of one's duty, the man who had delegated to James the task of handling her drunken brother. She sensed his tightness, his strictness, his control. "Will your punishment of Lieutenant Peck instill that quality of discipline and that sure sense of duty in him, Nathaniel?" she asked, holding his gaze with her eyes. "After all," she continued, "the professional officer trains himself for a lifetime of discipline and duty. The volunteer officer agrees to put up with discipline and duty only in the course of what, to him, will be at best an interruption of his normal career."

"Do I detect sympathy for an insubordinate officer, Lucille?"

"Not at all," she said, smiling, bowing her head slightly. "I'm interested in your feelings on this."

"May I believe that?" he asked quietly, looking directly at her.

"You're avoiding an answer, Nathaniel," she taunted him. "That, on the part of a disciplined soldier, surprises me."

Bachmann turned to face the judge's daughter. Lucille felt, to her surprise, an attraction to the man, to his confidence, his control, his power. "You're still avoiding an answer," she reminded him.

"Punishment seldom helps the one on whom it is inflicted," he said, his voice lower. "It does serve as a deterrent to others."

"Then your punishment of Lieutenant Peck is an empty gesture, as far as he is concerned?"

"I wonder," Bachmann said, stroking his beard.

"You wonder?" she asked, watching the strong fingers working against the dark whiskers.

"At your interest in Lieutenant Peck, Lucille."

She dropped her gaze quickly, the fun of trifling with the officer gone. She understood she could be exposing James to Nathaniel Bachmann's anger. "I was interested in your feelings on discipline," she hedged.

"My feelings on discipline," he repeated, considering, strong fingers stroking dark whiskers. "I may find that disciplining my subordinates could become an interesting exercise if it brings your attention around to my feelings."

"I expected more of you than that, Nathaniel!" she snapped. She looked away. She felt vaguely fearful.

An aide to the governor stepped into the room and beckoned to Bachmann, nodding toward the staircase.

"I must leave," the captain said, leaning slightly forward. "With your permission, of course."

Lucille nodded, unable to speak. An almost physical sensation of power seemed to radiate from the man. He made her feel off balance, at once attracted and repelled.

Judge Faircloth approached. "I kept him as busy as I could, Captain Bachmann," the jurist said.

The officer bowed slightly to Lucille, to the judge. He turned and went up the stairway.

"And how does the captain compare to your Lieutenant Peck?" asked the judge.

Lucille turned to her father. "I'm not sure," she replied.

15

The morning of the third Sunday in June, 1861, was bright and warm and clear. James rented a mare and carriage and drove to the Faircloth home, approaching the house at its coach door entrance. He tugged the mare to a stop and tied the ends of the reins to the base of the whip stock.

James Peck had known Lucille Faircloth for three weeks. He was sure he was in love with her.

The law clerk sat in the carriage seat and listened. Voices carried through the open window of Judge Faircloth's library, harsh, angry, raised voices.

Lucille came through the door carrying a picnic hamper in her arms. James jumped down and took the hamper, stowing it in the rear of the carriage.

"I'd ask you in to say good morning to my father," Lucille said, not smiling. "As you can hear, he and my brother are having a discussion."

"I couldn't help but hear." James smiled.

"Half of Madison can't help but hear!" she snapped.

"I'll see your father another time," he told her, determined to let nothing ruin this morning. "I'd like to meet your brother again. At a safe distance next time."

She smiled. "Good morning, Lieutenant Peck," she greeted him, starting over.

"Good morning, Miss Faircloth," he responded, taking her hand and helping her up into the carriage. He climbed in and took his seat beside her. Her bright smile thrilled him. He was certain she was the loveliest creature alive.

"Drive north from the city," she told him, taking his arm. "Around the shore of Lake Mendota. There's a point of land where we can picnic and have a fine view of Madison."

James chucked the mare into a brisk walk down the long drive and into the street. He drove east from the city across the marsh of the Yahara River and beyond. Fields and small farms edged the road on the right. The water of Lake Mendota lapped the shore in the near distance on the left. After an hour James followed Lucille's directions and turned the mare into a narrow lane that led to a wooded arm of land jutting into the lake.

"Didn't I promise you a lovely view of Madison?" she asked, as he drew the mare up close to some large rocks on the shore.

He nodded. He jumped from the carriage and took the hitching iron from the floor, snapping the long rein to the iron, giving the mare freedom to graze.

"That's the dome of the capitol," Lucille said, pointing across the water from her seat in the carriage. "Camp Randall will be behind those hills, there to the right. That's the roof of North Hall at the university on the hill above the sailboats."

James looked in the direction she pointed. It was a fine view of Madison. It was also a more secluded and intimate spot than any he'd have selected. Pleased that she'd chosen it, he turned and reached up to help her from the carriage. She took his hands and stepped lightly down, turning into his arms. James held her tight, tasting her lips, feeling the exhilarating closeness of her body. Lucille slipped her arms up and around his neck. His heart hammered and his bruised cheeks and nose throbbed gloriously.

Lucille lowered her face to the breast of his gray uniform coat, her arms still around his neck. She pressed her forehead against the fabric, lifted her head away and gazed at him, then rested her head on his chest. James buried his face in the full scent and substance of her thick, dark hair. He breathed, feeling the pounding of his heart, listening to the chirp and whistle of birds in the thickets.

"Lieutenant Peck," she whispered. "Kiss me again. Then, release me. If we return without eating our picnic dinner, there will be a scandal in Madison city."

James did as he was told.

Lucille stepped back from him. She reached and touched his bruised face, nodding to herself, confirming something. "Go," she told James. "Get the hamper from the rig. Bring it to those rocks."

The law clerk swallowed, his throat tight. Stiffly, he walked to the carriage and brought the hamper. Lucille showed him where to spread the blanket on the beach.

"We have plates and silverware," she told James, very businesslike and much in charge. "A bottle of wine from my father's cabinet that he doesn't know is missing. Put that in the lake water to cool. We've cold chicken and some special tarts. Fresh vegetables from our garden. Hard rolls that were baked at Stumpf's Bakery this very morning. A basket of fruit and a selection of preserves. We've a jar of cold tea. Is that standard fare for a soldier in the field?" she asked, grinning at him.

"It's standard fare for a platoon of soldiers in the field." He returned the grin.

Lucille settled herself on a corner of the blanket and smiled up at him.

James felt self-conscious. He sat busying himself with a napkin. He perspired in his wool clothing.

"Take off your cap and coat," Lucille told him. "Hang them on a branch. I promise not to tell Nathaniel Bachmann that one of his officers was running around the shore of Lake Mendota out of uniform."

James gratefully took off the gray coat. He unfastened the stud at the collar of his shirt and rolled up his sleeves.

Lucille served from the hamper. She ate and watched him. She'd unbuttoned the sleeves of her light gown, turning the cuffs back over her wrists. She thought of her comment about telling Nathaniel Bachmann one of his officers was out of uniform on the lake shore. She wondered if that would bring disciplinary action from the professional soldier. She wondered whether the professional soldier would derive pleasure from inflicting that discipline. She put Nathaniel Bachmann out of her mind for the moment.

James talked as they ate. He told Lucille about his early life, how we was raised by an aunt after his parents died. He told of coming to Baraboo through a connection his aunt had with Judge Blane. Lucille nodded encouragement as he spoke of his determination to complete his reading of law and open his legal practice. James described the men of the Baraboo Guards, his duties at Camp Randall. He spoke of Nathaniel Bachmann with distant respect. She understood as he talked that it was the law clerk from Baraboo who carried responsibility for the company of volunteers and not the graduate of West Point.

James ate and talked and Lucille examined her feelings for the man across the blanket from her, with his bruised face and uncertain manner. Confidence would come with accomplishment, she predicted. Personal strength and courage and basic honesty were already there, if as yet untested. She'd been impressed by the way he'd taken the distasteful task of handling her drunken brother and done that quietly and with discretion, even if he had suffered a broken nose in the process.

They worked together packing the remnants of the meal into the hamper. Their hands touched. They smiled and laughed.

"We've cold tea," she told him when they'd finished. She sat with her back against a large rock. "Or, we have the bottle of wine in the lake. Which will it be?"

"The wine!" he insisted.

"The bottle has drifted," she told him, pointing to where the neck bobbed thirty feet from the shore. "You'll have to wade to retrieve it."

James sat and took off his shoes and stockings, rolling his gray trousers to the knee. "Is the water deep?" he asked.

"I don't know," she admitted.

"I'll wade for you," he told her gallantly. "If the water is deep, I may have to drown for you. I can't swim."

"Be sensible. We'll have cold tea."

"Not till I test the water."

"Then be careful!"

James sloshed into the lake. The water was shallow. He waded to the bottle, enjoying the feel of water on his legs and sand under his feet, knowing he had the attention of the woman on shore. He waded back holding his trophy high.

Lucille had removed her own shoes and stockings. She sat with her skirts drawn up on her thighs, kicking and splashing her feet in the pool at the base of her rock. Her toes and calves dripped.

James stared.

"Do I shock you, Lieutenant Peck?"

"At times, you do."

"When I was a little girl," Lucille told him, taking one foot from the water and watching the drops fall, "Father would take Preston and me to his cabin at Devil's Lake near Baraboo. We'd swim and play in the water every day, naked and getting brown as Indians."

"You can swim?" James asked, astonished.

"Like a fish."

"You must teach me!" he blurted.

"Here?" she asked, grinning. "Now?"

James flushed. He waded the last few yards to the sand, found a cork screw in the hamper, and carefully worked the cork free. Stepping toward Lucille, he saw that she now was the one unsettled. She had both hands behind her back. Her eyes were not meeting his. "Are you all right?" he asked, concerned.

She looked away from him.

"What's the matter?" James asked, kneeling beside her.

From behind her back, Lucille brought a square box wrapped in blue paper. "I hope you won't think this forward of me," she whispered.

"What is this?" he asked, settling the wine bottle in the sand.

"I asked everyone what a soldier's most prized possession was," she said. "This is what they told me. I hope you like it."

"I'll like it whatever it is."

He tore the blue paper and opened the box. It held a pint-sized tin cup with a wide handle.

"I don't know what to say," he admitted. Murphy the Drummer had a tin cup and kept it fastened to the strap of his haversack.

"Look inside," she told him. "On the bottom."

He tipped the cup to better catch the light. He read

J. PECK
1 LT.
BARABOO GUARDS
REMEMBER ME
L. U. F.
16 JUNE, 1861

"I don't know what to say."

"Don't say anything," she suggested, relieved that he seemed to like her gift. "And, James Peck," she ordered, "don't dare ask what the U in my name stands for!"

"I won't," he promised. "What does the U in your name stand for?"

"Ursula! I hate my middle name!"

"I think I like your middle name."

"You think you like my middle name?" she teased. "You aren't sure?"

"I'm not sure about your middle name," he told her, meeting her eyes. "I am sure that I love you."

"Don't say that lightly," she begged.

"I'm often not sure about things in my life," James confessed to her. He looked at the tin cup he held in his hands. "I am sure of this. I do love you."

"Pour some wine," she said, her heart beating hard. "We'll christen your cup."

James poured the cup half-full and offered it to Lucille. She sipped, offering it back. James turned the cup and drank from where her lips had touched the soldered rim.

"I don't know where I'll be when I drink from this cup in the months to come," he whispered. "I'll think of you every time."

"You'll have a hard time not thinking of me!" she giggled. "With my initials staring up from the bottom at you!"

"You thought of that?"

"I did."

"You continue to shock me, Miss Faircloth."

"You never had a chance, Lieutenant Peck."

"I'd like to think that," he toasted, raising the cup.

"There's a small clearing beyond where the mare is grazing," she said evenly. "Spread our blanket there. Then leave me for a while. Watch the lake. Drink some wine."

James carried the blanket to the clearing. He pulled a few weeds from the center and kicked the sand level. Kneeling, he spread the blanket, straightening its edges. He came back and stood beside Lucille, both of them silent and looking out onto Lake Mendota. Lucille touched his hand and turned away.

James watched the sailboats tack and turn out on the lake. He listened to the birds chirping and singing. He finished the wine in his new tin cup and walked to the clearing.

Lucille had rolled her light gown into a bundle and placed it neatly to one side. Her petticoats were spread on the picnic blanket. She lay on their pallet of linen and lace.

James stared at her. Her breasts were large, round and firm and pink-nippled. Her waist was tiny, her hips wide. She had a glory of thick, dark hair at the base of her stomach.

James took off his trousers and his shirt, setting them next to Lucille's gown. He slipped off his drawers and dropped them beside the blanket. He lay beside Lucille and put his arms around her, drawing her close.

Lucille put a hand to his breast, lightly resting the tips of her fingers on his skin.

Her touch stirred him.

Lucille drew her leg up inside his legs, slipping her thigh against his groin. He rolled onto his back and drew Lucille onto him. Her breasts hung before his face, heavy, full, inviting. He tasted, suckled.

Lucille straddled him, her legs spread wide around his hips. James felt her warm moist softness. She moved her thighs for him and he slipped into her. Lucille shuddered. She gasped, grinding down onto him, forcing him further inside her. James felt movement against himself, warm and wet and tight. He held her in his arms, covering her face, her neck with kisses. Lucille moved, quickening, held in the grip of some force beyond or within herself, beyond James. Her pelvis, her thighs took on a frenzied rhythm, an urgency. James held her closer, feeling things happening inside her, wanting to help her. His own feeling rose. He pushed deep inside her, his passion breaking. Lucille cried out. James didn't know if he caused her pain or ecstasy. She rose above him, struggling and then collapsing in stages, coming down from some high place. Her head settled onto his shoulder, her breathing shuddering and then calming. He heard the birds singing.

After a time, Lucille moved, raising her head to look down into James' face. Her eyes searched his. Carefully, she raised her hips. James felt coolness when air touched where her warm wetness had covered him. Lucille slipped down to lie beside him. He nestled her head on his breast, his arms around her shoulders. He wanted her to know he loved her. "Lucille . . ."

"Hush," she whispered. "Hold me." She didn't want to share what had happened inside herself, not even with James.

They lay together and dozed in the sunlight of the June afternoon. Wagon and carriage traffic passed on the road at the end of the lane. Boats tacked close to shore near the point of land. James woke. He didn't know how long they had slept. He kissed Lucille on the forehead.

She opened her eyes.

"It's getting late," he whispered.

Lucille sat up, shaking her dark hair loose where it had matted on her neck and shoulders. She studied James' naked body. She got to her feet, standing beside him, stretching, her legs wide, her arms high. James stared at her body in wonder.

"Come, Lieutenant Peck," she said, bending from the waist to the pile of linen and lace, sorting through her petticoats. "Get into your things."

Dressed, they walked hand in hand to the shore and sat on one of the rocks, watching the sun drop toward the western shore of Lake Mendota. They finished the bottle of wine, drinking in turn from James' tin cup.

It was dark when James drove the carriage into the city. At the Faircloth home, Lucille kissed him and sent him on his way to return the mare and rig.

Judge Faircloth called to her as she carried the hamper to the kitchen. "Rather long picnic, wasn't it?"

Lucille set the hamper on the table in the hall and walked into her father's library.

"Yes," she answered distractedly, "it was a long picnic."

The judge watched his daughter. He understood.

Lucille's eyes were on the glass of cognac her father had poured for her. Her mind was back on the shore of Lake Mendota.

"'Cille," the judge said softly.

She gathered her thoughts and looked at him.

"They leave for Washington on Thursday."

"He didn't say . . ."

"He didn't know. The orders came by telegraph this afternoon." The judge stepped toward his daughter. "There will be a battle in weeks, 'Cille. The enlistments of the ninety-day regiments expire at the end of July. Lincoln has to send the army against the Confederates before that happens." He touched her shoulder, patting the sleeve of her gown. "I'm sorry."

She placed the glass of cognac on the table and stared at her hands.

"It had to come," the judge added. "That's what brought him to Madison. To become a soldier, to train, to go to war."

She couldn't speak.

"I'm sorry, 'Cille," he said.

16

WASHINGTON, D.C.—June, 1861.

The Baraboo Guards rode a thousand miles by rail across America.

At Chicago, as at every junction city, the men climbed down from the cars of one railroad and formed to march across the city to the terminal of the next railroad that would carry them on toward Washington.

At Toledo, the Baraboo Guards were the first company in line at a huge breakfast prepared and served by the citizens of the city.

At Cleveland, girls in bright dresses waved red, white and blue ribbons at the men from Wisconsin and passed out sweets and fruit as the regiment marched down the broad avenue toward the distant terminal.

At Harrisburg, the companies of the Second Wisconsin detrained at midnight and marched to the Federal arsenal. The men filed past a shed in the weak glow of hand-held lanterns. Regular army ordnance sergeants issued each man a leather cartridge box, a leather percussion cap box, a sheathed bayonet, and a heavy musket. Quartermaster sergeants issued each man a wool blanket and a canvas shelter-half.

Nathaniel Bachmann joined the colonel and the lieutenant-colonel of the Second Wisconsin in protesting the poor quality of the muskets, cumbersome imported Austrian .75 caliber pieces that were older than most of the men in the regiment. The ordnance officer in charge at the arsenal listened patiently. When the protest ended, he politely told the Wisconsin officers to take what he had or to go on to Washington unarmed. He had more regiments coming through than he had weapons to issue. Bachmann advised the colonel and the lieutenant-colonel to do as the ordnance officer suggested for the time being.

Adolph took James shopping at the arsenal's officers quarters. The lawman found an ordnance major willing to sell James a long .44 caliber Colt revolver. From the furtive whispering involved, James was sure the major had stolen the weapon. James bought the revolver, a holster, a cartridge box and a hundred cartridges.

At Washington, the men from Wisconsin, stiff, sore, and gritty after five days of rail travel in wooden coaches, climbed down from the cars onto a platform crowded with the men of other arriving regiments.

"Form up!" Carl Elsasser shouted to the Baraboo Guards, pushing men into line.

"Damned if I'll ride the cars back to Sauk County," Jack Black told Herby Auchter. "My ass hurts. I'll walk the return trip."

"I ain't been this knocked and rattled since my wedding night," Herby told Jack.

"Sergeants!" Carl called out. "Get your men into line!"

"Hey, Gus!" Andy Shoate pointed. "Let's go capture that lady in the brown dress!"

"Stay where you are, Shoate!" Carl threatened.

"Company K!" Nathaniel Bachmann shouted, striding from a meeting of the regiment's company commanders at the far end of the depot platform. He motioned impatiently at James and Adolph, who were working with Carl to get the men from Sauk County into ranks. "Attention!"

The Baraboo Guards came to order in a fashion, the unwieldy Austrian muskets at their sides.

Speeches were offered by congressmen and officers at the terminal, well out of the hearing of the men from Sauk County, who were at the far end of the line of companies on the platform. The men fidgeted and whispered. They'd been penned inside the wooden coaches for five days and didn't want to stand in ranks while politicians gave speeches they couldn't hear. Carl's grim glare held the more boisterous of the men in their places.

The speeches ended. The regimental band struck up a tune and paraded down the line of companies behind the color guards, tall sergeants carrying the blue flag of Wisconsin and the red, white and blue national colors. As the band passed, each captain in turn yelled orders and brought his company into column of fours, the unfamiliar Austrian muskets carried at many variations of the right shoulder shift. The Baraboo Guards brought up the rear, marching for the first time behind their full compliment of officers, their captain and their two lieutenants.

The column moved into the wide, muddy, rutted avenues of Washington. The capitol building was to the left of the men from Wisconsin, its great dome unfinished, long arms of derricks and cranes reaching up into the sky from the open rotunda.

Soldiers crowded the streets of Washington and delayed the regiment's passage. Soldiers strolled the walkways and stood at intersections. Soldiers gathered in the doorways of taverns and hotels and stores. Soldiers wandered in two's and three's or marched in companies or battalions or regiments. Mounted couriers threaded their horses through the masses of uniformed men, dispatch cases strapped behind their saddles. A battery of regular artillery blocked the regiment's way for a while, red-chevroned gunners sitting upright on limber chests in front of gleaming brass guns. Lines of heavy supply wagons moved slowly along parallel streets.

A soldier in blue sat in the dirt at the entrance to a tavern and waved a bottle as the Baraboo Guards marched past. "Hey!" he cackled. "Who are you?"

"We're the Second Wisconsin!" Johnny Makepeace shouted.

"Could be damned rebels in them gray uniforms!"

"Who are you?" Gus asked the soldier.

"Second Damned Maine! Out of Bangor!"

"Go back to Bangor!" Gus shouted. "Wisconsin's here to win the war!"

"Oh, yeah?" the soldier grinned. "Hey! Where is Wisconsin, anyway?"

The ten companies marched through the city and out to its northwestern suburbs. By the late hours of the afternoon the men were hungry and thirsty and frustrated at the stopping and starting that making way through the crowded avenues and streets involved. It seemed to Ethan that every vacant lot and open field was filled with soldiers, tents, wagons, or mountains of piled supplies. At dusk, the lead company turned from the street and marched into a meadow.

Under Carl's shouted orders, the Baraboo Guards broke ranks, stacked muskets and pitched shelter tents.

Nathaniel Bachmann called James and Adolph to him. The captain held a document which he studied carefully in the fading light. "Gentlemen," he said as the lieutenants approached. "I must leave you. I've matters to attend to in the city. You'll remain with the company. Keep the men in this camp. You'll receive any orders from Major Ross, the adjutant, until I get back. Send a party to find water. Set some men to digging a latrine. Any questions?"

James was furious that the captain would leave the company within minutes of its arrival at the camp in the meadow. He turned to Adolph. The lawman chewed tobacco and frowned.

"I may not be back for several days," Bachmann said. He returned the lieutenants' salutes and walked quickly toward a carriage that waited for him in the street.

Adolph spat. "We're on our own, again."

"I assume Captain Bachmann has business to attend to," James said without conviction.

"Business, my broad ass! He's got politicking to attend to! What the hell do you two want?" Adolph demanded of the Shoate boys as they approached.

"Carl told us to put your tent up for you, Sheriff," Andy Shoate said. "You want us to?"

"Damned right!" the fat man growled. "Get my half off my knapsack. Give them your half," he told James. "They'll do a better job of it than me and you."

"Some of the boys got a fire burning," Dewey Shoate said, pointing toward the center of the meadow. "Carl said to tell you they got some coffee cooking."

"'Evening, Sheriff," Johnny Makepeace greeted as the two approached the glow of the small fire. "'Evening, Lieutenant Peck. Want some coffee?"

"Where the hell'd you get the pot to make it in?" Adolph demanded, unbuckling his tin cup from the flap of his haversack.

"The Irishman found it," Ethan told the lawman. "He said he liberated it."

"Liberated it? I sure as hell hope it was a rebel sympathizer he liberated it from! Where is the Irishman?"

"He said something about going on a reconnaissance," John Barks said, pouring steaming coffee into the lawman's cup. "What's a reconnaissance, Sheriff?"

"For that Irishman, you can bet it's something having to do with getting drunk and getting laid," the sheriff growled.

"Are the men settled in?" James asked Carl, holding his tin cup out to John.

"As well as can be expected in a meadow, Lieutenant Peck," the tavern keeper reported. "If we get rain, they'll miss the swine shed at Camp Randall. Think I should hold a roll call, sir?"

"You'll come up short," Adolph interrupted before James could respond. "Look around you."

James could see, even in the advancing shadows of the late evening, that there were far less than a hundred volunteers present. "The men weren't supposed to leave the camp, Carl," James complained, recalling his fright on the road from Baraboo to Madison when he hadn't known how many men were with the column of Sauk County wagons. What would he do, he wondered, if Captain Bachmann returned and discovered men were missing from the company this night?

"I should've posted guards," the tavern keeper admitted.

"Wouldn't have mattered," Adolph interjected. "They'd still have run off and they'd have taken most of your guards with them. They've been cooped up in the cars for five days. The city was too much temptation. They'll be back, come morning."

"Sheriff?" Johnny Makepeace asked, to get the conversation away from those of his friends who'd given in to the beckoning lights of the city. "Might the rebels attack us here?"

"I don't think so," the lawman said. "There's a Federal army between them and us."

"That's Virginia," Ethan told the student. "There, across the river. That far ridge."

"That's the Confederacy?" Wayne Roohr wondered, looking across the shadowed valley of the Potomac River.

"Are there Rebs over there?" Johnny Makepeace asked the lawman. "Looking over here at us?"

"Count on it, boy," the Adolph replied.

"Should we have this fire?" the student asked.

"No harm in it. It's one among thousands."

"I'm going to sleep real close the that old gun they gave me," Wayne said.

Adolph stepped back from the fire and turned to James. "You've nothing to say?" he asked.

James started. He'd been thinking of Lucille Faircloth. He wanted to be back in Madison with her. He was serving no purpose here. The men ignored him. Instinctively, they turned to Adolph, looked to Adolph. James had no place in the company. He'd told Judge Faircloth that his role in all of this was to help Captain Bachmann command the Baraboo Guards. Captain Bachmann was seldom with the Baraboo Guards and the men seemed to prefer Adolph to himself.

"Let's take a walk," the sheriff said, putting a strong hand on the law clerk's arm. Adolph stepped off, pacing around the edge of the meadow. James had to walk quickly to keep abreast of him.

When they were beyond hearing of the men at the fire, the sheriff stopped and turned to face the law clerk. "You coming down with a case of the sorrows?" he demanded.

"I'm wondering what I'm doing here."

"If you're starting to feel sorry for yourself, you better get off that!" the lawman declared. "You're commanding the Baraboo Guards, that's what you're doing here. Nate Bachmann hasn't been doing it, that's for sure!"

"The men don't listen to me!" James argued. "They listen to you. They listen to Carl. They ignore me."

"Damn you!" the sheriff exploded. "I told you a long time ago I came with the boys from Sauk County! That's what I do. They listen to me because they're comfortable with me telling them what to do. Until they get comfortable with you telling them what to do, most of your job here is to stand around and look pretty and try to stay out of my way!"

"That isn't why I left Baraboo and Madison!" James protested.

"Why the hell did you, then? I asked you once and you couldn't tell me!"

"I still don't know!" James shouted. "I wish I hadn't come!"

"Back down some," the sheriff said. "You're working this too hard."

"I just don't know, Sheriff," James sighed.

The sheriff took the law clerk's arm and they paced the edge of the meadow as those Baraboo Guards who had not forayed into Washington city made ready for the night.

"Sheriff?" James asked after a while.

"What?"

James stopped pacing. "Have you been married?"

"So, that's what's digging at you? Hell!" the lawman laughed, spitting tobacco juice. "Twice! And, let me tell you, that was one time too many."

"Are you married now?"

"Now? Hell, no. That first time, it was good. I cared so much for that lady. Lost her and the baby both. Quack doctor killed them, a'birthing. I thought I'd found it again, the second time. She ran off after a year. Took my money, everything. Never did see my way to trying it the third time. I get along."

James walked beside the lawman.

"Kind of fun, the first time, isn't it?" the sheriff asked.

James stopped walking. He stood blushing.

"I'll be God-damned!" the sheriff laughed. "Guilty conscience and all! I didn't mean it that way. I meant falling in love the first time. Well, hell, you're going to have to live with the memory of whatever you brought along with you for a while. You've got other things to think about. Did you ever load that revolver you brought from that army thief back in Harrisburg?"

"Should I?"

"Might be a good idea."

"The package of cartridges is in my pack. I'll load the revolver in the morning."

"Your knapsack is no place for cartridges. You bought a cartridge box. You start carrying that revolver loaded and a dozen cartridges in the box from now on."

"I won't need a loaded gun for a while, will I?"

"Best have it ready when the time comes. Here's our tent. I'm going to turn in. That trip out on the cars was hard work for an old, fat man. You want a tug on a bottle before you go to sleep?"

"Sure," James said, responding more to the offer than to his need for a drink. He felt Adolph had been almost considerate to him over the past few minutes.

The lawman got down on all fours and crawled into the shelter tent the Shoate boys had rigged for the two of them. He rustled in his knapsack and handed out a bottle of brandy. James poured a measure into his tin cup.

The sheriff pulled off his shoes and stuck his stockinged feet out the front of the little tent.

James sat and sipped from the cup Lucille had given him. When the cup was empty, he crawled into his side of the shelter tent, resting on the ground next to the snoring mound of the sheriff of Sauk County.

17

Army supply wagons brought rations to the camp the following morning.

Murphy, hung over from his reconnaissance into the city, took charge when the Baraboo Guards drew their allotment of fresh beef, salted bacon, white bread, peas and potatos and onions, sacks of dried white beans and roasted coffee beans, candles and vinegar and lard and molasses and boxes of hard white crackers.

The suffering Irishman had the men organize themselves into twelve messes of eight or nine men. He spread twelve blankets on the grass and divided the bulk rations onto the blankets in twelve roughly equal piles. At his direction, Carl stood with his back to the piles and, as the Irishman pointed to the piles in random order, the tavern keeper called out a number between one and twelve, also in random order. The mess with that number drew the pile of rations to which the little man had been pointing. The Baraboo Guards agreed that Murphy the Drummer had come up with a fair method for dividing the issue.

John Barks' mess consisted of himself, Gus, Ethan, Hans and Olaf Larson, Robert and Willis Wright, and the Irishman.

"What are these?" Gus asked, gnawing on one of the white crackers.

"That'll be hardtack," Murphy advised, busy with an iron skillet, a dutch oven, an iron pot and a pan he'd acquired in the course of his reconnaissance.

"Hard what?"

"Hardtack. You'll be wanting to keep a package of it in your haversack."

"What the hell for?"

"One good reason will be staving off starvation when the rest of the food runs out," the Irishman advised. "Another good reason will be to have it handy to throw down the barrel of a cannon. It wrecks havoc when fired into the ranks of the on-coming foe."

"Try biting it!" Gus complained. "It's hard as wall plaster!"

"Aren't you the bright one, now," Murphy jibed. "Figuring what they bake it of, and so soon!"

"I'm not eating wall plaster," Gus declared.

"You'll be eating it. You'll be getting to where you're looking forward to the taste of it," Murphy assured the men of John Barks' mess. The Irishman kept his hands busy as he spoke, pouring water and molasses and beans into his dutch oven. He added half a cup of vinegar, stirring the potion with his bayonet.

"What're you doing?" Gus asked, still gnawing on the hard cracker.

"I've introduced you to the first friend of the marching infantry, the hardtack. I'll now introduce you to the second, the army bean."

"We aren't eating beans!" Gus objected. "Beans make you fart. You'll have us farting all over the place."

"Ah, my young tiger," the little man crooned. "You haven't smelled anything 'till you've smelled the farts of ten thousand cases of the cramps marching ahead of you, all brought on by the eating of the army bean. Be that as it may, Gus, get yourself busy digging me a pit in the sod of this meadow, about three hands deep and so far around. The rest of you, get scattering about and gather me a great pile of sticks and branches for fire wood."

"Hold on a God-damned minute, Murphy!" Gus countered. "Who hung sergeant's stripes on your sleeve? Who are you to be giving the rest of us orders?"

"Will you be cooking the beans, Mister Gaard?" the Irishman asked, stepping in front of the blond and looking up at Gus.

"I don't know how to cook beans."

"I do!" the Irishman declared. "You'll dig me the pit. The rest will gather fire wood."

"I don't have a shovel." Gus told him, finding an excuse.

"You have that lovely bayonet the army was thoughtful enough to give you."

"It's not for digging holes in the dirt."

"What's it for, then?"

"Stabbing Rebs!"

"How often, now, in the course of one day will you be doing that?"

"I don't know."

"How often, now, in the course of that same day will you be wanting to eat?"

Gus thought about that. He pulled his bayonet from its scabbard and set to work scouring a pit. John and the men scattered into the trees around the meadow to gather armloads of branches.

Murphy got a fire going in the pit. When he had coals, he set the dutch oven in and shoveled earth and embers onto its iron lid using the blade of

Gus' bayonet. "One of you fetch me back a pail of water," the Irishman ordered.

"What'll you need more water for?" Gus wanted to know. "You've already got the beans going."

"Will you be having coffee?"

Ethan volunteered, taking the Irishman's pail.

The little man waved the rest of the men close and showed them how to cut thin strips of meat from the side of fresh beef. These he rubbed with salt and pepper he took from an oil cloth sack. He wrapped the strips of meat loosely on the iron ram rod of John's musket. He held the ram rod over the coals of the fire. The men followed his lead, slicing and broiling seasoned strips of beef, catching the dripping fat on chunks of white bread.

"Murphy," John said, chewing bread and broiled beef, "you'll have us cooking and eating everything now. There won't be anything left for tomorrow."

"There'll be nothing left of the beef for the morrow after the heat of the day starts working on it, lad. There'll be nothing left of the bread and stuff after the rains. We'll be eating it when we get it. We'll leave worrying about the morrow to the commissary officers."

"You just got yourself elected to be the cook for our mess," John declared.

That was seconded by the nodding heads of the men who chewed strips of seasoned broiled beef and munched bread rich with drippings.

"Aye," the Irishman confirmed. "And, that'll be with the perquisites that go with the office and the honor."

"What's that mean?" the carpenter asked.

"I do the cooking," the little man told all of them. "I draw the rations. I work my own magic to come up with what cannot be found over the tail-end of an army supply wagon. The rest of you carry the pots and pans on the march. You gather the wood and fetch the water. You clean up when I've finished with my work. You share my fatigues and my watches among yourselves."

"What the hell does that leave for you to do, Murphy?" Gus argued. "Cook, march and fight? That's all?"

"Aye."

"That's not fair," Olaf said. Hans agreed with whatever his brother thought.

The Wright brothers shook their heads.

"Share and share alike is our way," Ethan told Murphy.

The little man turned his back on the men. He straddled a log and took the side of bacon. He cut small squares and sliced onions and mixed more molasses and water in his pan. Lifting the lid of the dutch oven, he dumped the concoction into the bubbling beans. He took another oil cloth sack and added a cup and a half of brown sugar to the beans, stirring the aromatic mixture with the blade of Gus' bayonet.

Olaf and Hans drooled at the scent of the bubbling beans.

"All right, Murphy," John said, speaking for the men. "We'll try it your way. For now."

18

Four mornings later, two hours after midnight, the drummers beat out the long roll. The men of the Second Wisconsin woke and rose, rolling their blankets into their shelter halves, strapping that load to the tops of their knapsacks and forming by companies in the darkness.

Ethan took his place in the ranks of the Baraboo Guards on the right of the line of companies with Murphy's dutch oven slung on a rope over his right shoulder. Gus bore the Irishman's coffee pot tied to his waist belt. Hans carried the iron pot in his left hand. Olaf carried the pan. Robert Wright tucked a cloth sack of spices and utensils into the front of his coat. John studied the cumbersome iron skilled that was his to bear for the day. Remembering that he was a sergeant, he pulled rank and handed the skillet to the already burdened Hans Larson. The simple boy studied the tapering handle of his added encumbrance and solved its transportation problem by sticking the handle down the muzzle of his Austrian musket, coming to attention bearing the only circular bayonet ever carried on campaign.

"Captain Bachmann!" Major Ross called out, striding toward the Baraboo Guards. The major carried papers, reading them in the light of a lantern carried by a corporal from Company B.

"Lieutenant Peck," James introduced himself. "Captain Bachmann is detained in Washington city, sir."

"Detained!" the major spat. "With our colonel and our lieutenant-colonel, he's detained! Damn! All right, Peck. I'm commanding the regiment until they see fit to join us. You have Company K. Your men are formed and ready to march?"

"Except for Captain Bachmann, sir."

"Forty rounds of cartridges? Percussion caps? Water in the canteens?"

James stared at the major. He had no idea what the men carried. He glanced at the sheriff. Adolph shrugged. Nothing had been said to either lieutenant about ammunition or percussion caps or water.

Behind James, Carl came to attention and saluted. "Forty rounds in the cartridge boxes, Lieutenant Peck. One hundred percussion caps. Water in the canteens and hardtack in the haversacks. The men are ready, sir."

"Thank you, First Sergeant," James said, relieved. He returned Carl's salute. "Sir," he said to the major, "the Baraboo Guards are formed, equipped and ready."

"You're Company K of this regiment, Peck!" the major snapped. "Remember that. Have your company follow along behind Company I. Don't let any of your men fall behind. Don't let an interval form between Company I's rear rank and Company K's front rank. You're the last company in the regimental column. If you come on stragglers from the companies ahead, bring them along. There will be four supply wagons following you. Any man too sick or too weak to march will be brought along in those wagons but only on your specific order. Is that understood?"

"Yes, sir."

"Mister Peck?" Major Ross asked, peering into the darkness over James' shoulder. "Is that man carrying a frying pan in the muzzle of his musket?"

James turned and saw the grinning Hans Larson.

"I think he is, Major," James said.

"God help me," the major prayed, shaking his head. "Be ready to march in three minutes, Peck."

"Sir?" James asked. "Where are we going?"

"You're going where the ass-end of Company I leads you!" the major snapped, turning and marching away with his corporal, shaking his head over men carrying frying pans in the muzzles of their muskets.

James looked at Adolph. The fat man spat tobacco juice into the trampled grass of the meadow. The men in the ranks made shuffling, nervous sounds. James wished desperately that Captain Bachmann were where he belonged, at the head of the Baraboo Guards.

The major called commands from the center of the regimental line. In darkness, the companies stepped off, tramping from the meadow into the street, the men carrying their heavy Austrian muskets at the right shoulder shift, slanted to the left across the backs of their necks.

The Baraboo Guards followed Company I through the sleeping suburb of Georgetown, downhill and westward to the bridge that spanned the Potomac River.

Cannon were placed behind log breastworks on the Columbia side of the bridge, their black muzzles pointed across the river at the dark ridges of Virginia. Regular gunners lounged near the pieces, sitting close to their watch fires, staring silently at the men in Wisconsin gray who stepped onto the bridge and began the march across the river. Provost officers, standing in the light of hand-held torches, recorded the passage of the Second Wisconsin from the inner defenses of the city.

Adolph marched beside James, listening to the hollow sounds of shod feet on the boards of the bridge, counting campfires on the Virginia hills. "Christ," he murmured, "I wonder if those are Reb fires?"

"Should we have the men load their muskets?" James wondered.

"Don't ask me!" the lawman growled. "That smart-ass major should have told us where we're going and what we're supposed to tell the boys to do."

"Captain Bachmann should be here."

"Well, he isn't! Let's do what that major told us. We'll go where the ass-end of Company I leads us." The sheriff glanced up at the shadowed ridges rising above the river. "It sure is dark over here with the lights of the city behind us."

James licked dry lips. He paced beside the fat man, his eyes searching the darkness, barely able to make out the knapsacks of the men in the rear rank of Company I. He felt inadequate, not knowing where he was taking the Baraboo Guards, not knowing what dangers might await the men from Sauk County in the shadows ahead, not knowing what was expected of himself. He stepped off the Virginia side of the bridge and led the company up a winding dirt road that climbed the first ridge.

Dawn broke as the Second Wisconsin halted at an encampment of blue-clad soldiers in the fields around the unfinished earthworks of a large fort. Men were crawling from shelter tents, lighting fires, making their way to the latrines. James felt foolish at his earlier fear—all along the Baraboo Guards had been marching in darkness through what appeared to be a large Federal army.

James gave the men the order to bring their muskets down from their shoulders and to stand at ease in the road. There was no banter from the ranks. The fact that they were surrounded by thousands of Federal soldiers did not ease the concern that they were miles inside the land of secession.

"Lieutenant Peck!" Major Ross called, approaching. "The regiment will go into camp here. This is Fort Corcoran. We'll work with the other regiments here to complete what still has to be done on the fortification. The other regiments, by the way, are the Thirteenth, the Sixty-ninth and the Seventy-ninth New York. With us, they make up Sherman's Brigade of Tyler's Division. Can you remember that?"

"The Thirteenth, Sixty-ninth and Seventy-ninth New York?"

"No! Sherman's Brigade of Tyler's Division!"

"I can remember that, Major."

"Do so. The regiment will camp further down this road. I've special orders for Company K. While the other nine companies work on the fort, you'll be the regimental guard company. Pitch your tents there, along that line of trees. See where I'm pointing?"

"Over there? Yes, sir."

"Picket this road where it runs into the trees. Put your sentry lines along the edge of the woods, from the road to that fence."

"Yes, sir."

"From there on, security is the responsibility of the Thirteenth New York. No one is to be allowed through your picket post without a pass signed by Colonel Sherman or his adjutant. No one, whomsoever, is to cross your sentry lines. If anyone tries to do either, have your men take him into custody and escort him to the officer of the day."

"Yes, sir."

"Any questions?"

"What if someone won't stop when my men try to take him into custody, sir?" James asked.

"In that case, Peck, have your men shoot to kill."

James stared at the officer.

"Shoot to kill! We're the invading army, here, Peck. We face a hostile enemy. Anyone with legitimate business to conduct will travel the roads and have the proper passes. Anyone without, or anyone trying to sneak across your sentry lines, will be assumed to be a danger to your men and your cause. If that person tries to flee, have your men shoot to kill."

James and Adolph saluted the major as the officer turned and marched away.

"Jesus," the sheriff said, drawing his revolver and checking the loads in its six cylinders. "This is getting serious."

James nodded, watching the major until he was out of hearing. The law clerk cursed Captain Bachmann for not being with the company where he belonged. "Sheriff," he said to the fat man, "get the men busy pitching their shelter tents. Send someone to find water. I'm going to go learn what a picket post and a sentry line are."

"Learn?" Adolph demanded. "You let that major think you knew all about that! Why didn't you ask him when he was here?"

"He seemed to have enough on his mind without me adding two stupid lieutenants. Have Murphy the Drummer step over here."

Adolph chewed his tobacco. The boy was starting to give orders. For a moment, the sheriff was tempted to put him in his place. He decided not to. "Carl! Have the men fall out and pitch their tents along that line of trees. Line them up like the other companies are doing. Have Murphy fall out and join Lieutenant Peck here."

The Baraboo Guards broke ranks, stacked muskets and dropped knapsacks.

Murphy approached, eyeing the young lieutenant cautiously. James motioned for him to follow several yards down the road.

"The Lieutenant is wanting to see me, sir?" Murphy asked.

"I have to talk with you," James said, looking into the little man's pinched, red face. "You've been in the army."

Murphy squirmed, squinting at the taller man. He was still burdened with musket and knapsack. He didn't like being singled out from the rest of the men and taken for a stroll with an officer. Murphy wondered if he could talk circles around this one. He decided to try. "Army, are you saying, sir?" he queried, watching the law clerk's eyes. "What would make the young lieutenant think that, sir?"

"You know too much about all this, Murphy. That business with the plank and the stick at Camp Randall. Organizing the men into messes. Teaching them how to divide their rations. You learned that in the army."

"Ah, now, Lieutenant Peck, sir, with all due respect, aren't you reading too much into what you're seeing?" the little man asked, wiping his nose on the sleeve of his gray jacket. "Didn't I learn all that in the local chowder and marching society as a lad, sir?"

"You're lying, Murphy."

"Sir?"

"You've been a help to us," James said, trying another approach to the man. "I don't want to have to worry that I'll wake up some morning and find you've left us."

"What would make the lieutenant think that, now, sir?"

"You've deserted before."

The little man wiped his nose on the back of his hand. He squinted his eyes. This one was prying too close to where the silver lay buried, he was. "I think that a man's past is his own affair. With no disrespect, sir."

Murphy's words convinced James that he was correct. "As long as that past doesn't interfere with the welfare of the Baraboo Guards," he said, "I don't care what you've done. I know you didn't volunteer for this like the rest of us. You were brought along in irons. You've every right to want to be away from us and away from here. But, you're here and we need you. What do you fear?"

"Won't that be my own problem, now, sir?"

"You're one of the men of this company, Murphy," James said. "I'll help you when what you fear catches up with you. If you run from us, I'll come after you and bring you back to face it, whatever it is. I promise you."

The little man shifted his musket to the other shoulder and scratched his backside with his free hand. He was hoping his sainted mother in heaven was in a kindly mood, for it would be her interceding with the Virgin on his behalf that he'd be needing soon. "How can I help the young lieutenant?" he asked, committing himself.

"What's a picket post?"

"That'll be eight men to the side of the road. Four standing to the guard, the other four resting but ready. You'll want to relieve them every four hours. It's how the army will guard the entrance to a place."

"A corporal in charge?"

"Aye."

"What's a sentry line?"

"That'll be as many of the lads as it'll call for to be giving each of them his own piece of path to guard. Say, a hundred feet. They'll be walking up and down their paths, meeting their opposite numbers at each end. No one passes over a sentry line. You'll want to have as many more men, to twice the number, in a guard tent to relieve the sentries every four hours and to turn out if one of the lads calls the alarm."

"Anything else?"

"I'd have the lads stay away from harsh spirits while they're on guard. I'd warn them to stay awake. It's the staff officers who like to find a lad who's snorting or snoring. Or, it might be some wandering rebel, out to be slitting the throat of a drowsing sentinel."

James swallowed.

"It won't be the waltz that guard duty was back at Camp Randall, Lieutenant. With all respect, sir, when you marched them across yon bridge, you brought them into the war."

"I appreciate your help, Murphy."

"Just so the young lieutenant appreciates the promise he made to come running should your humble servant have the need to call."

"I'll remember that," James confirmed. "You keep the rest of my promise in mind."

19

VIRGINIA—June, 1861

Robert Wright was the corporal in charge of the picket post where the road ran into the trees. The farmer from south of Baraboo had rolled into his wool blanket off to one side of the road. Wayne Roohr, Johnny Makepeace and Peter Everett slept on the ground next to the farmer. On the road, Robert's brother Willis, Alois Swartz, Hollis Oostendorp and Edgar Pendar stood with bayoneted muskets. The boys clustered around a lantern and snickered at dirty stories Edgar told. Robert wished they'd shut up. The farmer was tired, filled with a good supper, ready for sleep.

"Robert!" Willis cried from the road.

He sat up, letting his warm blanket fall away. If Willis and the boys on the road were playing a trick on him, he was going to hit someone pretty hard.

"Get up here, Robert!" Willis shouted.

"What do you want?" he demanded angrily.

"Horses! Horses coming! Lots of them! We can hear them! Get up here!"

The farmer stood and picked up his musket. He kicked the boys who slept near him. The three crawled from their blankets and groped for their muskets in the dark.

"They're coming fast!" Willis cried.

"They better slow down when they get here," the farmer said, twisting his bayonet onto the muzzle of his Austrian musket. "Alois, swing that lantern. The rest of you, line up on both sides of the road."

Robert listened. The sounds of galloping hooves came from the deep shadows where the road ran into the trees. "Get your blades up in the air where they can see them," he shouted at the boys. He wondered what he should tell them to do if the oncoming riders turned out to be Confederate cavalry on a raid. "Alois! Swing that lantern!"

Seven riders burst from the trees and rode for the men at the picket post.

"Whoa!" Robert shouted. "You slow down! Now!"

The lead rider, a spare man with a short beard, pulled his horse up inches from the point of Wayne Roohr's blade. The following horsemen had to scatter to the sides of the road to keep from riding their leader down.

"Good God, Colonel Sherman!" one of the horsemen cried. "They're wearing gray! They're Rebs!"

"Hey!" Robert shouted. "We ain't Rebs! Hold on now!"

"What's the meaning of this?" the same officer demanded, swinging his hand at Willis' blade.

"Best hold on, Mister," Willis advised the officer. "Lest you want skewered."

The officer, a major, swore and glared, holding his mount's reins with one hand, reaching for a saddle holster with the other.

Willis cocked the hammer of his musket and raised the weapon to point into the major's face. "I wouldn't!" he told the officer.

"Who are you men?" the major demanded, his hand high in the air, away from the holster.

"We're the picket post of the Second Wisconsin," Robert told him. "Who're you?"

"This is Colonel William Sherman, man! Your brigade commander! We're his staff! Clear this road!"

"Well, now," Robert said, lowering the butt of his musket to the dirt of the road. "I'm Bob Wright and that fellow with the blade in your face, he's my brother, Willis. This here is Johnny Makepeace and over here . . ."

"I don't want introductions, you dolt! Are you in charge here?"

"Sure as hell am!"

"Tell your men to clear this road for Colonel Sherman and his staff!"

"I'm not going to do that, Mister."

"By God!"

"Now, don't get all wrought," the farmer told the officer. "Adolph Zimmerman put us here. He told us not to let anyone through without a proper pass. Adolph, he's the sheriff of Sauk County. That's back in Wisconsin. He's our second lieutenant down here. We do what he says. Now, you show me a pass and I'll let you go by. Otherwise, you haul those horses around and go back the way you came.

"You're in the presence of your brigade commander!"

"Well," Robert said, spitting into the dirt. "I'm not sure who my brigade commander is, you see. I sure as hell know who Adolph Zimmerman is and I've seen him kick three men's asses all at one time. So, Mister, you show me a pass or you haul out of here. Otherwise, I'm going to take you into custody and send you to the officer of the day, just like Adolph told me."

The colonel held up a hand to forestall further argument. "Major, this is wasting valuable time," he told the officer. "Give me your dispatch book and a pencil." The colonel wrote hastily, using the pommel of his saddle for a desk. He tore the page from the book and leaned down to hand it to Robert. "Will that satisfy you, Corporal?"

Robert looked at the page in the light of Alois' lantern. "Well, hell, I guess so," he said. "Are you really Colonel Sherman?"

"I am. May we continue on our way?"

"Shit, sure, Colonel. Hey, boys, I got a pass signed by Colonel Sherman himself. We're glad to be part of your army, Colonel. When're you going to give us a lick at them Rebs?"

"May we pass?" Colonel Sherman asked impatiently.

"Hell, yes. Willis, take your blade out of that man's face. Nice to have had the chance to meet you, Colonel."

The brigade commander spurred his mount forward, his staff following. The galloping horses showered the men at the picket post with clods and dust. The party rode in the direction of Fort Corcoran.

"How about that one man?" Willis asked. "I was close to letting some darkness inside him."

"He was staring down the blade of your bayonet, Willis," Johnny Makepeace said, yawning. "That's no way to start a friendship."

"See him try to pull a holster gun on me?"

"You're something, Willis," Alois said, turning down the wick of his lantern.

"I'm a wing-ding when I get my blade up in some man's face!"

"One of them's coming back," Edgar called.

The men in the road watched the major ride into the dimmed circle of light from the lantern.

"Corporal," the officer spoke, addressing Robert.

"You forget something, Mister?"

"You're to come with me, Corporal."

"Can't do that. Can't leave this post until I'm relieved. Adolph Zimmerman told me that."

"You won't be leaving your post, Corporal. You've only to come a few rods down the road with me. Colonel Sherman wants to speak with you."

"Don't go, Robert!" Willis warned. "They're going to hang you for stopping them!"

Robert looked at his brother, wondering.

"Going to pull your head off with a rope!"

"I assure you, Corporal," the major said. "You've nothing to fear."

Robert motioned for Willis to take charge of the post and followed the mounted major down the road, trailing his musket at his side.

Colonel Sherman stood in the road holding the reins of his horse. His staff, still mounted, clustered behind him. Sherman held a short cigar in his teeth. He blew small, fast clouds of smoke into the air in front of his face.

"You want to see me, Colonel?" Robert asked.

"What did you say your name was, Corporal?"

"I'm Bob Wright. Me and my brother back there, we farm land south of Baraboo in Sauk County. Say, Colonel, I'm sorry if we got you riled. We do like Adolph Zimmerman tells us. We're pretty serious about this war thing, you know."

"I can see that you are, Corporal Wright. You were doing your duty like good soldiers back there. I want you to continue to do what your officers tell you. We'll come through this war well if you do that. You can return to your post now. That's all I have to say to you."

"Well, hell, Colonel Sherman," Robert said. "I thank you for the compliment. Listen, now, you take care, hear?"

Sherman threw his cigar into the dirt of the road and mounted his horse. He faced his staff. "That, gentlemen," he shouted, pointing to the farmer from Sauk County, "is the first positive thing I've seen since I took command of this brigade!"

20

Some distance from the picket post on the road, Murphy stood at his cooking fire. The little man kept his hands busy as his mind worked around the edges of his problem. Murphy larded the inside of his dutch oven and lined the pot with dough he'd made from flour, water, a little salt and some rendered fat for shortening. He puffed on his briar pipe, his fingers slapping the dough into a shell around the bottom of the oven.

To be selling his soul for the answers to what was a picket post and what was a sentry line, now! Damned and be gone with him, he'd sold his soul for that! To a boy lieutenant and a company of sod busters who were saying they were needing him. Needing him, indeed! Who were they to be needing him when he had his own need for a few more years in this vale of tears? And for the price of a promise! When the fat sheriff of Sauk County knew it was iron shackles alone that would suffice to be bringing him along, hadn't the boy lieutenant thought to be keeping him from running off with the bounds of a promise! Words, no less! What would words be doing for himself when they were bending him over the bench and touching the hot iron to his skinny arse? Murphy took the briar pipe from his mouth and spat into the coals of his cooking fire. Would young Lieutenant Oh-Promise-Me be there to stop the tips of the lash from tearing the muscle from the bones of his back with words? Words had never come to the aid of this son of Ireland in the past.

Murphy took dried apples and peeled them with his clasp knife, cutting long, even lengths of wrinkled skin that curled down as his fingers worked. He cut into the dried pulp, letting the slices fall into the shell of dough, pausing now and then to throw sugar and to sprinkle molasses and cider onto every layer.

Off and away he should be taking himself. They'd managed to get themselves enlisted into the marching infantry without his help. Let them be getting themselves through the fighting on their own.

Murphy felt eyes on his person. The Larson brothers had sidled up to his cooking fire and were watching him, open-mouthed, as he fingered the dough to form the top of his pie. Murphy slit the dough for vents. Hans timidly reached out a finger and wiped molasses from the edge of Murphy's cup. The Irishman snarled. He flipped his clasp knife, sinking the point of the blade into the log next to the simple boy's wrist. Olaf grabbed his brother, pulling Hans back to safety, away from the tempting cup of molasses.

"Off with you!" Murphy shouted.

The boys backed away.

Ah, now, he thought. What was he doing throwing his knife at the dummy?

Wouldn't he be turning on the whole of them soon enough, were he letting the haunts take hold of his soul? He put the dutch oven into the coals of his fire, shovelling hot earth and embers onto its lid with the blade of his bayonet.

There was coffee in the pot. Murphy poured some into a clean cup, adding again as much whiskey to the brew.

They needed him! He spat. For him to be wiping their arses, they needed him! What need had he of them?

His own need was to be off and away. His own need was for room to be maneuvering and keeping well away from the welcome home and how have you been since we parted that the jolly Corps of Marines would be making ready for himself. Oh, what a grand and glorious parade that would be!

Again, he felt the eyes on his person. He glanced up. It was the simple Larson boy, standing safely off from the fire and drooling, his eyes fixed on the cup of molasses. Murphy watched him. Had not that one been dragged along with the rest of them, manacled to his brother as much as Murphy had been manacled to the brace of the wagon box? Weren't they all in chains, be they of whatever metal, he thought.

The little man sniffled at the run in his nose. He took the molasses to Hans, handing the cup of sweets to the simple lad.

Be damned to the lot of them, he cursed, returning to his fire. He'd be staying with them as long as he felt it safe and then off and away he'd be.

He considered maybe he'd be strolling over to the camp of the Sixty-ninth New York when his pie was baked. The Sixty-ninth were Irish. Some of them spoke the old Gaelic tongue. He'd sit with them and listen to that for a while. He'd drink some whiskey with them and he might even get into a fight, giving and taking a bash or two.

Needing him, they were saying! Indeed!

21

The morning of July 15, 1861, couriers galloped the roads between the Federal camps.

Supply wagons arrived with food and equipment for the regiments at Fort Corcoran. Rations and ammunition were issued. Shoes were inspected and cobbled if necessary. Armorers set up benches and checked muskets, making repairs on the spot.

After supper, James and Adolph were called to a meeting of regimental officers at the major's tent. The law clerk hoped he'd meet Captain Bachmann there. He didn't. He did meet Thad Able, who was acting as secretary for the gathering. James and Adolph sat on the grass among the more than thirty officers of the Second Wisconsin.

"Gentlemen," Major Ross began. "If I may have your attention. Our colonel sends his regrets that he can't join us this evening. I'll leave the inspirational talk to him. Let me only say to you for myself that it's been a long journey from Camp Randall to here. That journey is over. Our time of preparation is past. We march against General Beauregard and his Confederate army at three in the morning."

The officers on the grass cheered. Thad Able looked up from his notetaking and grinned across the jubilant assemblage at James.

"Not only do we march in the morning, gentlemen," Major Ross went on, "but we lead the way. Tyler's Division has the advance of the army. Sherman's Brigade has the advance of the division. The Second Wisconsin has the advance of the brigade."

The major turned to a map he'd pinned to the canvas wall of his tent. "We march," he said, pointing, "from Fort Corcoran, here, by way of Ball's Crossroads, Vienna, Fairfax Courthouse, to Centreville, here, where General McDowell, the army commander, intends to establish his base in the field. Get this route fixed in your minds, gentlemen, in case any of your companies become separated from the main column. We'll move in light marching order which means the men will carry only their weapons and ammunition, their haversacks and canteens, their blankets. Nothing else. We'll leave our tents standing and our baggage and packs behind. The garrison of Fort Corcoran will provide a guard over our things. Regimental officers, meaning me, will be mounted. All other officers will be on foot and with their companies. Are there any questions?"

"Where are the rebels?" the captain of Company H asked.

"Here," Major Ross pointed, "at Manassas Junction where the Orange and Alexandria Railroad meets the Manassas Gap Railroad. Their field positions are somewhat forward of the junction itself, here along the banks of a stream called Bull Run."

"How far is that from here?" another captain wanted to know.

"About twenty-six miles."

"We're going to have to walk some to meet them."

"We've come a thousand miles," the major stated. "Another twenty-six won't matter."

"Are they any good?" the captain asked. The other officers booed him.

"We don't know how good they are," the major replied. "I expect we'll meet them and we'll beat them. That's why we've come this distance from our homes. Any other questions?"

The officers were too excited to ask further questions.

"I remind you to stay with your commands on the march and to keep your men under control," Major Ross continued. "Straggling is a punishable offense. Keep your men away from private homes and private property. If the people we meet on the way out aren't bearing arms against us, they aren't our enemies, and that applies to their chickens, their pigs and their fence rails. Gentlemen, I'll see you in formation at three in the morning. Good evening. Good luck."

At fifteen minutes to three on the morning of July 16, 1861, infantry drums beat out the roll and the camps at Fort Corcoran came alive with the bustle of soldiers preparing to march.

By candlelight in the tent that served as company headquarters, James finished a letter to Lucille. Dropping the letter into the sack on the field desk, he buckled on his belt and holster and checked the loads in the revolver's cylinder. He slung his haversack and canteen over his right shoulder. Lucille's tin cup was fastened to the strap of his haversack. He pulled his blanket roll over his left shoulder and tied its end with cord.

"Baraboo Guards!" Carl called. "Fall in!"

The men from Sauk County lined up, jostling and talking, excited and nervous.

"Sergeants!" the tavern keeper shouted, himself burdened with musket and blanket roll and equipment, "check your men! Water and hardtack and ammunition! Cut the horseplay! Jack Black, no one told you to fix that bayonet!"

"Letters, boys!" the regimental chaplain chanted, carrying the mail sack. "Last opportunity for letters to the folks at home!"

"You don't have an envelope big enough to mail me back to Prairie du Sac, Parson," Willy Schoming laughed.

"I didn't come all the way down here to write letters," Stepan Fedkenheuer told Ludwig Axt. "I came down here to whip the Confederates!"

"Hey, Gus," Johnny Makepeace wanted to know, "How do you say, 'thank you, ma'am,' in Reb?"

"You stay close," Olaf told Hans. He took the jumble that was his brother's blanket and made a neat roll of it, slipping it over Hans' head and tucking the ends under Hans' arm.

Murphy the Drummer struck a match on his brass belt buckle and lit his briar pipe. He glanced at the stack of precious cooking equipment beside the flap of his shelter tent. If they returned and it was gone, there was more to be had.

"All set to take some rebel scalps, Ethan?" Gus asked.

"I have a headache."

"Here? Now?"

"Here and now, Gus. I don't schedule them," the merchant said quietly.

"This's no place to have a headache. Taken a shit lately?"

"Matter of fact, no. Not for three, four days."

"Want a little drink of whiskey?"

"Will that help?"

"Can't hurt."

"I'll pass, Gus. I didn't have this problem until I left Baraboo and started drinking again. It might be the liquor."

Orders were shouted at the center of the regiment. James couldn't hear nor could he see what the lead companies were doing. When Company I on his left came to right shoulder shift, he called out the same orders to the Baraboo Guards. The law clerk's heart hammered and the palms of his hands were damp as drums rolled and fifes twirled and the steady tramp of army shoes on the soft earth of Virginia came to him as company after company of the Second Wisconsin marched past. Following Company I, he called orders and the men from Sauk County wheeled into line and marched away from Fort Corcoran.

The eager volunteers soon settled into the drudgery of the march. A thick cloud of road dust swept into the air and hung there, maintained by the shuffling passage of thousands of marching feet. Even in the cool hours before dawn, the men were sweating. The blanket roll over the left shoulder crowded the neck. The heavy Austrian musket weighed down the right shoulder. Haversack and canteen straps began to tug. Cartridge boxes flapped on the hip. Bayonet scabbards rubbed calf and thigh. The wool uniforms grew warm and itched. The high, stiff shakoes held in heat from the head.

The volunteers marched south through woods and past orchards and fields. Regiments camped along the route were only now forming up as the men from Wisconsin marched by.

Ethan plodded, thinking of Lily to keep his mind off his heavy cartridge box, his rasping scabbard, his cumbersome musket, his shoes that were slowly filling with dirt. He couldn't keep his mind off the heaviness in his bowels and the headache that pounded in his skull.

An hour out, Company I, ahead, halted on the road. James raised his hand to hold the Baraboo Guards. "Stand at rest!" he called. "Stay on your feet!"

Adolph wiped the perspiration that cut channels down his dust-grimed cheeks. The fat man took off his cap and fanned his florid face.

Major Ross rode his mare along the column, speaking to each company commander in turn. "Lieutenant Peck," he greeted, cantering toward the Baraboo Guards.

"Sir?"

"Have your men fall out and rest. No fires. No straggling away. We'll be here for a while. Be ready to resume the march on three minutes notice."

"Yes, sir," James responded. "What's the problem, Major?" he asked, immediately regretting the question, recalling the major's abrupt answer to him when he asked the regiment's destination back in the meadow.

The officer pulled his mare to a halt and took off his cap. He wiped the inside band with his fingers, flinging away drops of sweat. "Some of the following regiments are late getting off," he told James. "We don't want to get too far out in front of them. By the way, I have word for you. Captain Bachmann will join you when the regiment gets to Centreville."

"I'm relieved to hear that, sir."

"You're doing all right on your own," the major told James, wiping dust from his face and neck with a bandanna.

James nodded. He'd be relieved when Captain Bachmann arrived and took command of the company.

The regiment remained resting in the weeds at the side of the road for two hours. The sun was well up in the clear sky when the order to resume the march came down the line.

At noon, the column reached Ball's Crossroads where a quartet of anxious cavalrymen pointed the lead company onto a dirt pike that ran to the left of the original line of march. Once past the crossroads, men from Company B were sent from the column into the fields to serve as flankers. They worked forward, well out from the road, climbing fences and wading streams, probing into hollows and depressions in search of lone Confederate sharpshooters or groups of riflemen who might fire at the marching column, exposed as it was on the road. The flankers soon lost discipline as they became fatigued and many took to berry picking.

"Carl!" Jack Black, marching in the sixth rank of four, called out. "I've got to shit!"

"Stay in ranks!" the tavern keeper ordered, trudging at the side of the company formation.

"He does, Carl," Johnny Makepeace agreed, marching and sweating next to Jack.

"All right," Carl relented, blowing dust and sweat from his upper lip. "Take your shit and get back in place! Fast! Run to catch up!"

Jack threw his musket to Johnny Makepeace and ran for the bushes beside the road, grappling with straps and equipment as he went.

Men from the companies ahead of the Baraboo Guards had been scampering for the bushes for some time. The men from Wisconsin were learning that the first day's march tended to set a man loose.

Ethan tramped in his place in the second rank of four. The merchant envied the men who ran for the bushes. His head pounded and his blood felt thick. He contemplated what portion of his worldly goods he'd readily part with in return for one good dump. Ethan watched the flankers out in the fields beside the road. Their work was hard. They had to trot to keep pace with the companies marching on the pike but they moved free of the enveloping cloud of road dust and they were able to fill their canteens from the streams and pick berries as they went. Ethan wondered what a cap full of tart, rich berries would do for his problem with elimination. He'd volunteer to trot through fields and climb fences, even run the risk of stumbling onto a Confederate ambush, if a cap full of berries gathered in the process would help his problem.

Ethan wondered if he should have written a note to Lily. He could have written a few lines to tell her that he was in good health and going into battle, that he was thinking of her. His health was not what he wanted it to be with his constipation but he wouldn't put that in a letter to Lily. He wondered if his conscience would be any lighter if he'd written. There wasn't room in his skull for a heavy conscience and a booming headache.

The merchant listened to the shuffle of army shoes on the dirt road. He smelled the stink of many men perspiring in wool uniforms. He heard the *tink-tunk* of equipment striking equipment. His straps tugged at his chest, his musket weighed heavily on his shoulder. Murphy the Drummer had used a term that Ethan remembered, the marching infantry. He'd thought the term romantic when the Irishman said it. He knew now what Murphy meant. There was nothing romantic about the marching infantry.

He was thirsty but there was no water left in his canteen. He licked dry lips and immediately wished he hadn't done that. His tongue was covered with dust that turned to gritty mud in his mouth.

Ethan shifted his musket to his left shoulder. He concentrated on placing one dirt-filled shoe ahead of the other. He tried not to think about his solid bowels. He kept his mouth shut to the penetrating dust. He fixed his eyes on the blanket roll of the man ahead. Left and right, he ordered his tired legs. Left and right.

Well after noon, well into the heat of the day, the companies ahead stumbled to a stop. Men on the road brought muskets down and leaned on the muzzles, eyes unfocused, mouths open.

James halted the Baraboo Guards. Those with water in their canteens found the water warm and tasting of tin. Those without water hawked brown globs of mucus and mud from their lips. A few men dropped to the road, white-faced. Friends fanned them with shakoes and handkerchiefs.

"Lieutenant Peck!" the major called, forcing his sweating mare through clusters of men on the road.

James looked up at the mounted officer, the sun blinding him.

"One hour to rest and eat, Peck. Coffee and hardtack. Put pickets fifty yards back down the road. Send one man in six to find water."

"Sir," James mumbled. He felt hot, thick, wrapped in something that was smothering him.

Adolph took the law clerk's arm and led him to the side of the road where bushes offered some shade. The sheriff nodded to Carl. The tavern keeper went off to organize the picket and canteen details.

James blinked. He stared at the lawman.

"You're feeling the sun, boy."

James rubbed his cold, clammy hands together. "How far have we come?" he asked, forcing the words with a thick tongue.

"Eight, maybe ten miles."

"In all this time?"

"We've been standing still more than we've been marching. You feeling any better?"

James nodded. He did feel cooler in the shade of the berry bushes. He stared at the coating of dust on his shoes. He dozed, then slept soundly.

After half an hour, Carl joined Adolph. The tavern keeper settled into the weeds, dropping the lieutenants' filled canteens. He offered Adolph a drink from his own.

The lawman drank, wiping drops from his chin. "Think we ought to wake the boy for some of this?" he asked.

Carl looked at the exhausted law clerk. "I'd let him sleep."

"He's doing all right," Adolph sighed.

Carl nodded.

"How are the rest of the boys?"

"They're doing well," Carl said, drinking from his canteen, "considering what they're being put through. They're beat. They aren't ready for long marches. We haven't lost any to straggling."

"They're good boys," the fat man said.

"There's not enough water along the road," Carl said, removing his shako and wiping perspiration from its leather band.

The day was well on toward darkness when the regiment arrived at the village of Vienna. Carl kept his sergeants on their feet long enough to set out sentries and name their reliefs. The men not called to walk the first tour of guard duty dropped where they stood in the fields beside the road, most not even bothering to take off their blanket rolls.

22

Drums rolled again at three in the morning.

The Baraboo Guards woke, raising themselves from the earth on which they'd slept, groping in the darkness for equipment, for muskets.

"Fall in!" Carl chanted. "On the road! Get your stuff together and fall in!"

"Ethan," Gus grumbled from inside his blanket. "Tell that ass to wait till it's morning, will you?"

"You better get up, Gus," the merchant said quietly. His head pounded and his stomach felt solid. He concentrated on tying the ends of his blanket roll together in the darkness.

"It's still night," Gus mumbled. "I'm still sleeping."

"It's the start of a new day, Gus. The army gets to things earlier than civilized people do."

"Tell Elsasser to wake me when the sun touches the horizon," Gus sighed.

Carl strode to Gus' prone form and swung his right foot. His heavy army shoe took Gus squarely on the buns.

"Ow!"

"On your feet, Gus," the tavern keeper ordered.

"Ethan!" the blond shouted. "He's no right to kick a man!"

"No right at all," Ethan agreed, hoisting his blanket roll to his shoulder. The merchant bent and found his musket in the grass. He wiped dew from the barrel with the sleeve of his jacket. "Carl's getting ready to kick you again, Gus. I'd get up."

Gus rolled onto his back and pulled the blanket from his face.

"On your feet, Gus," the tavern keeper repeated.

"Kicking a man who's down is poor sport, Elsasser!"

"Fair warning," Carl stated. "The next one will be to your jaw."

"I'm moving," Gus assured Carl. "You can go kick someone else now."

"Keep him on his feet, Ethan," Carl warned the merchant.

"Get your things together," Ethan said, stepping close to a tree and unbuttoning his fly to piss. He'd advise Gus. He wouldn't stand between Gus and whatever retribution the blond had coming.

The companies of the Second Wisconsin formed in darkness on the pike. The massed bands of the four regiments of Sherman's Brigade sounded off with a tune. The lead regiment, today the Thirteenth New-York, stepped out and marched west. The other regiments followed.

The Baraboo Guards, at the rear of the Second Wisconsin, settled into the business at hand, tramping the dirt pike from Vienna to Centreville via Fairfax Courthouse.

Murphy the Drummer paced himself. He marched comfortably, his blanket roll tucked back, his musket balanced on his shoulder. The little man puffed on his briar pipe. His belly lifted and dropped as he strode. The lads, he saw, were fighting the natural rhythm of the marching. They'd learn to be drifting into it. Ah, they'd be learning. Meantime, the Irishman had nothing to occupy his fertile mind. Tum-tum-tiddley-tum-tee-day, he crooned. Tum-tiddley-tum-tee-day.

Ethan got the urge three miles out. He threw his musket to Gus and ran for the bushes. His headache left him as he squatted in a sassafras thicket.

General Irvin McDowell's Federal army was moving on the village of Centreville on several roads. With no staff worthy of the name, McDowell set his force in motion for the Confederate army at Manassas Junction at the insistence of the president and the secretary of war. It was politically important that the Federal army in front of Washington take the field and face the rebel force under General Beauregard before the enlistments of the ninety-day volunteers expired. McDowell set out from Washington with his ammunition and ambulance wagon trains accompanying each division but with his supply and commissary wagon trains waiting behind in Alexandria to follow after the army cleared the roads. Those supply and commissary wagons were still at Alexandria, held there by a dispute between haggling generals.

When the rations the men in the marching columns carried in their haversacks ran out or spoiled in the intense heat, there was no resupply. Discipline on the march deteriorated the second day. Chickens, pigs, geese and ducklings disappeared from farms along the route. Officers, who should have stopped the men, didn't know or didn't care. The officers, like the men, were hungry, thirsty, tired and footsore. The march of McDowell's Federals soon broke down into a wandering, berry-picking, chicken-stealing, pig-killing, plundering saunter of exhausted, undisciplined, hungry, thirsty men.

Late in the afternoon of Wednesday, July 17, Colonel William Sherman formed his four regiments after a short rest at the village of Fairfax Courthouse and, an hour after dark, sent his brigade forward to take possession of Centreville, a poor village at a crossroads eight miles from Fairfax Courthouse. Centreville overlooked the valley of the stream known as Bull Run.

The Confederate brigade in observation at Centreville withdrew as Sherman's men moved into and beyond the village.

The fields around Centreville showed the signs of long use by large numbers of men. The earth and grass had the trampled, dusty look of an old camp. Piles of horse droppings littered the dirt. Garbage and camp debris were heaped about. Sherman's men helped themselves to stacks of firewood left behind by the withdrawing Rebs and built fires to boil their coffee. Few in Sherman's regiments had anything left in their haversacks but coffee.

Ethan trotted out into the fields beyond Centreville, assigned with Gus and others to form a line of skirmishers between the village and Bull Run. Ethan settled himself behind a small tree and looked into the falling shadows westward across the wandering stream. He was aware that the Confederate army waited among the dark ridges and valleys a few hundred yards from him. For the first time since he'd been issued the cumbersome weapon, the merchant clenched his Austrian musket close.

Behind Ethan, at Centreville, the Baraboo Guards slept in fields where Southern boys had slept the night before. The rest of McDowell's Federal army came up during the night with the tramp of twenty thousand pairs of army shoes and the rattle of two thousand wagons and went into camp near the Second Wisconsin.

23

General McDowell held his Federal army in the camps at Centreville all Friday and Saturday. Officers galloped the roads west of the village and peered across Bull Run through telescopes. Cavalry squadrons cantered along the Warrenton Turnpike as far as the stream and scouted the farm roads to the northwest and southeast. Couriers dashed from camp to camp with messages and orders.

The hungry men in the Federal regiments sat at cooking fires and gnawed the last of their hardtack. They made coffee from beans already three times boiled. They watched the officers and the cavalry squadrons and the couriers and they wondered at the mass of confusion and disorder about them.

On Saturday afternoon, the supply and commissary trains came up from Alexandria and rations were issued. Murphy got a mess of beans and bacon going in a dutch oven he had mysteriously acquired. John Barks and Ethan Evans commiserated with a squad of Massachusetts infantry who came through the Wisconsin camp searching for a dutch oven that fit the description of the one bubbling away under earth and embers not a dozen feet from there the Bay Staters stood. One could never tell about dutch ovens, the Irishman explained to the carpenter and the merchant after the Massachusetts men left. They did tend to look alike.

The drums roused the men from their blankets at two o'clock on Sunday morning. They rose and found their equipment and weapons in the darkness.

Adolph joined James in front of the Baraboo Guards, strapping his holstered revolver around his ample middle. James was nervous, his throat dry, his palms damp.

Adolph stared past James toward the circle of lanterns that had formed around Major Ross. "Well, Christ come early in the morning!" the sheriff swore. "Look who decided to join us!"

James looked in the direction of the lawman's stare. Nathaniel Bachmann marched past the gathering of officers.

Adolph spat. "Send the son of bitch back to Washington city, boy! We don't want him around here!"

"He's our commanding officer," James cautioned. "He said he'd be here when we went into battle. I'm relieved that he is. Captain Bachmann! Over here!"

The captain joined his lieutenants. "Mister Peck! Mister Zimmerman! I see you have the company formed and ready. Good! Good!"

James glanced at the lawman. Adolph spat tobacco juice.

"Knew I could count on you," Bachmann stated, slapping leather gauntlets against his thigh. "Great to be back on campaign! In the field with troops. I've missed this. Been years since I've felt the excitement that comes when the battalions form in the darkness before dawn, ready to do battle with the foe. This is what I've spent my life training for!"

"Lieutenant Peck!" Major Ross called, striding along the fronts of the companies.

"Here, sir," James answered. "Major Ross, Captain Bachmann has resumed command of the company."

"Bachmann?" the major asked. "We've missed you. I expected to see you at the head of your command before this. Now that you're here, I've orders for you. This regiment will bring up the rear of the brigade. Your Company

K will bring up the rear of the regiment. Let no stragglers from the companies ahead get behind you."

The captain clicked his heels.

"Is Company K formed and ready?" Major Ross asked him. "Equipment? Ammunition? Rations? Water?"

"I shall inspect the men personally, Major, and report to you immediately," Bachmann assured the officer.

"It's too late for that!" the major snapped.

"Captain Bachmann," James interposed. "First Sergeant Elsasser has inspected the men. The company is present, equipped and ready, sir."

"James," Bachmann said, "you continue to impress me. Major Ross, there you are. I expect you to call on Company K for the most arduous of duties, sir."

"Just follow behind Company I and don't let any stragglers get behind you!"

"Sir!"

Major Ross marched away, shaking his head.

"The major is testy this morning," Bachmann said, slapping the gauntlet on his thigh.

"The colonel and the lieutenant-colonel haven't been with the regiment since we arrived in Washington, Captain Bachmann," James explained. "This has placed a burden on Major Ross, having to assume command in their absence."

"No reason to let it show in front of the men. His situation is no different than your own. Duty of the subordinate, to be ready to assume the responsibility of command in the absence of the superior. I don't see you throwing little tantrums over having to assume the command of Company K while I've been involved in added duties at the behest of the governor of Wisconsin."

James looked away. Adolph spat.

"Difficult for the inexperienced subordinate to appreciate the demands that command places on one until the subordinate has borne those burdens himself."

"Yes, sir."

"Shit," the sheriff murmured.

"Regiment!" the call came from the center of the line of companies. Drums rattled. Officers ran to their places in darkness. The color guards uncased the flags and loosened them to the slight breeze.

"Attention!"

Nathaniel Bachmann took his place at the front-center of the Baraboo Guards. James moved to the left-front, Adolph to the right-front.

"Column of companies!" Major Ross called. "By the left flank, march!"

The Baraboo Guards brought their muskets to the right shoulder shift and swung into column, four abreast, on the Warrenton Turnpike. Following the three New York regiments of Sherman's Brigade, the Second Wisconsin marched into the shadows of early morning.

The mass of the Bull Run Mountains loomed ahead, touched by the sun's early rays. James realized that the Confederate army lay in the darkened valley of Bull Run between him and where the sun touched the crests of those far ridges. He had momentary thoughts about whether he should be where he was. He put those thoughts out of his head. It was far too late for them.

Ethan's bowels had not moved since the march to Centreville. He tramped and sweated and thought of Lily. He shifted his musket to the other shoulder, wanting the day to get on. The smells of marching men came over him as the breeze died—perspiration, damp wool, leather, dust, and stomach gas. The merchant shook his aching head. He had no idea what would happen when the Federals met the Confederates on the far side of Bull Run, but he wanted it to happen, whatever it was, and be over with.

A cluster of officers on horseback conferred at the right of the pike where a country lane ran off toward the north.

Bachmann pointed out the personalities as he led the Baraboo Guards past the road-side conference. "There's General McDowell," he told James and Adolph, "the large, portly man. There's General Tyler, our division commander. Colonel Hunter. Colonel Heintzelman. Our own Colonel Sherman. Colonel Keyes, who commands the first brigade of our division, and Colonel Schenk, who commands the other brigade. Mark that sight well in your memories, gentlemen. That is the power of this mighty army, the division and brigade command, working out strategy with the army command. Captains and lieutenants such as us seldom get to share the same place on earth with men such as them."

"Hey, Colonel Sherman!" Willis Wright shouted as the middle ranks of the company marched past the gathering of officers. "Remember me? My brother's the one arrested you back at Fort Corcoran!"

The Baraboo Guards hooted and cheered. Colonel Sherman raised a hand in remembrance. The officers with him grinned at the idea of the fiesty brigade commander being arrested by gray-clad militia.

"What was that, James?" Bachmann insisted. "Arrested? Some of our men arrested Colonel Sherman?"

"Sir, some of our men stopped Colonel Sherman and his staff at our picket post," James explained. "I don't think it amounted to arrest, sir."

"I should hope not! I assume those men were properly punished. I've missed some things, I see."

"You have, sir," James agreed.

"I must say to both of you, James, Adolph, that you've done surprisingly well with the company as far as you have gone. Being totally without training or experience at handling recruits, that is. I take full credit, of course, for selecting you. Mark of the commander, you know, the ability to select good subordinates."

James glanced at the perspiring lawman.

"Shit, Nate," Adolph mumbled. "You're too humble."

Carl, marching at the side of the column, glanced over his shoulder, then stepped down into the ditch and turned to face the rear. Regiments that had been following Sherman's Brigade since leaving the camps at Centreville were turning off the Warrenton Turnpike into the country lane where the conference of officers had taken place. Carl trotted forward to the three officers. "Adolph," he said.

The lawman blew dust and sweat from his upper lip and looked at the tavern keeper.

"Adolph, the rest of the army has been following us. They've turned off the pike. There isn't anyone behind us like there's been since we left Centreville."

James looked back.

"What do you think?" Adolph asked him.

"Captain Bachmann?" James asked, redirecting the question.

"Don't we have orders to follow Company I?"

"Yes, sir."

"Then, why this discussion?"

James glanced at the sheriff.

Adolph shrugged at Carl.

The tavern keeper stepped to the side of the pike and let the leading ranks of fours pass him.

"Carl's in deep shit!" Gus cackled as he tramped by. "Hey! Carl lost the rest of the army and got his tail knotted for talking about it!"

"Deep shit!" Dewey Shoate echoed.

Several men grunted. A few snickered.

"Ethan," the tavern keeper growled. "Do you plan to keep this son of a bitch as a brother-in-law for long?"

"That's enough, Gus," the suffering merchant said. He had his headache and his stomach felt as solid as dried mud. He had no time for Gus' antics.

"James," Bachmann said to the law clerk.

"Sir?"

"Best not to permit banter among the men on the march such as this. Silence in the ranks, you know. The orders we carry out are decided at the command level, not by negotiations among enlisted men."

"I'll remember that, Captain Bachmann. Sir, where do you think the rest of the army has gone?"

"I have to assume the rest of the army has gone where General McDowell sent it, carrying out its orders as we are carrying out ours. And, James, I have to assume it did that without discussion between officers and enlisted men."

Ahead on the Warrenton Turnpike James noticed movement to the right. The New York regiments were turning off the pike, marching onto the crest of a ridge that sloped toward the valley of Bull Run. The New Yorkers halted and formed there, the Sixty-ninth farthest to the right, then the Seventy-ninth and the Thirteenth. The leading companies of the Second Wisconsin followed, taking position between the left flank of the Thirteenth and the pike. Aligned, the four regiments faced west, four thousand men standing in the high grass, clover and bramble that covered the ridge.

To James' left the pike ran down the slope of the ridge and crossed Bull Run on a stone bridge. Across the bridge, close under a high hill to the left, the pike ran straight as far as the law clerk could see. To his right the land climbed gently upward toward a range of wooded hills.

The regular artillery section attached to Sherman's brigade rattled up and went into battery across the pike from where James stood. The law clerk watched the gunners unlimber their brass cannons. Crews ran the caissons twenty paces to the rear. Horse holders led the sweating teams further back. The gunners fell to work aligning their guns, turning elevating screws, loading charges into the barrels and ramming them home. Artillery officers studied the woods across the stream and called out aiming points. Then, like Sherman's four thousand infantrymen, the artillerymen stood and waited.

The sun continued its climb into a perfectly clear sky and the temperature rose. Men in wool uniforms sweated. Birds sang, their twirling and chirping reminding James of the birds in the clearing on the shore of Lake Mendota four Sundays past.

Nathaniel Bachmann left the two lieutenants to join a meeting of the company commanders with Major Ross.

"What do you think?" Adolph asked, balling a wad of tobacco and fingering it into his cheek.

"I don't know," the law clerk admitted. "We're here. We're ready. The gunners across the pike are ready. They've brought us a long way to have us stand around and watch the woods on the other side of that stream. I thought going into battle would be a little more lively."

"Think we ought to ask our company commander what's happening?"

"He'd probably tell us something about the mark of the good subordinate being not to ask what's happening."

"We don't need that son of a bitch!"

"He's here, Sheriff. He's in command. I'm relieved that he is."

Adolph snorted.

Carl Elsasser approached.

"What is it, Carl?" James asked.

"Many of the men are out of water, sir. Can I send a couple with a load of canteens back to a well behind this ridge?"

James looked at Adolph. The sheriff nodded.

Carl waved to Olaf and Hans Larson. The farmhands moved along the lines of men taking empty canteens. The brothers trotted over the ridge to where Olaf had found the well.

Nathaniel Bachmann strode through the high grass toward James and Adolph. The captain carried his pocket watch in his hand. "In a few minutes, gentlemen," he announced, "you will bear witness to the beginning of the end of the rebellion!"

"What's going to happen in a few minutes, Nate?" the sheriff asked.

Crack-boom! a cannon across the Warrenton Turnpike fired. Crack-boom! Crack-crack-crack-crack-boom! boom! boom! boom! the other guns in the section roared.

James watched the shells arc high, smoke trailing from burning fuses. Whoomf! Whoomf! Whoomf-whoomf-whoomf-whoomf! they exploded in the air over the trees across the creek, puffs and flashes and smoke seen by the volunteers several seconds before the sounds reached the line. James swallowed.

"Are there Rebs over there, Nate?" Adolph asked.

"Most assuredly, Lieutenant Zimmerman. In the trees, beyond the stone bridge."

James searched among the trees, now shrouded with gray powder smoke. He saw no signs of Confederates.

The gunners south of the turnpike worked steadily, laying their pieces, swabbing and loading and ramming and firing. Crack-boom! Crack-crack-crack-crack-crack-boom! boom! boom! boom! boom!

"Just watch what regular artillerymen can do, gentlemen!" Bachmann cried, pointing.

James kept his eyes on the far side of the shallow valley. The gunners across the pike changed from shell to solid shot, their iron balls now uprooting whole trees and sending them tumbling, digging long, raw furrows in the earth where quiet woodland and undergrowth had stood minutes

THE BARABOO GUARDS 125

before. The section of guns changed, again, to canister shot, and the charges beat the foliage across the stream like huge flails, tearing away branches and throwing up showers of twigs and leaves and splinters.

"Isn't it beautiful!" Bachmann demanded, slapping a thigh with a gauntlet. "Trained regulars, going at their tasks as if they were just a job of work! Drill, training and discipline, gentlemen! No substitute for drill, training and discipline!"

"Captain," James asked, "what are we doing here?"

"Impatient, Mister Peck?"

"Curious, sir."

"As to why the Confederates across the stream are silent?"

"Well, yes, sir."

"Saving their ammunition. We're no threat to them as long as we don't try to cross the steam. And, James, they're asking the same question you are."

"Where the rest of General McDowell's army is?"

"Exactly!"

"Where is the rest of General McDowell's army, sir?"

"Soon, James," the captain smiled. "Soon."

Crack-crack-crack-crack-boom! boom! boom! boom! Crack-boom! Crack-boom! the guns fired.

Over the ridge, Olaf and Hans found the well next to a fallen log structure that once had been a corn crib. Olaf dropped the moss-covered pail into the well and listened to the splash at the bottom of the shaft. He jiggled the rotting rope several times to upset the pail and then turned the windlass to raise it. "The canteens, Hans!" he cried to his brother. "Take the stoppers from the canteens! Fill them!"

The roar from the guns on the pike rolled over them. Hans dropped to the earth, shaking.

"Fill the canteens!" Olaf shouted.

The sound of another barrage came from the pike.

"'Laf!" the simple boy shrieked. "Don' like, 'Laf!" Hans was petrified by the blasts of the guns.

Olaf knelt and took his brother's hand. Hans was shaking. Olaf watched Hans' gray Wisconsin uniform trousers turn dark with pee. "'Laf," the boy pleaded.

The six guns roared. The simple boy gagged.

Olaf looked around. He studied the corn crib. He dragged Hans into the shelter of its fallen logs. He took Hans' blanket and unrolled it, tucking it around his brother. "Stay here," Olaf told Hans. "I'll come back for you. Don't go anywhere until I come back for you. Understand?"

"Hans not go!" the boy repeated.

"That's right. Stay here. I'll come back for you."

"Back for me!"

"Yes."

The artillery fired again. Hans winced, his eyes tight. "Don' like, 'Laf!"

Olaf studied the ridge. There were no Federal soldiers in sight to see what he was doing. He touched Hans on the head and ran back to the well. He filled the canteens. It was better this way. He'd leave Hans at the corn crib and come back for him when the day ended. Olaf pulled canteen straps over his neck and shoulders and trotted back up the ridge where the men from Sauk County stood in line watching the gunners south of the turnpike blast away at the woods on the far side of Bull Run.

On the ridge, Adolph took off his cap and wiped perspiration from his head. The lawman blinked.

"What is it?" James asked, worried that the fat man might be suffering from the heat.

"Something," Adolph said, his face intent.

"Something?"

"Hush!"

James held his breath and listened. There was something, not as much a sound as the sensation of a sound, like distant thunder on a humid day.

"Look!" a man in Company I shouted, pointing across the valley at the range of hills that rose to the right of the Warrenton Turnpike. A brown mist of dust and smoke rose beyond the hills there, billowing into clouds that rolled and spread down into the valley.

James heard noise now, waves of noise that grew steadily, mixtures of layers upon layers of sounds, the grumble of artillery fire, the snarl of musketry, the shouting of men, the screams of horses.

"There's the answer to your question, James!" Bachmann cried. "There's the rest of General McDowell's army! He's marched around the far flank of the Confederate line and he's attacking their left! He's sweeping them, James! While we've stood here and held their attention, he's struck! Look! See them run!"

James watched, fascinated, as men and horses and wagons moved into the broad valley across the stream. There was confusion, even panic, over there. Formations of men fled from his right to his left, mobs of men, crowds and stragglers and wounded. Shells from Federal guns behind the far range of hills to the right broke over and among the retreating Confederates. Men dropped, fled their formations, ran across the valley floor toward the high hills to the south.

The gunners across the pike from James now worked in a frenzy, their brass Napoleons roaring flame and smoke and iron as fast as the regulars could swab and load and point and fire.

The men in the regiments from New York and Wisconsin shouted and cheered as shells exploded. It was obvious to even James' untrained eye that the Confederate army across Bull Run was in retreat. The Federal army under General Irving McDowell had struck hard and was winning a great victory.

"Hey!" Gus shouted. "When do we get our turn?"

"I haven't been sleeping alone to come here and watch Rhode Island get all the glory," John Barks told Carl.

"Gus," Jack Black decided. "They're saving us to do the ravishing."

"Look!" Johnny Makepeace cried, pointing. "There are our boys! See the Stars and Stripes!"

James watched blue-clad formations march into the valley from behind the hills to the north. Through the smoke and dust he could see flashes of Federal flags.

"God damn it, boy!" Adolph cried. "Isn't that something to live to see!"

James was startled at how quickly the scene across Bull Run had changed. An hour before, the Warrenton Turnpike had run between clean fields and grassy slopes. Now, the land was torn and blasted, littered and scored. Broken wagons and over-turned gun carriages marked the line of the Confederate retreat. Muskets and packs, blankets and haversacks, the bodies of men and horses lay scattered throughout the valley. As James watched, a galloping Federal gun and limber raced into his vision, postillions whipping the horses, gunners holding to the handles of the limber chests for their lives. The whole action, horses and wheels and gun and limber and men rode into an explosion of flame and smoke and James couldn't tell as he watched which of the pieces that flew into the sky were of horse or wheel or gun or man. He felt sick. He looked at Adolph but the sheriff was watching some other horror across the valley. James swallowed. His throat was dry.

Olaf hurried along the line of the Baraboo Guards, returning canteens heavy with water. No one asked him about Hans.

A drum rattled briefly where Colonel Sherman had his headquarters. Bachmann touched James on the arm and motioned for the law clerk to take charge of the company as he ran toward the gathering of officers forming around the brigade commander.

"I think we're going to be getting into some of that," the sheriff said, pulling his revolver and checking its loads.

"Hey, Gus!" Johnny Makepeace cried out. "Bullets, bayonets and rifle butts!"

Gus waved his musket over his head and let out a wild Indian yell.

Murphy the Drummer tapped the dottle from his briar pipe and tucked the pipe into a pocket of his trousers. It was good, he considered, that the boys were feeling fiesty. They'd soon be learning. Tum-tum-tiddley-tum-tee-day, he crooned. Tum-tum-tiddley-tum-tee-day.

"Bring on those Southern belles!" Andy Shoate cried, clutching his scrotum.

"Won't be a virgin left in the Confederacy by night!" Jack Black promised Johnny Makepeace.

Major Ross stepped away from the conference around Colonel Sherman. He saluted the brigade commander and led the Wisconsin captains back to their commands. The major motioned for his orderly to lead his mare to the rear. He marched to the front and center of the Wisconsin companies, turning, facing them, drawing his sword. "Regiment!" he shouted. "Attention!"

"Where's Captain Bachmann?" James asked Adolph.

The sheriff glanced around the field.

"He was just here!" James cried.

"I don't see him," the lawman said. "Get out in front. Take his place."

"He was just here!" James screamed. "Where is he?"

"He isn't here!" the lawman shouted. "You just got the company back! Get out in front and take his place!"

"He promised he would be here!" James shrieked, grabbing the lawman's arm.

"He isn't!" Adolph shouted, throwing off the law clerk's hand. "Do it!"

"Where is he?" James begged.

Major Ross glared down the line of companies.

"Captain Bachmann isn't here!" James screamed at him.

Major Ross pointed with his sword, first at James, then at the place in the high grass where the company commander should be standing.

"He promised me he would be here!" James shouted.

Major Ross held his sword steady, pointing it in front of the company.

"He isn't here!" James sobbed.

"We'll follow you, boy!" the sheriff shouted, looking over his shoulder at the men from Sauk County.

"Peck!" Gus called out.

"Peck!" Ethan joined his brother-in-law.

"Peck!" Murphy added. The Irishman saw the need for the lad to take command of the company.

"Peck! Peck!," the rest of the Baraboo Guards shouted.

"Captain Bachmann promised me he would be here!" James shouted at them.

"Company K!" Major Ross threatened, his sword pointed down the line.

Adolph stepped to the front, pulling the law clerk by the arm. "Company!" the fat man shouted. "Attention!"

"Regiment!" Major Ross ordered. "Column of companies from the right! Forward, march!"

The companies of the Second Wisconsin wheeled to the right, forming into columns of fours.

"Come on, boy," Adolph said, marching, holding James by the arm. "We don't need that son of a bitch! We've come this far without him. We'll do fine."

"He promised me he'd be here!" James cried, gagging, stumbling to keep pace with the fat man.

"God damn it!" Adolph cursed. "He isn't here!"

"He . . . he . . ." James stuttered, looking up into the fat man's fierce eyes.

"Get in step," Adolph said. "Let's make the boys think we know what the hell we're doing."

James wiped his eyes and his nose on the sleeve of his coat. He shuddered, trying to get control of his emotions, trying to get in step with the fat man.

Crack-crack-crack-boom! boom! boom! the guns south of the Warrenton Turnpike fired. Crack-crack-crack-boom! boom! boom!

Major Ross led the march toward a farm lane that ran down the slope of the ridge to a ford across Bull Run. The sergeants of the color guard followed him, the deep blue of the Wisconsin flag and the bright red, white and blue of the national colors rustling in the warm late morning air.

"Are you all right?" the sheriff asked, tugging on the law clerk's arm.

James nodded, sniffling. "Ah, back there," he shuddered, "I'm sorry. He said he would be here."

"I told you he was a son of a bitch, didn't I?"

James nodded, ashamed of his weakness.

Major Ross strode through the shallow waters of Bull Run at the ford, wet to his knees. The sergeants of the color guard followed, wading to the far bank. Company A, the Citizens' Guard from Columbia County, cheered as the men splashed into the cool water.

Ethan trudged through the water with the Baraboo Guards, his head pounding. He climbed the far bank and marched past an overturned wagon, its dead team lying tangled in the traces. The horses' flesh was hacked and slashed, their pink and gray entrails spilled out on the dirt, drawing flies.

Off to his right, the merchant saw men from Federal regiments crossing the valley, men from the units that had made the long march around the Confederate left and rolled up that flank of the rebel army. Ethan was shocked at the condition of the men from the flanking regiments. They'd been marching and fighting since three o'clock in the morning and they were dirty, dusty, tired, dulled. Many of the units were without officers, without leadership. Wounded men wandered in the valley, looking for friends, for surgeons, for help.

Colonel Sherman rode to the head of the Wisconsin column and leaned from the saddle to shout to Major Ross, pointing to the high hill south of the Warrenton Turnpike. The rolling sounds of battle came from there. Major Ross nodded, stepping back and saluting. Colonel Sherman pulled his horse around and galloped toward the Thirteenth New York.

Olaf sensed that something was going to happen. He was satisfied he'd hidden Hans at the corn crib. The farmhand gripped his musket and marched in his place behind Gus Gaard. Sergeant Barks hadn't asked him what had become of Hans. Maybe the carpenter hadn't noticed. Olaf had done what was best.

Murphy the Drummer marched steadily. Ah, he thought, but for the sweet solace a sip of good whiskey would bring to the parched tongue of a man at a time like this. The Irishman noticed the direction of march was toward the high hill south of the turnpike. The lads would have no idea what was waiting for them there. It was better they did not, the first time.

For himself, he considered, shouldn't a veteran of many a battle on land and sea be contemplating the possibility of coming down with a terrible case of the stomach cramps? He'd just be stepping to the side of the line of march and dropping his trousers, squatting in the position known to all men, and letting the farmers from Sauk County march on by. Once out of their sight, it would be back over the stream and mixing in with the crowd of stragglers and wounded around Centreville until this fight went into the books.

Murphy glanced to his right, to scout out the lay of the land. He looked directly into the hard eyes of the grim first sergeant. It would not be like that harsh man to be letting one of the lads out of the line of march to be taking a dump when the Baraboo Guards were striding toward their first taste of glory.

Murphy considered. If the tavern keeper would be stumbling and breaking a leg, it would be but an act of human compassion for himself to be volunteering to carry the bastard back to the surgeons and be saving his life.

The tavern keeper seemed quite adept at not stumbling and breaking his leg. Well, the little man decided, there was naught to be gained by worrying on a fact that would not come to be. He hefted his musket a little higher on his shoulder and crooned, tum-diddley-tum-tee-day. Tum-tum-tiddley-tum-tee-day.

Gus marched beside his brother-in-law, wishing Ethan would speak to him. Gus was frightened. This was not what he had imagined battle to be, walking forward in a column of men, tramping in smoke and dust and confusion, one man among thousands.

Gus glanced down at two shapes that he'd taken, at first, to be bundles fallen from some wagon. The bundles were, or had been, men. They wore gray, the same shade the men from Wisconsin wore. They lay side by side, as if placed there by friends, crumpled, broken, deflated. Blood and dirt discolored their features. One man's eyes stared up into the clear sky. The other had no eyes. Gus swallowed. A man back in the column saw them and stepped to the side and retched. Gus wished Ethan would speak to him. He didn't want his fear to show and he didn't know how to hide it.

Major Ross led the column to where the Warrenton Turnpike was cut close into the side of the high hill. He climbed the berm and waved his arms right and left to the Wisconsin companies. "Form line of battle in the road!" he shouted. "Color guards! Front and center! Here, up on the hill!"

The color guards scrambled up from the road, waving the flags back and forth.

"Close up!" Major Ross shouted. "Dress right! Officers to the front!"

James and Adolph climbed the bank in front of the Baraboo Guards. James could see, from the vantage of the hillside, the Thirteenth New York forming in the road to the left of the Second Wisconsin. The Sixty-ninth and the Seventy-ninth New York formed in fields behind the regiments in the road. The law clerk looked at his hands. His fingers were shaking. He breathed deeply, trying to calm his shuddering. He'd been shocked by the absence of Captain Bachmann. He felt the captain had betrayed him.

Major Ross backed up the hill, his eyes checking the alignment of his ten companies. "Second Wisconsin!" he shouted.

The men in the road looked up at him.

Major Ross turned and waved his sword toward the crest of the ridge. "Forward!" he called.

The drummers struck up the roll. The company officers shouted orders and started the march up the hill behind the major, drawing their own swords and revolvers. The front ranks climbed out of the cut, aligning on the sergeants, and paced up the hill in time to the incessant beat of the drums. The second rank followed, climbing out of the road, aligning, marching upward.

James saw nothing before him but the grassy slope. He drew his heavy revolver and glanced to his left where Adolph lumbered up the slope on the left flank of the Baraboo Guards. The fat man's face was bright red, his mouth open, his chest heaving. Beyond the suffering lawman James saw the blue lines of the Thirteenth New York sweep forward, moving up the hill slightly behind the gray lines of the Second Wisconsin.

James cleared the top of the hill.

Six brass guns of a Federal battery stood alone on the plateau. In the high grass around them James saw the gunners and the horses sprawled on the earth. A few gunners struggled to pull themselves away from the bloody scene among the wheels of the cannon. A few horses kicked, weakly. James realized, stunned, that the men and horses had been shot down. Across the fields beyond the battery he saw a farm house and barn in flames. Through the smoke and wavering heat of the fires he made out men moving into lines in front of trees. Battle flags waved along the far line. As James watched and marched forward, men ran from the trees and took their places on the flanks of the formations, extending the lines to the right and left. The law clerk realized, horrified, that the men in the far formations were Confederates. James shouted to Major Ross to warn the officer, to tell him to stop the onward movement of the men from Wisconsin.

Major Ross marched steadily, his sword over his right shoulder.

James saw a horseman wearing a gray uniform ride slowly forward from the Confederate line. James stared at him, unable to stop his legs from moving in time with the beat of the drums. The horseman pulled his small horse up and stared across the plateau, appearing to gaze directly at the law clerk. The rider raised his right forearm, as if in greeting or in warning. James marched, watching the horseman, unable to stop his legs, unable to command his mind, unable to make his body do anything but pace forward in time with the beat of the infantry drums. The man turned his mount and cantered back toward the Confederate lines.

James counted battle flags across the plateau. Four, six, nine flags, fourteen, more. Each flag spoke for a thousand men. James looked at Major Ross, who marched steadily forward, his head up, his sword over his shoulder.

The Confederate lines rippled, moved, sunlight striking bayonets and musket barrels as the front ranks knelt and the rear ranks stepped forward into the intervals. Both ranks brought their weapons to the shoulder.

Major Ross halted and turned. He raised his sword.

The men from Wisconsin halted. They stood ready, Austrian muskets over their shoulders, watching the major.

"Present!" Major Ross shouted.

The thousand imported muskets swept from the shoulder to the horizontal.

"Aim!" Major Ross screamed.

The Confederate regiments got their volleys away first. White billows of smoke rolled out across the plateau, flame dancing back and forth along the lines, thousands of lead balls humming toward the men from Wisconsin.

Herbie Auchter from west of Reedsburg felt as if a horse had kicked him in the chest. He dropped his musket and clutched at the front of his gray jacket. He fell, sitting hard. The farmer carefully showed his bloody hands to Ottis Blumenfeld who lay dead in the grass next to Herbie. The farmer looked up in time to see Ludwig Axt shriek and fall, his left arm shattered. Herbie wanted to remember something. He couldn't. He slipped into warm darkness.

"Fire!" Major Ross cried. "For God's sake, fire!"

The Wisconsin muskets roared and filled the air with flame and powder smoke and lead balls. Men dropped in the Confederate formations across the plateau.

"Reload!" Major Ross called. "At will! Fire! Fire! Fire!"

Ethan dropped the butt of his musket to the ground. The merchant pulled a paper-wrapped cartridge from the leather box on his hip. His headache pounded. He stared at the cartridge. He couldn't remember what it was that he should do with it. He dropped it and took another. His fingers worked by themselves. He bit the end of the cartridge, tearing the paper, and stuffed it into the smoking muzzle of his musket. He couldn't think. He couldn't remember what to do next. The merchant winced as the Thirteenth New York volleyed off to his left. Ethan saw swaths of men fall in the far rebel lines.

A man in Company I bucked and heaved and threw his musket into the air, falling to the grass and screeching. Jack Black, white with fear, watched him. The man screeched again and the sounds tore at Jack's mind. He dropped his musket and turned. He looked into Carl Elsasser's stern face. The tavern keeper leveled his bayonet at Jack. The dark man cried out in terror and ran past Carl, arms pumping, eyes wide with panic.

Carl cursed Jack. He'd been ordered to cut down any man who ran from his place in the line but he couldn't shoot a man from Sauk County.

Gus thumbed a brass percussion cap onto the nipple under the hammer of his musket. He raised the weapon and took careful aim. There was a tall color sergeant across the plateau waving a scarlet battle flag. Gus held his breath for a second and slowly squeezed the trigger. His musket roared. The scarlet battle flag continued to wave. The blond dropped the butt of his musket to the grass and began the reloading process. Gus was no longer frightened, now that he could shoot.

Olaf aimed and fired. He'd been right to have Hans hide at the corn crib. The boy couldn't have stood the noise and the shouting and the smoke and men falling. If Sergeant Barks found out and beat him for hiding Hans, that would have to be. It was best this way.

Murphy the Drummer loaded, aimed, fired. Dum-diddley-dum-dee-day, he crooned to keep his mind from thinking. Dum-diddley-dum-dum. Dum-diddley-dum-dee-day.

Alois Swartz jerked and buckled. His stomach ached sore bad. He was dead before his face hit the trampled earth at his feet.

Men in the Wisconsin line began to step back as they loaded and fired. Officers shouted at them. Sergeants shoved them forward, swearing at them. They ignored their leaders, loading and firing and stepping a few paces to the rear.

Major Ross saw what was happening. "Back!" he ordered. "Fall back and take cover under the hill!"

The two ranks moved to the rear. A warbling tenor cheer rose from the Confederate formations across the plateau of Henry Hill.

James stumbled down the slope and fell to his knees. Adolph grabbed the law clerk and pulled him to his feet. "You all right, boy?" the fat man demanded.

James stared into the sheriff's face. He licked dry lips. He'd been frozen with fear on the hill top, petrified, unable to move. He'd shut his eyes and sobbed, biting into his bottom lip, waiting for the musket balls to slam into his body. He wanted to tell the sheriff. Adolph would know what to do. James tried. He couldn't form words.

Sauk County's farmers and townsmen sprawled on the grass of the hillside, sucking at canteens, spitting dust and smoke and the taste of black powder from their mouths. They were numb, shaken by what had happened on the plateau. Few of them spoke. Many stared at their hands, at their feet, off into the distance.

"Second Wisconsin!" Major Ross cried, running from company to company. "We're going back up this hill! Captains, form your men! We're going back!"

Gus looked at Ethan. Gus didn't want to go back up the hill. Ethan didn't speak. The merchant hadn't fired his musket since the first volley. Gus saw the cartridge still in the muzzle of his brother-in-law's weapon. He took Ethan's musket and completed ramming the cartridge home and capping the nipple. Gus had been frightened until the firing started. His hands were steady when he handed Ethan's musket back. He didn't want to go back up the hill but he'd go if Ethan would.

"Up!" Carl shouted, running among the men from Sauk County. "Form up! Load up!"

The drummers struck up their rattle and roll. The color guards stepped out. The two ranks of the Second Wisconsin swept back up Henry Hill, the men chanting in time with the beat of the drums, crying out anger, rage, fear, determination.

The Confederate lines volleyed into them before they cleared the top of the hill. Men in Wisconsin gray screamed, fell, tumbled back down the slope.

"Fire!" Major Ross shouted, pointing with his sword in the direction of the rebel formations. The front of the Wisconsin line exploded with its own storm of flame and flying lead.

The regiment advanced, the men loading and aiming and firing as they paced forward, shouting, howling, cursing. The companies drew up where they had stood before on the line marked by crumpled, broken, moaning forms, many of which lay where they had fallen. Some men crawled through the advancing companies toward the rear, seeking the safety of the hillside. A few in the high grass pleaded for help, crying out or raising hands to friends in the firing line.

James stood before the Baraboo Guards, clutching his revolver close to his side. His eyes were tightly closed. He wept, breathing in short, terrified gulps.

"Steady, now," Adolph chanted, walking the length of the company line behind the rear rank. "Aim low. Fire slow. You can do it. Hey! Let that man lay!"

Dewey Shoate fell, his forehead carried away in a spray of pink matter that splattered over men in the rear rank. Andy Shoate stared in shock at what had been his brother.

"Steady, now," the sheriff told the men. "Aim low. Fire slow."

"We need some help," Ethan told Gus. The merchant was composed now, loading and aiming and firing.

"We're all alone out here!" Henry Calef cried.

"Too many of them over there," Johnny Makepeace told John Barks, capping and aiming his musket. Johnny fired and stepped several paces to the rear before thumbing another cartridge into the muzzle.

The withdrawal began without orders from the officers or the sergeants, the men loading and firing and steadily moving back.

Major Ross cursed the men, cursed the Confederate formations across the plateau, cursed the Federal command that put Sherman's Brigade on a hill that was wide enough for only two regiments to come on line at a time. He shook his hands in the air and threw his sword on the ground. "Fall back!" he ordered. "Gather on the side of the hill!"

The Sixty-ninth New York advanced through the men from Wisconsin, who tumbled down the slope and lay on the grass, breathing heavily, sucking canteens, staring.

James stumbled back with the Baraboo Guards, walking blindly. "Hey, you!" a voice called out at him. James looked. Two New Yorkers stood before him with Jack Black struggling in their grips. "You want this one, Lieutenant?" one of them asked. "We caught him charging in the wrong direction."

James looked at the two men, not comprehending. He tried to make himself think. He saw Carl and waved for the tavern keeper to take Jack from the New Yorkers.

Adolph came to him, reloading his revolver. The fat man was perspiring, panting, his gray coat open and his shirt dark with sweat and dust. "Are you all right?" the lawman asked, finishing with his revolver and holstering it.

James stared dully at the sheriff. He tried to swallow. He put his own revolver, unfired, away. He'd tell the sheriff how terrified he'd been some other time. Just now, he couldn't think. He felt the need to say something. "What should we do?" he managed, wiping weakly at his forehead.

"Do? For Christ's sake, let's hold a roll call and see how many of us didn't come off the top of this hill! We better see if we can get to any of them up there and bring them down. These here, the ones that are hurt, we ought to send to the surgeons. Carl!"

"I heard you, Adolph," the tavern keeper said. He gathered his sergeants and put them to work on the roll calls. He sent Andy Shoate, who was still in shock from the gruesome sight of his brother's death, off to find where the surgeons had set up. Carl loaded his musket and trotted up the hill, stooping under the whiz and hum of lead balls that flew past his head. He straightened to look for gray uniforms in the high grass. A hammer blow took Carl on the side of his head. The tavern keeper saw a thousand bright lights. He felt the world turn beneath him and he fell face down among the Wisconsin bodies on the plateau of Henry Hill.

Below the crest Adolph took James by the arm. "Look down there," he said, pointing into the valley.

James looked.

The Federal army was going back. Lines of men were making their way along the Warrenton Turnpike heading for the stone bridge over Bull Run. The floor of the valley was carpeted with the waste of battle. Equipment littered the fields and roads. Dead horses and dead men lay on the torn sod. Where trees had stood, shattered trunks remained. Broken gun carriages and overturned wagons blocked the movement of men marching in formations among the thousands who wandered singly, in pairs, in threes. There was no sign of panic or rout. General Irvin McDowell's Federal army had marched and had fought and had been winning the day until the very end. Now it was leaving the field. The men had been without food or water since leaving Centreville before daylight that morning. They were thirsty, hungry, tired, and confused. Many were without ammunition and most were without officers to tell them what to do. They had marched and they had fought as best they could. They were heading back.

The sun dropped toward the hills to the west. The fierce heat of the day began to ebb.

"We'll go," Adolph told James, walking among the men from Sauk County. "We'll try to keep the boys together."

James followed Adolph. He had no ability to do anything but follow the fat man.

"Where's Carl?" John Barks asked.

"I sent him up the hill to look for our boys there," Adolph told the carpenter, looking through the crowd of men on the hillside. "I don't see him. John, take over for him until he gets back. He might be anywhere. Get our men formed on the road. Let me know what the roll calls tell us."

The Baraboo Guards slid down the hill. Sergeants and corporals aligned the men. John took the reports from the sergeants. He made notes in his book and then joined James and Adolph, his face drawn, his jaw clenched.

"Well?" the lawman asked.

John swallowed, staring uneasily at the sheriff.

"How bad is it, John?"

"Fifteen!" the carpenter blurted. "We lost fifteen men!"

The sheriff turned away and looked across the fields in the direction of Centreville.

"We lost fifteen men, Adolph!" John cried.

The fat man wiped his face.

"Carl's gone! I can't find him! No one has seen him!"

"Take over for him, John," Adolph ordered. "Until he comes back."

"Will he come back? Good God, Adolph! I saw Dewey Shoate and Ludwig Axt fall! Auchter! Blumenfeld! Good God, Adolph!"

"Get hold of yourself," the sheriff said gently. "Form the men. Put someone on Jack Black. I'll take care of that son of a bitch later."

Major Ross joined James and Adolph. "Lieutenant Peck," he said. "Lieutenant Zimmerman. You both did well. Company K did well. There were too many of them for us. What were your losses?"

James cringed at the major's praise. He couldn't answer. He couldn't tell the major he'd lost his nerve on the plateau of the hill. He waved a weak hand to Adolph.

"Sauk County lost fifteen of its boys, Major Ross," the lawman stated.

"Fifteen," the officer echoed. "By God, Lieutenant Zimmerman, Wisconsin paid dearly for its moment of glory this afternoon!"

"Glory?" James was able to croak, his throat tight. "That was glory?" he pleaded, pointing up the hill.

"No, Lieutenant Peck, that wasn't glory! That was slaughter! Simple slaughter! It's over. There's nothing more we can do. I'm taking the regiment back to Centreville. Try to keep your men together if you become separated from the rest of us. If we don't meet at Centreville, I'll see you at Fort Corcoran. I doubt if this army will stand anywhere this side of the Washington forts. Look to your men. Do the best you can. That's all I ask of you."

"Jesus!" Adolph blurted angrily as the major walked away. "I didn't know it would be like this! We brought them all the way from Sauk County to get killed in a losing battle! They were willing! By God, they were willing! But to get killed like this!"

James looked down at the coating of dust on his shoes. He had nothing to say.

Two men in Wisconsin gray struggled past the law clerk and the sheriff, their muskets forming a litter with a blanket. A body sagged between the weapons.

"Who is that?" Adolph asked, wondering if the body might be that of one of the missing Baraboo Guards.

"Our lieutenant," the man at the front of the litter said.

"What company are you?"

"Company A. The Citizens' Guards. We're from around Beaver Dam in Dodge County."

James lifted a corner of the blanket and saw Thad Able's broken face, the eyes fixed on some point high in the darkening sky.

"Can we get on?" the man at the rear of the litter asked. "We want to get Thad's body across the creek before the Rebs set their horsemen on us."

James reached into Thad's coat pocket and found the flask from which the two were going to drink their toast to victory. He nodded for the men from Dodge County to move on.

James gripped the flask in both hands. He recalled the boy asking that night at the Dorn House if the preservation of the Federal union was worth going to war. James sobbed, tears cutting into the dust and powder smoke on his face.

Adolph put a hand on his arm.

James wiped his eyes with the sleeve of his coat. He gathered himself, drawing back and throwing the flask far from the hillside. There was no victory to drink to. There was no grinning, gleeful law student from Beaver Dam to drink with. There was only shame at what he had been a part of.

"The other companies are moving," Adolph told him. "We'll want to follow. Are you in charge now?"

James looked at the fat man. He nodded.

The skies darkened as the sun set. Heavy clouds rolled low over the valley of Bull Run.

Across the stream there was little of the confusion and congestion that was taking place along the Warrenton Turnpike west of the stone bridge. As the afternoon shadows lengthened Nathaniel Bachmann made his way alone from the stand of trees in which he'd hidden and walked quickly in the direction of Centreville. He saw a troop of Federal cavalry in the distance and ran to take cover behind a fallen structure. He waited there for several minutes until the troopers rode from sight.

He sensed movement behind himself. Alarmed, he turned rapidly, losing his cap, drawing and cocking his revolver. A form rose before him, a strange form wearing a blanket.

The form mumbled. The blanket fell away. Hans Larson smiled reassuringly at Bachmann. The simple boy reached toward the captain, to let him know how grateful he was that Olaf had sent the captain to find him. He'd been frightened by the noise and the movements during the long day but he'd done as Olaf told him. He'd hidden under the blanket and waited. Now the captain had come to take him back to Olaf. Hans was happy.

Bachmann thought quickly. He searched for some way to turn his desertion into something beneficial through this lad. He couldn't think of a way to do that. He shot Hans through the forehead. Looking around to see if the sound of his revolver had drawn notice, he strode on toward Centreville. He couldn't leave a witness to his cowardice. Besides, the boy was a dummy.

West of Bull Run on the crowded turnpike the companies of the Second Wisconsin became separated in the mix and flow of men, artillery, wagons, ambulances, and carriages. Stragglers and officers without commands shoved their way into the formations. Horsemen threaded through the marching ranks. A massive traffic jam developed at the stone bridge. Beyond the span lay Centreville and the safety of the reserve division stationed there.

As the Baraboo Guards approached the mass of men and vehicles at the bridge, three Confederate shells burst low in the air over the heads of the crowd. A wagon driver whipped his frightened team. The horses bolted, upsetting the wagon and spilling the wounded men it carried onto the road. Men and animals surged against the wagon, trampling the wounded and jamming the wagon sideways between the stone sidings of the bridge, blocking the way. Men on the pike suddenly became a stricken mob of individuals desperate to get across the barricaded bridge and away from the unseen dangers the lengthening shadows of evening might hold.

"Cavalry!" an officer screamed, pointing south of the pike where a regiment of rebel horsemen cantered into line and formed for a charge.

Murphy grabbed Ethan and Gus and pushed them forward on the road. "Follow me!" he cried to James and Adolph, pushing them toward a battalion of regular infantry that was marching into the field beside the road. Several Baraboo Guards followed the Irishman.

The regulars kept their discipline and order as the mob at the bridge panicked. The hard-faced men in blue frock coats and tall black hats maneuvered to form a hollow square, facing outward. The first rank of regulars knelt, bayoneted muskets angled upward. The second and third ranks stood behind the first, bayoneted muskets held level.

Half a dozen Baraboo Guards formed behind Murphy, loading and capping their muskets and taking places in the third rank where there were gaps in the lines of regulars.

The commander of the rebel cavalry circled his large horse, shouting to his men and pointing with his saber toward the hollow square of infantry between his riders and the milling mob at the bridge.

The Confederate squadrons charged, the riders bending low, spurring their mounts, yipping and hallooing and warbling high-pitched cries.

The somber regulars cocked their muskets and aimed for the chests of the on-coming horses. The Confederate lines swept toward the hollow square. The regulars stood waiting the order to fire. The rebel commander waved his saber back and forth and the charging cavalry split into two waves, each veering to one side of the square. The regulars fired on command. Horses and men in the surging cavalcade crashed to the earth in the roaring billows of smoke and flame and lead. The momentum of the charge carried most of the Confederate riders past the hollow square and into the mass of people and animals and vehicles on the pike. The rebel riders wailed and yelled and cheered, shooting and sabering and riding men down. Their charge tore through the mob and on into the fields and shadowed hills to the north of the pike.

"Well, now," Murphy said, wiping his red nose on the sleeve of his gray jacket. "That'll be enough for one full day, I'm thinking."

James stared at the little man. The Irishman acted as if he'd finished a job of work and was ready for a strong drink and his supper. The law clerk turned his gaze onto the field at the flailing legs and heaving bodies of horses and the moaning, shrieking riders who had fallen before the disciplined musketry of the regular infantry. He was too stunned to react.

"We'll want to be moving along," Murphy told him. "In the direction of the ford we crossed this noon. We'll stay away from the mob at the bridge. Those riders will be coming back this way."

James nodded, his mind dull.

The battalion of regulars broke its hollow square and formed into marching ranks.

"You lads," Murphy told the men from Sauk County. "You'll be following the lieutenants and staying close together." The little man reloaded, nodding for the rest of the Baraboo Guards to do so.

"Murphy," James said as the regulars started their march eastward, striding easily to the tap of a single drumstick.

"Lad?" the Irishman asked, returning his ram rod to the carrier rings under the musket's barrel.

James swallowed. His throat ached. He had to force the word. "Thanks."

"Not to mention it, Lieutenant. 'Twas common sense to form on them that knew what they were doing. We'll be off now. We won't do any good for ourselves staying on in this place. Whaawk!"

The little man's face began to turn bright red. A large sergeant in regular blue stood behind Murphy with his hands around the Irishman's throat, choking life's breath from him. James had seen the sergeant step from the ranks of the departing regulars.

"Ha ha!" the sergeant shouted, holding Murphy, lifting the Irishman's struggling body into the air. "I've finally got you, Mickey O'Fallon, you bastard!"

James stared at the sergeant, at Murphy. He looked at Adolph who stared back at him.

"I've got you, Mickey!" the sergeant crowed, swinging Murphy back and forth in the air. "You won't get away from me this time!" The sergeant wore the blue frock coat of the regulars but with white cross belts over his chest and a tall shako topped with a red pompon. The chevrons on his sleeves were red, different than the light blue of the regular infantry. The sergeant tightened his grip on Murphy's throat. The little man's eyes bulged. "You murdering scum!" the sergeant roared. "You deserting, thieving, murdering scum! I've got you, Mickey O'Fallon, and you're going to hang!"

Murphy's eyes fixed pleadingly on James'.

"What is this?" the law clerk asked, his throat dry, his voice rasping.

"This is Mickey O'Fallon," the sergeant roared, shaking Murphy. "One of my own, he once was! Weren't you, Mickey?"

Murphy gurgled in the sergeant's hard grasp.

"Who are you?" James demanded, his anger rising. He needed to take command of what was happening. He'd promised Murphy.

"I'm Sergeant Callahan of the Corps of Marines! This one in your pretty militia suit is Mickey O'Fallon, whatever name he might have given you when he signed on. He's a murderer, a thief and a deserter from my own Corps of Marines, he is! He's going back with me to face what he brought on himself. He deserted me once. He'll never do that again. You've no cause to concern yourself with him, Lieutenant. This one is a dead man!"

Murphy struggled in the man's hands. His eyes begged.

"Release that man," James told the sergeant, his voice still dry and rasping.

"Oh, no, sir!" the sergeant smiled. "Mickey and I, we'll be leaving and I'll be marching this one back to Washington city. To the quarters of the Commandant of the Corps, himself." The sergeant turned Murphy around in his hands and shouted into the little man's face. "You know what you've got coming, Mickey! You'll be whipped, branded and hanged! With the blessings of the commandant, I'll be doing the bloody three to you myself!"

Adolph, Ethan, Gus, Olaf, and the rest of the Baraboo Guards stood in the high grass, muskets in hand, not knowing what to do.

James drew his revolver. "Release that man, Sergeant," he repeated, his voice still weak.

"He'll die here first!" the sergeant snarled, raising Murphy's feet from the ground and shaking the little man.

James cocked his revolver and pointed it at the marine's chest. "I order you to release that man," he managed to say, his voice shaking.

"Order me?" the sergeant shouted. "You back-country militia shit! You order me?" He threw Murphy to the ground and looked around, searching. He strode several feet and grabbed up a bayoneted musket from where the regulars had formed. He turned and leveled the weapon at James.

"Put that musket down!" James croaked. He raised his revolver.

The marine grinned. He stepped, putting his left foot forward.

"Watch!" Murphy screamed from the ground. He knew the bayonet drill, knew what was about to happen.

The sergeant stepped with his right foot and carried the musket forward with a snap. The bayonet took James in his left shoulder, grinding to the bone as it went in. James felt the shock, the tearing entry, the hard thrust that threw him backward. He fell to the earth, his shoulder throbbing and flaring in pain. He dropped his revolver.

The marine jerked the bayonet free and stepped back. He snarled and braced, then lunged forward and down.

Adolph raised his revolver and shot the sergeant through the chest. The marine fell, his bayonet thrusting into the earth beside the law clerk's throat.

"Ah, my God, my God!" Murphy wailed. "What have I brought you all to?" The Irishman sat in the high grass, rubbing his aching throat, looking up at the men from Sauk County who stood above him.

"You've brought us to nothing we didn't bring ourselves to," Adolph said, holstering his revolver. "That man attacked our commanding officer. I shot him, as well I should have shot him. Shut up and get something to bandage that hole in the boy's shoulder." Adolph turned to the men around him. "You all saw what happened!"

The men nodded.

"Adolph . . ." James gagged, lying on the earth, the pain from his shoulder radiating down his arm and his back.

"God damn it, boy!" the lawman cursed. "You should have shot the son of a bitch when he didn't obey you the first time!" He bent and picked up James' revolver, shoving it into the law clerk's holster. "Can you stand?"

"I hope so," James whispered. He grimaced when Murphy folded a sweat-soaked neckerchief against the bleeding wound inside his undershirt. He groaned when Gus and Ethan pulled him to his feet. He bent and vomited into the high grass.

"Which way to Centreville?" Adolph asked the Irishman.

"East," Murphy nodded. "Into the darkening of the day."

"Let's move," Adolph told the men. "I don't want us here when that Reb cavalry comes back. We'll stay off the pike and away from that crowd at the bridge. We'll move through the fields. Ethan, go find that ford we crossed at this noon. Can you walk as far as Centreville?" he asked the law clerk.

James wiped his chin. "I want to try."

"We can carry you."

James shook his head. It was important that he walk.

"Gus," the lawman ordered. "Get out in front of us. Wayne, off to the right. John, behind us. All of you make sure we're in your sight and keep your eyes open for Rebs. The rest of you, load up and keep quiet."

The small group moved away from the field south of the road. Ethan found the ford across Bull Run. The men from Sauk County waded the creek as day passed into night.

James stumbled in the ford. Murphy pulled the law clerk onto his back.

"Sorry to be such a burden," James sighed when Murphy put him on his feet on the far bank.

"You're no burden, lad," the Irishman said. "You promised to come, were I to be needing you. You came."

"All I managed to do was get in the way of a bayonet."

"I'm owing you for being able to look forward to life this night, lad. You and that terrible man of a sheriff. I'll be staying with you, Lieutenant Peck. You're to have no concern about that from now on."

James wavered. He fought to keep his balance. His shoulder flared, throbbed. He bit his lips to stifle a moan. Turning to the Irishman he said, "We need you, Murphy. Or, is it Murphy? That sergeant called you O'Fallon. Which is your name?"

"Truth, lad, it's neither. What's a name but a sound to go with a face?"

"We'll keep it Murphy," James decided. He staggered and was about to fall when the sheriff grabbed his right arm and held him. James steadied himself. He found he was able to walk with help. Ethan and Gus walked with him.

Adolph led the men through the fields east of Bull Run where the regiments of Sherman's Brigade had formed during the morning. He stepped close to Olaf and pulled the farmhand to one side.

"Where did you hide Hans?"

Olaf had hoped no one had noticed that Hans was not with the men on Henry Hill.

"It's all right, Olaf," Adolph said.

"In a corn crib," Olaf whispered. If the sheriff were to beat him for hiding Hans, that was as it should be.

"Where?"

"Over this ridge. Near the well where we filled the canteens. Was I wrong, Sheriff?"

"You weren't wrong, boy. Let's go find him."

Olaf checked the percussion cap on the nipple of his musket and trotted to his left into the shadows. Adolph motioned for John Barks to keep the men heading in the direction of Centreville. He lumbered after the farmhand, drawing his revolver.

Olaf approached the fallen structure carefully. Confederate sharpshooters could have taken cover there to harass the retreating Federals. He hoped they had not. That would frighten Hans. Olaf stepped into the corner where he had put his brother. "Hans!" he whispered.

Adolph stood several yards away with his revolver in his hands. He let Olaf do the searching. The lawman watched for wandering Confederates.

"Hans!" Olaf hissed.

"Where did you leave him?" Adolph asked. He wanted to find Hans and get back with the men from Sauk County who were moving across the fields.

"I left him here. I told him not to go anywhere until I came back for him."

"Could he have wandered off?"

"No. He wouldn't leave until I came for him."

Adolph looked around, close. He saw a shape in the grass. "Olaf."

"What?"

"Here. In front of me. You look, boy."

Olaf knelt beside the form in the high grass. It was Hans. Olaf drew his brother's head into his lap and cradled him. Hans was cold. He'd been dead for some time. Olaf took his brother's hands and crossed them over Hans' chest as he'd seen a preacher do for a neighbor who'd been killed by a falling tree. Olaf had not thought of Hans dying when he brought him to the war. But Hans had died and that was as it would be. He searched about in the darkness for Hans' cap to cover his brother's face. He couldn't find the stiff shako. He found a soft kepi. He felt the fabric of the kepi, working his fingers through its fabric, remembering the kepi from when Captain Bachmann talked to the men at the post office in Delton. Olaf slipped the kepi into the front of his jacket so the sheriff wouldn't notice. The farmhand didn't know why Captain Bachmann's kepi would be next to his brother's body at the corn crib on the ridge in Virginia. Now was not the time to ask.

"Do you want to bring him along so we can bury him?" Adolph asked.

No, Olaf shook his head. He had come to the war and he had brought Hans with him. Hans had been killed in the war. It was as it was. He buttoned the front of his gray jacket, tucking away the officer's kepi.

Pickets of the reserve division in front of Centreville challenged the Baraboo Guards when Adolph brought the men from Sauk County into the Federal lines. The pickets almost fired into the group until their gray uniforms were explained.

The disorganized battalions of General Irvin McDowell's Federal army wandered past Centreville, taking the dirt roads that led back to the camps at the Washington forts, twenty-three miles away. The dark skies clouded and rain fell heavily. Roads that had been firm and dusty on the march out turned into tracks of tenacious mud. The dispirited Federals hunched their shoulders against the rain and trudged, hands in pockets, mud tugging at their shoes.

Gus found an army surgeon working under a tarpaulin hung from the branches of a tree beside the road. The primitive surgery was lighted by two lanterns. Lines of wounded men lay in the rain in a field next to the surgery. Some of the wounded were covered with blankets. Many lay exposed to the rain.

The surgeon wiped bloody hands on a leather apron and studied the rip in James' coat. "Sword?" he asked. "Bayonet, then. Don't see many bayonet wounds. They tend to be fatal. Help me get the lieutenant's coat and shirt off."

Adolph and Ethan worked with the surgeon. The wound in James' shoulder was a dark, oozing pucker.

The law clerk sat on a box, biting his lips to keep from screaming at the agony of the surgeon's probing and kneading fingers.

"You're fortunate, Lieutenant," the surgeon said, wiping his fingers on his stained apron. "Nothing I see that needs taking out or taking off. Major blood vessels are intact. You'd be dead by now if they weren't. You'll hurt for a while as this heals. If it heals."

James declined the offer of a drink from a brown bottle.

"I'll put a dressing on it. That's all I can do. Have another surgeon look at your wound when you get to Washington. I bandage what I can," the surgeon told Adolph, "and cut off what I have to. The ones who might make it, I line them up on the sides of the road in case ambulances or wagons come along. The ones who won't make it, I put them over there in that field where they can die in peace. I asked the farmer down this lane if I could put them in his barn but he ran me off. Said he had two sons with Beauregard and he hoped all us Yankees would roast in hell. Do you want to wait for an ambulance or a wagon, Lieutenant?"

James shook his head. "I want to stay with these men."

"Just as well," the surgeon shrugged, throwing a bloody pad into a pile of stained bandages at his feet. "Ambulances and wagons I see from here on most probably will be Confederate. Was it bad up there?"

"It was bad," Adolph told him.

"My own regiment is back at the forts," the surgeon explained. "Heavy artillery. Garrison duty. I rode out here on my own to watch the fight. I got this far before I got run off the road by the mob. I heard, earlier, that we were winning."

"Earlier, we were," Adolph grunted.

"You better get on. Good luck to you. Have the lieutenant see a surgeon when you get to where you're going. Here, that man is dead. Put him over there in that field. Bring on the next one."

James walked the twenty-three miles in falling rain, his agony compounding as fever set in. He leaned on Murphy part of the way. Gus tried to carry him but the law clerk insisted he could walk.

24

Carl Elsasser felt rain falling on his face. He woke, realizing that he was soaked through and cold. Pain split his head. He heard voices.

"Master," one soft voice said. "There's one of them moving."

Carl rolled onto his left side. He saw low clouds, thick and gray. Gritting his teeth against the throbbing pain in his skull, he managed to sit.

"Cover him, Bushrod," another voice said. "He's wearing gray but he ain't one of ours."

Carl slipped back toward unconsciousness, the pain in his skull overwhelming. He struggled to gain control of himself. He blinked. That helped. He put a hand to the side of his head and felt caked blood. He blinked again. He was able to see more clearly. He was sitting just below the crest of the hill. There was something he was supposed to do on the hill. He couldn't remember. He saw legs, a pair of boots, shoes. He blinked at an officer and four Confederate soldiers standing a few yards from him. One of the soldiers held a bayoneted musket pointed at him.

"You're fortunate, Sergeant," the officer said. "We almost buried you." The officer wore a rubber cape. The four soldiers had no protection from the rain. They, like Carl, were soaked through.

The officer nodded and two soldiers came down the hill. They grabbed Carl and pulled him to his feet. The tavern keeper gagged and bent over, drooling bitter bile.

"Take your time, Sergeant," the officer said. "You've taken quite a bang on the head. Willy, give the sergeant a pull on your canteen."

Carl accepted the offered wooden canteen and took a swallow of the harsh whiskey it contained. He exhaled, breathed deeply, shuddered. He felt better. He could see behind the officer and soldiers parties of Negroes spading shallow graves in the earth and rolling bodies into the holes. The bodies were limp, distorted things, bloated and soft. They seemed to collapse as they rolled into the holes. Carl noticed that the bodies were without shoes. Most had the pockets of their trousers turned out.

"Who are you, Sergeant?"

Carl blinked again. Beyond the burial parties, men and wagons moved slowly, gleaning the battlefield, picking up muskets and pieces of equipment.

"Who are you, Sergeant?" the officer reminded the tavern keeper.

Carl touched his head where the blood had hardened. That was where his pain seemed to be centered. "Ah," he sighed, shuddering. "Ah, Elsasser. Carl Elsasser. First Sergeant, Company K, Second Wisconsin."

"You're a far piece from Wisconsin, Sergeant. I fear that you're our prisoner. Will you drop your belts?"

"Belts?" Carl asked stupidly.

"Your belts. Cartridge box and cap box. You won't be needing them. You're going to Richmond, to prison, Sergeant."

"Prison?"

"It's better than being one of these." The officer nodded in the direction of a limp corpse the Negroes were rolling into a rain-filled hole.

"Yes," Carl agreed. "I take it, we lost?"

"You lost. You gave us a bad time for a while. In the end, your men couldn't break Professor Jackson's stone wall of Valley troops. Your people left after that."

"I see," Carl said. He didn't see. He didn't know what the officer meant by the stone wall of Valley troops. "I'd like to look at the bodies," he asked. "I'd like to see if any of my men are here."

"We've already buried the men from your side who wore gray."

"I see," Carl repeated, not seeing.

"Bushrod," the officer said to the soldier with the musket. "Take Sergeant Elsasser back to Manassas Junction. Turn him over to the provosts. You'll join some of your people there, Sergeant. We took a parcel of prisoners. Move along, now."

"Were there many like these?" Carl asked, nodding at the corpses.

"About five hundred on your side. Three hundred or so on our side. It was a costly day, Sergeant."

Carl nodded. "Well, Bushrod," he said, still the first sergeant. "Let's go."

25

Adolph brought the group to Fort Corcoran late on Monday morning, the day after the battle.

The sheriff had a cot set up in the conical Sibley tent that served as company headquarters. James was delirious when the men stripped off his wet uniform and put him into warm bedding.

Murphy got a fire going in spite of the rain. He boiled water and washed the law clerk's wound, bandaging the shoulder with clean cloths. The little man disappeared for an hour and returned with a sack of food and a bottle of whiskey. Murphy made tea. He spooned that, well-sugared and laced with whiskey, into the feverish law clerk. James slept fitfully, hot and dry.

Olaf spent the day alone in the shelter tent he'd shared with Hans, holding Captain Bachmann's kepi in his hands, thinking things through. Hans had been shot where there had been no fighting. Captain Bachmann's little cap had been on the ground under Hans' body. Captain Bachmann hadn't been with the men from Sauk County during the fighting and hadn't come back to the camp with the men. It could be that Confederate men had found and killed Hans but Olaf didn't think that was the case. If it were, Captain Bachmann's kepi wouldn't have been under his brother's body. At the end of the day Olaf put the kepi into his knapsack and joined the men who sat at Murphy's cooking fire. Hans was dead. That wouldn't change. Olaf would think about what must have happened at the corn crib. He'd talk to no one. He'd remember and he'd work this out for himself.

By Wednesday, three days after the battle, men were still straggling into the camps at Fort Corcoran. Some had been carried along in the retreat of the Federal army all the way to Washington city. They wandered into the camps without weapons or haversacks, without shoes, blankets, coats, canteens. General Irvin McDowell's army had lost much of its equipment and a great deal of its pride on the long retreat from Bull Run.

When the final tally was taken, the Second Wisconsin had suffered severely. Twenty-three men were known to be dead. More than sixty were known to be wounded, many of whom had been left on the field and captured by the Confederates along with another sixty who had been captured during the confusion of the retreat. In all, the Second Wisconsin lost a hundred and fifty of its thousand men at Bull Run. The losses of the four regiments of Sherman's Brigade were the highest brigade losses in the Federal army.

Murphy showed remarkable skill in caring for the wounded law clerk. He pressed men into nursing duty and forbade the sheriff of Sauk County from bringing surgeons to see the patient. The Irishman changed the dressing daily, wiping the soreness of the wound with cooling whiskey, using cloths that had been boiled clean. The little man kept a pot of broth simmering and had the men he assigned to nurse James spoon broth and tea and whiskey into the law clerk every few hours.

Wisconsin's governor, Alexander Randall, had been in New York City when he read the news of the battle and heard of the high losses the Second Wisconsin Regiment had suffered. He took the first available train to Washington.

When the Baraboo Guards joined the other companies to parade for the governor, James, still feverish, his shoulder sore and suppurating, was barely able to sit up in his cot in the Sibley tent.

He worked on the decision he'd been struggling with since he'd climbed Henry Hill the first time. He'd been useless at the head of the Baraboo Guards. He'd let Captain Bachmann's desertion unnerve him. Adolph had to take command of the company and lead it. James had been frightened into immobility on the plateau. He'd been unable to act, to speak, to even open his eyes most of the time. His one attempt at taking command had resulted in his being bayoneted.

James couldn't keep the memory of the plateau of Henry Hill from filling his thoughts. He recalled the shattered Federal battery atop the hill and he remembered the lone horseman who had ridden from the Confederate lines, seeing that man again through the smoke and wavering heat of the burning farm. James saw the man pull up his small horse and look directly across the fields, appearing to stare at him. James saw the horseman raise his right arm as if in greeting or in warning. He recalled his agonizing wait for the musket balls to strike into his body.

James would tell Adolph that he'd lost his nerve and given in to his weakness. The sheriff would understand. He'd help him. James would resign his commission and return to Baraboo. He dreaded the day he'd have to tell Lucille Faircloth that the man she loved was a coward.

The flap of the Sibley tent was thrown open. Alexander Randall stepped into the tent, stooping under the slope of its roof. Major Ross and Adolph Zimmerman followed the governor of Wisconsin. "Is this the young officer I've heard so much of?" Alexander Randall asked Major Ross, as he walked to James' cot.

The law clerk struggled to sit up. He got as far as his elbows could push him. Adolph stepped forward and placed a knapsack behind James.

"Stay as you are," the governor insisted.

"Governor Randall, I . . ." James started to say.

"Let me do the talking, young man," Alexander Randall said, sitting on a stool next to the cot. "Politicians are good for few things. Talking is one of them. Leave that to me. First, though, tell me, how are you feeling?"

"Sore, sir," James admitted. "And beaten."

"Not beaten," the governor corrected. "Not beaten by any measure! You boys went out there on Sunday and you made Wisconsin proud. The other side got the best of the day but you'll go back at them. You'll beat them next time. Do you have any idea what the news of Bull Run has caused to happen back in Wisconsin? I have more volunteers than I can equip or train. You boys proved to our state and to our nation that you can take a pounding and still be ready to come out fighting again. You have much to learn but you were not beaten. Not by any measure."

"The men tried, sir," James offered weakly.

"That's all our state can ask. Do you feel strong enough to have a short talk with your governor?"

"Yes, sir."

"Colonel Ross? Lieutenant Zimmerman?"

The officers saluted the governor and left the Sibley tent, dropping the flap behind them.

"You addressed Major Ross as a colonel, sir?"

"I've appointed William Ross to the colonelcy of the Second Wisconsin Regiment. Captain Vaughan, of Company D, will be the new lieutenant-colonel. Captain Bache, of Company F, will be the new major. The former incumbents will be returning to Wisconsin with me. I made some mistakes in my original appointments. They are good men, each in his own way, but they are not officers capable of leading Wisconsin troops in battle."

"I'm pleased to hear about Colonel Ross, sir."

"Yes. But, young man, I want to talk to you about Captain Bachmann."

"Sir?"

"I understand that Nathaniel Bachmann was not with his command at Bull Run. I understand that he's seldom been with the company since its muster in Baraboo. I have to bear the blame for the shortcomings of Nathaniel Bachmann. I found in him an able assistant and a knowledge-able aide. However, while he was doing my bidding, the burden of his command fell on your shoulders. That's why I'm replacing him and appointing you to the captaincy of Company K."

James stared uncomprehendingly at the governor.

"Not qualified?" the governor phrased the question.

"I'm not worthy, sir!"

"You've proven your worth."

James shook his head. He couldn't tell the governor he had lost his nerve on Henry Hill. He wanted to talk with Adolph. "The men, sir," he offered, "they signed on to fight under Captain Bachmann. They won't follow me."

"The men of your company, Captain Peck, are drawn up at this very minute in front of the tent waiting for you to speak to them."

James shook his head. This was all wrong. He couldn't tell the governor why.

"I don't condone what Nathaniel Bachmann did at Bull Run," the governor continued. "I have to overlook that. I have to use every resource that is available to me in this war. Nathaniel Bachmann is one of those resources. As the commander of an infantry company, he proved himself to be without merit or honor. He'll return to Wisconsin with me. He'll serve on my staff there. That's what he's best fitted for. You, young man,

will serve here. This is what you are best fitted for. We have to do with what
we have, Captain Peck."

James swallowed. His throat was dry, constricted. His face was bright
with fever.

"Can you walk to the door of the tent if I help you, Captain?"

"Don't do this to those men," James pleaded.

"I intend to appoint Adolph Zimmerman the first lieutenant in your place
if that meets with your approval."

James nodded. He'd try to correct all this later.

"Lieutenant Zimmerman thought you'd agree to my appointing Sergeant
John Barks as the second lieutenant."

The law clerk was being carried forward by something he couldn't control.

"Let me help you stand, Captain Peck. Lean on me. Now, young man,
meet your command." The governor threw back the tent flap and motioned
toward the Baraboo Guards, who were formed in the street.

James stood unsteadily before the men from Sauk County in his flannel
shirt and his long underwear, holding tightly to the governor's arm to keep
from falling.

Murphy marched to the front of the company and snapped to attention.
The little man saluted James, presenting the law clerk with a box. On pieces
of white paper lay the shoulder straps of a captain of infantry, two gold bars
on a blue background.

James accepted the box, leaning on the governor.

The Irishman stepped back, saluting again.

"Peck! Peck!" Adolph shouted, repeating the call the men had used to
signal their willingness to follow the law clerk into battle.

"Peck! Peck!"

"Let's go back to Bull Run!" Gus called out.

"Whenever you're ready!" Johnny Makepeace shouted.

"We'll kick some ass next time!" Willy Schoming confirmed.

"Peck! Peck!"

James struggled to stand on his own. He was deeply touched. He could
think of only one thing to say to the men. He painfully raised his right hand
to his eyebrow. "Men of the Baraboo Guards!" he called out to them. "I
salute you!" He dropped his hand to his side. Then he fainted.

26

On Friday, two days later, James, still feverish and stiff, cautiously made
his way to the regimental headquarters tent. He scratched on the canvas at
the flap.

"Come in, Captain Peck," Colonel Ross called. "Have a seat. How's that shoulder?"

"It's healing, sir. It's sore. You wanted to see me?"

"I'd have come down to Company K's area. No need for you to have walked all the way up here."

"It's good for me to be up and around, Colonel."

The regimental commander studied the law clerk. "I've two topics to discuss," he said. "The first may not be pleasant. I have a report of the killing of a sergeant of marines on the field after Bull Run. What do you know of it?"

James felt light-headed from the exertion of his walk. He wasn't as strong as he'd thought. He wet his dry lips, pausing, wanting to be sure what he told the colonel was correct. "The sergeant was the man who wounded me, sir. He refused to obey an order. He attacked me after I drew my revolver on him. He was about to finish the task when he was shot."

"To save your own life, Peck?"

"Yes, sir."

"Have you witnesses?"

"Yes, sir. However, the responsibility for what happened is mine alone, sir."

The colonel considered, tapping the edge of the document he held in his hand. "All right, Peck. I'll tell headquarters I'm satisfied this was done in your own defense. Let's hope that's satisfactory. I wondered about your wound. You didn't have it when I last saw you on Henry Hill."

"I was wounded after the Confederate cavalry charge at the stone bridge.

"Yes. Now, this other matter. Governor Randall has arranged for the seriously wounded men of the regiment who can be moved to return to Wisconsin. Most of our wounded, as you know, were left on the field to the mercy of the Confederates. I have to appoint an officer from the regiment to take charge of the return of those we were able to bring back with us. I want you to be that officer, Captain Peck, if you feel up to making the trip."

"To Wisconsin?" James asked. He'd said nothing yet to Adolph about his intention to resign his commission. The return to Wisconsin would give him time to think through what he felt he had to do.

"I want you to see to the care of our men on the way and I want you to see to your own care also. You can use the rest. Take three or four weeks leave."

"I've just taken command of the company, Colonel."

"You took command of your company when it mustered in Baraboo three months ago, Peck. Your men can spare you. Lieutenants Zimmerman and Barks will see to them. This army has been given a new commander, General McClellan. It'll take him months to get us into shape before we can go back out and fight. I doubt if the Confederates are in any shape to come in after us among these forts. The ninety-day regiments are mustering out, going home. New regiments are coming in every day. They have to be brigaded, trained, equipped. We'll do little in the coming weeks that will require your presence. You won't mind a few weeks in Madison, will you?"

"No, sir," James agreed, thinking of the time the journey would give him to work through his decision but fearing the acceleration toward when he would have to tell Lucille he was a coward. "I won't mind a few weeks in Madison at all, Colonel."

"Then, go. Let your wound heal. Enjoy yourself."

"Thank you, sir."

"There's a matter I want you to see to while you're in Madison, Peck. You've made a favorable impression on Governor Randall. I want you to take advantage of that and intercede with him for replacements for the regiment's Bull Run losses. We lost a hundred and fifty men. Governor Randall admitted he's flooded with volunteers. I want a hundred and fifty of those volunteers to replace the men we lost last Sunday."

"I'll try, sir."

"You might give my regards to Judge Faircloth," Colonel Ross smiled. "You will be seeing Judge Faircloth?"

"I hope to, Colonel."

"Go, Captain. Care for our men on their way home. Take care of yourself."

James saluted and left the headquarters tent. He didn't know if he cherished or dreaded the thought of seeing Lucille at the end of his journey.

James spent a few minutes with Adolph and John, who hurried him on his way. He rode one of the ambulances carrying the Wisconsin wounded to the depot where he supervised the loading of the stretchers into specially equipped baggage cars. There were no coaches. He turned down the crew's offer of a ride in the caboose in order to stay with the wounded.

The four days and nights in the cars with the wounded men of the Second Wisconsin were agony for the law clerk. He was weak with a persistent fever. His shoulder was stiff and sore, inflamed, the punctured flesh and bruised bone healing slowly but draining strength from his body as they did so. He carried his left arm in a sling Murphy had fashioned for him.

He helped the orderlies with the wounded men, many of whom had had legs or arms amputated, washing them when they fouled themselves, feeding them, giving them water and whiskey. Three men died on the journey and were removed from the cars at Pittsburgh.

James delivered the wounded men to the surgeon in charge of the general hospital in Milwaukee and spent the night there having his own wound examined, probed, drained, dressed. He took the train for Madison the following morning, ignoring the surgeon's warning not to travel.

He wanted to see Lucille, to hold her, to bury his fears and his failings in her embrace. He did not want to tell her he was a coward. He was ashamed of his lack of courage, at the turn his life had taken in those few minutes on the plateau of Henry Hill where fear had overcome will, ability, mind and body. Things would be so simple, he considered, if he'd died on Henry Hill, but he wanted very much to go on living. Even, he decided bitterly, if that meant living the life of a coward.

He'd telegraphed from Baltimore that he was traveling to Wisconsin with the wounded men of the regiment. By return telegraph, Judge Faircloth insisted he stay at the Faircloth home during his leave. He dreaded the time when he would have to tell the judge and his daughter about Bull Run but he accepted the fact that he owed them the truth. He wished it were over. He assumed the hospitality of the Faircloth home would be withdrawn when he informed them of his cowardice, of his intention to resign his commission and leave the army.

The Faircloths, father and daughter, were waiting for him on the depot platform. Lucille saw James when he stepped down from the car. She ran to him, smiling, her dark hair shining in the sun. Her light, wide-skirted gown set off her narrow waist and full bosom. Her smile froze when she saw his arm in the Irishman's sling.

"You've been injured!" she gasped. "You didn't say you'd been injured in the telegraph!"

James reached and took her with his good arm. People on the platform smiled at the scene—the lovely lady, the wounded officer.

Lucille pulled away. "Are you all right?" she asked. "What have they done to you?"

"Young man," Judge Faircloth interrupted. "Has that wound been attended to?"

"Good day, Judge Faircloth," James greeted the jurist, leaning heavily on Lucille's arm. He tried to stand on his own. "In Milwaukee, sir," he said with difficulty. The platform, the people, seemed to waver in his vision. "A surgeon there." He noticed he was trembling and perspiring. "Ah, it was last evening."

"We'll have Doctor Yeager join us this very afternoon," the judge stated. "Come, I have my carriage waiting. Congratulations on your promotion, by the way. Always did think you had it over that man, Bachmann."

"Thank you, sir," James mumbled. He was feeling very weak. The judge and Lucille helped him into the carriage. He collapsed when he tried to use his left arm to pull himself into the swaying vehicle.

Judge Faircloth sent a boy for Doctor Yeager, to tell the surgeon to come immediately to the Faircloth home.

Mary Schmelzer, the serving girl, helped the judge and Lucille bring James into the house. The three eased the law clerk into a chair in the judge's library. James was embarrassed, light-headed. He was trembling.

"Cognac?" the judge offered.

"Ah, please," James said faintly. "I apologize for being a burden." He wiped his forehead with a shaking hand. "I felt a little weak there. For a moment. I hope I'm not disturbing your home. I could stay at a hotel."

"We won't hear of that," the judge replied, handing James a glass of cognac.

Lucille sat on a stool in front of James, her hands on his knee. She studied his face, his wrinkled, stained uniform. She noted with pride the charred tin cup strapped to the flap of his haversack.

Mary Schmelzer ushered in Doctor Yeager, a short, bald man carrying a black valise. "The boy said I should come at once."

"Yes, John," the judge waved the surgeon into the room. "This is Captain Peck of our Second Regiment. He's suffered a wound and needs your attention."

Doctor Yeager bent over James' shoulder, touching the torn fabric of his coat, feeling the dried blood. "Bull Run?" he asked.

James nodded. He couldn't speak.

"Ten days ago," the surgeon told the judge. Addressing James, he asked, "Has a surgeon attended your wound, Captain?"

James nodded. His vision was fading.

Doctor Yeager put his hand to the law clerk's forehead. "Dry," he said. "There's the heat of fever. Let's get the captain into a bed, Judge Faircloth. I'll examine him immediately."

"Our guest room," the judge ordered. "Top of the stairs, then to the rear of the house. Mary, help us. 'Cille."

"I, ah, I can walk," James slurred. He was having trouble understanding what the people hovering over him were saying. He struggled to stand. He couldn't do it.

"Easy, now," Doctor Yeager cautioned. "Judge, take his right side. I'll take his left. Let's lift carefully and guide Captain Peck to the stairs. That's it."

Doctor Yeager joined the judge and his daughter in the library an hour later.

"How is that boy?" the judge asked. He handed the surgeon a glass of cognac.

"He's sleeping. I gave him laudanum. I don't think he's slept much in the last ten days."

"How serious is his wound?" Lucille asked.

"It's quite serious. A bayonet wound always is. Bruise to the bone, trauma to the tissue and sinew. Suppuration, which is to be expected. I didn't find anything that won't heal. He'll be weak and uncomfortable for a few days. I suggest he continue to carry his arm in that sling to keep pressure off the healing muscle. Rest and nutrition, of course." Doctor Yeager looked at Lucille. "I don't think his shoulder is his primary injury."

"What do you mean?" she asked.

"He's come from a battle, 'Cille. He's come from a bad time. He's been hurt in his body but he's also been hurt inside. He wouldn't talk to me about it. He may want to talk to you. If he does, don't pry. He's carrying the usual reactions of guilt and shattered innocence. Battle is a terrible experience for a young man, seeing his comrades killed or maimed. The survivor tends to feel he should have done more, something that would have prevented what he saw happening. A good listener is the only prescription I can write for that. I will have more of your excellent cognac, Judge Faircloth."

"What can I do for him?" Lucille asked.

"You can look in on him from time to time. He won't wake for a while with the laudanum. When he does, I suggest a bath and some clean linen. He came here straight from the camps. Shall I send over a nursing woman?"

"No!" Lucille snapped.

"I'll leave him in your good hands, 'Cille, Judge. I'll be off to my practice. Call me if you need me. I doubt you will."

Judge Faircloth saw John Yeager to the door. "James can wear Preston's suits while he's here," he said when he returned. "They'll fit. His uniform will require a great deal of airing and brushing before you can show him off to Madison city in it."

"I'll sit up through the night with him."

"I'm sure he doesn't require that, 'Cille."

"Of course he doesn't," she told her father. "I do."

27

MADISON, WISCONSIN—August, 1861.

James opened his eyes and looked up at the plastered ceiling of a strange room. He was in a bed, naked. He had no idea where he was nor how he had come to be there. The sound of rain striking a window pane had wakened him.

He turned his head. Lucille sat on a chair beside the bed gazing at the window, watching the patterns the rain made on the glass. He remembered where he was, how he had come to be here. He remembered what he had to tell her. For the time, he put that out of his mind. "Don't tell me this is a dream," he whispered.

Lucille turned to him, smiling. "Good evening!"

"Have I slept long?" he asked, noting the shadows in the room.

"Since yesterday and through most of today. How are you feeling?" She studied his face. He looked drawn, tired, sallow.

"I'm feeling better. I've missed you."

"How long will it be," she asked, "before you have to go back?"

"They can do without me for a few weeks," he answered, turning away from her, away from the thought of returning to the army in Virginia.

"That's such a short time."

"A short time," he echoed.

"Can you eat?"

"I'm starving, I think."

"I'll have Mary prepare a tray," she told him. "While she does that, I'm going to shave you. I love you more without the whiskers. Are you well enough for me to shave you?" she grinned.

James ran his right hand across his chin. He hadn't shaved since the battle.

Lucille sensed the tension. Doctor Yeager had told her not to pry. She wanted to help but she didn't know how. She stood, looked down at him, touched his hand. She left the room to find the serving girl.

James stretched his full length in the bed. His shoulder throbbed but his fever had broken. He'd have to tell her soon. There was no way to avoid telling her. The longer he put it off, the more it would hurt her. The longer he put it off, the longer he would have to dread telling her.

Lucille returned with hot water and a barber's set. She shaved James and trimmed his hair. She took the supper tray from Mary at the door of the room and fed him, sitting on the side of the bed and eating with him. After their supper she drew the sheets and the coverlet from the bed. She took water and cloths, soap and towels, and bathed James on the bed. She slipped out of her gown and underthings and carefully made love to him, watchful of his wound. After, she lay with him, his good arm around her shoulders. She slept, her breath lightly touching the hairs on his chest.

When she woke, later in the evening, she slipped into a dressing gown and lit two lamps. She drew a chair close to the bed and sat, studying him. She had been told not to pry. She wanted to help him if he would open his troubled soul to her. "Will you tell me about it?" she asked gently.

He didn't answer. His heart hammered in his chest. He couldn't look at her.

Lucille waited.

"I lost my nerve," he whispered, speaking with his eyes closed.

She watched him, saying nothing.

"Adolph had to pull me along by the arm," he made himself say. "He led the men. He told them what to do. I was so filled with fear that I wept."

Lucille reached and touched his face.

He turned away from her. "I was a coward."

She didn't know what to say.

"When we were on the hill, I couldn't make myself move. I shut my eyes so I wouldn't have to look at the Confederate lines."

"Alexander Randall told us you led your men into battle," she offered.

"I was there. Adolph made the decisions and told the men what to do."

"You were wounded in the battle."

"I was wounded by a Federal marine after the battle," he said, bitterly. "I couldn't even do that right."

She looked at him. She could think of nothing to say to him.

"I'm going to resign my commission," he told her, turning from her gaze. "I'll go back to Baraboo. I'm not fit to command those men. They don't know. They cheered when Governor Randall told them I was to be their captain. They have no idea how weak I am. They deserve more than what a coward has to give them."

"Whatever you think, James, you're not a coward," she said, taking his right hand in both of hers. "I won't let you condemn yourself."

"They're good men," he told her. "They tried to be good soldiers. They marched up Henry Hill. They stood and they fought and they fell. They were driven off the hill and they went back the second time. There were too many rebels on the plateau for them but they were brave, Lucille. They were willing. They fought."

"Did you go back with them the second time?" she asked.

"I couldn't help going back the second time. I didn't know what I was doing. I followed Adolph, as they did."

"Don't blame yourself." she urged.

"Good men died on that hill."

"Could you have changed that?"

He shook his head. He didn't know. "Thad Able's dead."

She nodded, watching him. "I read his name on the list of casualties in the newspaper."

"I was there when his men carried him off the field."

"You weren't the cause of what happened, James," she said, wishing she knew some way to convince him.

"I should have been better than I was."

"I think you'll find, in time," she said, looking into his eyes, "that you did as much as you could. That's something you'll have to learn for yourself. I can't help you with that, James. I intend to go on loving you as you come to learn it. Do you want to get up?" she asked, changing the direction of the conversation. "You can go down and sit with my father. He wants to talk to you."

"I'll need some clothing," he said, relieved that the time he had dreaded was over. He felt purged, as if some bad thing had gone out of him.

"Mary is brushing your uniform. If the day is bright, she'll hang it out to air tomorrow. For now, one of my brother's suits will fit you."

"I'm ashamed to have to tell you what I have," he said, meeting her eyes. "I don't deserve you."

She bent over the bed and kissed him. "Let me be the one to decide that," she smiled to him. "Get up and get dressed, Captain Peck. You've slept the night and most of the day. I've slept only a few wonderful minutes in your arms. I'm going to go to bed and sleep the rest of this night and I'm going to dream of you. Go, talk with my father. May I make a suggestion?"

He looked at her.

"Don't decide what you're going to do this evening. Give yourself time. You've several weeks. Let things work."

"Will anything change?" he asked.

"Why not give yourself time to find out?"

James dressed slowly and carefully in one of Preston Faircloth's suits and made his way to the stairs. He felt weak but relieved. She hadn't condemned him, rejected him. Not yet. He went down the stairs, leaning heavily on the banister.

Judge Faircloth was standing behind his large desk, looking out the window at the falling rain.

"May I join you, sir?" James asked.

"Come in, young man! Tell me, how do you feel?"

"Much better, sir. Rest and food have helped. I apologize for the disruption I've brought to your home. I'm grateful for your hospitality."

"Don't mention it. We in Wisconsin are proud of you boys in the Second Regiment."

"The men will be pleased to hear that, sir."

"So," the judge said, turning and facing the law clerk. "Bachmann didn't work out?" The jurist noted that the young man looked much better than he had the day before.

"Captain Bachmann will be serving on the governor's staff here in Madison, Judge Faircloth."

"You'll command your Baraboo Guards in his place?"

James looked away. He didn't answer.

"Will you command them?" Judge Faircloth asked. "Will you go back?"

"I haven't decided, sir," James said. He didn't want to put his doubts into words. "I don't know."

The jurist studied him. "So, they won their victory," he said.

"We lost our battle, sir," James said. "Our army will fight them again."

The judge offered a cigar which the law clerk refused. The judge lit his. "I want to speak with you."

"May I sit down, sir?"

"Please. I don't know how to begin this," the judge continued. "I care for 'Cille very much."

"I'm sure you do, sir."

"If you return to the army in Virginia, you'll be involved in the very fighting you've predicted. You'll be gone from 'Cille for months. Possibly, forever. I'll be very frank with you. If you go back to the army, I think your chances of coming out of this war are pathetically slim."

"I understand that, sir."

"I don't want to see her hurt."

James didn't answer.

"I can get you appointed to Alexander Randall's staff," the judge said, leaning toward the law clerk. "You don't have to go back. You've fought your battle. You've shed your blood. You've proven yourself."

"I've proven nothing, sir."

"Let others decide that. Stay here in Madison with her."

"Like Nathaniel Bachmann?"

"What is he to you?" the judge demanded. "James, look at Bachmann as I do. He's here. He's safe. He'll live through this war. He'll do important work that Wisconsin's regiments in the field will depend on. He'll be part of this state's war effort and he'll be that here in Madison. If 'Cille cared for him, I'd approve the match at once! Be sensible, damn it! Anyone can carry a musket!"

James looked away.

"Am I asking too much of you?" the judge persisted. "For her?"

James shook his head. "Sir, ninety days ago I was a law clerk in Baraboo," he explained. "Today, I'm the commander of a company of infantry with the army in Virginia and I have the love of a wonderful woman. I'm not sure how this happened. There's much to it that I just can't comprehend. I appreciate your concern and your offer, Judge Faircloth. I have to do this my own way. Lucille and I spoke on this earlier this evening. She concurs."

"She concurs!" the judge exploded. He was thinking of the spouse his daughter would bring into the family to carry on the future of the Faircloth holdings. "You refer to her concurrence as if there were an agreement between you! No father in his right mind would permit your suit for the hand of his daughter!"

"Yes, sir."

Judge Faircloth gazed across his desk at the law clerk. He settled into his leather chair, lowering his head. "Be kind to her, James," he sighed. "And, for God's sake, take better care of yourself!"

"Thank you, sir."

"Alexander Randall wants to talk to you," the judge said.

"I want to talk to Governor Randall. Colonel Ross has charged me with bringing back a hundred and fifty volunteers to replace the regiment's Bull Run losses."

Judge Faircloth shook his head. "Alexander Randall has his heart set on a Wisconsin brigade commanded by a Wisconsin brigadier general. His direction is toward more Wisconsin regiments, not toward replacing the losses in existing ones. Even now, the Sixth Wisconsin is training at Camp Randall."

"The governor must replace the Bull Run losses, sir."

"The governor must do nothing, young man. He's a war governor. A king upon a throne to hear him tell it. However, you may try. He'll be calling here later this evening. He hopes to convince me to lend him support from the judicial branch for his creative interpretation of his presumed war powers under the state's constitution. He'll fail in his quest as you most probably will fail in yours. Alexander Randall will find that in a republican democracy, even in the midst of a terrible civil war, a king upon a throne is still subject to the whim of a judge upon a bench."

"I'll look forward to meeting the governor again, sir.

"Tell me that after your meeting. I should warn you. Nathaniel Bachmann will accompany the governor this evening. Are you up to meeting your former commanding officer?"

The law clerk didn't answer. He didn't know.

"I have a cabin at Devil's Lake near Baraboo, James. Why don't you spend part of your leave there? The quiet will help your recovery and the fishing is superb."

"I'd enjoy that, sir. I don't wish to leave Lucille."

"She intends to go with you."

"Ah, sir, ah . . ." James stammered.

"Let's not feint with each other, young man."

"I love your daughter, Judge Faircloth."

"I'm sure you feel that you do." The judge wondered if 'Cille would change her mind after a week or so alone with the law clerk at Devil's Lake. "For the present, enjoy your time together. You have love and time. Both are jewels of great worth. There is something I'd ask of you."

"Sir?"

"My son, Preston."

"We met. Once."

"Yes. Your nose and his fist. I remember. I'll ask that you try to see him."

"Now, sir?"

"No. He's not here. He's at Camp Randall with the Sixth Regiment. They've been ordered to Washington to join your army."

"Is Preston an officer with the Sixth, sir?"

"He's a private soldier. He enlisted. He wouldn't take the commission I obtained for him. He'll have nothing to do with anything I arrange for him. If you go back to the army in Virginia, James, will you look in on him if you can?"

"I will, sir. If I go back."

"I'll be grateful."

Alexander Randall and Nathaniel Bachmann arrived at the Faircloth home at ten.

The judge greeted the governor and stood for a few minutes with him in quiet conversation in the foyer.

James stared icily at Bachmann. The former commanding officer of the Baraboo Guards bowed stiffly. He said nothing.

"Captain Peck," the governor greeted James as he walked into the library. "I must say, you look a great deal better than you did when I last saw you. Is Judge Faircloth taking good care of you?"

"The judge has been most hospitable, Governor."

"You gentlemen will join me in cigars and cognac," the judge insisted. "Captain Bachmann, will you serve?"

"Captain Peck," Alexander Randall said, "I want you to know how grateful the people of Wisconsin are for the care and attention you gave our wounded men on the journey from Washington to Milwaukee. John Yeager tells me that you should have been on a litter, yourself. Colonel Ross couldn't have chosen a more capable and caring officer for that important command. Your own wound?"

"It's healing, sir."

"Good!" Alexander Randall said, taking a cigar from the humidor Bachmann offered and lighting it at the lamp on Judge Faircloth's desk. "Now, be very frank with me. Tell me what happened to our Wisconsin soldiers at Bull Run."

"Sir, my version would be very limited. You already have the reports of the other officers who were there."

"I want to hear from you."

The law clerk hesitated.

"James?" Bachmann asked.

James looked at the officer who was prodding him for a report he would be giving himself had he not run from his command. James addressed the governor. "We thought the battle had been won when they sent us across Bull Run, sir, about noon." He glanced at Bachmann, tempted to add words to the effect that the time would be shortly after Bachmann had deserted his command. "The Confederate army was retreating. We could see that. Somehow, after we waded the stream and began the move up Henry Hill, they'd lined up on the plateau and were waiting for us. It was obvious they'd been reinforced."

"Yes!" Alexander Randall cried. "By troops from the Valley of Virginia under their now-famous Stonewall Jackson! He brought them in by railroad, I've been told."

James recalled the rider on the small horse across the plateau from him. "We attacked on the right of our line," he went on nervously, uncomfortable at recalling the memory. "The Thirteenth New York attacked on our left. We couldn't advance further than the crest of the hill. There were just too many of them. Our men fought well." James was tempted to add words to the effect that those men from Wisconsin who didn't run away had fought well. He glanced at Bachmann.

The captain sat, watching him, unconcerned.

"We're all proud of what the men of the Second Regiment did at Bull Run, Captain Peck," Alexander Randall said. "Tell me, though, why didn't Sherman attack with his full brigade? Was he at fault?"

"The plateau of the hill was only so wide," James said. "There was room for only two regiments on a front."

"Could Colonel Sherman have supported you better? Bachmann asked.

"I don't know," James admitted, looking at the governor. "I remember seeing a battery on the plateau when we got up the hill. The gunners and the teams had been shot down. I don't know if more guns could have been got up to support us or not. I just don't know."

"Your lack of military experience is understandable," Bachmann said patronizingly.

"It would appear that I have more first-hand experience in what took place at Bull Run than you, Captain Bachmann!" James replied angrily.

Bachmann flushed.

"Gentlemen!" Alexander Randall cautioned. "I seek information that will help me guide this state in a distant and difficult war. Both of you, keep your remarks impersonal. Sherman has a reputation for instability, Captain Peck. Some say he's crazy. Did he spare the New York regiments in the attack?"

"They suffered the same losses we did, sir."

"Sherman's Brigade took the heaviest brigade losses of the day," Bachmann added.

"Colonel Sherman's four regiments went in against fifteen or more massed Confederate regiments!" James argued. "Any other brigade would have suffered the same casualties in the same place."

"Are you defending Sherman?" Bachmann asked.

"Of what are you accusing him?" James asked pointedly.

Bachmann didn't respond.

"The issue remains, gentlemen," Alexander Randall interposed. "Wisconsin's regiments cannot be sent to war to fight under the command of officers from other states. We must have a Wisconsin Brigade commanded by a Wisconsin brigadier general."

"What would the men of the Second Regiment think of that?" Bachmann asked.

"They'd be proud to be part of a Wisconsin brigade," James said, addressing the governor.

"We're working on just that, Captain Peck," Alexander Randall said. "Captain Bachmann has already drawn up the plan."

Bachmann smiled and bowed slightly.

James addressed the governor. "Sir, Colonel Ross has instructed me to plead with you for replacements for the Second Regiment's Bull Run losses. We lost a hundred and fifty men, sir. Fifteen percent of our strength."

"I'm aware of the regiment's losses, Captain Peck. I have no troops to send to Colonel Ross. The Sixth Regiment is about to leave Camp Randall for Washington. The Seventh Regiment is mustering and will report to Camp Randall in a week. We're a small state, Captain Peck, with limited manpower. Colonel Ross will have to do with the men he has. It's important that Wisconsin put as many regiments into the field as it can. I can't spare companies from the new regiments to serve as replacements for the old ones."

"Colonel Ross will be disappointed, sir."

"Would Colonel Ross rather have a hundred and fifty new men, James, or a new regiment?" Bachmann asked.

"There are new regiments coming into Washington every day," James suggested.

"Don't be impertinent, Captain Peck!" the governor warned. "They aren't Wisconsin regiments!"

"Have you named your Wisconsin brigadier general, Alexander?" Judge Faircloth asked to change the subject as he saw the governor's color begin to rise.

"Rufus King," the governor announced.

"General King will report to the army at Washington within the week," Bachmann said.

"Judge Faircloth," Alexander Randall said, "why don't you and I step into your garden? I want to have a few words with you in private. We'll leave Captains Peck and Bachmann with your cigars and your cognac. I'm sure they have much to discuss."

"Captains?" the judge asked. "You'll excuse us?"

Bachmann poured cognac for himself as the governor and the jurist left. "You're recovering from your wound, James?"

"You ran!" the law clerk blurted. "You deserted us!"

"Of course I did."

"You held yourself out to the men of the Baraboo Guards as a soldier and an officer and a leader!"

"James, they wanted to be organized and marched off to war. They were. I owe them nothing."

"You never intended to lead that company into battle!"

"Are you disappointed?"

"You lied to them! You lied to me!"

"Oh, come, James. You let yourselves be lied to," Bachmann said, sipping cognac. "Why this anger? This war is the greatest opportunity you or I will ever see in our lives. Power and wealth are to be taken from it. Don't let some childish sense of honor and trust stand in the way of seizing your share of it. I certainly won't. Here, sit beside me. We have much to discuss."

James remained standing.

"Come," Bachmann urged. "Sit with me. We have so much to plan out."

"Sir," James said, "I respected you. I followed you. I believed in you. Now, I find that I despise you. We have nothing to plan out."

"Sit and have a drink with me, James."

"I think not, Captain Bachmann," the law clerk said as he made his way from Judge Faircloth's library.

28

Well out from the shore on the still waters of Devil's Lake, the rowboat drifted without motion. James stretched sideways in the stern seat, shirtless. The sun warmed his chest and the pink gnarl that was the wound in his shoulder. He wore a straw boater hat, the brim well down over his eyes.

Lucille sat in the prow of the boat on cushions and a blanket. She, too, wore a straw boater. The bodice of her light gown was open to below the swell of her bosom. Her skirts were drawn up on her thighs, resting on unstayed hips and bare legs. Lucille studied the man in the stern of the boat. She wished she could reach inside him and find the root of his torment, sooth it, make it go away.

James sensed her eyes. Without taking the boater from his face, he said, quietly, "I didn't want it to happen the way it did."

She didn't respond.

"My whole life changed in those few minutes on that hill."

She watched him.

"I wanted to be brave. I wanted to do what had to be done. I couldn't. I counted on Nathaniel Bachmann being there when we went into battle. He wasn't, and I was unprepared for that." James sat up and looked across the water at the granite bluffs along the shore.

She said nothing, watching him.

"I couldn't move. I couldn't act. I couldn't make myself open my eyes and look at the enemy."

"You didn't run away."

"I couldn't run away!" he replied, shaking his head. "I was frightened beyond the ability to move."

"Give yourself time, James," she urged.

"While good men die?"

"While you gain the confidence that comes with experience."

"They need someone who can lead them now. Adolph can do that. They deserve more than I have to give them."

"Let them decide that."

He looked away from her. "I feared I'd lose you when I told you this." He thought for several minutes, gazing across the smooth water of Devil's Lake. "Am I a coward, Lucille?"

"I can't answer that."

"You won't reject me?" he whispered.

"I love you."

"I'm going to go back to the army in Virginia. My place is there. I'm not sure I can explain."

"You don't have to explain."

"I won't want to leave you."

"Let's not talk about it. We still have days here at the lake. We'll need the memories in the months to come."

29

James left Madison the morning of the third Sunday in August, 1861. It was just three months since the Second Wisconsin had marched from Camp Randall to take the cars for Washington.

Lucille slipped into his room an hour before dawn, taking him in her arms, touching him, loving him. She cried out softly when her passion came. She curled at his side and slept. James held her closely.

Later, he gently freed himself from her, cautious not to wake her. He rose and dressed in his worn gray uniform. He drew the sheet over Lucille and kissed her damp shoulder.

Even though it was close to daybreak, a lamp was burning in the judge's library when James came down the stairs. Judge Faircloth sat behind his desk in a cone of amber light. He'd been reading Latin through the hours of the night. In the dim light, with the gray stubble on his unshaven cheeks, he looked, James thought, very tired, very old.

"Come in," he greeted the law clerk. "Join me."

"Have you slept, sir?" James asked.

"At my age, young man, you'll try to spend as many hours awake as you can. I've been reading, as you can see. I find order and familiarity in the classics, the Latin, the Greek. Shall I wake Mary to prepare coffee and bread for you before you leave?"

"Thank you, sir. No."

"I'll walk with you toward the depot, James. Will you mind walking instead of taking the carriage?"

"I'll enjoy walking with you, sir."

"Why don't we leave now? We can watch the early morning sun come up over Lake Monona. There's plenty of time for you to get to the depot for the cars."

"I want to thank you for your hospitality, Judge Faircloth."

The old man waved a hand, dismissing the gratitude. He closed his Latin text and stood. "There's something there on the table for you," he said nodding. "You'll probably throw it away the first chance you have but 'Cille and I wanted you to have it."

"Sir?"

"On the table."

James stepped to the library table. Shining in the weak glow from the oil lamp on the desk, an infantry officer's sword lay in a tangle of straps and hangers.

"I don't know what to say," James confessed. "I'll carry this in memory of you and your daughter."

"Carry it in health and safety, if one can do that with a sword."

"I shall, sir."

"Go ahead. Put it on. I couldn't figure out where all the straps and buckles went."

James removed his belt and revolver holster and strapped on the new belt and shoulder strap. He hung the sword and scabbard on the carrier hook.

Judge Faircloth poured a large glass of sherry and drank it quickly. He took a walking stick from the vase beside the door and led the way out the front door into the morning.

The jurist and the law clerk walked in silence to the capitol park, where they watched the sun break through low clouds over the water of Lake Monona.

"It's lovely, James."

"It is, sir."

"Madison has much to offer. When this insanity is over, come back here. Finish your reading of law. Live here. Practice here. Add to what we've begun. 'Cille loves Madison, you know. You'll find here the finest of things, James. A woman. A place. A purpose."

"Yes, sir."

"I'll leave you now. I might make the walk to the depot with you. I couldn't to that and then walk all the way back home. That would be a little too much for a man of my age and condition. Take care of yourself. Look in on my son Preston if you can. And, James, come back to her."

"And, to you, sir."

"No," Judge Faircloth said. "I won't see you again. I pray you live through this terrible war. I won't live through the coming winter. I'm dying, James. Some men fall to bullet or blade or shell. Others fall to a part of their body that ceases to perform as it should. I'm content. I'm ready. I do fear the pain of the passage but I look forward with great curiosity to what may lie beyond. Have no sorrow for me. I've held the woman I loved. I've built my home and my place among men I respect. I've watched the results of my work grow. My only sorrow is that I let my own loss come between myself and my son. You can help me with that, James, if you will."

"I'll try, sir."

"Go, then, young man. Walk on toward those frightening fields you soon must march over. Don't help the hand of fate claim you before your time, James, but don't shirk from what you must do. Do you believe in God?"

"I'm not sure, sir."

"Nor am I. I'll pray for you, in case that helps. Go with God, James, if there is one."

"And you, sir."

"Yes. Soon, I expect."

James walked to the railroad depot from the capitol park, his new officer's sword in his hands, his eyes filled with tears. He remembered little of his journey back to the army in Virginia. He bought a bottle of whiskey in Milwaukee and stayed drunk until he got into a fight with four provost guards in Washington city. The provost guards delivered the young captain to the regiment at Fort Corcoran in the back of an army supply wagon.

30

VIRGINIA—September, 1861–March, 1862.

The Second Wisconsin had been resupplied and reequipped. The lightly wounded from Bull Run had recovered and returned to the companies. Under Colonel Ross' leadership the regiment pulled itself together and settled into a routine of drill, sentry duty, picket duty and more drill.

The day after the defeat of the Federal army at Bull Run, General George McClellan had been called to Washington from western Virginia to take command of the Army of the Potomac, replacing General Irvin McDowell.

"First thing he did," Adolph reported, "was to make the regulars into provost guards and send them into the city. They rousted everyone out. Show a pass or get hauled back to camp, like they did with you last night. Same thing I'd have done. He got the regiments together and working. I hear the saloons and whore houses in Washington city are going broke. We're getting supplied, we're getting fed and we're getting our asses drilled off."

"I take it this General McClellan means business," James said.

"Damned right! Wait till you see him riding through the camps with about ten thousand cavalry for his escort. The men cheer themselves hoarse when they see him coming."

"And, Cap'n," John Barks, the new second lieutenant, added, "we've got a Wisconsin brigadier general."

"Yes, I know. General Rufus King."

"How did you find that out?" John asked, disappointed that his announcement wasn't news to the law clerk.

"Governor Randall told me."

"Say, Cap'n, did you get to Baraboo? Did you get to see my Peggy?"

"I did, John. I spent a day in Baraboo. Mrs. Barks said to tell you she'd write you a letter that very evening."

The carpenter grinned.

"Who else did you see in Baraboo?" the sheriff asked.

"The Larsons. Old man Larson wanted to know how much the government would pay him for the loss of Hans' services on the farm. How's Olaf?"

"He's getting over Hans' death. He's been quiet, moody."

"I saw the Shoate family. Axt's folks. The Auchters and the Blumenfelds. I spent some time with Carl's wife and son. Any news on Carl?"

Adolph shook his head.

"I visited with Ethan's wife. I have a letter for Ethan with me."

"I suppose you saw your Miss Faircloth?" the sheriff asked.

"Judge Faircloth extended the hospitality of his home to me while I was in Madison. I couldn't turn him down."

"Spend most of your time with her?"

"Truth, Sheriff, I spent all my time with her."

"You're doing all right. See Nate Bachmann?"

"I saw Captain Bachmann," the law clerk admitted, not elaborating. "He's serving on the governor's staff."

"I don't think we've seen the last of that son of a bitch."

"The Fifth Wisconsin has come down here," John said, "and the Sixth is on the way. They say the Seventh is coming, too."

James told the lawman and the carpenter about Alexander Randall's plan for a Wisconsin brigade under the command of Wisconsin's Brigadier General Rufus King.

"That's good to hear," Adolph nodded. "We've heard something else. It's got the men madder than hell. We've got to turn in our Wisconsin gray uniforms and draw Federal blue."

"I think that's a good idea," James considered. "At Bull Run most of the Federals were in blue and most of the Rebs were in gray. We should all be in blue. Why would the men be mad about that?"

"They have to pay for the new uniforms out of their clothing allowance. Some of them were counting on saving that and sending the money home."

"I hope that Federal blue is as good as Wisconsin gray, Cap'n" John added. "Winter's coming on."

In September, wearing their new Federal blue, the Second Wisconsin marched back across the Potomac River to Kalorama Camp on Meridian

Hill in Washington and joined the Sixth and Seventh Wisconsin Regiments of Rufus King's Brigade. In spite of Alexander Randall's dream and Nathaniel Bachmann's plans, the Fifth Wisconsin was ordered away. The Nineteenth Indiana became the fourth regiment of King's Brigade. The Hoosiers of the Nineteenth were not from Wisconsin but they were, at least, Westerners, as the primarily eastern men of McClellan's Army of the Potomac called anyone from the far side of Pittsburgh.

In October, the four regiments packed up and marched to Fort Tilling-hast, an encampment on the Virginia side of the river a mile south of the Second Wisconsin's old camp at Fort Corcoran. There the men from Wisconsin and Indiana built log huts and settled into their winter quarters.

James walked to the camp of the Sixth Wisconsin on a cold, rainy afternoon late in October. "Can I help you, Captain?" the duty officer in the headquarters tent asked.

"I want to see one of your men. Private Faircloth."

"His company, sir?"

"I don't know. He's from Dane County."

"That'll be the Anderson Guards, sir. Company I. I'll have him sent for."

"Just tell me where to find him," James said. "This isn't official."

"Company I will be at the end of this street. Ask anyone there and they'll point you the way."

The muddy street ran between rows of log huts. As in the camp of the Second Wisconsin, canvas shelter halves served for roofs. Wattle and daub chimneys rose at the rear. Some of the dwellings showed ingenuity and craft. Most bore crude signs over the entrances, "Johnson's Resort," "Beloit City Hall," "Camp Randall-East," "For Rent-Ladies Only."

"Where can I find Company I?" James asked a sentry who sat on a stump with his musket across his knees.

"You're here, Captain. Who're you after?"

"Preston Faircloth."

"What in hell do you want with him?"

"I'm a friend."

"Ha!" the sentry snorted. "If you're his friend, you're his one and only, Captain. Last hut on the left there. It's ours. We had a drawing and we lost. We had to take him in."

James found the hut and pushed aside the hanging blanket that served as a door. In the dim interior, James saw two rows of bunks along the sides. Boards were laid on the earth for flooring. Two crude stools made from ration boxes sat before a mud hearth that held the coals of a fire.

"Faircloth?" James called.

"What?" a voice answered from one of the upper bunks.

"Are you Preston Faircloth?"

"What if I am?"

"I want to see you."

"There isn't much to see."

"I'm James Peck."

"I don't care worth a damn who you are. Go away."

"I can't do that. Please come out of the bunk."

"Go to hell, James Peck."

James hadn't known how Lucille's brother would receive him. He wasn't prepared for the surly reception. "Get out of that bunk!" he ordered. "You're being addressed by a Wisconsin officer!"

Preston's head rose from the blanket. "Why didn't you say so?" the boy grumbled, sitting up, swinging his legs over the side of the bunk. He dropped to the floor, unsteadily holding the frame of the bunk for support. He was drunk.

"Come out into the daylight with me," James told him.

Preston followed the law clerk into the street.

"What happened to your face?" James asked, pointing at a bruised eye and forehead.

"I fell."

"Onto someone's fist, you fell! You're drunk!"

"I fell onto someone's fist. I'm drunk. Is that all you have to tell me, Captain?"

"No."

"Can I go back to my bunk? It's cold out here."

"I want to talk with you. Where can we walk?"

"What's wrong with right here?"

James held his temper. "Let's start over, Faircloth. I saw your father and your sister in Madison a little over a month ago. I promised your father I'd look in on you. That's why I'm here."

"Oh, I know who you are! You're 'Cille's boyfriend from Baraboo. You're the one whose nose I broke that night. Want to try for twice, Captain?"

"I didn't come here to fight with you. How did you manage to get that beating?"

Preston shrugged his shoulders. He coughed and spat into the mud.

"I asked you a question," James said.

"Aw, they're a bunch of abstainers I have to live with. They got mad at me for being drunk at inspection. They had to stand extra guard duty because of that. They beat me up."

"I understand they lost a drawing and had to take you in with them. You haven't added to the welcome, have you?"

Preston shrugged.

"Are you proving something with all this?" James asked.

"I don't think that's any of your business, Captain."

"I spoke with your father before I left Madison."

"Did that old fool send me any money?"

"He's dying."

Preston turned abruptly and walked several steps along the muddy street. James watched him.

"None of us will live through the coming battles," Preston said, staring across the camp. "Why should he go on living when we have to die?"

"Will you write to him?"

"What for?"

"He'd appreciate a note from you."

"Go away, Captain Peck. Leave me alone."

"Will you write to your sister?"

"I'll write to my father's attorneys."

"Even that . . ."

"To ask them how much of the estate I'll get when the bastard dies!"

James turned away from the boy and walked up the company street the way he'd come. He regretted promising to look in on Preston.

31

One morning in late January, 1862, Murphy puttered at his cooking fire working on a dutch oven of lamb stew. The Irishman looked up from slicing onions. He took the briar pipe from his mouth. "Sweet Mary, Mother of the Christ!" he whispered.

"What's that?" Gus asked, sitting at the fire and concentrating on darning a hole in the heel of a stocking.

"It's himself," the little man said. "Himself, and he's come back from the dead."

"Whose self?"

"Get the captain!"

"Murphy, what in the hell are you talking about?" Gus asked.

The little man pointed with the stem of his pipe down the length of the muddy company street.

A dirty, bearded, emaciated Carl Elsasser, hollow-eyed, clad in rags, stumbled toward Murphy's fire, his steps uncertain, his hands groping in front.

"Holy shit!" Gus shouted. "Ethan! Olaf! Get Adolph! Get Captain Peck!"

Carl staggered toward Gus. He opened his mouth to speak through a mat of filthy beard. The tavern keeper stumbled, fell to his knees.

"Get him!" Murphy barked.

Ethan and Olaf ran to Carl and took him in their arms. They carried him to the cooking fire, setting his gaunt frame on a cracker box. Carl smelled of something sour and thick. His hair was in matted strings, his flesh caked with layers of grime. Carl looked from man to man as the Baraboo Guards gathered around him.

"You're late for breakfast," the Irishman chided.

Carl tried to smile. His filthy face quivered. His lips trembled.

"What's going on out here?" Adolph demanded, stepping from the head-quarters tent. "Damn! James! John! Come out here!"

Murphy poured coffee into a tin cup and added a healthy measure of whiskey to the brew. "Here, now, First Sergeant, be putting yourself on the outside of this. You lads, stand back and give the poor man some air who's just returned from the terrible times he's been having."

Carl took the cup and clutched it in dirty claw-like fingers. He sipped. His hands shook. He tried to speak. His throat was constricted.

James stepped from the tent, pulling on his overcoat. "Carl," he said, holding out his hand. "Welcome back."

Carl tried to rise.

"Sit!" the Irishman ordered.

Carl sat. Tears flowed from his eyes and muddied the grime on his face. He wept, shaking.

"How are you?" James asked.

The tavern keeper wiped at his eyes, smearing the dirt on his face. "I'm all right, Captain," he said, slowly. "I'm all right. Now."

"Do you want us to get a surgeon?" Ethan asked.

The tavern keeper shook his head. "I prayed for this day, Ethan," he whispered. "I prayed for this day."

"You're back," the merchant told him.

"Where have you been?" Adolph asked.

"Richmond. I've been a prisoner in Richmond."

"Richmond!" Gus exploded. "This whole army's trying to fight its way to Richmond and you just went there and came back!"

"It was a hard trip, Gus," Carl sighed.

"We thought you were dead," Adolph told the tavern keeper.

"Close to it, Adolph. Close."

"What happened to you at Bull Run?" Ethan asked.

"I was shot. Here," the tavern keeper said, touching his temple where an ugly crease of scar tissue showed under layers of dirt and matted hair. "A Reb officer and some soldiers took me in the morning after the battle. There were a lot of prisoners. They took us to Richmond on the cars. Men died on the way. We had to throw the bodies out the doors. They marched us through the streets for the people to see. Locked us up in an old warehouse. It was bad, Ethan, bad. Not enough food. Some of the men caught and ate rats. Some of the men killed themselves. I didn't. I knew I'd make it back. I prayed. The other day they came and got us. Exchanged us for some of their own men. So, here I am."

"You're back, Carl," James said.

"I keep remembering," the tavern keeper went on, shaking his head. "On the hill after the battle, I watched them bury our dead. Shallow holes filling with rain water. They just threw the bodies into the holes."

"You're safe now, Carl," Ethan assured the tavern keeper.

"What'll you be having, First Sergeant?" Murphy called out. "Bed? Breakfast? Booze? Bath? To tell you the truth, man, you're in dire need of all of them. What'll you have first?"

Carl managed to smile. "A bath. I'm crawling with Confederate lice."

"We'll be burning those proud Wisconsin rags you're wearing. We'll be bathing you in turpentine to kill the crawling creatures. We'll fill you with good army food and strong whiskey and we'll be tucking you into a warm bed. We'll be letting you drift with the angels for one day and one night. But, mind you! You'll be taking the roll call at formation the following morning! There's been enough of your shirking your duties since the battle of Bull Run! We'll have no more of that in the Baraboo Guards!"

"Does your wife know?" Ethan asked.

Carl nodded. "They let me send a telegraph message from Fortress Monroe where they exchanged us."

"It's good to have you back, Carl," James said, putting his hand on the tavern keeper's filthy arm.

Carl clutched the law clerk's hand, holding it in both of his. He sobbed. James put his arm around Carl's broad shoulders and held him until he quieted.

32

In February the Baraboo Guards turned in their cumbersome Austrian muskets and were issued new Springfield muskets rifled to fire the conical minie ball.

Earlier in the winter Rufus King's western brigade had been joined by a battery of regular gunners, Battery B, Fourth U. S. Artillery, under the command of a testy regular, Captain John Gibbon. Gibbon and the gunners of Battery B had marched overland from their post in Utah to join the army in Virginia.

Toward the end of February the level of activity in the camps and forts increased. Organizations and reorganizations took place. Drill schedules were stepped up. Battalion and regimental drills gave way to brigade and division drills. Target practice was introduced.

James received a letter from Lucille that contained the news of Judge Faircloth's death. The jurist, Lucille wrote, had died in pain but with dignity, with the plea on his lips for forgiveness from his son.

James tucked the letter away and pulled on his overcoat. The day was bitterly cold. The wind had an edge to it. He pulled up the wide collar of his coat and buttoned its shoulder cape. He walked to the camp of the Sixth Wisconsin and went directly to Preston Faircloth's hut. He met the boy carrying a pail of water from the regiment's well.

"Captain Peck," Preston addressed James. He set the pail of water in the frozen mud of the street, waiting for James to come to him. He tucked chapped hands into his pockets and hunched his shoulders against the cold. He wore no coat, only his blue flannel shirt against the cold.

"Your father . . ." James began.

"I know. I got a letter from 'Cille."

"I'm sorry, Preston," James told the boy. "I respected Judge Faircloth."

"Captain Peck, I didn't respect him at all."

"I thought I could help," James answered. "I was wrong. Good-bye, Private Faircloth." The law clerk turned and walked away.

"Captain Peck!" Preston called after him.

James turned.

"Look, I don't like you," the boy said, walking toward James. "I don't know why you're making me your personal cause of concern. Still, I don't think you mean any harm. I apologize for the way I acted when we last met. I don't want to talk to you about my father. Can you understand that?"

"Yes."

"Then, let's part. We won't have to see each other in the future."

"All right."

"Oh," the boy conceded. "When next you write to 'Cille, you can tell her that I was deeply touched by my father's death."

"Even that untruth might make her feel better."

"It's not an untruth. He was my father. Tell her, also, that my hut-mates have stopped beating me up. I've learned to stay out of their way."

"That's good."

"It's merely an accommodation I've found it expedient to make."

"I wish you well, Private Faircloth."

"You, too, Captain Peck."

33

MADISON—March, 1862.

Nathaniel Bachmann called at the Faircloth home a week after the judge's funeral. "My condolences, of course," he told Lucille. He sat in the parlor and accepted a cup of tea. "Your father was a renowned and respected man. An inspiration to all who knew him."

"Thank you," Lucille said, sipping tea. The captain had not called at the Faircloth home since his meeting with James seven months earlier.

"If there is anything I can do," he said.

She shook her head.

"One never knows."

"Thank you for the offer, Nathaniel. There's nothing." She remembered the conversation she'd held with the captain at the governor's reception shortly before the regiment left for Washington. He'd both attracted and frightened her then. Lucille wondered if Nathaniel had any power over James' fate now that he was established in Madison on Alexander Randall's staff. She held in her mind the fact that Bachmann had deserted his company at Bull Run.

"Are you all right financially?" he asked.

"Father left things arranged quite well." She wondered whether his inquiry was an offer of assistance or a query to determine the extent of the Faircloth holdings.

"Yes, he would have. You must call on me if there is anything I can do. Your brother, Preston? May I apply for his release from the army in Virginia?"

"Preston has chosen to stay with the army," she said. She didn't say that she was assuming this. Her brother had not written to her.

"One would think, with your father's passing . . ."

"Preston has his life to live, Nathaniel. We must all turn to getting on with our lives. Father would insist on that."

Bachmann placed his cup and saucer on the table next to his chair. He turned to face Lucille. "I find the thought of you living here alone uncomfortable. I'm quite concerned about you."

"There's no need for concern, Nathaniel. Mary Schmelzer is company for me."

"Hardly adequate. You have the need for a man's presence. A man's guidance. Now that your father is gone and your brother away, a woman alone, well . . ."

"Well, Nathaniel?" she asked, angry at his demeaning tone. "What are you offering?"

"You're aware, of course, of my affection for you," he said leaning forward. "This close to your father's passing, I wouldn't press my suit were it not for my concern and my affection. Here, alone, you're exposed. Madison, you know, has turned into an armed camp. The regiments are coming and going. Men passing through. There have been assaults on lonely women. I handle the reports of them, investigate them. And, dear Lucille, your father was a wealthy man. He had holdings, timber, land, investments. There'll be decisions you'll have to make that will affect your security in the years to come."

"I asked you, Nathaniel," she said holding her temper, "what are you offering?"

"A firm hand at the helm, my dear. Protection in a society that has gone awry. A guide through the mystifying complexities of finance and investment. Do I have to mention that the hand I offer is experienced? Successful?"

"You've always impressed me, Nathaniel, with your ability to make the most of any given situation."

He paused, ignoring the possibility of sarcasm in her words. "There's an option on four thousand acres of timber that your father held. That option must be picked up by his estate tomorrow or it'll be lost. Will you direct your banker to release eight hundred dollars from your account to me so that I can pick up that option in your name?"

"Is that a sound investment?" she asked, impressed that Bachmann had known of it.

"Most sound."

"I wasn't aware of it."

"As I said earlier . . ."

Lucille studied the officer. A sense of power and self-assurance radiated from the man. Bachmann had none of the doubts and questions that confounded James. She felt a certain attraction. She rose and walked to the judge's library. "I'll write a note to the bank."

34

VIRGINIA—Summer, 1862

The second week in March, 1862, brought orders confirming the rumors that had been circulating in the Federal camps for weeks. Confederate General Joseph Johnston had pulled his rebel army back from Manassas, abandoning the lines along Bull Run and withdrawing into the defenses of Richmond, the Confederate capital, a hundred miles to the south.

When the marching orders came, Murphy had the men in his mess stow what would keep in their haversacks: coffee, sugar, hardtack and bacon, salted meat and dried fruit. He set to work with the remainder and served up a feast of baked beans, fresh beef stew, ash cake and white bread, boiled potatoes and rice pudding. He assigned his precious pots and pans to pairs of men to be carried on the march, one day on, and the next day off.

On the morning of March 10, 1862, King's Brigade set off on firm dirt roads to march west into the hills and ridges of northern Virginia.

The Baraboo Guards bivouacked at Fairfax Courthouse that evening, tired and worn. They had not made long marches during the winter. Their thirty pounds of pack and weapons, ammunition and rations and water, clothing and blankets bore down heavily. The dust from the road had filtered into their shoes and helped to rub heels raw.

There was none of the straggling and berry picking that marked the march of General Irvin McDowell's army on the same roads eight months earlier. General George McClellan's army was better trained, better disciplined, better led than the crowd of ninety-day militia that had moved on Manassas in July, 1861.

The following day King's Brigade marched into Centreville and occupied the abandoned Confederate fortifications there, chagrined to find the formidable embrasures armed with great logs painted black to look like cannon.

"Wooden fucking guns!" the new men of the Sixth Wisconsin protested.

"Wait'll you come up on real fucking guns!" the veterans of the Second Wisconsin replied.

The brigade camped at Centreville for four days as the weather turned cold and wet. Then, without explanation to the men in the ranks, it marched back to the capital in heavy rain. Roads turned into muck. Men slipped and fell, weighed down with sodden clothing and equipment. Wagons sank up to their axles in mud. Whole platoons had to push the wagons and pull the guns when they mired down and blocked the road.

Lysander Cutler, the crotchety colonel of the Sixth Wisconsin, took command of the brigade when Rufus King was promoted to division command. Cutler brought the four western regiments into Alexandria, marching the men through the old city and into the camps at Fort Tillinghast on Sunday night, a week after their departure.

On the march through Alexandria the Baraboo Guards had seen the masts and spars of the huge fleet being assembled in the Potomac River. Rumor had it that General McClellan was planning to take the army against

Richmond by sea, sailing down Chesapeake Bay and disembarking on the peninsula between the York and James Rivers to approach the Confederate capital from the east. The following morning the Baraboo Guards received orders to pack and march to Alexandria with Cutler's Brigade for embarkation. They camped in the city and waited for two weeks as men, guns, horses, supplies and munitions from other brigades were loaded onto vessel after vessel.

James stormed into the headquarters tent one morning early in April, his face florid.

"What's got into you?" the sheriff asked.

"We aren't going!"

"What?" John asked, looking up from a letter he was writing to Peggy.

"We aren't going!" James repeated, throwing off his belts and dropping his sword and holster onto his cot.

"What's that mean?" Adolph asked.

"We aren't going against Richmond with General McClellan and the rest of the Army of the Potomac! We're staying here! To guard the capital!"

"Hell, Cap'n," the carpenter argued. "We're one of the few veteran regiments in the army."

"It doesn't matter. We're staying behind and, what's worse, we'll be under the command of General McDowell again."

"This isn't right," Adolph said after a moment. "This just isn't right."

"You'll have to tell that to the president and the secretary of war!"

"The boys'll be disappointed," Adolph considered. "They're anxious to get another crack at the Rebs for what they did to us at Bull Run. They think we're the best outfit in the Army of the Potomac."

"We aren't in the Army of the Potomac any more," James replied. "We're part of McDowell's Army of the Rappahannock, whatever that is."

"The boys won't like this when they hear it, Cap'n."

"I know that, John. Tell them, will you? I can't."

"Yeah," the carpenter said, pulling on his cap. He didn't like the task. "Sure."

"It's been almost a year," James complained as John left the tent. "We've been gone from home for almost a year. What do they give us when things are about to begin? Guard duty! Some of the men in the regiments going with General McClellan were plowing furrows on their farms two months ago. We've been here, training and waiting, for almost a year. It's wrong!"

"Sit down and have a drink," the sheriff said. "Things will change. They always do."

"Have the men pack up," James said, sitting and holding out his tin cup as Adolph poured whiskey into it. "General McDowell has ordered a movement south and west from Washington. At least we'll be heading in the right direction even if we aren't going very far."

On April 4, 1862, General George McClellan disembarked the Army of the Potomac from the fleet of transports at Fortress Monroe, Virginia, and began a cautious approach up the peninsula between the York and James Rivers toward Richmond.

That same day the Baraboo Guards marched from Alexandria to Fairfax Courthouse on what was becoming a familiar road. This time the march continued past Centreville, across Bull Run and beyond Manassas Junction. Two nights later the men from Sauk County bivouacked at Bristoe Station on the Orange and Alexandria Railroad.

McDowell's army stayed at Bristoe Station for a week, camping in incessant rain. When they weren't on guard duty, the men huddled in their little shelter tents, wet and cold.

Gus shivered, wrapped in overcoat and blanket, in the tent he shared with his brother-in-law. "Jesus, Ethan," he complained, "I'm cold."

"You're wet," Ethan told him. He had no sympathy for Gus. Ethan was constipated.

"Of course I'm wet!" the blond countered. "I've been walking back and forth in a berry patch in the rain for four damned hours! You get wet doing that! Next time Elsasser puts me on guard in the rain, I'm going to find me some shelter where I can stay dry and go to sleep."

"Stay on your feet and awake when you're on guard, Gus."

"What the hell for? There aren't any Rebs out there in the rain. They've got more sense. My walking up and down in a dripping berry patch isn't going to protect Irvin McDowell's broad ass one bit."

"It'll protect your own. You can be shot for sleeping on guard duty."

"I can die from a bout of the grippe from getting wet and cold."

"There's a chance of recovering from a bout of the grippe. There's no chance of recovering from a bout with a firing squad."

"Well, you're right about that. Want a drink?"

"A drink is not that I want right now."

"What is it you want?"

"Right now, Gus, I want nothing more than to be able to go out into those cold, wet woods and take myself one good dump."

"Got the solids, huh?"

"I have the solids."

"Well, hell," Gus wound up. "I always say a good romp in the hay is what keeps a man loose. It's good for just about anything that can ail you. Jesus, Ethan, it's been about three weeks for me. Can a man turn back into a virgin after three weeks?"

"I think virginity is a one-time thing, Gus. Like a bout with a firing squad."

"You might be right about that. Well, hell, I can dream about it. Hey, remember that Schurz family that lives up near Delton, back in Sauk County?"

"I know the family."

"That Ellie Schurz is something. She's got buns like baked loaves, fresh from the oven. Screamer, though. She'd set to screaming from the time I got my fingers into her drawers until I got her to where she wanted to be taken. I'd usually walk her way off into the woods. Screamed like wild Indians were about to take her scalp, I mean to tell you. Her brother took a shot at me once. Did I ever tell you that?"

"No."

"Yeah. Must have thought I was going to scalp Ellie for real. Hell, Ethan, I've been shot at by brothers and fathers and husbands. This war is just old times for me. You know, now that I think about it, the Rebs who were shooting at me at Bull Run were just piling up debts."

"I don't follow you."

"It figures. If you diddle their women, they have the right to shoot at you."

"That does make sense."

"It ought to work the other way around, too. If they shoot at you first, you should have the right to diddle second. Assuming they miss. Hell, Ethan, how many Rebs do you think were shooting at me at Bull Run? Ten, fifteen thousand?"

"There were that many shooting at me and I was standing right beside you."

"Damn! I have diddle-rights to ten, fifteen thousand Southern belles! I might not make it back to Sauk County for months after the war is over. I'll be collecting my past due accounts, know what I mean? Hey! Ethan! Where are you going? It's raining out there!"

"I'm going to take that dump," Ethan called over his shoulder, crawling from the tent and running for the trees.

"See!" Gus shouted after his brother-in-law, clutching his wet blanket around his head. "Even listening to stories about it can set you loose! I keep telling you, Ethan, it's good for you!"

Olaf Larson lay in the tent he shared with Johnny Makepeace. When the company marched past Bull Run on the way out from Alexandria, he'd wanted to go to the field where he'd left Hans, but Sergeant Elsasser had said no.

He wondered if he'd been wrong to bring Hans to the war. Hans would be alive back in Sauk County with their father and mother if he had not. No, he decided, he wouldn't have left Hans alone with their father. Their father beat Hans too many times. He'd never considered not bringing Hans with him. He'd brought Hans to the war and Hans was dead. That was so.

Olaf was sure, now, that Captain Bachmann had killed Hans. There was no reason for the captain's cap to be under his brother's body other than for the captain to have dropped it there and for Hans to have fallen on it. Olaf would wait. His revenge would come.

When the war was over, Olaf thought, he'd go to Kansas as he and Hans had planned. He'd buy cheap land there and he'd farm the land. He'd find a good woman and he'd take her to wife. He'd have sons by that good woman and he'd name his first son Hans. He'd name his second son after the father of his good woman. He'd name no son after the father of Hans and himself. And, he swore, he'd never beat his sons as their father had beaten them. For now, he decided as he rolled into his wet blanket, he'd wait.

Wayne Roohr stood behind a tree. The cross-eyed stage clerk carried his Springfield in the crook of his arm upside down to protect its action from the rain. He hunched his shoulders so the capelet of his overcoat covered the musket. Wayne wiggled his toes in his shoes, frigid water soaking his stockings.

There was a sound off to his left. Wayne threw the Springfield upright, cocking the hammer. He squinted his left eyelid. "Halt!" he shouted. "Who goes there?"

"It's Captain Peck," James called as he walked toward the sentry. "Are you all right?"

"Sure, I'm all right, Captain. I'm wet, lonesome, horny, cold and hungry. Other than that, I'm just fine."

"I'll take your post for a while. Run back to the guard tent and get some hot coffee. Bring it back here to drink."

"You don't have to do that, Captain. I'm all right."

"You're freezing. Go on. Take your musket with you."

James watched the stage clerk trot away through the dripping undergrowth. He pulled his broad-brimmed officers' hat low on his head and hugged his chest. Even wearing his rubber poncho, he was wet through. James knew he didn't have to go about relieving sentries. He did it to keep busy. Lying in the tent alone after Adolph had gone to regimental headquarters, he'd begun to think of Lucille.

James gazed into the wet bushes, wondering if Confederates were hidden in there. He opened the flap of his holster and thumbed the hammer of his revolver to half-cock.

'Cille, her father and brother called her. "'Cille," he spoke her name. He liked the sound. How long would it be, he wondered, before he could hold her in his arms and whisper that name to her? His body ached for her.

James was angry at the course of the war that kept him far from her but idle. He was willing to go into battle again, to risk the fear that had paralyzed him on Henry Hill. He'd thought much about that since his return to Virginia. He still didn't know what he would do, how he would be able to force himself to act the next time. He hoped he'd be courageous but there was the doubt. At least betrayal by Nathaniel Bachmann wouldn't be part of his next battle.

The Army of the Potomac was well to the south, fighting its way up the peninsula toward Richmond. Were he with that army, he thought, he'd know by now how he'd conduct himself in battle. He'd be doing something to justify the separation from the woman he loved instead of standing on a dripping hillside in a backwater of the war, accomplishing nothing.

"I'm back, Captain Peck," Wayne called out.

"Stay awake," James told the stage clerk, walking down the sentry line to relieve Willis Wright.

35

The weather broke and the roads dried. Lysander Cutler marched the brigade south along the Orange and Alexandria Railroad to Catlett's Station and had the men go to work on the tracks there, grading the roadbed and strengthening culverts.

Early in May, Captain John Gibbon of Battery B was promoted to brigadier general and replaced Lysander Cutler at brigade command. The Westerners didn't know what to make of John Gibbon. They didn't like being commanded by a regular officer instead of one of their Wisconsin volunteer officers. Gibbon, they learned, was a native of Pennsylvania who'd been raised in North Carolina and appointed to West Point from that southern state. He'd fought in the Mexican War and against the Seminoles in Florida. There were rumors he had family in the Confederate army. He wasn't much for words, the Westerners found, and the regular gunners of Battery B would only tell the volunteers from Wisconsin and Indiana that the man had sand, whatever that meant.

The brigade packed up and marched south to Falmouth, across the Rappahannock River from the colonial town of Fredericksburg, still wondering about its new commander.

John Gibbon inspected the four regiments after they settled into the camps at Falmouth. Colonel Ross called a meeting of the company commanders of the Second Wisconsin after the inspection. "Gentlemen," he greeted the captains, reading from some notes. "I'll review General Gibbon's comments after his inspection. Make yourselves comfortable. Smoke, if you wish. Captain Burke?"

"Sir?"

"Seven men from your Company E have been cited by General Gibbon for being exceptionally well turned-out for his inspection. I have their names. You're to issue them passes for twenty-four hours."

"To do what?" the captain of the Oshkosh Volunteers asked.

"Whatever they wish."

"Here? In Falmouth?"

"Yes."

"What can they do here for twenty-four hours, Colonel? Watch the Rappahannock roll by?"

"I don't care if they go off and pick blackberries. Issue the passes. The rest of you captains are to spread the word that seven of Captain Burke's men were issued twenty-four hour passes for being well turned-out at General Gibbon's inspection. Captain Peck?"

"Here, sir," James spoke up, wondering which of the Baraboo Guards had been well enough turned-out to warrant blackberry passes.

"When General Gibbon and I visited Company K's area, Captain Peck, we found several of your men using fence rails for firewood. You're familiar with the orders prohibiting the use of fence rails for firewood?"

"Colonel Ross," James said, "the men needed the wood to cook their rations."

"I understand their need, Captain Peck. That's not the issue. What is the issue is the disobedience of an order. Have all the men of Company K rebuild the fence."

"Colonel Ross!" James argued, getting to his feet. "It hardly seems fair for Northern soldiers to have to rebuild the fence of a Southern farmer who's probably in the Confederate army."

"I agree with you, Captain Peck. Hardly fair at all. Have your men rebuild the fence. All the men of Company K. Have it done before nightfall."

"God-damned regular army!" the captain of Company D, the Janesville Volunteers, growled. "Just who the hell does John Gibbon think he is?"

"He thinks he's our brigade commander, Captain," Colonel Ross said evenly.

"We might have to bring the governor in on this!"

"If you wish. For now, I suggest we try to get along with the man. I've spent the last two days with General Gibbon. I think he's tougher than we are."

"I heard he's a damned rebel himself," a captain shouted. "At least, some of his family are."

"I wouldn't say that to General Gibbon's face, Captain. Gentlemen, I share your concern that we don't have the Wisconsin brigadier general we hoped for. I agree that General Gibbon's order for Captain Peck's company to rebuild the fence seems unfair and capricious. Still, I suggest we try to get along with him. We aren't sharing the glory of General McClellan's army fighting on the peninsula before Richmond but we are under General Gibbon's command in the face of the enemy. There are Confederate soldiers picketing the far bank of the Rappahannock River in front of us."

"Think he'll get us a crack at the Rebs, Colonel?"

"That's his stated intention. Now, I have another matter to bring up. This, I think, will take some explaining to the men. General Gibbon has ordered that this brigade will wear the uniform of the regular army."

"What's that mean?" one captain asked.

"New uniforms."

"Is he going to pay for them?"

"The cost is to come from the men's clothing allowance."

"They just paid for their Federal blue uniforms! That'll be twice in one year they'll have to pay!"

"I said it will take some explaining to the men."

"Black hats and frock coats!" the captain of Company B laughed. "Good God, Colonel Ross, I can see the La Crosse Light Guards prancing around in white leggings and picking their noses with their white gloves! Believe me, those black hats will go into the roadside ditch on the first march from camp."

"Gentlemen," Colonel Ross cautioned his captains. "I think we should try to meet the man half-way."

The Westerners despised the new uniforms. Coming into the warm months of summer, they thought the long blue frock coats, light blue trousers and the white canvas leggings ridiculous. The morning after the men drew their new uniforms, John Gibbon woke to find his horse wearing white leggings.

The Westerners did take to the big black hats. Of felt, with a crown twelve inches high and a wide brim that would keep sun and rain off the face and neck, the Hardee hats, as they were known to the regulars, were turned up on the left side and pinned there with a large brass eagle plate. The hats were trimmed at the side with a cluster of rooster feathers and at the base of the crown with a braided light blue infantry cord. Within hours of the issue, John Gibbon's western brigade was known throughout the camps at Falmouth as the Black Hat Brigade.

For more than a month Gibbon's Black Hat Brigade labored on the railroad, grading and repairing. The men sweated in their new frock coats. They threw away the white gloves and leggings. They wished they were fighting with the Army of the Potomac under General McClellan on the peninsula before Richmond.

Early May passed without mention that the Baraboo Guards were now a year in service. The men from Sauk County were becoming used to soldiering, if living in army camps and working on the railroad when they weren't picketing the river bank were considered soldiering.

One night Ethan stood in a thicket next to the river. The water was high from spring rains, moving swiftly between its banks, gurgling and whispering and sighing. Ethan's head dropped to his chest, startling him awake. He'd been lulled by the sounds of the river.

He glanced to his right and left. He could see nothing in the darkness. He heard only the sounds of the river. Ethan hated picket duty at night. "Olaf!" he hissed.

"What?" the farmhand answered from behind a fallen log six yards to Ethan's right.

"Nothing. Just trying to stay awake."

"Me, too."

"Hear anything?" Ethan asked quietly. Once established, he didn't want to lose contact with another person.

"Just the sounds of the river."

"Ethan!" Gus whispered off to the merchant's left.

"What?"

"You all right?"

"Sleepy. I've got a headache."

"Got the solids again, huh?"

"Like a rock."

"Good drink of whiskey will set you loose."

"I wish something would."

"Hee-yah!" a high-pitched voice called from thirty yards across the river. "Hee-yah, Yanks!"

Ethan ducked down in his thicket and thumbed the hammer of his Springfield to full-cock.

"Whoa, now!" the voice called. "Ease up on them hammers!"

"Who are you?" Ethan asked.

"Couple of Rebs! All it takes to keep you Yanks on your side of the river."

"We'll come over when we're ready, Reb," Gus advised.

"Come ahead," the rebel laughed. "We'll be waiting. One of you got the solids?"

"Yeah," Gus called. "Ethan, here, he's got the constipations."

The merchant silently cursed his brother-in-law for announcing his difficulties at the top of his lungs to men on both sides of the Rappahannock River.

"A good blast of Confederate canister'll set you lose, Yank!"

"Show your head, Reb!" Ethan howled furiously.

"Now, y'all settle down over there, Yanks. No need for us to be pecking away at each other. Besides, you start shooting, you're going to lose. Old Lacey, here with me, he's the best shot in Calhoun County."

There was silence between the pickets for a while.

"Hey, Reb!" Gus eventually called out.

"We're still here, Yank."

"Have you got any Southern belles with you?"

"Shit, Yank! You think we'd come up to fight you and not bring along poontang?"

"I came down here to ravish some Southern belles, Reb!" Gus laughed. "I haven't seen any worth the effort so far."

"Ain't no effort for a fighting man, Yank."

"I hear they don't wear anything under their skirts down here."

"No sense putting on what they're going to be taking off."

"You're full of shit, Reb," Gus chuckled.

"Your friend, there, he's the one full of shit from what I heard you say."

"Who are you?" Ethan called out to change the subject.

"Attwater's Battalion. Virginia Infantry."

"What regiment?"

"No regiment, Yank. Don't take no regiment to keep you Yanks on your side of the river."

"Bullshit!" Gus guffawed.

"Who y'all?" another voice asked. Ethan figured that would be Lacey, the best shot in Calhoun County.

"Second Wisconsin," Gus answered.

"Where the hell is Wisconsin?"

"Some place you'll never go, Reb."

"Talk's cheap, Yank."

"We're going to be in Richmond in a couple weeks," Gus advised.

"You're going to be in your graves in a couple weeks, Yank."

"We're going to diddle your poontang on the way down."

"You'll diddle a pig's ass!"

The pickets were silent for several minutes. Ethan shifted his cramped legs.

"I hear you wiggling, Yank. You the one with the miseries?"

Ethan didn't answer. His problem was one he didn't want to banter back and forth across the Rappahannock.

"Hey, Rebs!" Gus called.

"Yo!"

"Were you at Bull Run?"

"Sure as hell were. Shot us a parcel of Yanks there."

"We shot back."

"Y'all there?"

"We were there."

"Your own good fortune y'all didn't come up against us, Yank. You wouldn't be here, for sure. We shot the shit out of a bunch of Yanks wearing gray . . ."

Crack! Olaf fired.

Ethan threw his Springfield to his shoulder and fired into the darkness across the river. He heard two other Springfields roar from the trees nearby. He reloaded as silently as he could.

"You all right, Ethan?" Gus whispered.

"Yes. Olaf?"

"I couldn't help that," the farmhand explained. "They killed a lot of our men at Bull Run."

"Forget it," Gus hissed. "Keep your head down."

"You do that, Yank!" the voice from across the river called.

"Fuck you, Reb!" Gus shouted.

"Fuck y'own damn' self, Yank!"

36

MADISON—June, 1862.

Nathaniel Bachmann spread sheets of paper across Judge Faircloth's desk. Lucille watched him from an armchair in front of the desk.

"You can see what I propose," Bachmann told her, motioning toward the papers. "Railroad stocks balanced by land investments. Keep the land you already have and the timber options, the state bonds. These were your father's largest investments. Wisconsin is growing. Railroads are being built. They'll require the land and the timber you control."

"You seem quite confident, Nathaniel."

The captain looked across the desk at the judge's daughter, meeting and holding her gaze. "I am," he said, his strong fingers slowly stroking his trimmed beard. Lucille felt a surge of attraction toward the stocky, dark man. She thought briefly of James. James, however, was a thousand miles away in Virginia. Nathaniel Bachmann was here, working on her investments.

"I suggest you sell the cabin and the land at Devil's Lake," Bachmann went on. "A woodland retreat is a luxury. You can use the proceeds for a cash investment."

"No," she said, unsure whether she wanted to keep the land or assert herself. "I won't sell the place at Devil's Lake. That was father's favorite spot. He loved it. I don't need the cash. Should I, I can sell it then."

"Of course, that's your decision. You know, Lucille, were you to grant me your power of attorney, I could act in your interests. As your agent, so to speak. I wouldn't have to bother you with these details."

"The details interest me, Nathaniel," she said.

"As you wish. Now, I've marked up this plot of Madison city showing the spread of building taking place in the direction of Camp Randall. These several lots, here, can be bought at a good price. I suggest acquiring them."

Lucille stepped around the desk, looking over the captain's shoulder. She thought of James but his image slipped from her mind.

"This lot would be ideal for a store. I suggest you contact your attorneys to find a grocer who will operate the place under contract to you. You'll have the land and the income."

"Which lot?" she asked, moving closer until her shoulder touched his.

"This one," Bachmann said, bending over the plot map. His strong fingers traced the outline of the property. "Do you agree, Lucille?" he asked, turning his face toward her.

"Yes, Nathaniel," she whispered, shuddering. She took his head and pressed his face between her breasts. "Yes, I agree."

37

VIRGINIA—June, 1862.

Carl Elsasser roused the Baraboo Guards at three o'clock in the morning. "Come on!" the tavern keeper shouted, running among the shelter tents. "Get up!"

"What's happening?" Gus asked, crawling from his blankets.

"General McClellan is moving up the peninsula!" the tavern keeper told him. "He's got Joe Johnston and the Confederate army pinned tight against Richmond from the east. We're going to come down from the north and cut Joe Johnston up! The whole war can depend on us!"

"It's about time," Gus snorted. "We've been acting like extra hands to McClellan's ranks long enough."

Murphy got coffee going in his iron pot. The men from Sauk County struck their shelter tents and drew forty rounds of new ammunition for their cartridge boxes. Ready to march, they sat at their cooking fires and waited. They were sure they could beat General McClellan's peninsula veterans to the Confederate capital if the devil was willing and let them have their way.

The devil, as it happened, was not willing. The devil, for that time and place, was an eccentric professor from Virginia Military Institute who wore a ragged gray coat, long leather boots and a crumpled cadet's kepi crushed down over his forehead and who ranged throughout the Valley of Virginia to the west and north of where Irving McDowell's army was preparing to march on Richmond. The devil was Thomas Jonathan "Stonewall" Jackson.

It had been Jackson's Valley Brigade that stood like a stone wall and held back the assault of Sheridan's Brigade on the plateau of Henry Hill at Bull Run, turning the Confederate defeat into victory and earning Jackson his nickname.

As General George McClellan's Federal Army of the Potomac closed in on General Joseph Johnston's Confederate Army of Northern Virginia in front of Richmond, Stonewall Jackson marched his little army up the Valley of Virginia, down the Valley of Virginia, and across the mountain range that rose in the middle of the Valley of Virginia and beat three Federal armies in the Valley, one every week. Jackson, hemmed in by those Federal armies in the Valley, was no threat to the Federal capital at Washington. But Jackson, victorious over those Federal armies, was the closest armed force to Washington, closer even than Irvin McDowell's Army of the Rappahannock, which had been created to guard the Federal capital. The administration in Washington panicked.

The Black Hats were two days out from the camp at Falmouth on the way to Richmond, to McClellan, and to glory when the regiments were stopped on the road.

James hurried to the Baraboo Guards after a hasty meeting with Colonel Ross and the other captains. "Sheriff!" he shouted. "We're going back!"

"To Falmouth? We just came from there."

"Back to Falmouth and then with all possible speed to Catlett's Station on the Orange and Alexandria."

"What's happening, Cap'n?" John asked.

"Jackson's gone wild in the Valley and we have to protect Washington."

"Damned guard duty again!" the carpenter cursed.

"Not quite, John. We're going to guard Washington by going after Jackson in the Valley. We're part of twenty thousand men detached from McDowell's army to find him and fight him. We still owe him for what he did to us at Bull Run."

"Damned right!" the carpenter agreed.

"How far is it to Catlett's Station?" Adolph asked.

"Forty miles by road."

"That'll be a march," John said.

"I want Company I to feel our breath on the backs of their necks all the way, John. We'll take the cars from Catlett's to the Valley but we have to get to Catlett's first. We march in one hour."

They marched. When the Baraboo Guards dropped to the side of the road that night they'd covered fourteen miles while weighed down with packs, blankets, muskets.

"Carl?" James asked, limping from a blistered heel. "How're they doing?"

"Four men straggled, sir. It's the heat. They'll be along. Sit down and let me take care of that heel."

"I'll be all right, Carl."

"You're one of my men, Captain. Sit down." The tavern keeper pulled off James' shoe and lanced the blister with his pocket knife. He drained the swollen bubble and poured some whiskey over the wound, bandaging it with a clean cloth.

"You didn't learn that behind your bar in Baraboo, Carl," James said, grimacing as the whiskey burned into raw flesh under the blister.

"I learned it up the road, sir, watching the Irishman. Half the men in the company have blisters. He's taking care of them. I just do what he does. Why don't you leave your shoe off for the night?"

"Stragglers are all in," John reported, dropping to the weeds as the tavern keeper walked away. "Do we have to post guards, Cap'n?"

"Company D is south of us, John. Company A is to the east. We have the night off. I don't want to have to order tired men out to walk sentry posts this night," James replied, laying back.

"The men need water," John said. "Think I ought to send scouts to find a well or a stream?"

James didn't answer. He was already asleep.

John stretched himself in the weeds. He'd let the scouts sleep. The men from Sauk County had marched themselves to exhaustion and there would be more of the same tomorrow. John was proud of them, proud to be one of them. He thought for a moment of his Peggy and then he, too, slept.

Before dawn the regiments were on the road. Olaf trudged in his place in the ranks, step after step. The farmhand carried his Springfield over his right shoulder, his left hand pulling the pack strap away from his chest. His haversack scraped his hip. His heavy cartridge box tugged on its strap over his left shoulder. Sweat formed in the band of his black hat. Dust turned to mud in the sweat of his face. His eyes were gritty, his mouth sandy. He had no spit, no water left in his canteen.

Ethan was too tired to talk with Gus, who marched beside him. He shifted his musket to the other shoulder and its hot barrel touched his ear. His shoes were filling with dirt from the road. The blister Murphy had lanced the night before threw arrows of pain up his leg with each step. He had the miseries. He'd never eat the Irishman's baked beans again. He was sure that it was baked beans that did it to him. He thought of Lily to take his mind from his agony—Lily, soft and clean. All he could see in his mind was her lovely body covered with road silt.

The Virginia sun bore down on the brigade column, four men wide, four regiments long, as the Westerners marched to the shuffle of army shoes and the clank of empty canteens.

"Get him!" Carl shouted.

Edgar Pendar had dropped to the road, landing hard. Murphy shoved his way through the ranks to the fallen boy. "Up, now, lad," the little man urged, holding the boy in his arms, pulling the pack straps away from Edgar's chest. The boy's face was white, his lips stretched tightly over his teeth, his eyes rolled back in his head.

"You'll be carrying his Springfield for him," Murphy ordered, handing Gus the student's musket.

"I'm carrying my own!"

"You're carrying his also. Will you want to be lending him yours when we come onto Johnny Reb?"

"I'll carry his also," Gus decided.

"You two," Murphy directed, nodding at Jack Black and Henry Calef. "Up with the lad. Keep him on his feet between you. We'll not be leaving one of our own at the side of the road."

"To hell with him," Jack challenged the little man.

"You'll be helping to carry the lad, Mister Black," Murphy stated quietly.

Jack squirmed. He hated the Irishman but he feared him. "Well, come on, Henry!" Jack turned to the farmhand. "Aren't you going to help?"

The column marched north. More men fell from the heat. By mid-day some men carried two or three muskets, three or four haversacks, an extra pack for comrades too exhausted to bear their own. Ammunition and commissary wagons at the rear of the column picked up those too weak to be helped along. Mounted officers led their horses, each of which carried a jaded man.

The Baraboo Guards came to a halt six miles south of Catlett's Station as darkness came over the ridges. The men dropped to the earth, sleeping where they fell. No fires were lit. No cooking was done.

Hours later James woke, opening his eyes to a sky filled with thousands of stars. He couldn't remember where he was. His body ached.

Something moved in the darkness off to his right. He blinked, fully awake now. He drew his revolver. He tried to swallow but his throat was dry, caked with road dust. He cocked the revolver. "Who's there?" he managed to croak.

"It'll be me," Murphy said from the shadows.

"What are you doing?" James asked. He knew now where he was. On the road to Catlett's Station. In the starlight he made out the forms of men sleeping all around him.

"Will you be shooting me or will you be putting that terrible weapon back where it came from?"

"Sorry," James said, sliding the hammer down.

"Seeing as you're not going to be shooting me, will you be having a dipper of cold water?"

"Where did you get cold water?"

"I found a bit of a grove next to the tracks. Searching about, I found a spring. Here, be spitting out the first sip to get the dirt of the road from your throat."

James took the metal dipper. He sipped, sloshed, spat, then drank deeply. He could not recall tasting anything as cold and refreshing as the water he drank that night from the little man's dipper. "Ah," he sighed, "thank you."

"'Tis nothing, lad. I'll be away now, making my rounds. Some of the boys will be waking and thirsting. We won't want them wandering the fields about, searching for what to drink when a tired sentry can't be telling a thirsting Black Hat from a prowling Reb."

"Do you ever sleep, Murphy?" James asked.

"I sleep."

"Why are you up and about with a pail of spring water and a dipper when you must be as tired as the rest of us?"

"Now, lad, are you asking me why I am what I am?"

"What are you, Murphy?"

"Ah, I'm but a soul that's been given a chance to help the likes of them along the way," the Irishman said, nodding toward the sleeping shapes.

"There's been those've been a help to me since I rode from the Sauk County jail chained to the brace of a wagon box."

"We've all had people who've helped us, Murphy."

"Lad," the little man explained, "what I'm saying is, for the first time in my life, I've the feeling of being needed. You said it to me your own self. All my life I've been on the run, dodging and hiding and trying not to get caught. I've had no purpose but to continue existing. Now, I've the feeling that others need me. It started with that piece of plank and the stick, showing them how to walk. Since then, I've been able to make living less a burden for them in some ways. They do need me, Captain, lad, and I'm finding I'm needing them."

James didn't respond.

Murphy looked closely at the law clerk.

James was sleeping.

Now, the Irishman thought, wasn't he the one to be running off at the mouth? He took a drink of cold spring water from his dipper. Here was the young captain, sleeping and dreaming of glory, be it on the field of battle or between the thighs of his lovely lady in Madison, and here was himself, prattling on about being needed, no less.

Murphy heard a man cough in his sleep, close to wakefulness. The little man moved toward the sound. That one would soon be needing a dipper of cold spring water.

The Baraboo Guards marched into Catlett's Station the following morning, dirty, sweaty, tired, but together.

James had sent John ahead to get orders. The carpenter waited for the law clerk and the sheriff a distance down the tracks from the milling throng of regiments gathered at the station.

"We're to camp in this field, Cap'n," John said.

"What's happening?" James asked, wiping perspiration from his face and watching the preceding Wisconsin companies file into the field.

"Nothing is what's happening, Cap'n. We're to wait for the cars. Some of the force has already gone into the Valley. There aren't enough cars to move all of us at one time."

"Shit!" the lawman spat, sluicing tobacco juice onto hot iron rails. "The boys marched their hearts out to get here. Now they have to wait?"

"They told me they're moving regiments into the Valley as fast as they can get the cars there and back. That's what the man said."

"The boys want their crack at Stonewall Jackson," James sighed. "They have that coming."

"We wait, Cap'n."

Wait they did. They learned that Jackson had turned on the pursuing Federals and beaten them at Winchester, at Cross Keys, at Port Republic.

They waited. They cooked rations and picketed the woods around Catlett's Station. They never did get onto the cars for the Valley of Virginia to go after Stonewall Jackson. By the time the government got the transportation problems straightened out, Jackson had finished with the Federal forces in the Valley and had stolen a march to the south and west of McDowell's army to come into line on the left of the Confederate forces facing McClellan's army in front of Richmond.

The Baraboo Guards went back on the road, marching to Manassas Junction and then to the pretty little village of Hay Market on the Manassas Gap Railroad.

By the end of June they were back at Falmouth on the Rappahannock River across from Fredericksburg whence they'd started.

38

Because of McDowell's failure to capture or destroy Jackson's force in the Valley, a new general, John Pope, was named to command the Federal armies in front of Washington. On the Confederate side, Ethan read in the newspapers that General Joseph Johnston had been severely wounded in the battles before Richmond and had been replaced by another Virginian, Robert E. Lee.

While the Baraboo Guards camped at Falmouth with the rest of John Gibbon's Black Hat Brigade, Pope moved south, where his army was caught by Stonewall Jackson's force at Cedar Mountain. Pope's Federals were mauled by Jackson's Valley veterans.

Gibbon's men were told that the two forces still faced each other on the battlefield. The Black Hats were ordered to march with all possible speed to Culpeper, forty-five miles west of Falmouth and five miles from Cedar Mountain. The Baraboo Guards took that to mean they'd get their chance at Jackson if they arrived in time.

They marched quickly along dusty roads in the August heat. Men dropped to the side of the line of march, worn out, as their comrades hurried by. At the halts some stragglers caught up. At every stream men threw themselves face down to suck water that had been stirred and muddied by the marching feet of the companies that had passed before them.

During a rest late the first morning James saw a familiar figure among a company of dirty, tired men from the Sixth Wisconsin. Preston Faircloth sat against a rail fence, his blue uniform and his face covered with dirt, his face blotched, red. The boy had his shoes off and was rubbing his stockinged feet.

James went to him and offered his canteen. Preston drank. "Thank you, Captain Peck," he said, corking and returning the canteen.

"I wrote to 'Cille," he added

"I'm glad you did."

"Take care, Captain Peck."

"You, too, Preston."

The first afternoon on the road the skies clouded over. The marching men were grateful for the respite from the glaring sun until torrential rains fell and turned the dirt roads into channels of mud.

The Baraboo Guards marched twenty miles the second day in heavy rain.

The evening of the third day on the road the aching men streamed into the village of Stevensburg, six miles from Culpeper. They were too tired to cook their rations. They chewed hardtack, drank from their canteens, and went to sleep in the rain on muddy ground.

During the night Stonewall Jackson quietly pulled his forces back and left the battlefield at Cedar Mountain to the Federals. When the Baraboo Guards marched onto the battlefield the following day, the stench was with them long before they arrived.

"Sweet Mother of God," Murphy whispered, shocked at what he saw. The Irishman dampened his neckerchief and tied it over his nose and mouth.

Federal dead on the field had been hurriedly buried in shallow graves that had washed open in the heavy rain. Confederate dead lay where they had fallen, the corpses bloated and misshapen. Carcasses of horses from both armies were strewn among the bodies of men. Flies swarmed and fed in open wounds, open mouths, open eyes.

Bodies lay in piles, in heaps, in lines, arms and legs thrown every way. Mixed with the stench of putrefication was the foul smell of human excrement from bodies that emptied themselves when death relaxed the sphincter muscles.

Ethan tied his neckerchief over his face as the Irishman had done. The rows of bodies that lay where they fell showed where firing lines had stood. He made out where a Confederate charge had stopped where the carpet of gray- and brown-clad bodies ended. He saw where a surgery had operated, with its neat rows of bloated corpses and grisly pits of stained bandages and white, blanched pieces of arms and legs.

Fifteen hundred Confederates lay dead on the field at Cedar Mountain, exposed and rotting. Half again as many Federal dead lay buried in hasty graves that concealed little.

James returned to the Baraboo Guards after a quick meeting with Colonel Ross. His face was gray. "Adolph! John! Carl!" he called harshly.

The sheriff, the carpenter, and the tavern keeper gathered around.

"I don't want to have to tell you what I'm about to," James gazed steadily at the sheriff. "Have the men stack their muskets and drop their packs."

"We aren't staying here?" Adolph asked.

"Carl," James continued, "have the sergeants draw spades and picks and axes from those wagons over there. Divide the men into parties. Some to bury the Confederate dead. Some to rebury the Federal dead. Some to burn the horses."

"My God," the sheriff shuddered.

"Those Rebs have been laying in the sun, Cap'n," John said. "For days. They'll break apart when we try to move them."

"We've been ordered to do this," James replied. "Get them to it so they can be done with it."

Murphy showed the men from Sauk County how to handle the tasks. He set twelve men to work digging pits six feet across and three feet deep. He sent the others, divided into groups of four, to find a Confederate overcoat or blanket and, using that, to roll a corpse onto it to be carried to the nearest pit. The digging men threw the dirt from the forward edge of the pit over the bodies laid behind. As the diggers progressed, the pit at their backs filled with buried men.

As the bodies in one area were interred, Murphy had the diggers move to another so the carriers wouldn't have to haul their bloated, reeking burdens any farther than necessary.

That was the worst of the chores, rolling decomposing bodies onto a coat or blanket and carrying them to the pits. After two hours, Murphy relieved the carriers, having them trade places with the men who were cutting wood and burning the horses.

Long after dark, having worked for hours in the flames and the bitter smoke of the horse fires, the Baraboo Guards turned in the spades and picks and axes and dropped to the ground near their stacked muskets. Murphy had a fire going and coffee for them. He'd even gotten whiskey from the regimental surgeon.

"I'll never wash the stench from me," Gus told Ethan.

The merchant didn't want to talk.

"I've never seen them up close," Wayne Roohr said. "They looked ragged and poor, the dead Rebs. They wore rags and tatters. Few of them wore gray," he babbled on, unable to stop talking. "Most were wearing that brown stuff."

"It's called butternut," Johnny Makepeace told Wayne. "Homespun cloth dyed with nut juice."

"Some of them didn't have shoes," Wayne continued. "They've been marching and fighting barefoot. God, they didn't look like much."

"They left a lot of well-dressed Yanks dead on the field," Ethan murmured. He wished Wayne would drop it.

"They were young," Wayne whispered. "I thought they'd be older."

"Here!" Murphy ordered. "Let it be! Drink your coffee and whiskey. The dram will help cleanse from your souls the sights you've had to see this day."

One by one, the Baraboo Guards left Murphy's fire to roll into their blankets. The stench hung in the air above them as they slept.

39

After Cedar Mountain, Pope retreated from a trap he belatedly realized Jackson was setting to lure the Federals into an ambush between the Rapidan and Rappahannock Rivers. Pope's army began a slow march up the line of the Orange and Alexandria Railroad in the direction of Manassas Junction, where its supply depot was located.

The Confederate high command, Ethan read in the newspapers, was showing aggressiveness and ability against McClellan's army east of Richmond. The former Confederate commander, Johnston, had been content to let the Federals come at him. The new Confederate commander, Lee, was carrying the fight to wherever the Federals happened to be.

Ethan read that McClellan had been ordered away from the gates of Richmond and directed to march his Army of the Potomac back down the peninsula to reembark on the transports and come north by water to reinforce Pope. Ethan wondered if Republican Lincoln's decision to recall Democrat McClellan to the aid of Republican Pope was based on military considerations alone.

Pope's army grew as McClellan's peninsula veterans arrived in northern Virginia. By the end of the week the Baraboo Guards were seeing battle-tried regiments from the peninsula, grim, knowledgeable men who felt they had fought the Confederates into their final defenses and would have taken Richmond and ended the war had not McClellan been harassed and interfered with by the politicians in Washington. George McClellan had organized the Army of the Potomac, had taken it into battle and would have led it to victory, the peninsula veterans believed.

The Federal troops became even more angry with the administration when they learned that Stonewall Jackson's hard-marching brigades had worked their way in between John Pope's army and Washington. The eccentric professor and his foot-cavalry, as his Valley veterans called themselves, marched west and then north behind the Bull Run Mountains and came wailing and keening their frightening rebel yell through Thoroughfare Gap into the village of Hay Market. Jackson had taken the Federal supply depot at Manassas Junction, and its immense store of supplies went up in flames and smoke and explosions to the cheers and laughter and enjoyment of the plundering Confederates.

No army on earth, staff officers told the men in John Pope's army, could march that far in that short a time and be in any condition to seize the depot at Manassas. The Baraboo Guards listened to the staff officers, not asking how Jackson's men had done what no army on earth could do.

Pope's army was scattered, some brigades holding the fords over the Rappahannock, others moving up the line of the Orange and Alexandria, while some marched on the ravaged supply depot at Manassas. McClellan's peninsula veterans were still arriving by water at Fredericksburg, at Alexandria, at Washington. Pope called for all segments of his army to concentrate at Gainesville, five miles from the old Bull Run battlefield. The Baraboo Guards hoped, as they had for more than a year, that the stunned Federal force at Manassas could hold Stonewall Jackson to the ground until they got there.

Marching past the depot at Manassas in the half-light of early morning, the men from Sauk County inhaled the sweet, tangy aroma of burnt pork and bacon and the bready smell of acres of hardtack that had been consumed in flames. They tried not to think of pork or bacon or hardtack as they marched, their empty haversacks flapping on their hips.

Pope couldn't find Jackson. He and his Valley veterans had disappeared, gone into the air like the smoke of the ravaged depot at Manassas.

No army on earth, staff officers told them, could vanish from the face of the earth. The Baraboo Guards listened and nodded. Staff officers, Gus told Ethan, seemed to know a lot about what no army on earth could do.

40

For the next few days, Federal cavalry lost Jackson. He was reported back at Manassas, but he wasn't there when Pope marched against him. He was reported at Centreville, at Bull Run, at some other places. He was everywhere. He was nowhere. Pope's army sought him and got scattered and confused in the process.

At mid-afternoon on August 28, 1862, the Baraboo Guards went into camp in a small wood west of Centreville. They drew an issue of fresh beef from the commissaries that had finally caught up with the marching columns. Murphy got his fires going to cook the beef before it spoiled in the heat.

"We going to have a stew?" Olaf asked. He loved Murphy's beef stew.

"No, my hungry Viking," the Irishman told him. "I doubt there'll be the time. I'm thinking there's more moving and marching to be done before this day's laid to its rest. We'll have the lads broiling the beef in strips on the ram rods of their Springfields before we're called away and have to leave it."

"Coffee's done!" Murphy called, pouring sugar into the pot from one of his oil cloth pouches.

"God damn it, Murphy," Gus intoned, taking a sip of coffee and dipping a hardtack cracker into the brew. "What more could a man want? Good food, fresh air, clean living, exercise."

"A man could want a crack at Stonewall Jackson," Olaf said, chewing beef.

"A man could want a crack at something in a skirt!" Gus countered.

"Carl!" James called, striding toward the men. "Pack up. We've got marching orders."

"Where're they sending us?" Adolph asked.

"Centreville."

"They think Jackson's at Centreville?"

"Sheriff, I don't think they have a clue where Jackson is. Carl, have the men fall in. Company A is moving off."

The Baraboo Guards marched east on the Warrenton Turnpike toward the old Bull Run battlefield. After an hour on the pike, Gibbon's Brigade was alone, the preceding brigade, Hatch's, having moved on and the following brigades, Doubleday's and Patrick's, not yet come into sight.

The late afternoon sun slipped toward the shadowed Bull Run Mountains at their backs as the Baraboo Guards tramped along. The Sixth Wisconsin had the lead of the brigade with General Gibbon riding up front talking to Colonel Cutler. The Second Wisconsin followed the Sixth with the Seventh Wisconsin and the Nineteenth Indiana coming along in that order. Battery B, the artillerymen of Gibbon's former command, trailed in the dust.

"Pretty place," Gus declared, nodding to his left at a farm the column was passing. "Reminds me of the Asbaugh place west of Baraboo. Know where that is?"

"I know the Asbaugh family."

"Asbaugh's Ash Pit, I used to call it. Know why I called it that?"

"I think you're going to tell me."

"I called it Asbaugh's Ash Pit because I went there to get my ashes hauled when I was in that part of Sauk County. Angeline Asbaugh! Glory, Ethan, that lady could strike sparks. Well, hell, I remember one time in the loft of her daddy's barn . . ."

Ethan looked at the farm while Gus rattled on. Amid the shuffle of shoes on the dirt of the road, the tink of bayonet scabbards striking canteens, and the stink and smell of men in the marching column, the sight of the peaceful farm with its house, barn and out-buildings helped the merchant recall Wisconsin and carry his mind away from the spitting, farting, swearing men of the marching infantry. Were he on a road in Sauk County this time of day, Ethan thought, he'd be driving his wagon up the lane to the place. The family would ask him in to join their evening meal. People in Wisconsin were like that.

"Rider!" Olaf shouted, pointing up the ridge toward a horseman a hundred yards away.

"Where?" Gus asked, interrupting his tale of Angeline Asbaugh.

"There!" the farmhand cried.

Ethan looked up the ridge. He saw the rider. The man cantered along the side of the ridge in front of the farm. He kept pace, studying the regiments of John Gibbon's Black Hat Brigade as the Westerners marched east.

"That man's looking at us," Gus told Ethan. "He isn't wearing Federal blue. What do you think?"

"Could be a Reb scout," Ethan said.

"That one'll be no scout," Murphy said, knocking the coals from his pipe on the stock of his Springfield.

"Why say that?" Johnny Makepeace asked.

"No scout would show himself so. Not as that one's doing. A scout would be seeing all he wanted to see of this marching column from back in the cover of the trees. That one's studying us too close to be a cavalry outrider."

"What are you saying, Murphy?" Ethan asked.

"Aren't you the one always reading the newspapers they're selling through the camps? Figure it out for yourself, lad. Is not yonder Reb a tall, rangy man on a small thing of a sorrel horse? Long coat and high boots? Is that not a cadet's cap he's got smashed all down over his face?"

Ethan looked from the Irishman to the rider on the ridge. "Is that man Stonewall Jackson?"

"Aye."

"Aw, shit, Murphy!" Gus nagged the little man. "Come on! If that rider is Stonewall Jackson, where the hell is his God-damned army we've been chasing all over hell and creation?"

"If the rider on yon ridge is the terrible Stonewall Jackson, my young stallion, I'm telling you his army will be within the sound of his voice. We'll be looking to the priming of these lovely Springfields the government was nice enough to be giving us."

"Captain Peck!" Ethan called out. "Rebel rider!"

James stepped out of the column of march and looked up the ridge in the direction the merchant was pointing. The law clerk wiped perspiration and road dust from his face. He saw the horseman.

The rider drew his mount to a halt and raised his right forearm as if to shield his eyes from the sun. James remembered the man from the plateau of Henry Hill. The law clerk was certain, again, that the two looked at each other. The horseman dropped his arm and turned his mount, trotting out of sight into the line of trees behind the farm buildings.

James stood beside the pike, letting the Baraboo Guards march by. He glanced along the Warrenton Turnpike. A rectangular wood ran down the ridge and touched the pike. The Sixth Wisconsin was passing the wood, the leading company of the Second Wisconsin approaching it. James took off his hat and wiped his forehead. He looked up the ridge to see if the rider had reappeared.

A Confederate battery, six guns hauled by three teams each, the horses whipped by howling riders, galloped from the trees on James' far right. The rebel cannoneers' voices were high, warbling and wailing, faint but certain in the distance. The gray-clad gunners wheeled the teams and unlimbered, running the guns forward as horse-holders struggled to lead the excited teams back to cover. Billow after billow of dirty smoke rose above the battery as each gun fired.

James ran up the pike to head of the Baraboo Guards. He took his place beside the sheriff.

Ahead on the Warrenton Turnpike, where the companies of the Sixth Wisconsin had passed the far edge of the rectangular wood, Confederate shells tore through the evening air and exploded over the heads of the men in the Sixth Regiment. Men in the column screamed and dropped to the road, clutching hands and arms and legs. The brigade halted without orders, the men loading their Springfields and twisting bayonets onto the muzzles.

Adolph stopped marching and stared up the ridge. James followed the lawman's gaze. A Confederate brigade in line of battle moved silently forward to take position behind the battery, crimson battle flags waving back and forth, burnished musket barrels and bayonets flashing.

"Christ come early in the morning, boy," the fat man whispered. "I think we found Jackson's army."

James swallowed. He didn't want to think about Bull Run, the place of his failure, six miles down the Warrenton Turnpike from where he stood. He couldn't help but think about it.

"Look," the sheriff said.

The law clerk saw a second, then a third rebel brigade move silently and relentlessly from the trees and form into line of battle on the crest of the ridge behind the farm. "It's Bull Run all over again, Sheriff," he said, noticing that his voice was calm. "They're uphill from us and they outnumber us."

Adolph drew his revolver and checked the loads in its cylinders

A mounted brigade officer galloped from the head of the column. "Clear this road!" he shouted, waving his arms. "Clear this road!"

The men in the company formations moved to the right and left into the ditches.

Battery B rattled forward, the regulars whipping their horses, anxious to take their guns into battle. Gunners clutched iron handles on the limber boxes and swayed as the teams surged forward. The six guns went into position beside the Sixth Wisconsin on the far side of the rectangular wood.

James drew his revolver. He put the pistol in his left hand and looked at fingers of his right. His fingers were steady. He felt calm, ready, alert.

Colonel Ross ran back to the head of the Second Wisconsin. The colonel shouted at the captain of Company C. Half the Grant County Grays brought their Springfields up and ran for the rectangular wood, angling back to come out of the trees on the side where the farm house and the barn sat at the end of the lane. The men from Grant County spread out in the high grass of the sloping meadow and started to work their way uphill as skirmishers.

Colonel Ross drew his sword. James remembered him in that same pose in front of the Second Wisconsin as the regiment advanced up Henry Hill more than a year earlier. James also remembered his terror.

Another series of shells from the Confederate battery on the ridge burst above the Sixth Wisconsin. Battery B, now in position, roared back at the rebel guns.

Colonel Ross raised his sword, pointing toward the rectangular wood. He swept his sword down and the ten companies of the Second Wisconsin angled into the trees following the line of skirmishers from Company C.

Clearing the trees, Colonel Ross marched backwards, motioning for the captains to bring their companies into line on the color guards who ran to the center of the meadow. Satisfied, Colonel Ross turned and began a steady march up the slope through tall grass, bramble and clover.

James marched in front of the Baraboo Guards, who were on the far left of the regiment. To the right of the company, John Barks paced forward, chanting to the men. To the left of the company, Adolph Zimmerman plowed ahead, shouting.

Confederates skirmishers rose from the high grass and fired into the half-company of Wisconsin skirmishers and then scampered up the hill to take their places in their own lines.

James looked to his left. The Nineteenth Indiana was marching forward, sweeping to the left of the Second Wisconsin. To his right, the Seventh Wisconsin was coming out of the wood and into line in the opening between the Second and the trees.

The Second Wisconsin behind Colonel Ross marched toward the gray and butternut formations on the crest of the ridge, ninety yards, eighty yards away. The men from Wisconsin paced forward with bayoneted muskets over their right shoulders. Ethan heard Confederate officers shouting orders and encouragement to their own men. He wondered how close Colonel Ross intended to take them toward that solid, overlapping Confederate line.

The colonel halted and turned to face the regiment. He raised his sword. The regiment halted.

"Present!" the colonel shouted.

The line of Springfields swept to the horizontal.

Ethan aimed into the mass of men atop the ridge.

"Fire!"

The Springfields flamed and roared. Men tumbled to the earth in the rebel line.

Ethan exhaled. He'd been holding his breath the last ten yards of the regiment's advance. He grabbed a cartridge from his leather box and bit its end, tearing the paper wrapping and thumbing the cylinder into the smoking muzzle of his Springfield. He pulled the ram rod from its carrier rings and thrust the cartridge home, returning the ram rod. He cocked and capped his musket, raised it and aimed. Crack! he fired. A man in the gray and butternut formation clutched his stomach, sat hard, then slowly rolled over in the grass.

The Baraboo Guards were firing uphill. Jackson's rebel veterans were firing downhill. Murphy had told Ethan that men tended to fire high when aiming downhill. The merchant listened to the whine and buzz of lead balls over his head and hoped the Irishman was correct. Not entirely, the merchant learned. Ethan heard the distinct thwack! of lead hitting living flesh. A man near him screamed and fell from the line.

"Steady, now," Adolph chanted, walking along the rear of the line. "You know what to do," he told the men from Sauk County. "Aim low. Fire slow. Take your time."

Murphy closed his mind. He filled his thinking with his dum-diddley-dum-dee-day. The Irishman fired and reloaded steadily, an experienced hand at this manner of work. He gripped his cold briar pipe in his teeth off to one side in his mouth so it wouldn't interfere with biting into the ends of the paper cartridges. Load. Ram. Withdraw. Cock. Cap. Aim. Fire, crack! Dum-dum-diddley-dum-dee-day.

Gus slowly squeezed the trigger of his musket. The Springfield bucked harshly against his shoulder. A tall sergeant with ragged sleeves and a large hole in the knee of one of his trouser legs went down in the rebel line. "Fall, you son of a bitch!" Gus roared. "Three tries but I nailed your ass!"

Jack Black sneaked a look over his shoulder. Captain Peck stood behind him, sword and revolver drawn. There was no way to run past the bastard, Jack decided. Having run at Henry Hill, Jack was sure Captain Peck would cut him down before he took three steps. He'd wait but he didn't like waiting with a bunch of Confederate brigades shooting at him. He wished the captain would walk away or fall down or get himself killed or something. Jack slowly reloaded his Springfield, sheltering himself behind Gus Gaard's broad back.

James had seen Jack looking at him. The law clerk had stared back at the dark man. Jack aimed his musket up the ridge and fired. James glanced at the fingers of his right hand wrapped around the walnut grip of his revolver. His fingers were steady. He felt confident. He paced back and forth behind the firing line and called out encouragement to the men from Sauk County.

Paul Azhar jerked and coughed blood over the front of his blue coat. Jack Black, standing next to him, winced. Paul looked at Jack, bloody drool dripping from his chin.

"I didn't do that to you!" Jack screamed at the laborer from Reedsburg. Paul lowered his face and slumped into the grass.

"What'd he look at me for?" Jack shouted to no one.

Olaf sighted along the barrel over the tip of the front sight where it stood above the socket of his bayonet. A rebel up the ridge in the act of capping his musket came into the farmhand's vision. Olaf rested the tip of his front sight where the rebel's belt buckle would be and gently squeezed the trigger. His musket roared and bucked against his shoulder. Through the smoke of the blast Olaf saw the rebel fall. He reached for another cartridge. Four, he thought. That's four.

Frederick Auerbach pointed his musket up the ridge and fired, his eyes closed, tears forcing their ways through the lids.

"Frederick!" John Ausmann called.

"Aye!" Frederick shouted. He was relieved to hear John's voice among the shouting and the shooting. Frederick blinked away his tears and reloaded. It was all right when he could hear John's voice. He wasn't alone when he could hear John. Frederick cocked and capped his musket. He fired, his eyes closed, his nose running. He wiped his nose on the sleeve of his coat and reached for another cartridge.

John Ausmann grinned at Frederick. John drew a bead on a man in the Confederate line and held his front sight steadily as he put pressure on the trigger of his Springfield. A lead ball smashed into his face. John threw his hands into the air as if to grab something high above him. His unfired musket fell to the ground. John crumpled to the earth, his eyes wide open.

The regimental major ran to James, who stood at the left of the Baraboo Guards' line.

"Captain Peck!"

James looked at the officer.

"How's your ammunition?"

James stepped forward and lifted the flap of Henry Calef's cartridge box. "Less than half, Major."

"A working party from Company A is bringing cases of cartridges from the ammunition wagons. When you see them, send two men from Company K to bring up one case to your men. Have those two distribute the cartridges along your line. Keep the rest of your men firing."

"Yes, sir."

"Colonel Ross is dead, Captain," the major added. "Lieutenant Colonel Vaughan commands the regiment."

James stared at the major.

"Colonel Ross fell at the head of his regiment," the major said, wiping sweat from his face. "Look to your own command. That's why you're here."

James breathed, sighed, shuddered. "Yes, sir."

The major grunted and staggered, then turned slowly. He slipped to his knees. Blood dripped from a pierced hand. James ran to the officer.

"Please help me, Captain Peck," the major said calmly. James tugged his sweat-soaked neckerchief from his collar and tied it tightly onto the major's hand, staunching the flow of blood. He helped the major back to his feet.

"Thank you, Captain Peck. Now, tend to your duties with Company K." The major walked away along the rear of the firing line, stepping carefully over the many blue-clad bodies that lay in the grass.

Adolph paced behind the line chanting his litany, "Aim low, now. Fire slow. You're doing fine."

"Sheriff!" Johnny Makepeace cried. "I'm out of cartridges!"

"Take some from the bodies of the boys at your feet," Adolph told the student. He patted Johnny on the arm. "Don't fire so fast."

Wilfred Bland, the farmer from Reedsburg, raised his arm to ram a cartridge. His elbow shattered. Wilfred fell to his knees, screaming, clutching his arm. He bit into his lip against the fierce pain.

James ran to him. "Give me your cartridge box!" he shouted. "Let me help you get the strap over your shoulder. Can you make it back down to the road?"

"It hurts, Captain!"

"I know it hurts. Can you make it back down to the road?"

"I'll try, Captain. God, I never knew it would hurt like this!"

Wallace Dean crawled back from the firing line, his right hand holding what was left of his jaw. Red matter seeped through his fingers. The farmhand's eyes were glazed, unseeing.

"Wilfred, help Wallace," James ordered. "Take him back with you. Use your good arm. Help me get him on his feet."

James pulled the gagging farmhand upright and lifted his left arm over Wilfred's shoulder, taking Wallace's cartridge box. The wounded pair joined the streams of men making their way down the slope of the ridge to where the brigade surgeons had set up a dressing station in the trees of the rectangular wood.

Ethan felt a tug at his belt.

"Cartridges, Ethan," Henry Calef shouted to make himself heard over the roar of musketry and the wail of voices. Henry tried to force two packages of cartridges into the merchant's cartridge box.

"Stick them in my pants pocket!" Ethan shouted, aiming. Crack! he fired. "How are you doing, Gus?" he asked, speaking aloud in a world full of noise.

"Sure would like a drink!"

"Olaf?" Ethan shouted, biting into the paper wrapping of a cartridge.

"Here!" Crack! Seven, the farmhand counted. I've got seven of them so far. Seven, by damn!"

"Murphy?" Ethan called, ramming the cartridge home.

"I'm at the sides of you!" Crack! Dum-dum-diddley-dum-dee-day.

Adolph paced the rear of the line. "Aim low, now. Fire slow. You've got all day. Take your time."

John Barks met the lawman at the center of the firing line. "They're doing fine, Adolph!" the carpenter shouted.

"They sure as hell are!"

"See those bastards dropping up on top of the ridge, Sheriff?"

"Dropping like flies come the winter, John," the lawman agreed, taking his red bandanna and wiping his perspiring face. "We'll pay those sons of bitches back for what they did to us at Bull Run!"

"Sauk County's finest!" John crowed, turning away from the fat man to retrace his steps along the rear of the line. John heard the zip-thwack! of a bullet striking into flesh. He looked to see who had been hit.

Adolph Zimmerman lay full length in the trampled grass just behind the men in the firing line.

"Sheriff!" John screamed, running to the lawman.

Adolph's eyes were open. He looked at the carpenter.

"Can you get up?" John asked.

The sheriff shook his head. The front of his coat was open. His flannel shirt was dark with perspiration and blood. Adolph coughed. Blood dribbled from his lips. "Oh, shit, John," he sighed. "This sure as hell isn't a good place for an old, fat man."

"I'll get men to carry you back to the surgeons!"

The sheriff shook his head. "Don't tell the boy," he ordered, clutching the carpenter's sleeve. "He's got his hands full as it is. He's doing fine. You tell him I said he's doing fine."

"God, Sheriff!" John sobbed. "Don't die on us! Hey, you two men! Come over here!"

Stepan Fedkenheuer and Peter Everett stepped back from their places and knelt beside the carpenter. "What do you want, Lieutenant Barks?" Peter asked, taking off his black hat and wiping sweat and powder granules from his face.

"Carry Sheriff Zimmerman back to the surgeons!" John cried. "He's been wounded!"

"Lieutenant," Stepan said. "Sheriff Zimmerman's dead."

John stared at the peaceful face of the sheriff of Sauk County. His sightless eyes were open. There was bloody drool at his mouth and chin above the gore that had been his chest. "Go back into the line," John told the two men. "Don't say anything about this."

"Sure, Lieutenant," Peter said, capping his musket.

John knelt beside the lawman. He felt tears rolling freely down his cheeks. He bit into his lip to keep from screaming.

Ethan tore the end of a cartridge and shoved the load into the muzzle of his Springfield. The merchant's mouth was foul with the taste of black powder. "Getting on toward dusk," he told his brother-in-law.

"This won't be going on for long," the Irishman said, digging another cartridge from his pocket. "Look along the line."

Ethan looked as he capped his musket. Less than half the Baraboo Guards were on their feet and firing. Blue bodies carpeted the grass along the rear of the firing line. From where the merchant stood, he saw the situation was the same all along John Gibbon's brigade lines. Half the Black Hats were down.

Ethan noted how bright the muzzle flashes along the Confederate line seemed in the falling shadows.

With darkness, the firing slowly receded, then stopped.

Gus was exhausted. He lowered the butt of his Springfield to the ground and leaned on its hot muzzle, desperately wanting a drink of whiskey.

Ethan, his musket in his hands, looked up the slope of the ridge and wondered what he would do if the Confederates should charge.

Murphy sucked on his cold pipe, closing his ears to the pitiful moaning of men lying at his feet.

Olaf aimed his Springfield, sure he could get one more Confederate before total darkness came over the field.

Carl leaned on the muzzle of his musket, sure in his soul that he had been a fool to follow Nathaniel Bachmann off to fight in Abraham Lincoln's war.

An officer from Company I, holding a neckerchief to a bleeding cheek, approached James. "Orders from regiment, Captain Peck. In half an hour pull your men back to the wood. Take up a position there where you came out of the trees this afternoon. Carry as many of your wounded with you as you can. Keep your men silent. Company I will leave a skirmish line to cover our withdrawal."

James nodded. He felt numb. He was satisfied the he'd conducted himself well.

John and Carl came to the law clerk.

"Fall back to the trees in half an hour," James repeated the orders to the carpenter and the tavern keeper. "Where's the sheriff?"

John's lips quivered.

"Adolph?" James asked, begging the question not to be fact.

John nodded, openly crying.

Carl looked away.

James covered his face with his hands.

Carl stepped forward and put his arm around the law clerk's shoulders. "I'll have some of the boys bring his body with us when we leave, Captain Peck."

James stepped away, shaking his head. He'd thought the fat man indestructible. He shook himself, forcing away his shock and grief. "Let him be, Carl," he sighed. "He came with the boys from Sauk County, he always told me. He fell with them today. He's where he'd want to be. John, have the men fall back by sections when we go. Carl, take the lead. I'll follow. Later."

"Sure, Cap'n," the carpenter said.

James found Adolph's body in the trampled grass a few feet behind the scattering of corpses that marked where the Baraboo Guards had stood on the firing line. The fat man looked like he was resting, sleeping off one of his powerful drunks. James took the sheriff's calloused hand, sitting on the ground beside him.

"Help me!" a voice pleaded. "Please help me."

"Who are you?" James asked, brought back from his reverie.

"Azhar," the voice whispered. "Paul Azhar. Is that you, Captain Peck?"

James found the laborer in a clump of blue bodies. "Where are you hurt, Paul?"

"My chest. It's hard to talk, Captain. I think I passed out for a time. Where is everyone?"

"We've pulled back. Can you get up if I help you?"

"I think so. Don't leave me!"

James helped Paul to his feet and supported him down the slope. The dark meadow was littered with bodies and equipment. James stumbled several times, eliciting moans from the wounded boy.

In spite of the danger of drawing fire from the Confederate brigades on the ridge, the brigade surgeons had strung lanterns from tree limbs and hung blankets and tarpaulins to make a field hospital in the wood close to the turnpike.

A surgeon's assistant took Paul Azhar from James. Carl found the law clerk. "Well?" James asked.

"We mustered eighty-two men this morning, Captain. I count fifty-three tonight. We've lost twenty-nine men, dead, wounded or missing."

James swallowed. "Does this place have a name?"

"The locals call it Groveton, sir."

"The Baraboo Guards will remember Groveton, Carl."

"Murphy has a small fire going in the ditch beside the road, Captain. He's making coffee."

"Where's John?"

"With Murphy. We'll make that company headquarters if that's all right with you."

James followed Carl to Murphy's fire. Ethan and Gus were there, the Wright brothers, Jack Black and Olaf, Johnny Makepeace and Wayne Roohr, others. The men sat on the earth, dark shapes in the soft glow of the little man's fire. The flames reflected from their grimed faces, their tired eyes, their musket barrels and bayonet blades. A few men dozed. Most stared into the fire.

Carl took James' tin cup from the strap of the law clerk's haversack, filled it with coffee, and brought it to James along with a handful of hardtack crackers. James sipped the brew and chewed the crackers. They had no taste. He drank from the cup, draining it. He couldn't see the letters stamped into the bottom of the cup but he knew they were there. He thought of her, so far away from where he stood.

"Captain Peck?" an officer called.

"I'm Peck."

"We're leaving, Captain. We're going back to Manassas. Have your men wrap their cups and canteens and anything else that might make noise. Take all the wounded that can walk or that you can carry."

"What about the wounded we can't carry?" James asked, thinking about Paul Azhar.

"The surgeons are going to stay with them. We have to hope for mercy from Jackson's men. Be ready to leave in ten minutes."

The Black Hat Brigade formed on the Warrenton Turnpike after midnight and moved west, half the strength it had been when it strolled casually east on the same pike the day before. Gun carriages, caissons, the teams of Battery B and the horses of brigade officers all carried wounded men. Some of the volunteers passed their muskets to comrades and carried the wounded in litters made from branches and blankets.

The column moved silently in the darkness away from Groveton. A few tired men in the lead companies drank what water remained in their canteens and checked the priming of their Springfields, then trotted out from the column to serve as flankers and skirmishers in case the rebel brigades on the ridge came down in pursuit.

James walked unsteadily, exhausted, not sure with each step that he wouldn't fall to the road before he could put the next foot out in front of himself. He felt sick in his soul.

"You all right, Cap'n?" John asked, shifting his load of four Springfields.

"I'm all right," the law clerk answered. "I'm sick at what I've seen."

"What are you thinking, Cap'n?"

"I'm thinking of an old, fat man," James whispered, shuddering.

"Here!" Murphy interjected. "Be letting go of it now! Have it out of your mind! You've a company of infantry to be thinking of!"

"There's little more than a platoon of us left," James sobbed.

"There's a company of us left, my young Captain! Numbers won't make a difference to the burden of command you've to bear. Would himself, that terrible man back there, be wanting to see you keening a wake for him? Ach!

That terrible man would be telling you that you was doing fine and then he'd be off and seeing how the rest of the lads are faring, wouldn't he?"

"He'd be doing that, Murphy," James agreed, wiping his eyes.

"Then get yourself busy looking to the welfare of your men. The dead will do a fine job of mourning themselves. You've other things to be thinking about. Get your spine straight, lad."

James forced himself to march steadily. He'd come through the fighting without losing his nerve but he felt no pride in that. He'd seen too many men die. He walked through the ranks in the darkness and spoke to the men, touching them, talking with them, letting them know the Baraboo Guards existed and that he was in command. For twenty minutes he carried the corner of a blanket litter so Ethan could rest his weary arms.

Murphy trudged along, wishing for a sip of whiskey. The little man shifted the three Springfields he carried to his other shoulder. He cursed himself. He shouldn't have been harsh on the young captain. Wasn't he but a lad and hadn't the sheriff been like a father to the boy? Ah, it was life that made a man into what he was, the Irishman thought. It was life that made these weary farmers into the sorry dregs of battle they were this night. They should all be at home in their Sauk County, swilling hogs or plowing fields like the good farming stock they were. Or, like the lads they were, contemplating in their young minds getting a finger or more into the drawers of the maiden down the lane. They'd no business carrying muskets on the march and killing other men in fields.

Hadn't they stood to it this day and given back as much as they'd taken like regulars of the line? Regulars of the line wouldn't have stood and faced such fire. The farmers from Sauk County hadn't known the hopelessness of the thing. They'd not known enough to run away. Veteran infantry would have gone from that terrible meadow with honor and lived to come back to fight another day. Trained officers would have marched them off, retreating before a superior force with no thought of shame.

Murphy wondered if he'd done good or evil by staying on with them and showing them the way. The guilts were coming on him. He sensed them. He longed to be able to crawl into a dark corner of one of the fields he marched by and drink his soul into unconsciousness where the guilts could not find him. The guilts would bring on the haunts and the little man didn't want the haunts on a night as dark and dreadful as this one. To make it as bad as it could be, he hadn't a drop of whiskey on him. Well, he considered, what was one to do? Tum-tiddley-tum-tee-day, he crooned. Tum-tiddley-tum-tee-day.

At dawn, John Gibbon's Black Hats went into camp beside the Warrenton Turnpike.

At noon, a flag of truce came in and the Confederates delivered the wounded men and the surgeons from Groveton in wagons.

James couldn't find Paul Azhar among the wounded men the Confederates had sent in. He learned that Paul was among the dead.

41

The line of pickets stretched in darkness across the Warrenton Turnpike. Men of the Second Wisconsin and the Seventh Wisconsin manned the picket line, neither regiment alone able to muster enough for the task. To the left of the picket line rose Henry Hill, where the Second Wisconsin had fought more than a year earlier.

General John Pope's Federal army retreated through the picket line, heading east for Centreville. Second Bull Run, the men were already calling the battle that began with Stonewall Jackson's raid on the Federal depots at Manassas, followed by the savage fighting around Groveton, ending four days later with the smashing defeat of the Federal army.

General Robert E. Lee had come up from Richmond with Major General James Longstreet's First Corps, hard on the heels of Jackson's thrust, and had caught Pope's forces between Jackson's and Longstreet's divisions. It took three days and ten thousand casualties to convince John Pope that he wasn't fighting one detached wing of the rebel Army of Northern Virginia.

After the bloody struggle on the slope at Groveton, the Baraboo Guards were posted with the survivors of the Second Wisconsin supporting some batteries.

Gus leaned on the muzzle of his musket. His head was heavy. His eyes wanted to close. He yawned and scratched his crotch. The little devils were at work down there in the sweat and grime of his private parts. He figured he must be home to about a hundred of them. He was too tired to get mad as the little devils crawled and bit and made him itch. Gus just wanted to close his eyes and sleep. Even standing, leaning on the fouled muzzle of his Springfield, he could sleep if only he dared close his eyes. Even a bottle of Elsasser's brandy wouldn't keep him awake if he could close his eyes. Not even Miss Doris Studemacher from Reedsburg, he thought, could keep him awake. He wondered, leaning heavily on his musket in the darkness, if a combination of Elsasser's brandy and Miss Doris Studemacher from Reedsburg together could keep him awake.

That was a pleasant thought.

Hell, he argued with himself, he'd have to pour half the bottle of Elsasser's brandy over his private parts to kill off those little devils down there before Miss Studemacher would let him touch her. She wouldn't let him get close if she had any idea what was crawling around his private parts. She was one for being clean, Gus remembered. She always smelled so nice. He wouldn't want to be responsible for having those little devils get on her and start crawling around her pretty places. Now, he caught himself, there was another pleasant thought. Gus wondered what it would be like to be one of those little devils crawling around the pretty places of Miss Doris Studemacher.

"Hey!" a man in the column of retreating infantry called out. "Black Hat!"

Gus raised his head from the muzzle of his musket and forgot Miss Doris Studemacher from Reedsburg. "What?"

"Who are you?"

"Second Wisconsin," Gus yawned. "Who're you?"

"One-Oh-Five Pennsylvania! You been out here for a while, Wisconsin!"

"Since First Bull Run!"

"We heard you Black Hats kicked Stonewall Jackson's ass on Thursday!"

"He kicked back."

Murphy walked up to Gus. "Here," the little man said, handing Gus a shape. "Put this between your backbone and your belt buckle."

"What's this?"

"White bread, fresh baked."

"Where in the hell did you find white bread in a retreat?"

"From a bakery wagon, would you believe it? Will you be eating it or arguing about it, Mister Gaard?"

"I'll be eating it," Gus assured the Irishman, biting into the loaf, ripping away and chewing the sweet, doughy crust. Gus was hungry. Other than coffee and hardtack, he hadn't eaten since the issue of beef the afternoon before the fight at Groveton.

Olaf moved down the picket line to stand beside Gus. The farmhand chewed on a loaf. "That damned Irish!" he said. "He found bread. He can find anything. He'd find a willing maid in a monastery."

Gus nodded, biting into the crust. He watched a battery of guns pass on the road. The battery was followed by a long column of ambulances and wagons filled with moaning, weeping wounded men.

"Bastards!" Olaf swore, watching the wheel spokes turn slowly as the vehicles moved by him. "It's better to let them lay. They'll get better or they'll die. Putting them in wagons and hauling them from place to place only makes more of them die."

"They do what they can, Olaf."

The two stood and chewed and watched the army pass.

"Gus?" Olaf asked.

"What?"

"Do you turn to dirt when they bury you?"

"What?"

"Hans is dead. They'd have buried him. Will he turn to dirt?"

"I don't know. I guess so."

"He'll turn to dirt," Olaf decided. "That's good. Dirt's good. Plow it. Plant it. Grow wheat in it. Hans was a good farmhand, Gus. He liked to work the dirt."

Gus chewed. He didn't know what to say.

"Maybe we'll all die before this is over," Olaf sighed. "Maybe we'll all turn to dirt." He'd counted eleven men who fell before his aim in the fight at Groveton. He didn't hate the Confederate men he shot down. He'd shoot as many of them as he could, but he wouldn't hate them. They hadn't killed Hans. Captain Bachmann had killed Hans. Captain Bachmann had gone back to Wisconsin. The Confederate men were here in Virginia. If the Confederate men didn't kill him, he'd go to Wisconsin after the war and kill Captain Bachmann.

The retreat of Pope's Federal army continued. Gus couldn't understand how a force so large and well-equipped could have been so soundly whipped by the tattered, bearded, bare-foot scarecrows in butternut and gray who fought under Jackson and Longstreet and Lee.

The last regiment of the Federal army passed through the picket line. John Gibbon brought his Black Hat Brigade across the stone bridge over Bull Run and up the eastern slope of the valley to Centreville. They went into camp in the fields the Second Wisconsin had occupied more than a year before.

Ethan woke the following morning to rain falling on his face. The merchant sat up in the mud, his blanket roll still tied across his chest. He'd slept as soon as he'd stopped marching the night before. Ethan rubbed his face. Around him in the fields near Centreville the beaten Federal army was trying to bring its scattered segments together.

Ethan had lost the brass eagle plate that held up the side of his black hat. He wore the brim turned down all around like a Wisconsin farmer. Rain dripped from the brim, chilling him. The merchant unrolled his blanket and wrapped it around his shoulders like a shawl. He was wet and cold and had the tightness in his bowels. He got to his feet and wiped rain from his Springfield with a dry corner of his blanket.

Murphy worked at a smoking fire of wet wood, trying to coax a flame by fanning the meager coals with the brim of his black hat.

"You need dry wood," Ethan told the little man, sniffling at the run in his nose.

"Here!" the Irishman snapped. "I'm being advised I'm needing dry wood! Where would a man be finding dry wood on a day such as this, I ask?"

"The undersides of fence rails would be dry," the merchant suggested, shivering in his blanket.

"Dry, would they be? And, with our darling brigadier threatening the wrath of God onto the soul of the first man to be taking just enough tinder to be using to get this poor fire blazing? Just enough, mind you, to be boiling a pot of coffee for the warmth of the lads of the marching infantry?"

Ethan looked at the Irishman.

"I'm asking you, Mister Evans!"

Ethan sniffled and spat. He nudged the shape lying in the wet grass at his feet. "Olaf," he said. "Get up. Come on, we got to go commit a crime."

Olaf rolled and sat up, pulling his muddy blanket over his shoulders. He blew his nose with the fingers of one hand, wiping his fingers on his jacket. He put up the other hand and the merchant tugged the farmhand to his feet. The two walked toward the far tree line, where a rail fence snaked along the border of the field.

The rest of the Baraboo Guards began to wake. Gus stood, barefooted in the mud, and looked at the sky through holes in the soles of both shoes. "Where's the cobbler's shop?"

"The trains'll be coming up," Murphy told him. "They're waiting till the fighting's done before bringing up the trains. There's fewer men to give the replacements to when the fighting's done."

"Where's Ethan?"

"Out plundering the countryside."

"Good for him! Hey, Murphy, why does it always rain after a battle?" Gus asked, squinting and looking up into the falling rain. Dirt and powder smoke dissolved and ran down his face.

"Some say it's the good Lord's own way of cleansing His earth of the sight of the terrible things His creatures been doing to the land."

"Makes sense. I sure could use a drink, Murphy."

"I've not a drop, lad. Facts being what they are, what you're carrying in your haversacks is what we'll be living on until they get the commissary trains up."

Ethan and Olaf returned, each dragging two fence rails.

"You find a rail tree in the woods?" Gus asked his brother-in-law.

"Big one," the merchant answered straight-faced. "Tore these branches off it."

"Get to breaking them up," Murphy urged. "We'll have our fire going and we'll have your plunder out of sight."

James joined the men at Murphy's fire.

"Morning to you, Captain," the little man greeted. "We'll have a spot of coffee for you in a couple shakes."

"Thanks, Murphy," the law clerk said, ignoring the fence rails being broken for firewood. "Are we all here, Carl?" he asked as the tavern keeper rolled out of a muddy blanket.

"We're here, Captain Peck. I'll call the roll. It won't take long this morning."

James nodded. He knew it wouldn't.

The law clerk watched the Baraboo Guards straggle into line. There were less than fifty of them. Some had no blankets to wrap around their shoulders against the rain and the chill. Some, like Gus, had no shoes. They stood with shoulders hunched forward, hands in pockets, muskets under their arms. To James they didn't look like a company of Federal infantry. They looked like a pack of uncared-for orphans from some poor institution.

"Forty-seven present, sir," Carl reported.

"Have the men stand at ease," James said. "Have them gather round."

The men shuffled in close, standing in a circle. Auerbach, the cobbler, had lost his friend John Ausmann at Groveton. George Ball, the farmer, wheezed from congestion in his chest. Jack Black shivered, wiping his running nose. Henry Calef and Preston Christensen shared a blanket, both farmers wet and dirty. Ethan and Gus stood together, the merchant constipated and wet, the blond barefooted. Peter Everett and Stepan Fedkenheuer had lost their black hats. Rain washed unchecked down their faces. Hollis Oostendorp and Wayne Roohr stared blankly, their faces showing the horror of the past days. The Wright brothers stood back to back for warmth. Neither had a blanket. Henry Schoming, hot with fever, leaned on the muzzle of his Springfield.

In the distance other companies of the Second Wisconsin formed, holding roll calls, starting the business of the day. Men fanned fires of wet wood. The smoke from their futile efforts floated low across the fields around Centreville. James shivered.

"I'm proud of you," he told the Baraboo Guards. "You've done well. Last night as the army retreated through your picket line men called out to you Black Hats. The whole Federal army knows what you've done. They think of you with pride. Stonewall Jackson, on the other side, won't forget the fight you gave him and his veterans at Groveton. You met him close to here a year ago. This time, you gave him back what he had coming and then some. You took losses doing that. Men you know and marched with have died. The people of Wisconsin are proud of you. I'll get blankets and shoes for you as soon as I can. Food, too, when the commissary trains come up.

Until then, try to keep warm and dry as best you can. Take care of your-selves. That's all I have to say to you."

James nodded to Carl and walked away from the circle of men. He did feel great pride for his Baraboo Guards and he also felt great fear. There would be more fighting, more losses.

James gazed over the fields. What was the purpose? In fifteen months the Baraboo Guards had fought two battles that had accomplished noth-ing. In fifteen months, half the Baraboo Guards had fallen.

42

The demoralized brigades of Pope's army marched from Centreville to the protection of the Washington forts. As they approached the camps of the peninsula veterans of McClellan's army they saw men throwing caps and haversacks into the air, shouting and tearing the gray, wet skies with whoops and cheers. McClellan, the men learned, had been reinstated to command the army in place of John Pope. McClellan's men were delirious with the news. They'd had no faith in Pope. Even Pope's own men had little faith in him and were satisfied with the change. Everyone, it seemed to the Baraboo Guards, liked George McClellan. Everyone, the Irishman cau-tioned, except the president and the secretary of war.

With the reorganization that followed McClellan's assumption of com-mand, General Rufus King of Wisconsin was relieved and General John Hatch took King's former division. Over Hatch, Joseph Hooker took com-mand of what had been McDowell's army, now the First Corps of the Army of the Potomac. John Gibbon's Black Hats became one of nine brigades in the First Corps.

After the Baraboo Guards settled into camp, James looked in on Preston Faircloth. Preston had come through the fighting at Groveton and Second Bull Run unharmed. He wore two chevrons of a corporal on the sleeves of his frock coat. The boy mentioned to James that he'd written to Lucille. James left Preston sitting at the fire with his mess mates. The law clerk promised himself he'd try to keep in touch with Preston.

"Major wants to see us," John told James when he returned.

James led the way to the command tent and scratched on its canvas wall. "You wanted to see us, Major Bache?"

"Yes, Peck," the officer said, sitting at a field desk, his right hand ban-daged from the wound he'd taken at Groveton. "Come in. You, too, Barks. Be seated. How are the men of Company K?"

"We've been resupplied, sir," James reported. "The men finally got shoes."

"Good. I have much to discuss with you. There'll be changes, of course, with the death of Colonel Ross. Lieutenant Colonel Vaughan has resigned and will be returning to Wisconsin."

"I hadn't heard that, sir," James said.

"No announcement has been made, at his request. I've been appointed to the colonelcy and given command of the Second Wisconsin."

"Congratulations, Colonel."

"Thank you, Peck. Captain Ford, of Company B, is the new lieutenant colonel. You, Peck, are the new major."

"Sir?" James asked, startled. "I don't know about that, sir. I don't know that I want to leave the Baraboo Guards."

"You've no choice, Peck. I need you here. The Baraboo Guards will be in excellent hands. Barks, you've been promoted to captain and will command them."

"Aw, hell, Colonel," the carpenter objected. "I wouldn't know anything about being a captain. I've been stretched trying to act like a lieutenant. I was stretched just being a sergeant."

"You were a good sergeant, Barks, and a good lieutenant. You'll do well as the commanding officer of Company K. Gentlemen, I have to work with what I'm given. I've already sent your names to Madison for confirmation by the governor. Captain Barks, I'll accept your nominations for lieutenants to replace yourself and Sheriff Zimmerman."

"I'd like to talk with the men about that, Colonel," John said. "With a whole new batch of officers, I'd like them to have a say in this."

"I want the names in the morning, Captain. Major Peck, I'll expect you here at noon, tomorrow, to assume your new duties. There's a matter that lends urgency to our reorganization. Lee has taken his rebel army into Maryland. After defeating us at Second Bull Run, he's striking north, possibly heading for Pennsylvania. I don't have to tell you how important it is that this war be contained inside the Confederacy. They started it. We intend to let them bear its burdens. We'll be setting off in pursuit of Lee soon. Captain Barks, I want Company K ready to march on six hours' notice. Major Peck, I want you working with the other captains to bring their companies to the same state of readiness. For now, gentlemen, that's all I have for you. Good day."

The law clerk and the carpenter saluted and left the tent.

"God damn!" John swore as they walked to the camp of the Baraboo Guards.

"You'll do fine," James assured him, hearing the echo of an old, fat man.

"The boys are going to miss you, Major Peck. You've been in command from the beginning, even when Nate Bachmann was still around."

"I'm going to miss being with them, John. Who'll you talk to about the lieutenancies?"

"Carl and Ethan."

"You couldn't ask better men."

Neither the tavern keeper nor the merchant would consider promotion. Carl was comfortable as first sergeant. Ethan was determined to remain a private. In the morning John sent forward the names of Robert Wright, the farmer from south of Baraboo, and Castle Newton, the tanner's son.

James sat with the Baraboo Guards at Murphy's cooking fire after supper as darkness fell, listening to the men, sipping coffee.

"Will you be having more coffee, lad?" Murphy asked.

"What?" James started, brought from the reverie into which he'd slipped. He'd been thinking of the months since the company had mustered. "Oh, no, thanks."

"Is your mind already heavy with the burden of command?" the little man asked. "You're not assuming those new duties till the noon of the morrow."

"I don't even know what the burden of command will be, Murphy. I was thinking about the men, about the ones we've lost, about the sheriff, about a lot of things."

"Leave off with too much thinking, now! You'll be bringing on a haunt!"

"Maybe. Where are the men? They were here a while ago."

"They've been slipping off, two and three at a time so you wouldn't be noticing. They've left me to be bringing you along to a bit of celebrating they want to share with you away from the constrictions of the camp. Be taking a tug on that bottle, there, and come with me. It'll do you good to break out of the funk you've let yourself slip into."

"I don't want to go anywhere, Murphy. Tell the men for me . . ."

"I'll tell them nothing! You'll be taking your orders this night from me, young Major Peck! On your feet, sir!"

The Irishman led his charge west from the camp to a farm house at the end of a lane off the Leesburg Turnpike near the village of Falls Church. As they approached the house James heard the lilting music of a fiddle.

"Murphy?" he asked apprehensively as the two stepped onto the porch, "is this all right and proper?"

"Seeing as you're asking, lad," the little man said, spitting off to one side, "if we're getting caught, don't be giving the right name."

"Here goes my promotion," the law clerk sighed, following the little man into the parlor of the farm house. The Baraboo Guards were waiting.

"Hip! Hip!" John called out.

"Hooray!"

"Hip! Hip!"

"Hooray!"

"Company!" Robert Wright, the new first lieutenant, cried. "Attention!" The men stiffened.

James was touched. He swallowed. He knew what to say to them. They'd heard it said before. "Men of the Baraboo Guards!" he called, raising his right hand to the brim of his hat. "I salute you!" James held the salute, turning left to right as he faced them. He dropped his hand sharply and Gus slapped a bottle of whiskey into it. James toasted the Baraboo Guards and took a long pull on the bottle.

A black man playing a fiddle struck up a tune. Gus whirled past the law clerk, a woman in his arms. Several women, James noticed, were among the men from Sauk County, drinking and dancing and laughing with them.

"Glad you came, Major Peck," Carl said, standing behind a bar made from a plank and two barrels. The tavern keeper had tucked a towel across his front and was tending bar.

"I couldn't not come, Carl," James said, taking a light sip from his bottle. "I was ordered here by a superior officer. An Irishman. Carl," James asked, "does an Irishman outrank a major?"

"Sir," the tavern keeper confided, "that Irishman outranks everyone."

43

MADISON—August, 1862.

Lucille held Preston's letter, her mind overflowing with conflicting thoughts. In the letter, Preston asked her in their father's name to forgive him.

Her brother wrote that he'd come to accept and live with the anger their father held against him for the loss of his wife and their mother. Preston understood, he'd written, that their father had been wrong, but Preston admitted his own guilt for adding to the bad situation by living and acting as he had. He gave credit in the letter to James for his reconciliation with himself and wrote that he hoped the three of them could work together when the men returned from the war to build on the Faircloth holdings and continue the work the judge had begun. In his final paragraph he wrote that he'd sent their father's attorneys instructions naming her as his beneficiary in the event of his death.

Lucille touched the edges of the sheets of paper, wishing in her heart that her brother had come to his reconciliation while their father was alive.

She folded the letter and placed it in the center drawer of her father's desk. She poured a glass of sherry.

Preston had been alienated from their father all his life. His change of heart, though welcome, was late. James had returned to the army in Virginia to find the answers to his own problems. He was a thousand miles from her when she needed his love, his body, his counsel and his help. Neither Preston nor James had been available to her when the options had to be picked up, when the bonds had to be exchanged, when the opportunities had to be taken. Neither had been available to her when the days grew long and the nights grew empty. Nathaniel Bachmann had.

She'd done what she wanted to do at the time, or at least what she thought she wanted to do. She'd given herself to the dark, stocky, commanding man.

She sipped sherry, her mind whirling. She forced herself to be honest.

She'd given herself to Bachmann because she was attracted to him and because she desired him. She'd taken him into her life, into her bed, into her body because she'd wanted him there. It did her no good to wonder what she'd have done had Preston and James been in Madison instead of Virginia. It did no good to blame Preston and James for their distance from her. It did no good to blame Nathaniel Bachmann for being the present and persistent help he'd been. She faced herself in the mirror above the table. She had a serious problem and for the first time in her life she didn't have her father to turn to. She understood that the day would come when Preston and James would return and look to her to be the focus of their lives after the years and the horrors of war. She knew that Nathaniel Bachmann would be an unwelcome presence then.

She'd allowed herself to bring him into her present life to provide counsel and excitement. She'd have to begin working the officer out of her life. Lucille knew that would be difficult. Nathaniel Bachmann had touched the Faircloth holdings and found them enticing. He'd touched her and found her satisfying. He wouldn't be easily sent packing as her earlier suitors had been.

She heard Mary open the front door and admit Nathaniel Bachmann to the house. She looked to be sure Preston's letter was safely concealed in the center drawer of her father's desk.

Lucille had a lot of thinking to do. For the remainder of the evening she'd put that out of her mind. She turned to the mirror, pausing for a moment to see to her face and hair. Her breathing quickened in anticipation of the evening to come. She smiled reassuringly at her reflection and walked into the foyer to greet her visitor.

44

MARYLAND—September, 1862.

Robert E. Lee had gone north, taking his butternut and gray Confederates across the fords of the Potomac River, west and north of the Federal army in front of Washington. His fifty thousand warriors were loose and about in Maryland. There was a rumor that Lee was at Frederick, fifty miles from the Federal capital.

A week after taking command of John Pope's beaten army, George McClellan swung the ponderous weight of the Army of the Potomac northward.

The Baraboo Guards took to the road, leaving the camp at Upton Hill, marching over the bridge into Washington city, then through the Maryland suburbs and out into the rolling country beyond. The Baraboo Guards went into camp south of Frederick, three days and fifty exhausting miles from their starting point.

On Saturday, September 14, 1862, they marched through Frederick to the shouted welcome of its loyal citizens. Lee and his Confederates had marched through the city three days before.

Crowds lined the streets and cheered the steady tramp of the regiments of weathered, worn Federal soldiers. A little girl ran into the street and kissed Ethan. The Baraboo Guards roared their approval. The stocky merchant blushed.

"Here, boys!" an old man in a black suit shouted, trotting into the ranks with a pail of iced lemonade.

"Hey, Sis!" Gus called to a pretty brunette with freckles. "Throw me a kiss!" The blond was showered with kisses thrown from the women in the crowd.

"God bless Abraham Lincoln and the Constitution!" a fat man cried, waving his walking stick.

"You'd better ask God to bless John Gibbon and the Black Hat Brigade," Colonel Bache countered.

Girls ran through the striding ranks to tie red, white and blue ribbons to the men's muskets. Flags waved from the porches of Frederick. The citizens had witnessed in sullen silence the passage of Lee's Confederates through their town. They gloried, now, at the march of the regiments of Federal fighting men.

"Here comes Little Mac!" Lieutenant Colonel Ford called.

General George McClellan, escorted by two squadrons of lancers, reined his large horse and lifted his little cap to the dusty Westerners. "Black Hats!" he greeted them. "Are you men bully!"

The Black Hat Brigade roared its agreement.

"Black Hats!" McClellan shouted at them, spurring his horse forward beside the column, the lancers trotting behind.

"Never saw McDowell or Pope stop and talk to us like that," Johnny Makepeace told Wayne Roohr.

The Federal army marched west from Frederick and topped the ridge known as Catoctin Mountain. Over Catoctin, the Baraboo Guards saw the solid mass of South Mountain that ran to the north into Pennsylvania, where it was known by that name, and to the south into Virginia, where it was known as the Blue Ridge. In the valley between Catoctin and South Mountain the Baraboo Guards swung off the National Road into fields and dropped to the grass, tired, worn, dusty and filled with enthusiasm and excitement.

James ran to where the Baraboo Guards lay. "No time to boil coffee, John!" he shouted to the carpenter. "The Rebs hold the pass over South Mountain. Gibbon's Brigade is going to open it up."

"I've been smelling a fight since we left Frederick, Major," the carpenter grinned.

"Fall the men in. Load and fix bayonets. We'll follow the Nineteenth Indiana. Take care of them, John. They're good men."

"They're Sauk County's finest, sir!"

Gibbon's four regiments formed on both sides of the National Road that ran up the eastern side of South Mountain to a depression at the top known as Turner's Gap. There the road crossed over the mountain and ran down the western side. The Nineteenth Indiana formed forward to the left of the road, the Second Wisconsin behind the Hoosiers in support. To the right of the road, on its northern side, the Seventh Wisconsin faced up the ridge, the Sixth Wisconsin behind.

South Mountain rose gently but steadily toward Turner's Gap. Cultivated fields, broken here and there with woodlots and stone walls, covered the slope. Gunsmoke at the gap and along some of the stone walls indicated the locations of Confederate batteries firing on the Federal formations in the valley between Catoctin and South Mountain.

John Gibbon rode to the front of the Nineteenth Indiana and raised his right arm. He swept the arm down, pointing to the gap. "Forward!" the fiesty brigadier called. "For-ward! Forward!"

The Nineteenth Indiana stepped off up the slope, cheering and shouting. Across the National Road, the Seventh Wisconsin moved forward in line of battle.

Skirmishers ran out ahead of the marching regiments, single men, trotting alone, stopping to fire and reload, keeping well to the front of the advancing lines.

Shells from rebel batteries broke over the heads of the Black Hats. One fell into the right companies of the Nineteenth Indiana, maiming or killing twelve men. A sharp fight rattled and clattered across the National Road when the Seventh Wisconsin came up against a strong Confederate force behind a stone wall. The Seventh cheered and charged, taking the wall and driving away the yelling Confederates.

The Second Wisconsin marched upward, muskets at the right shoulder shift. Ahead, men from Indiana chased swarms of rebel skirmishers and overran lightly defended fence lines.

James, at his place on the left flank of the Second Wisconsin and in front of the Baraboo Guards, who were the left company, watched as the Nineteenth Indiana halted. A long stone wall ran at right angles to the National Road and across the line of the Indiana advance. The stone wall erupted into a billowing storm of flame and smoke.

The Hoosiers faced left and marched, then halted and faced again to the front, making room for the Second Wisconsin to come forward between them and the road. The Second Wisconsin advanced and halted. The two Black Hat regiments faced the wall.

Colonel Bache marched to the front, motioning for the captains to dress their companies on the color guards.

James drew his sword and revolver, watching the colonel. The law clerk felt calm, controlled, confident in himself. He thought of Lucille. He closed his eyes for a moment and recalled the scent of her dark hair. He opened his eyes and brought his mind back to the slope of South Mountain in Maryland.

John strode back and forth in front of the Baraboo Guards. "Hold your fire until you're close to them," the carpenter told the men from Sauk County. "After you fire, don't stop to reload. When you get to the wall, go over it with your bayonets. Don't stop to help any wounded men. I'll be right there with you. You know what to do."

On the left the Nineteenth Indiana moved forward, shouting. The Confederates behind the wall fired into the Hoosiers. Men fell in the Indiana lines, but others from the rear ranks moved to take the place of their fallen comrades. The blue lines swept forward like waves, closing on the rebel force behind the wall.

"Charge!" Colonel Bache cried, waving his sword.

The Second Wisconsin shouted and ran up the slope of South Mountain.

Ethan ran, his eyes fixed on the point of his bayonet as the blade swept back and forth over grass and bracken. The merchant heard the zip and whine of bullets singing past his head when the rebels behind the north end of the wall rose and volleyed into the charging Wisconsin companies. Men fell beside him. He ran on, his lungs aching for breath, his legs throbbing. He saw only the thick white cloud of gunsmoke at the wall and the wavering point of his bayonet before him. Closer, he made out stabbing flame, men, movements behind the stones. An arm. A face. Ethan fired. The face shattered and fell from his sight. He ran full into the stone wall and bounced back from it. He was confused for a moment. Men in blue near him shouted and fired and tumbled over the stones, roaring in rage and fury and fear. Screeching men in butternut and gray moved in and out of Ethan's vision. The merchant climbed clumsily over the wall and watched the point of his bayonet slide into the straining throat of a rebel in brown rags. Ethan jerked his Springfield back and the gory blade came free. Gus ran in front of Ethan, swinging his musket by the muzzle like a wheat flail. A skull crunched and a man went down howling. Ethan heard himself shouting senseless sounds. A bayonet came at him from the smoke and confusion and drove into the loose canvas of his haversack. Inches from his own, Ethan saw the face, the open mouth, the straining eyes of the rebel who wielded the weapon. Ethan couldn't hold his balance. The point of his own bayonet scraped across the rebel's face. The man dropped his musket and grabbed at bleeding eyes. Ethan thrust his bayonet into the man's stomach and, putting a foot against the man's chest, withdrew it. The rebel dropped heavily to the trampled grass behind the stone wall.

"Form up!" James shouted at the captains.

"Baraboo Guards!" John shouted hoarsely.

"Get into line!" Carl roared, pushing men into their places.

"Forward!" Colonel Bache ordered, swinging his sword to point up the slope of South Mountain. The regimental color guards ran ahead, waving the flags back and forth.

Ethan panted, gulping in air. He looked around. The fight for the stone wall was over. The rebels had fled, falling back up the mountain to a new fence line. Mangled bodies and a few surly prisoners were all that remained.

The Baraboo Guards marched on, the men loading and capping their muskets as they climbed, some sucking on canteens. Ethan trotted to his place beside Gus, breathing heavily.

The Westerners climbed, pausing and forming to charge and take Confederate positions behind stone walls and rail fences and then move on. The sun dropped behind South Mountain.

Ethan saw ahead, silhouetted against the setting sun, the heads and arms and muskets of the Confederate line at the top of the ridge. Battle flags, black against the evening sky, waved, taunting the men from Wisconsin and Indiana to come on. Streaks of flame stabbed out from the lines. Men shrieked and fell. Ethan aimed and fired and moved on.

John formed the Baraboo Guards as the regiment took up its line below the top. "Cease firing!" he shouted. "Hold your fire! Save your ammunition!"

Ethan glared at the carpenter. He wanted to go on fighting, to go on killing. It was important to him to go on killing.

Gus grabbed him and shook him.

Ethan struggled against the blond.

"It's over!" Gus shouted.

Ethan looked at Gus, then up the hill where the Confederate line stood in the falling darkness. He shuddered. He breathed deeply, several times. He nodded.

"Load up," Gus told him.

Carl appeared. "How are you for cartridges?"

"The last one I've got is loaded," Gus told the tavern keeper.

"Ethan?"

The merchant felt in his cartridge box. He had three. He gave one to Gus.

"Olaf?"

"I'm out."

"Murphy?"

"One and it's loaded."

"Check the dead and wounded at your feet," Carl told them. "Take what they have. Reb cartridges will fit your Springfields. Now, listen to me, all of you. If they come down at us, stay and use your bayonets. Keep your formation. The nearest cover is forty yards down the slope and we'll never make it if we break and run."

Murphy put his cold pipe into his mouth. He had nothing to add. They were learning, they were, he observed to himself.

Full darkness came over South Mountain. Firing on the right and left of the Baraboo Guards died away. The men from Sauk County stood in line, leaning on the carbon-fouled muzzles of their muskets. They could hear soft voices of Georgia and Alabama officers in the rebel lines sixty yards away.

After midnight, men from the Second Corps came up to relieve the Black Hat Brigade. The Westerners walked slowly down the slope of the mountain, searching in the darkness for the bodies of injured or dead friends. This time their wounded wouldn't be left to the mercy of the Southerners.

The Second Wisconsin lost thirty men in the assault up South Mountain. The Baraboo Guards lost three. Preston Christensen was dead. Andy Shoate had been hit in the arm and would live if gangrene didn't set in after the surgeons sawed off the shattered bone above his elbow. Johnny Makepeace was gut-shot.

Gus and Wayne Roohr carried Johnny to the hospital tent, where the surgeons shook their heads over the student from Baraboo. Gut-shot meant hemorrhage and peritoneal poisoning, they said. They could do nothing.

Gus and Wayne carried Johnny back to Murphy's fire. Murphy gave Gus two bottles of whiskey for the boy.

"He shouldn't drink," Wayne cautioned. "Not with a stomach wound."

"Should he not, now?" the Irishman asked, lighting his pipe and walking into the night. He'd seen gut-shot men die before. He'd gain nothing from watching again.

Johnny bled into his stomach cavity and the poisons began their work. Gus sat with the boy through the night, giving him whiskey to sip, holding his shoulders when pain wracked his body. Johnny Makepeace died when the sun came up over Catoctin. The Baraboo Guards buried him on the lee side of a stone wall on South Mountain.

James joined the men at Murphy's fire that evening. He sat and sipped coffee from his tin cup. He wanted to be with the Baraboo Guards this night, not with the officers at headquarters.

Lieutenant Colonel Ford found James. He accepted a cup of Murphy's coffee and sat on the log beside the law clerk. "Your boys from Company K did all right, Major Peck," he said. "So did you. I know that Colonel Bache intends to mention you in his report."

James didn't want to talk. He didn't respond.

"So," the lieutenant colonel said, lighting a cigar with a brand from the Irishman's fire, "we aren't the Black Hat Brigade any more."

James inhaled the smoke from Lieutenant Colonel Ford's cigar.

"Care for one, Major Peck?"

James took the offered cigar and a light from the lieutenant colonel's brand. He inhaled the rich, bitter Havana smoke. He exhaled, glancing up into the faces of several of the Baraboo Guards who had moved in closer to the fire. The men from Sauk County were staring at Lieutenant Colonel Ford.

"Peck?" the officer whispered, looking up at the circle of grim men standing about him. "What is this?"

"Gus?" James asked.

"This man better back up some, Major Peck," the blond growled, leaning across the fire.

"We heard what Lieutenant Colonel Ford said, Major Peck," John said, stepping in front of Gus. "About us not being the Black Hat Brigade any more. I think he better explain that."

More men gathered around the fire, circling the lieutenant colonel.

"Well, now!" the officer said. "I didn't mean anything wrong, men. Believe me. Entirely the opposite, I assure you. Let me explain. You see, General McClellan and General Hooker watched our fight for Turner's Gap yesterday. They were impressed. One of them, I don't know which, said that men who would advance so steadily and with such determination under such heavy fire had to be made of iron. Someone overheard that. The name caught on. Now, the whole army is calling us the Iron Brigade."

"Iron Brigade!" Gus snorted. "Shit! I don't like it! It sounds like something that'll rust!"

"Well, now, young man," Lieutenant Colonel Ford said. "You can't very well choose the name your commanders call you."

"We damned well picked the name the Rebs call us, Mister!" Gus insisted. "God-damned Black Hats! That's what the Rebs call us! That's what we taught them to call us!"

"I see," the officer said. "Well, then, it'll have to be the Black Hats of the Iron Brigade, won't it?"

"Too much of a mouthful," Gus argued. "I'll have to think on this. I don't like it."

The men drifted away from Murphy's fire, discussing their new name.

"Ah," Lieutenant Colonel Ford exhaled. "You left a rather democratic company when you moved up to regiment, Peck."

"A very democratic company, sir," James concurred, enjoying his cigar. "But, sir, I haven't left the Baraboo Guards. They're the men I came to war with. I'm still one of them."

"That's hardly the proper attitude for an officer of field rank to hold, Major Peck!"

"I agree with you, sir," James said, drawing on the cigar. "Hardly the proper attitude at all."

45

South Mountain was the beginning of an even greater drama.

Counting on George McClellan's customary caution, Robert E. Lee divided his invading army into three segments. He sent James Longstreet north from South Mountain toward Hagerstown to continue the threat of invasion aimed at Pennsylvania. He sent Stonewall Jackson and Ambrose Hill south, back across the Potomac River, to take the Federal garrison at Harper's Ferry, a move which would open the Confederate supply line from the Valley of Virginia and bag for the rebels ten thousand Federal prisoners and great quantities of sorely needed guns, wagons and supplies. With the balance of his small force Lee thought to delay the pursuing Federal advance through Turner's Gap over South Mountain. The audacious Lee had not expected the Federal pursuit to be as rapid and harsh as it became. The day after South Mountain, Lee desperately recalled the scattered wings of his Army of Northern Virginia. He chose the quiet town of Sharpsburg, on Antietam Creek, as his point of concentration. The rebel commander would be fighting with his back to the broad Potomac River there, but that didn't seem to bother Lee. He'd not yet been beaten by an army commanded by a Federal general.

John Gibbon's regiments formed on the National Road and once again marched up South Mountain. Men from regiments camped along the road cheered and waved.

"Black Hats!"

"Hey! Iron Brigade!"

"You kicked some Reb ass!"

"Hey, Wisconsin!"

"Hey, Indiana!"

Confederate batteries in fields beyond the mountain opened on Gibbon's column as the Westerners came down the far slope and marched through the open country beyond. By evening the four regiments had worked through wood lots and ravines and were camped in the fields of a farm owned by the family Poffenberger north of Sharpsburg on the Hagerstown Turnpike.

James joined the Baraboo Guards at Murphy's fire.

"Stay for supper?" John asked. "The Irishman has a stew going."

"Sure," James replied. "The food at headquarters is terrible. They pick the officers for our good looks and the orderlies for the size of their horses. No one thought to pick someone who could cook."

"Wet your whistle?" John offered, taking his canteen from his shoulder.

"Thanks," James said, sipping whiskey from John's canteen.

"What's the plan?" John asked, taking a drink for himself.

"Walk down the pike a bit with me. I'll tell you."

The carpenter slung his canteen over his shoulder and fell into step with the law clerk.

"See that farm south of us?" James asked, pointing.

"I see it."

"The cornfield to the left of the pike? The woods to the right?"

"Yes."

"John," James said, stopping in the road, "at this minute that cornfield and those woods are part of the Confederate States of America."

"The Rebs are there?"

"So they tell me. We'll go down the turnpike in the morning, Gibbon's Brigade leading with the rest of the First Corps following. We'll be two regiments to each side of the pike. There's another corps coming in on our left and one coming up from the south. We out-number them, we out-gun them. We'll pin them against the Potomac River and the war will be over by night time."

The carpenter looked into the law clerk's face. "Do you believe that?" John asked. "That it'll be over by night time?"

"No."

"That cornfield is probably holding a Reb division, Major Peck. Those woods, they can be holding three. This isn't going to be easy." The carpenter took a sip of whiskey.

"Do you miss Baraboo, John?" James asked.

"I wish to God I was back there right now."

"This is September," James said, taking the carpenter's canteen and sipping. "After tomorrow, the fighting will wind down for the winter. You're an officer. Why don't you take some leave and go back to Baraboo for a while?"

"Major Peck," the carpenter said, "I'll think about that after I get the boys through that cornfield and those woods, come tomorrow morning."

46

On the early morning of September 17, 1862, fog settled into low places along Antietam Creek and in the hollows and openings of the rocky, wooded ridges and cleared fields east and north of Sharpsburg.

John Barks and Robert Wright stepped away from the gathering of officers in front of Colonel Bache's tent and returned to the Baraboo Guards, who sat at their fires finishing their breakfasts of beans and coffee.

"Company K!" Robert called. "Fall in!"

"On your feet!" Carl ordered, throwing the last of his coffee into Murphy's cooking fire and buckling his tin cup to the strap of his haversack.

Murphy piled his cooking gear neatly beside his fire and forgot it. It would be there when the company came back this way, if it did, or it would not. If not, there was more to be had.

The Baraboo Guards formed, the men from Sauk County loading and capping their Springfields and twisting bayonets onto the muzzles without orders. They knew the drill.

The Irishman handed Ethan and Gus a paper-wrapped parcel. "Twenty rounds over what you're carrying in your cartridge boxes," he told the brothers-in-law. "Tuck these into your trouser pockets. Use them first."

"What are you up to, Murphy?" Carl demanded.

"Extra cartridges, First Sergeant," the little man explained, offering a parcel to the tavern keeper.

"Where were you with extra cartridges the other night on South Mountain when we needed them?"

"The memory of that bad time, First Sergeant, is why you're being handed extra this foggy morning. Will you be taking them?"

Carl took them.

John Gibbon marched his Iron Brigade to the fields that had been selected the evening before, forming the regiments on the left and right of the Hagerstown Turnpike, facing south. The Second and Sixth Wisconsin were on the east of the pike. The Nineteenth Indiana and the Seventh Wisconsin were on the west.

The Baraboo Guards waited silently, standing close, touching elbows. Traces of morning fog lingered in the space between the front and rear ranks, mixing with light dust kicked up from the plowed earth by army shoes. Ethan could see only a few yards along the line of blue uniforms, black hats, musket barrels and bayonets. He glanced at Gus. The blond was staring south into the mist.

Willy Schoming cleared his throat nervously, breaking the silence.

The Irishman put his briar pipe into his mouth and scratched a sulphur match on his brass belt buckle. The men grinned at him.

"Murphy!" John hissed.

"I'll be lighting my pipe, Captain Barks," the little man spoke out. "You can then be telling the general commanding he has my permission to be starting the ball." Murphy held the match to the bowl of his pipe and puffed clouds of smoke. He dropped the flaming match to the furrowed earth at his feet.

On cue, Battery B opened from its position on the Hagerstown Turnpike. Crack! crack! crack! boom-boom-boom! Crack! crack! crack! boom-boom-boom!

The Baraboo Guards turned their attention from the Irishman to the action of the gunners on the pike.

Battery B's shells exploded down the road between the cornfield and the woods.

Colonel Bache shouted. The color sergeants ran to the front of the center companies, uncased the flags and stepped out into the fog-shrouded field. The four regiments moved south along both sides of the pike with loaded, bayoneted muskets over the shoulder.

The mist lifted as the sun rose. A light breeze scattered the dust raised by marching feet. Drums rattled. The Westerners advanced in step.

James saw ahead an orchard, a small farm. Two companies from the Sixth Wisconsin ran forward, skirmishers to snoop into any place that might give cover to a Confederate sharpshooter. They approached the farm. White smoke billowed from the house and barn. The skirmishers fired back, aiming for the doors and windows. One gun of Battery B swung to point at the farm and blasted solid shot into the buildings, shaking the structures. Butternut and gray figures tumbled out the doors and ran, bending low, for the cornfield.

Rebel batteries down the pike, out of sight, began to fire on the Federal advance, their missiles bursting in the air over the heads of the marching men. One shell whizzed into Company D of the Second Wisconsin, exploding, sending seven men stumbling and screaming and falling to earth. The Janesville Volunteers closed ranks on the center and continued the march.

John Gibbon halted the two regiments on the east side of the pike and sent the Nineteenth Indiana and the Seventh Wisconsin forward, west of the road, against a rail fence behind which was a skirmish line of shouting rebels. The two regiments charged, clearing the fence, sending the Confederates scampering for the woods to the south. Reforming, the brigade resumed its steady advance, centering on the cornfield to the east of the road and on the woods to the west.

Battery B kept pace with the infantry, moving forward on the pike, coming about to throw shells over the cornfield and the woods, then limbering up to move to a new position from which to come about and fire again.

James paced at the left front of the regiment, watching the northern border of the cornfield, where the stalks stood high, glistening, waving slightly, heavy with ripe ears. He breathed evenly. For a brief moment he thought of the sheriff of Sauk County, then of Lucille. He could write to her and tell her he'd found the answer to his question of courage. His thought was interrupted when he saw movement among the stalks of corn. Before he could shout a warning, a roar of musketry exploded outward from the front of the line of corn stalks at the advancing Black Hats. In the Wisconsin companies men shrieked and stumbled, dropping to the earth in two's and three's and sixes.

"Halt!" Colonel Bache ordered. The men stopped, wavering, stunned at the violence of the fire being poured at them. Captains and sergeants called reassurances. The men steadied, aligning on the flags. "Present!" Colonel Bache called. The line of Springfields swept down and leveled, pointing into the rows of standing corn.

"Fire!"

The Springfields roared across the yards of plowed earth. Stalks were scythed down and men fell with them, some rolling out from the standing corn into the cleared field. Hands and arms working ram rods showed above the tops of the stalks as the Confederates reloaded.

Gus winced at the fire that poured into the Baraboo Guards. The blond crouched, as if to protect himself from a storm of hail. He loaded and capped, pointing his musket into the field of corn. He didn't have to aim. The field was crowded with cursing butternut- and gray-clad men who fired round after round into the blue ranks, shouting as they did so. Gus felt the buck of his musket against his shoulder when he jerked the trigger. He reloaded, cringing when someone near him gagged and cried and fell to the ground.

Gus heard the roar of cannon fire close by. He looked up from capping his musket and saw what seemed to be huge flails sweep through the standing corn, whipping great swaths through the stalks, throwing corn and heads and arms and weapons into the air. Battery B was pouring volleys of canister into the cornfield from an angle on the pike.

James saw the right of the regiment start to move. "Forward!" he shouted, starting for the corn, firing his revolver into the confused, swarming mass of green stalks and gray and butternut uniforms.

The blue line ran ahead, the men bending low as they trotted forward, pausing only to fire. Inside the edges of the cornfield mangled bodies lay in disorder on the earth. Gus trod on one body that groaned and sagged beneath his feet. He fired, his muzzle blast sending pieces of stalks flying. A gray figure rose in front of him, coming up from the ground slowly, deliberately, eyes staring into Gus' eyes, mouth open. Gus couldn't hear whether the rebel was shouting or not. He ran the man through, jerking his bayonet free as he pushed past the screeching form. Standing stalks whipped at the blond's face, the sharp edges of the leaves cutting his cheeks.

He ran on, not thinking, not understanding, trying to work his ram rod while the stalks slapped and grabbed at his arms.

A butternut soldier came at Gus from the right, his musket hauled back to club the blond. Gus couldn't stop running. Olaf shouted and bayoneted the soldier, the farmhand's blade taking the Southerner in the throat. Gus screamed and ran, thumbing a percussion cap onto the nipple of his Springfield.

Ahead, Gus saw the far edge of the corn. Clearing the last of the stalks, he faced an open field. He paused, gasping for breath. Gray and butternut figures were running across the plowed ground, others crawling or staggering toward the far tree line. Dead and dying rebels lay on the earth where they had fallen.

The color sergeants of the Second Wisconsin ran from the corn and cheered, waving the flags for the men to rally on. "Form up!" James shouted, shoving men into line as they came out of the corn.

"Fall in on me!" John called, grabbing men without regard to company, hauling them into line, yelling for Robert Wright and Castle Newton to keep the Baraboo Guards together.

"Forward!" the captains shouted. The blue line resumed its advance. Forms rose from the earth as the Westerners came on, forms with muskets leveled or held by the barrels to use as clubs. Some of the rebels had hideous wounds and still they struggled to fight, to strike at the men in blue. Gus shot one bearded, ragged creature who sprang from the ground with a huge knife in one hand, the other hand hanging at the end of a broken and useless arm.

Ethan trotted beside Gus, capping his musket. The merchant looked south across the plowed field as smoke rose and drifted away. Ethan swallowed. He grabbed Gus and pointed south. He couldn't speak.

Orderly formations of Confederate infantry moved out from the far line of trees. As Ethan watched, more gray and butternut formations came forth. There can't be that many of them, he wanted to shout to Gus.

"Form up!" James cried. "Load!"

"Steady, now," Carl cautioned the men, walking the line behind the Baraboo Guards and the men from other companies who had formed on the men from Sauk County. "Steady, now," the tavern keeper chanted. "You know what to do. Stand steady."

The Confederate infantry formed across the plowed field clear of the trees. A cloud of skirmishers drifted toward the Federal line. Officers galloped and pointed. The rebel regiments started forward.

Ethan swallowed hard.

Gus swore, sucking at his canteen.

The horizon seemed filled with line after line of butternut and gray formations, men with flashing musket barrels and flaring bayonets and waving battle flags. Thousands of Southern legs stepped and paused, stepped and paused. The lines rolled forward, coming across the plowed earth, across the rich farm land of Maryland. Ethan was certain the marching regiments were centering their advance on the spot where he stood. He gripped his musket.

The Southern lines halted. The front ranks rippled as tiers of muskets swept level to the ground. Gus realized and grabbed Ethan, hauling his brother-in-law to the dirt. The Confederate lines volleyed and thousands of lead balls whizzed through the air and rattled among the few corn stalks still standing behind the Federals. Gus heard the thwack-thump of lead striking into living flesh. Men screeched and howled, tripping, kneeling, falling heavily. The Confederate regiments erupted into their chilling chorus and charged. The blond jumped to his feet and aimed into the oncoming formations. He fired, breathing hard and fast, his heart pounding.

Ethan stood beside Gus and aimed carefully as his brother-in-law shouted and screamed and fired.

Olaf grabbed Gus by the strap of his haversack and pulled him backwards. "Gus!" the farmhand cried. "We're going back!"

"Like hell!" Gus screamed. "Those sons of bitches!"

"Yea, Gus, sons of bitches. Come on, we're going."

Gus glared at the farmhand. Behind Olaf the blue line was falling back through the wrecked field of corn. Gus shuddered, calming. "All right," he told Olaf, "we're going."

The advancing Confederates saw the Federal retreat and wailed their keening yell at the men in blue. They continued to swarm forward.

Gus followed Ethan and Olaf through the corn. Bodies hidden beneath fallen stalks made walking treacherous. Gus saw a form with a black hat over its face. He kicked the hat away. Jack Black's chest was a mess of gristle and gore. The dark man's eyes were open to the clear sky, his teeth bared. Beside Jack, the Wright brothers lay, their hands touching as if one had tried to help the other. Robert's officer's coat was riddled and bloody. Willis had been shot cleanly through the forehead.

Beyond the corn Ethan, Gus and Olaf formed on a captain who waved the regiment's flag over his head. None of the color guards were left. The last had been shot in the retreat through the corn. Men lined on the captain, paying no attention to company organization. Gus tried to estimate the number. There were very few. He couldn't see Murphy. Reloading, he counted the cartridges in his box. He was thankful for the extra parcel Murphy had given him.

He heard shouting and cheering, the deep Northern roar, off to his right. The Nineteenth Indiana and the Seventh Wisconsin had changed front and were now charging across the turnpike and attacking the advancing Confederate flanks.

The captain with the flag waved it back and forth vigorously and raced into the blasted field of corn. The blue line east of the turnpike shouted and followed. Gus, Ethan and Olaf joined in, running and shouting with the rest.

The Confederate formations halted, volleyed, wavered. Battery B galloped ahead on the pike and unlimbered, commencing a rapid fire with double-loaded barrels into the rebel ranks. The Confederate force withered, broke and retreated across the plowed field toward the trees.

Gus heard more firing and shouting to his right. The man running beside him choked and fell. Gus turned to look across the pike. A new Confederate force marched from behind wooded hills there, this time on the far right flank of John Gibbon's four regiments. The Nineteenth Indiana and the Seventh Wisconsin broke off their charge and maneuvered to face the new threat.

The rebel regiments that had fallen back to the trees south of the cornfield saw the new attack diverting Federal strength and took heart, surging back across the plowed field wailing their wild yell.

Gus aimed and fired and saw the Confederate he had drawn bead on fall. He ignored men crying out and falling at his side. He loaded and fired, aiming each shot. He fired until the barrel of his Springfield fouled with grime and carbon. He threw the Springfield away and grabbed up a Confederate Enfield from the ground.

On the pike, Battery B poured canister into the rebel lines. Still the screaming men in gray and butternut came on, companies closing on the centers as men fell away.

Gus saw men in the rebel ranks pointing at him. Balls whizzed past him. He fired. There was no time to reload. He reversed the Enfield, its hot barrel burning his hands. He swung it up, determined to take two or three of them with every strike. "Sons of bitches!" he roared.

"Son of a bitch, y'own damn' self, Yank!" a butternut scarecrow with a ragged beard shouted from twenty yards away. The rebel raised his musket and aimed at Gus.

"God damn you!" Gus cried, throwing his Enfield and hitting the man next in the rebel rank. The scarecrow in butternut fired and missed.

"Yankee bastard!" the rebel screeched, running forward. Gus pulled back his fist and hit the men full on the chin. The rebel fell.

"Back!" James shouted. The law clerk saw the uselessness of standing before the mass of Confederate infantry in the open field. He ran along the line pulling at men. "Fall back!" His revolver was empty and his sword blade was coated with drying blood. "Olaf! Fall back!" James grabbed Gus by a strap and tugged. "Back, Gus!"

"Not this time!" the blond cried, digging cartridges from his box and throwing them at the Southerners before him.

James cracked Gus across the temple with his revolver. Olaf caught the blond when he sagged. The Federal line broke and ran, Confederate musketry cutting men down as they stumbled through what remained of the corn.

On the pike, Battery B limbered up to gallop to safety with the retreating Black Hats. The team of one gun was down, lying in a tangle of horse hooves and harness straps. Volunteers from the Sixth Wisconsin ran for the gun at the same time a company of rebels spotted the stranded piece. The rebels raced the men from Wisconsin for it. The men from the Sixth got there first, raising the trail and turning the piece, pushing the spokes of the wheels, running it up the pike and out of harm's way. The rebels wailed their yell and fired several shots at the struggling Black Hats and the gun.

James watched in horror as one of the men from the Sixth Wisconsin stumbled, fingers at his throat, blood spurting. Preston Faircloth did a disjointed step and a half as more lead balls struck into him, dancing like a marionette with its strings cut. He dropped to the dirt of the Hagerstown Turnpike. Two men ran back from the group at the gun and knelt over the boy. James saw them shake their heads. They jumped and ran to join their comrades, bullets striking up dust balls at their feet.

The survivors of John Gibbon's Iron Brigade walked north, stumbling from fatigue, shock and wounds, small groups of dirty, thirsty, men. The Confederate formations did not pursue, but taunted the Westerners with their wavering yell and some long range musket shots.

A tremendous roar of gunfire from the south swept over the valley of Antietam Creek as a fresh corps of the Army of the Potomac came into the battle, too late to help the battered Black Hats and the other brigades of Hooker's First Corps.

Ethan sat on the earth in the yard of the Poffenberger farm, his head on his arms, his arms on his knees. Around the merchant the Baraboo Guards gathered, stricken by the shock that comes after battle when the juices are used up and the nerves are still stretched beyond all normal limits. Ethan felt numb.

"Are you all right?" Gus asked, sitting beside his brother-in-law.

"Yes," Ethan whispered. "I'm thirsty."

Gus fell back on the trampled earth. He stared into the sky. He could sleep for a week. He touched his temple. "My head hurts."

"It should," Ethan told him.

"I don't know if I'm grateful for Peck knocking me on the head or mad about it."

"You're grateful. You were taking on Jackson's corps all by yourself."

Carl stopped next to the brothers-in-law. He carried his roll book. "Ethan," he said, making a mark on the page. "Gus. Have either of you seen the Irishman?"

Ethan shook his head.

"He was beside me when we went into the corn the first time," Gus told Carl. "After the first volley, it got mixed up in there."

"No one has seen him," Carl told them, pushing his black hat back on his balding head. The tavern keeper looked down the pike at men who straggled north. "He must be out there."

Ethan got to his feet and loaded his Springfield.

"What are you thinking of doing?" Carl asked.

"I'll see if I can find him."

"Not with all that fighting going on down there. I don't want to lose any more men than I have. Either of you seen Olaf?"

"He's here," Gus said, standing and capping a Springfield he'd taken from the field. "He went to get water."

"The Wright brothers?"

"Dead, Carl," Gus said. "I saw them. Jack Black, too."

Carl made marks in his book. "Willy Schoming?"

Gus shook his head. Ethan shrugged.

"Wayne Roohr?"

"He's here," Ethan said. "He's back with the surgeons. Grazed ankle. It isn't serious."

"Henry Calef?"

Ethan shook his head.

"What's the butcher's bill?" Gus asked.

"I'm missing twenty men," Carl said bitterly. "I know twelve are dead. Some of the rest may straggle in. I hope to God it doesn't turn out worse."

Olaf returned and handed Ethan and Gus their filled canteens.

"We can't find the Irishman," Ethan said. "We're going to look for him." Olaf unslung his musket.

"There's no need for everyone to go," Carl cautioned.

"For me, he'd come," Olaf stated. "For him, I'll go."

"You're right," Carl agreed. He tucked the roll book into his coat pocket and capped the nipple of his Springfield.

The four walked slowly south, looking at blue-clad forms on the ground. The carpet of bodies lay thick as they approached the northern border of what had been the cornfield.

"Spread out," Carl told them. "We can cover more ground that way. Olaf, over there with Ethan. Gus, in between Olaf and me. Keep your eyes open. Some of these Rebs may be laying for us."

Gus moved slowly into the corn, looking carefully among the broken stalks and the bodies at his feet. A blue uniform moved. Gus knelt and rolled the man gently. "Willy! Willy Schoming!" Gus whispered harshly. "It's me! Gus!"

"That you, Gus?" Willy gasped, squinting. "I can't see real good."

"It's me. Where're you hurt?"

"Stomach, Gus," the brewer gagged. He was holding his stomach in with bloody hands. "Ah, Gus, it hurts. A drink. Give me a drink of water."

"Shouldn't drink with a stomach wound, Willy."

"Hell, Gus, what can it do to me? I saw Johnny Makepeace go at South Mountain the other day. I'm going to die. It's all right. Please, Gus, give me a drink of water."

The blond took Willy's head in his arms and uncorked his canteen. He dripped water into Willy's mouth through lips that were cracked and blistered. "Easy, now," Gus told him. "We'll take you back with us."

"I'm not going to make it. Hey, Gus, we run them bastards, didn't we?"

"We run them, Willy. Couple of times."

"You'll tell my father for me, Gus? You'll tell him we run them?"

"I'll tell him."

Willy started to say something. The brewer shuddered in Gus' arms and then lay still. Gus left the brewer from Prairie du Sac on the soil of Maryland. Gus glanced at the carpet of bodies around where he knelt. Blue and butternut, they'd all come a long way to die in a cornfield in Maryland.

Gus covered Willy's bearded face with his black hat. He sipped water from his canteen, listening to the aftersound of battle, the persistent moaning. He got to his feet and followed the others.

"Here!" Olaf shouted, waving his musket back and forth.

Gus and Ethan ran for the farmhand. Carl stood several yards off, covering the three with his Springfield. Parties of Federals and Confederates worked around the field warily eyeing each other as they searched for fallen friends.

Murphy lay on his back, his arms at his sides. Gus knelt. He saw no wound. The little man could have been sleeping. "Murphy!" he shouted.

"He looks drunk," Olaf observed.

Gus pulled the Irishman's black hat away and exposed a bump on the little man's forehead where a musket butt had struck. Ethan poured water from his canteen over Murphy's face. The Irishman opened his eyes. His eyes rolled. "Aaagh!" he moaned. "Ah, God! Ah, Gus, Ethan. What's happened to me?"

The brothers-in-law tugged Murphy to a sitting position.

"Awk!" Murphy choked.

Ethan patted the Irishman's arms and legs. "Nothing seems broken."

"Ah, lad, it's not my arms and legs I'm worrying about," Murphy sighed. "It's my head and my private parts."

"You have a bump on your head the size of a small melon," the merchant reported, sitting back on the ground. "As for your private parts, they're your concern."

"Ah, my God," the Irishman moaned, touching his forehead carefully. "What was it hit me?"

"Probably a cannon ball," Ethan said, standing. "I'll wager it bounced off when it hit. Can you stand?"

The little man put up a hand. Ethan tugged him to his feet.

"Whooo!" Murphy warned. "Here, give me something to hang onto for a mite." He wavered, clutching Olaf's arm. "Hooo! My head feels like I'm coming off a three-week's drunk. Ah, now, that's better, seeing the world settle into where it's supposed to be."

"Take him back, Olaf," Carl directed. "The three of us will see if any more of our men are out here."

The farmhand led the staggering Irishman north after finding him a musket on the field.

"Sergeant Elsasser!" a voice called.

"Where?" the tavern keeper asked.

"Here! Over here! It's me, Henry Calef."

"Where are you hurt, Henry," Ethan asked, kneeling beside him.

"My arm. My leg. I tried to walk, Ethan. I couldn't. I couldn't crawl. I prayed. I knew you'd come for me, I knew you wouldn't leave me to be taken in by the Rebs."

Henry's right arm showed through the ripped cloth of his blue coat, a swollen and discolored mess of flesh and shattered, exposed bone. Henry's left leg was bent outward unnaturally.

"We'll rig a litter for you," Gus told the boy. He took off his coat and slid the barrels of two muskets into the sleeves. Ethan did the same with his coat, pulling the butts through his sleeves. The brothers-in-law slung their own muskets across their backs and gently lifted Henry onto the litter. The boy screeched when they moved him as jagged bone grated against bone and flesh.

"Ready?" Gus asked, taking the muzzles of the muskets in his hands.

Ethan nodded, taking the butts. The two lifted the litter between them.

"Stand in your tracks, Yanks!" a Southerner's voice called.

The brothers-in-law looked to their left. Three Confederates stood several yards away in the debris of bodies and corn stalks. All the rebels had muskets in their hands.

Carl aimed his Springfield at the tallest of the rebels. "We're taking one of our boys in," he told them

"No more, you ain't," the tall one countered. "You're going to help us carry off some of our men. Best lower that Springfield, Sergeant."

Ethan stood helplessly, watching the Confederates. The merchant wouldn't drop his end of Henry's litter. He'd be dead before he could get his musket unslung. He looked at Gus. The blond, holding his end of the litter, shrugged.

"Our men mean as much to us as yours do to you, Sergeant," the tall Confederate told Carl. "That boy in the litter, he's going to die. Let him be. Help us get one of ours back to our surgeons and y'all help save a life. Either way, you're going back with us. We're taking you in."

"Ethan, Gus," the tavern keeper said slowly, his Springfield steady on the tall rebel. "Get along. I'll let these Rebs decide which of them is going to make the first move. That's the one I'm going to kill. I've been to Richmond once, Reb. I don't care to return. So, which one of you will it be?"

"And, won't we be taking care of the other two?" Murphy called out from where he and Olaf had circled round and come up on the flank of the three Confederates.

"You lose, Reb," Carl told the tall Southerner. "Back away. We'll keep you covered until you're out of range. Go on, now."

"Ambrose?" one of them asked.

"We'll back away," the tall one said. "You put up one hell of a fight, Yank. You're them God-damned Black Hats!"

"We are," Carl told him. "Iron Brigade."

"Look like flesh and bone up close, Yank."

"Who are you, Reb?" Gus wanted to know.

"Stonewall Brigade, and damn' proud of it!"

"We've met before," Carl told him.

"Probably meet again. We're walking off, Yank, this time."

"Be doing it ever so slowly!" the Irishman advised.

Carl, Olaf and the Irishman covered the Confederates. Gus and Ethan struggled with their litter, making their way carefully through the field of fallen men. They carried Henry to a field hospital in a barn east of the Hagerstown Turnpike.

A surgeon's assistant met the brothers-in-law in the muddy, manured yard. They set the litter on the ground. Henry's eyes were wide with fright and pain. The surgeon's assistant knelt and cut away the farmhand's sleeve with scissors, exposing Henry's arm. "This arm will have to come off," he decided. "There isn't enough for the surgeons to try to save. I don't know about that leg. Pick him up and bring him right in."

Ethan and Gus lifted the litter and followed the assistant. Gus gagged inside the terrible place. There were eight animal stalls. Eight tables were set up, one to the stall. Teams of surgeons worked on writhing, screaming beings on the tables. Orderlies struggled to hold contorting bodies down, gripping shoulders and arms and legs. The place smelled of animal dung, of chloroform and urine and blood and perspiration and whatever fear and agony smelled like. Ethan and Gus carried Henry past a table where a sweating surgeon sawed back and forth on a thigh bone with a short, bright blade that was coated with blood and gristle and fat.

"Bring that man here!" a surgeon shouted, pointing to a table in the last stall. The table and the surgeon's apron were soaked with blood. An orderly sloshed a pail of water onto the gory table. Strong arms took Henry from the litter and spread him on the wet boards. The men around the table ignored Henry's shrieks of pain and terror. One surgeon slit the farmhand's trousers. The flesh of Henry's leg was bruised, swollen, cut through with bone fragments.

Ethan and Gus stood at the foot of the table and watched, horrified.

A second surgeon slapped a wooden dowel between Henry's teeth, across the boy's jaws, tying it in place with a leather thong.

An assistant dropped a bandage onto Henry's face and dripped chloroform from a tin can into the fabric. Before the substance could ease Henry's feelings or fears, the two surgeons were slicing into the flesh of his leg, cutting away wide strips from around the exposed fragments of bone. A third surgeon grappled to tie off spurting blood vessels with silk thread.

"Jesus, Ethan!" Gus gasped. "Get me out of here!"

"Yes!" one of the surgeons shouted at Ethan. "Get him out of here! This is no place for you!" Glaring at the brothers-in-law, the surgeon put his scalpel between his teeth to free his hands for their work on the muscles of Henry's leg.

Gus staggered from the barn, following Ethan.

In the manure and dirt of the barn yard hundreds of men lay on litters or on the hoof-scarred earth, their faces shocked, frightened, dulled. In their eyes was bewilderment, a lack of comprehension, an avoidance of what had been done to them. They stared up at Ethan and Gus.

Gus stepped to the side of the barn and vomited.

47

For two days the armies watched each other across torn and littered farm fields and wood lots that bore the grisly harvest of thousands of men and hundreds of horses. No truce was asked to bring in the wounded, who lay suffering between the lines, or to bury the dead, who were beginning to decompose.

Then Lee withdrew his Army of Northern Virginia across the Potomac River and left the field to McClellan and the Army of the Potomac.

September 17, 1862, would be known as the bloodiest single day of battle ever to take place on the American continent. As the smoke drifted away and the guns cooled, counting the losses began. John Gibbon's Iron Brigade had lost half its men. The Second Wisconsin lost a hundred men. Carl reported to John that only twenty-nine of the hundred Baraboo Guards who had mustered in Sauk County sixteen months before remained.

The Federals buried the dead, their own and those of their foe, tended the wounded of both sides, and burned the butchered horses.

Murphy slowly recovered from his knock on the head and resumed the care and feeding of the men of the mess. Henry Calef died the morning after the surgeons amputated his shattered arm and broken leg. James wrote to Lucille and told her of Preston's death.

President Abraham Lincoln visited the army. The men dutifully cheered him as he rode past their formations in a carriage. They broke ranks and roared passionately when Little Mac, following the commander-in-chief's carriage, rode past on his spirited black charger.

James was depressed and sick at heart. Preston Faircloth and many other men he knew and cared for had died in the fighting and in the aftermath in barbaric surgeries set up in filthy barns, in school houses, in churches. They'd died of sickness brought on by wounds and exhaustion. Seventeen thousand men, Federal and Confederate, fell at Antietam, and when the fighting ended on that single, terrible day, the armies parted, paused, stared at each other across the horror of what they'd done and then began the process of regrouping, resupplying, reequipping and getting ready to fight each other again.

A week after the battle, James walked through a cold, driving rain to the camp of the Baraboo Guards. Murphy had rigged a tarpaulin between two trees to shelter his cookery and his pots. He wore an officer's cape over his skinny shoulders.

"Any chance of a cup of coffee?" James begged as he approached.

"Major Peck, now, is it?" the Irishman called back, waving the law clerk toward the warmth of his fire and the shelter of his tarpaulin. "Coffee, and maybe a drop of the spirits to sweeten it."

"What smells so good?" James asked, sitting on a cracker box and shaking rain water from his black hat.

"That'll be the oven. Full it is, to the brim, with stout army beans and a bit of pork, simmering and bubbling away and waiting for the call of reveille. The lads'll be having that for their breakfast come the morning."

"Breakfast?" James asked, obviously disappointed.

"Ah, you scavenger! If you can keep it a secret, I'll place a few spoons of it on a plate for you. Seeing as how you're weighted down so with the burden of command, there at regimental headquarters."

"I'm weighted down with the terrible food at regimental headquarters. Where are the men?"

"Standing picket duty along the river bank in the rain. Except for Gus. That one has found a little Dunkard girl who's interested in learning all there is to know of the flora and fauna of Wisconsin from Professor Gaard. That, and in the loft of her daddy's barn! Here, lad, give me your tin cup for the coffee. If you'll fish about in that pail of water to your right, you'll catch a lovely bottle bass swimming just below the surface."

James rolled his cuff and put his hand into the pail. He found the bottle. He pulled the cork and poured a good measure of whiskey into his coffee. "How's your head?"

"Mending. Taking its own sweet time about it, but mending."

"Have you seen a surgeon?"

"Ach! I'll not have the likes of them probing and poking at my head! They get into their habit of amputating anything that's ailing. I wasn't letting the surgeons near you, lad, when you were recovering from the wound you took for me after First Bull Run. I'll not let them near me now. I'll be bright as brass in a week."

"I heard you and some of the men almost got taken in by some Rebs after the battle."

"Aye. Gus is telling me there were three of them. I was counting six. I been seeing in doubles since I got this crack on the head. I'm telling you, Major Peck, I'm wanting to get myself in front of a large-breasted woman, I am, before I'm cured of this. I'm wondering what it'll be like to come face to face with four great teats. Here, lad, put yourself on the outside of this plate of beans. There's hard tack in the box on the stool."

"Thanks, Murphy."

"It's nothing, lad," the little man said, settling himself on a cracker box and lighting his briar pipe. "Now, tell me," he said, "how is himself, the young major?"

"I'm all right. I lived through the battle. I was lucky. We all were, we who lived. They say our army lost over ten thousand men, killed and wounded, the Confederates almost that many."

"Ah, now, lad, what's tens and thousands? Numbers won't mean a thing to the man who's getting himself killed. It won't matter to him if he's one of one or one of ten thousand. He's but himself when he's up to dying. We left good lads in that field of corn, Major. The numbers mean nothing."

James chewed the Irishman's beans, staring into the cooking fire. "I can't get it out of my head," he said after a while. "There'll be more cornfields and more killing. This battle didn't accomplish a thing. We're here. Lee and the Confederates are across the river. We'll fight again. For what?"

"Here!" the little man barked. "Take yourself a long pull on that bottle and get your mind off it! War is killing. It's nothing more, nothing less. If you didn't understand that when you signed on, you should've learned it by now."

James sipped coffee. He didn't want more whiskey. "How do you do it, Murphy?" he asked.

"How do I do what?"

"How do you get through the days and the dangers and the battles and the things we have to do and stay calm and settled in your mind? Doesn't this get to you?"

"Major Peck, lad," the Irishman said, striking a match to relight his pipe. "Living is one of the difficult things a man is born to do. Living in any time or place is never easy. Living is something that has to be done where a man is, wherever that might be. War is one place to be living, a place with a lot of killing in it. The killing will end some day. The living will go on for those left. I've been in many places worse than being here with the lads of the Baraboo Guards of the Sauk County militia. I'll admit to you not many of them were as bad that field of corn. But, lad, for now, for this night, that field of corn is over and done with. It's a part of the past, best forgotten. If there's to be another in one of our tomorrows, let it come upon us in its own good time. I'd not worry myself on toward it. It's best to live one day at a time with the pleasures and the troubles it brings. Drink whiskey when you have it, lad, and water when you don't. Do you get what I'm saying to you?"

James stared into the fire. He didn't understand all the little man had said. Murphy did tend to talk around all four sides of a subject at times. "Are the men all right?"

"Sure, they are. Carl, that grim man, is fine. Ethan and Olaf, they came through the fighting unscathed. And that great beast, Gus, isn't he fine also who's even now trying to be planting the seeds of his loins into the little Dunkard girl in the loft of her daddy's barn."

"Captain Barks and Lieutenant Newton?"

"Behaving as the officers and gentlemen they've been named to be."

"There'll be another lieutenancy open. To replace Bob Wright."

"Will we be needing the promotion, Major? Soon there'll be more lieutenants and sergeants in the Baraboo Guards than we'll have privates for them to be shouting at."

"I saw the returns. The Baraboo Guards muster twenty-nine men."

"Twenty-nine good men, lad!"

"Thanks for the coffee and beans, Murphy. And the wisdom."

James wrapped his poncho around his shoulders and walked into the falling rain. His shoes sloshed in the mud. Water ran from the brim of his black hat. He thought of the men of the Baraboo Guards who stood picket duty on the banks of the Potomac River. They'd be wet and cold when they came in. Murphy would have coffee and whiskey for them.

48

"Yes! Ah! Yes! It's good! Good!" Ilsa gasped and cried into Gus' ear. Her thick thighs wrapped around Gus' hips. Her heels and hands drummed on his back and legs. Gus thrust, driving himself into her, feeling his own passion build. He buried his face in her blond hair. The cold night air on his bare bottom contrasted with the hot, moist tightness that held him. He exploded and that drove Ilsa further along. She moaned and arched her back, crying out, gasping, "Ah! Ah! Good! Yes, good! Yes, Gus! Yes! Good, good, Gus, good!"

Gus collapsed on her, panting into the straw. Ilsa worked her hips beneath him, coaxing, pleading, seeking more of him. "Gus? Was it good? More?"

"Oh, Christ, Ilsa," Gus sighed. "No more. I have no more. No more for Ilsa."

"Was it good, Gus? Did you like it?"

"It was good. I liked it."

"Soon? More, soon, Gus?"

"Maybe," Gus half-promised. He rolled onto his back. Straw pricked his buttocks and the backs of his legs. His trousers were at his ankles and he was too pleasantly exhausted to reach down and pull them up. Ilsa threw a large, soft thigh over his groin and curled into the comfort of his arms. Her white breasts pressed Gus's chest. Her sex felt hot and wet against his hip. Ilsa wrapped her fingers around his soft, tender penis, holding him in her large hand. "More, Gus?"

"No more, Ilsa."

"You're nice, Gus."

Ilsa yawned and snuggled close into his arms. In minutes she slept, her breath pleasant on his breast. Without waking her, Gus reached out onto the straw and found the bottle of whiskey he'd brought along. He worked the cork with his teeth and spat it away into the shadows of the loft. He drank.

Gus wondered how long the brigade would stay in the camps at Sharpsburg. They could go into winter quarters here. He could be with Ilsa every night until the thaw. He wondered if he could survive being with Ilsa every night until the thaw.

Sated and slightly drunk, Gus dozed. Rain drummed on the roof of the barn.

Gus woke.

Ilsa still slept warm in his arms. Something had wakened him. His bladder was full. He began to work his way from the girl without waking her. Then, he froze.

There were sounds below in the barn. The sounds had wakened him, not his bladder. They weren't the sounds of animals in the stalls. They were the sounds of men. Gus reached out, carefully, for his Springfield. The musket was several yards beyond his fingers. Straw prickled his bare legs. His trousers will still down around his ankles. Gus listened, his heart beating, trying to hear over the sound of the falling rain.

Voices. Quiet voices, men talking in whispers.

Gus thought of the embarrassment of being caught by a provost patrol with his trousers down. He strained to hear. Footsteps. Movement.

"Captain?"

"Here."

"Everybody make it out?"

"We're all here."

Southern voices, soft, hushed. Gus tightened, his spasm causing Ilsa to turn in his arms. He prayed she wouldn't wake or call out in her sleep. He couldn't tell how many men were below in the barn.

"Captain, Paulie's bleeding!"

"Bad?"

"It's bad, Captain!"

"Cletus? Tommy? You able to walk?"

"Sure as hell going to try, Captain. Tommy, here, he's getting feverish."

A man below fell into a bout of hacking, rasping coughs. Ilsa stirred in Gus' arms.

"You don't sound good, Tommy."

"I'd sound worse in some Yankee prison!"

"Captain!" one of the voices hissed. "Paulie, he's bleeding something fierce! Where that Yankee butcher sawed off his arm!"

"Can you help him?"

"We're trying!"

"Do what you can for him. The rest of you, it's a couple of hours before first light. We've got to work our way up the river. We'll find a place to cross somewhere and try to meet up with our cavalry on the other side. Be quiet as you go. Yankee pickets are going to be thick as flies on horse shit along the river bank."

"Are we going to make it, Captain?"

"We're not going to spend the rest of the war in a Yankee prison camp. We're going to make it."

"Paulie ain't going to make it."

"How so?"

"He died, Captain."

"Damn! Damn! We're going to have to leave him."

"Take his cap, Cletus. His daddy in Albemarle County'll want it. Some damned Black Hat's going to pay for this! Some damned Black Hat!"

"Put Paulie in the corner. Close his eyes. The rest of you, follow me. Keep quiet. It's a long walk back to Virginia."

Gus listened. For several minutes there were no sounds from below, only the soft rattle of rain on the roof. He was sure they were wounded Confederate prisoners escaping from one of the many prison hospitals near Sharpsburg. Gus worked himself loose from Ilsa, careful not to wake her. He pulled his trousers up and found his Springfield in the straw. He climbed down the ladder, looking into the shadows of the stock room. At the door he peered out into the darkness and the falling rain. All he could make out were some footprints in the mud near the threshold.

In a corner he found Paulie, his one arm crossed over his chest. Gus leaned his Springfield against the wall and picked up the emaciated form, carrying the boy out into the night. He'd hide the corpse in a thicket. It wouldn't do for Ilsa to wake and find a decomposing corpse in her father's barn.

Paulie smelled terribly. His bare feet swung as Gus carried him. His ragged uniform, caked and matted with blood and filth, covered a gaunt body that Gus felt had to weigh less than a hundred pounds. When Gus placed him on the ground in a growth of elderberry bushes Paulie looked for all the world like a lost boy, caught in the woods, sleeping out the storm.

Gus wondered at the ragged, barefoot, hairy Confederates who fought and died while wailing their terrifying rebel yell. Wounded and captured, Paulie and his comrades had broken out of a prison hospital to face the dangers of an enemy army and a swollen river standing between them and their home state, where they would rearm and refit and come back to fight again. Gus looked down at Paulie. He'd heard one voice in the barn swear vengeance on the Black Hats. Gus wondered how many of John Gibbon's Black Hats Paulie and his comrades had already brought to vengeance before this rainy night beside a small barn in Maryland.

49

MADISON—October, 1862.

James commanded the Second Wisconsin while Colonel Bache and Lieutenant Colonel Ford were on leave for three weeks. When they returned he requested and was granted a month's leave to return to Wisconsin.

He tried to talk John Barks into coming with him. The carpenter pleaded the demands of the Baraboo Guards. James remembered their conversation on the Hagerstown Turnpike before the battle. He wondered if the carpenter really did fear not being able to return to the army after a time in Baraboo.

James rode to Frederick on a borrowed cavalry horse. He took the cars to Baltimore, where he checked into a hotel and had a bath. He sat up late talking and drinking with officers in the bar until the porter had to help him up the stairs to his room. He caught the morning train to Pittsburgh and was in Madison three days later. He'd telegraphed ahead to tell Lucille he was coming.

The Madison depot was crowded with soldiers and civilians when James stepped down from the first car of the Milwaukee train.

A fresh regiment was boarding other cars, bound for the war in the west, where Federal armies under a general named Grant were cutting the Confederacy in half, steadily reclaiming the Mississippi Valley. James watched the men, youngsters with bright faces and new uniforms.

In contrast, at the far end of the platform another train was unloading wounded men from the Eighth, Fourteenth, Seventeenth and Eighteenth

Regiments, broken and bloodied remnants of Wisconsin farmers and townsmen brought back from the heavy fighting at Iuka and Corinth in Mississippi. They were bound, James learned, for the general hospital at Camp Randall.

"James!" a voice called. Nathaniel Bachmann strode toward him in a splendid uniform of perfectly tailored blue wool. "I couldn't believe my eyes when I saw you!" the officer declared. "Tell me, how are you?"

"I'm fine, Major Bachmann," James said coldly, noticing the gold leaves on the former captain's shoulder straps.

"I see you, too, wear the leaves of majority," Bachmann smiled, nodding at the tarnished straps on the shoulders of the law clerk's stained, worn coat. "Where one has led, the other followed! Right?"

James started to step around the major. He had no wish to spend time talking with the man.

"Yes!" Bachmann continued. "The Second Wisconsin of the famous Iron Brigade! How I wish my duties would have permitted me to return to my fierce warriors!"

"Return?" James blurted, incredulous.

"Now, James," Bachmann confided. "Wisconsin has a new governor, a new administration. No need to carry the burdens of the past into these new times, is there? We each have our peccadillos to live with or forget. Forget, James, is by far the most advantageous course. I want to buy you a drink," Bachmann continued, taking the law clerk by the arm and steering him toward the depot bar. "There's a matter you and I must discuss before you leave here."

James allowed himself to be drawn along, wondering what the two could possibly have to discuss. Bachmann ordered whiskey for both.

"Well, now," Bachmann said. "Tell me. How are my Baraboo Guards?"

James bridled at the possessive term.

"With you serving at regiment, who commands the company, James?"

"Captain Barks commands the twenty-nine men who remain, Major," James said curtly, taking a sip from his glass. The affrontery of the man beside him amazed the law clerk.

"Barks? Barks? A carpenter, as I recall. Some kind of tradesman."

"He was a sergeant."

"Yes. Twenty-nine, you said? Well, one expects losses, doesn't one? Hard fighting makes for hard losses. Axiom of war. Tell me, how is Sheriff Zimmerman?"

"Adolph Zimmerman is dead, Major Bachmann. At Groveton, in August."

"So? Rather old and heavy for infantry work, wasn't he? Too bad. But, James, you've prospered. From law clerk to major of a famous fighting regiment in, what? A year and a half? Brought you into the military way under my direct tutelage, young man. Ability to spot and foster talent, James. Mark of the officer."

"You taught me a lot, Major," James agreed pointedly.

"Good sign, that, James. Like to see gratitude in a subordinate."

"I believe we hold equal rank, Major Bachmann."

"What? Oh, of course. I was referring to before. You know, James, I want us to maintain our close relationship. We have a future. You do realize that."

"No, I don't."

"Why, James! With the base of power that I'm developing here in Madison while you accumulate laurels on the field of battle! Think of it! We'll lay claim to high reward when the war is over. I have plans, James. Even now, in my position as commander of Camp Randall, I'm making contacts and developing political resources that will stand us in good stead later."

"I don't think so, Major Bachmann," James said, finishing his drink and turning to leave the bar.

"James, think! A hundred thousand veterans will return to Wisconsin after the war, willing to follow their former commanders into whatever financial or political direction they are led!"

"You don't seem to understand, Major Bachmann," James said quietly. "I despise you."

"Oh, personal animosity is no reason for two capable entrepreneurs not to join forces for their mutual benefit. Now that I have access to the Faircloth name and fortune as a financial base, James, just think of what we can do!"

James stopped.

"What? You seem startled? Has Lucille not written to you? I'm astounded! Certainly she's written to tell you that she and I . . ."

James swung his right fist into Bachmann's face, hitting the major solidly and knocking him to the floor of the bar room. The law clerk reached for his holstered revolver. Men at the bar grabbed him, holding his arms.

Bachmann looked up at James from the floor, wiping a trickle of blood from his lips. "I suggest, Major Peck," he said as he was helped to his feet, "that you have a talk with your former inamorata." Bachmann jerked his blue coat into place. "A short talk. I intend to see Miss Faircloth later his evening, myself."

James struggled against the arms that held him.

"Major Bachmann," a captain offered. "Will you prefer charges?"

"Of course not. Major Peck merely became distraught. We'll speak later," he told the law clerk. He turned and left the bar, several officers following him.

The men holding James released him. The bartender offered him a fresh glass of whiskey. James drank it in one gulp and walked quickly from the bar toward the Faircloth home.

He was in shock. What Bachmann had inferred couldn't be true, his mind insisted. The thought of her in Bachmann's arms made him want to retch.

She stepped into his sight from the gazebo in the Faircloth garden.

He stopped on the board walk.

"James?" she asked cautiously. "James?"

He didn't answer.

"You've spoken with Nathaniel Bachmann," she confirmed, lowering her gaze.

Lucille walked to the kitchen doorway. She left the door open for him to follow. Inside, she stood before the dry sink, arms at her side, head up, waiting.

"He said . . ." James blurted.

Lucille put her hands to her face.

"Tell me!" he shouted.

She turned to face him.

"Tell me," he begged.

"You went back to the army," she began, looking away from him. "Father was dead. Preston was away. I needed someone."

"Bachmann?"

She nodded.

"Have you taken him to your bed?" James demanded, his voice cold.

She nodded.

"There are a thousand new men every month at Camp Randall you could have taken into your bed!" he shouted, pointing in the direction of the camp. "Why Bachmann? Why him? Why?"

"It happened," she whispered.

"I won't impose on you any more," he told Lucille. "Major Bachmann suggested I have a short talk with you. This has been short enough. Goodbye."

"Don't leave!" she pleaded, turning to him, frightened, guilty, confused.

"I've no reason to stay."

"You've every reason to stay!" she sobbed, running to him. She threw her arms around his shoulders. James stood unmoving, his hands at his sides. "Help me, James!" she begged. "Before God, I need you! Don't, oh, please, don't leave me!"

"Your caller will be here soon, 'Cille," James said, pulling her arms from him. "I won't share your presence with him. I tried to draw my revolver on him when he told me. Men at the depot bar prevented that. If I see him here, there'll be no one to stop me. I'll kill him."

"He's not worth that!" she cried, shuddering. "I'm not worth that!"

"You'll have to let me decide that."

"I said that once to you, James," she reminded him desperately. "When you came back from Bull Run, you said you didn't deserve my love. I asked you to let me decide that. James, if I helped you at all then, for God's sake, help me now!"

"In these few minutes before he comes?"

Lucille thought frantically. She couldn't let this man go. She grabbed at an idea. "Devil's Lake! We'll go to Devil's Lake! Now! Immediately! We'll be alone there, James! We'll have time! Give me, give us, that time!"

James looked at her. She wasn't the object of his anger. His anger was directed at Nathaniel Bachmann, who'd used her as he'd used him. He reached out and took her hand.

50

MARYLAND—October, 1862.

The regiments of Gibbon's Iron Brigade formed and marched to a meadow east of Sharpsburg. The Second, Sixth and Seventh Wisconsin and the Nineteenth Indiana numbered in all less than nine hundred men, less than a quarter of their original four thousand volunteers.

The Westerners lived out of doors, each with a single ragged uniform. They marched from one place to another, in sun or rain, sleet or hail. They were subject to the vagaries of quartermaster issue when they drew replacements for clothing worn out or lost. As a result, the four regiments appeared to be an assemblage of tramps, honest men but poor. Their one consistent item of dress was the black hat.

Drums sounded across the meadow. Infantry marched behind a cavalcade of officers that included General Gibbon and the colonels of the four regiments.

"What do you think?" Gus asked Ethan.

"It's a new division."

"That'll be fresh fish for Johnny Gibbon's Iron Brigade," Murphy advised.

"Why do you say that?" Ethan asked.

"Be looking at them. New uniforms. White faces. That'll be a new regiment."

"That can't be a regiment," Ethan argued. "There're more of them than there are of us and we're four regiments."

"Look for yourselves," the little man said, nodding toward the silk flags the approaching color guards carried. "Twenty-fourth Michigan. That'll be their name, embroidered on their banners for you and all the world to see."

"Seems like a lot of men to be one regiment," Gus observed.

"What do you think they're doing here?" Ethan asked.

"From the parading and the posing that's going on," Murphy said, "I'm thinking they'll be joining our brigade."

"It's more like our brigade is joining them," Gus offered.

"Twenty-fourth Michigan," Wayne Roohr said, squinting his left eyelid. "I read about them. They're bounty men. They enlisted for bounty money."

"What do you mean, bounty money?" Gus asked the stage clerk.

"States are paying men bounty money to enlist. Something about avoiding what they call the draft."

"They got paid money to enlist?" Olaf asked.

"So I read."

"Well, hell," Gus declared. "We won't have that in the Iron Brigade! Look at them. They're virgins! They don't even have holes in the knees of their pants. They're wearing the kepi. They can keep it. They haven't earned the black hat! No black hats for them!"

The Baraboo Guards heard Gus and set up the chant. "No black hats!"

The chant ran along the ranks of John Gibbon's brigade. "No black hats!"

"No black hats!"

The Michiganders had been proud when told they were to reinforce the renowned but decimated Iron Brigade. It hurt them to be jeered by the veterans of the famous fighting outfit. They didn't understand that the men of Gibbon's four regiments were selective about their hard-won fame and its emblem, the black Hardee hat. They would have to prove themselves before they could wear it.

"One way to look at it," Murphy decided. "We're twice the strength we were this morning."

"Bounty men!" Gus objected.

"Meat for the cannons, Gus. Bait for Reb bayonets. It won't be mattering where they came from or what it was brought them here. If they'll fight, we'll make room for them."

"Can we count on bounty men to fight?"

"Doesn't that remain to be seen, now?" the Irishman replied.

51

WISCONSIN—October, 1862.

James dipped the oars into the calm water of Devil's Lake and pulled. The boat slid forward. Trees on the shore at the base of the rock bluffs were bright with their fall colors. Dryness in the air promised cold weather.

"You mustn't see him, James," Lucille said from the stern.

He looked at her without answering.

"He's a danger to you."

"I'm more a danger to Bachmann than he is to me."

"I beg you to think carefully about him," Lucille replied. Her voice was somewhat hesitant. The course of the rest of her life would be decided by what was said in the remaining hours of the afternoon. She had to be careful. "He has power in Madison, James. If you harm him you'll face charges. Satisfaction for what has happened will only cause you more harm. He's not worth that. I'm not worth that."

"How far has this gone?" he asked, facing her.

Lucille stared at the far bluffs. She wanted to control what was about to happen, to manage it, to make it work her way. She remembered the Sunday she and James had picnicked on the shore of Lake Mendota, the day they'd given themselves to each other. She'd barely known James that day, yet she recalled sensing that the man was honest about himself, his life. Untested, but honest. She could never refer to Nathaniel Bachmann as untested but honest. There was no choice but to be honest now. Were she to manage to keep James with deception, she wouldn't be able to live with him from day to day wondering how long her deception would last against his basic honesty. Were she to give in to deception, she realized, she should seek out Nathaniel Bachmann and enter into a life of that and little else.

"I want you to tell me how far it's gone," James said.

"He helped me with some financial matters. It went well beyond that as you know. I thought I could control it."

James leaned on the oars and studied her. "Is he involved in your finances?"

"He's made investments. He wanted me to give him my power of attorney."

"Did you?"

"I didn't."

"He has his mind set on controlling the holdings of your father's estate, 'Cille. The man is determined to have money and power. I think you're rather incidental to that."

"I was a fool," she admitted.

She was a fool to take him into her bed, James thought. Yet, she was able to look at him and admit it.

"I won't see him again," Lucille promised.

"Will you be able to avoid seeing him?" James demanded. "Bachmann is a man who seems able to make things like that happen."

Lucille lowered her eyes. Nathaniel Bachmann had used her and taken advantage of her but he had not made her take him to her bed. That had been her own doing. She wanted to believe the officer was the cause of her problems. She knew better.

"He's the kind of man who will take advantage of every opening he's given, 'Cille. You gave him openings and he took advantage of them. So did I and he took advantage of me."

She studied the far shore of Devil's Lake, dreading the question she had to ask. "Have I driven you from me?"

James pulled on the oars. He didn't respond.

Lucille closed her eyes. Her heart was hammering. She couldn't stand the silence. "Will you return to the Army in Virginia?"

He thought for a long moment. "I will."

Lucille's mind worked desperately. "Preston bequeathed his share of my father's estate to me. If we marry you'll control the Faircloth holdings."

James pulled harder on the oars.

"God forgive me, James, for saying it that way!" Lucille gasped. "I didn't mean to offer you the price of Nathaniel Bachmann's interest in me! I meant that would block him from any further interest in our lives. I've been trying to be so honest with you."

"I've thought of that," he said.

"Can you ever trust me again?" she begged.

He didn't know the answer. He rowed the boat silently.

52

MARYLAND—November, 1862.

An autumn storm raged over the Federal camps at Sharpsburg. Sheets of rain lashed through the trees, whipping and twisting bare branches and dead leaves. Lightning flared in the evening sky. Thunder rolled and crashed like so much heavy artillery. Wind tore tents loose and rain drenched the huddled occupants. Men gave over the futile task of resetting tent pegs in mud and wrapped themselves in blankets and coats, sitting back to back for warmth and support. Wind pelted them and water ran from their hats and onto their soaked uniforms.

Murphy scuttled about trying to defend his tarpaulined cookery from the ravages of the storm until, with a great snapping and ripping and flapping, the canvas broke away and was carried off into the darkness.

The little man cursed. He shook his head in disgust. There were times when a man was but a man in the face of the force and the power of nature and this October night was one of those times. Murphy wrapped himself in an overcoat that was several times too large for his frame and settled himself into the mud with his back against a tree, a bottle of whiskey in his hands. He'd make himself as comfortable as his miserable condition would permit and he'd wait out the storm.

Ethan, Gus and Olaf ran through the downpour to the Irishman's cookery, coming in from picket duty on the river. The three were soaked through and cold.

"Jesus Christ, Murphy!" Gus shouted, looking at the ravaged site. "We're wet and starving and you're sitting on your ass under a tree getting drunk! Where the hell's the coffee?"

Murphy jerked his head savagely in the direction of the drowned fire pit.

"This is a hell of a note!" Gus declared. "You got anything for us to eat?"

"Aye!" the little man snapped, glaring at Gus from under the dripping brim of his black hat. "I've leaves for you to eat! Twigs and bark from the trees! All the mud you're wanting and rain water to wash it down!"

"Hell," Gus replied, glancing at Ethan and Olaf. He was shaken by the Irishman's tone. "I just asked."

"Ah, you're all too soft for hard soldiering!" Murphy barked. "It's my own fault for spoiling the bunch of you. Pull up a puddle and sit by a tree. It'll be a long night, Private Gaard, and I'll not be listening to you whine through it!"

The three hadn't seen the little man like this.

"It's just as wet and cold for Johnny Reb," Olaf shouted.

"That helps me?" Gus asked, settling his hips into the mud and leaning against Murphy's tree. "You going to drink that bottle all by yourself?"

Murphy glared at him.

Gus dropped the line of questioning.

Ethan settled down, squirming in the mud.

"You bound up?" Gus asked, smarting under the Irishman's rebuke and wondering what had caused the little man to turn on his mess mates.

"I'm bound up like a bottle with a cork," Ethan complained. "I only get loose when we're marching or fighting. We haven't done any of that for a while."

"Good for you the Baraboo Guards don't run," Olaf giggled. "We'd leave you with your trousers down and your bum showing to Johnny Reb."

"I appreciate your concern," the merchant growled.

"Did you hear them across the river tonight?" Gus asked, tipping the brim of his black hat to spill out water.

"They said Little Mac got fired," Olaf told Murphy.

"How can they know if we haven't heard ?" Ethan asked. "How do they do that?"

"How?" Gus barked. "How does Johnny Reb do most of what he does? His ass sticks out the back of his pants. His elbows are out of the sleeves. He goes barefoot, eats green corn and ain't worth a damn. Then, he out-marches us, out-fights us, takes the shoes from our dead and by next morning he's thirty miles off raising hell at the other end of the line."

"It's sounding to me, Private Gaard," Murphy accused bitterly, "that you're taking on an admiration for the creature."

Gus shook his head. He wouldn't let Murphy provoke him. "We'll whip him one of these days."

"Aye," Murphy said, changing his manner. "Some time or other. All we'll be needing is to borrow some of his generals for a while."

"Man for man, we can handle the Rebs," Ethan told him.

"The Baraboo Guards are the best there is," Olaf assured the Irishman.

"Sure, aren't we the best!" Murphy argued. "But, my bloody Viking, be telling me! Would even our Baraboo Guards be good if we were sent charging over meadow and farm with our arses sticking out the back of our pants and our backbones rubbing against our belt buckles?"

"All right, Murphy!" Gus exploded, finally provoked into anger at the little man. "They're tough! They're good! Do you want to join the Confederate army?"

"Not on your life!"

"They aren't much different from us when we're talking across the picket lines," Ethan said.

"Sure, and they're lovely lads," Murphy mumbled.

"It's too bad Little Mac got fired," Olaf suggested, shivering.

"Hell, why not?" Gus asked, tipping his hat again to drain water from the brim. "They fire them all, sooner or later. McDowell. McClellan the first time. Pope. McClellan the second time. Hell, they've got a lot of generals."

"Little Mac was good," Olaf said.

"He wasn't good!" Murphy insisted. "His job was the taking of Richmond or the taking of the rebel army in the field. We buried many a good lad while he was taking his time doing neither!"

"Lee buried a lot of men, too," Olaf countered.

"Aye, he did. Well, we'll see what bumbler they're sending down to us next. Whoever, he'll have us marching over the face of the earth until we stumble into another fight for the rebels to win. After that, they'll send down another. So it will go, on and on."

Ethan looked at Murphy. The Irishman's head was down, his face hidden in the collar of his over-sized overcoat. The little man's voice had broken. "Is that it?" Ethan asked.

Murphy didn't answer.

"Is that it? Thinking the war will go on and on?"

Murphy sniffled inside the collar. Ethan realized the little man was sobbing. The merchant looked at his brother-in-law.

"It's all right," Gus said gently.

"Ah-ah," Murphy shuddered, wiping eyes that were filled tears. "Ah, I've got to be asking all of you your forgiveness," he mumbled, his voice unsteady.

"Nothing to forgive," Gus said. "Not for telling us how you feel about this God-damned war going on forever."

"It's not that," Murphy sniffled. "It was pouring it out on you, my mates."

"That's all right," Gus assured the little man. "Hell, we're friends. That's what counts."

"It counts, you're saying? With me drinking the last of the whiskey in the larder and saving none for you, it counts?"

53

MADISON—November, 1862.

It was well into afternoon.

The judge's library was lit by the soft light of an oil lamp. Outside, shadows gathered as the autumn evening came on.

Lucille sat on the sofa, her hands in her lap.

James sat behind the desk.

Neither of them had spoken for a while.

She'd been the one who'd believed in him, he thought. She'd been the one who gave him the reason to find his way back from his fears. She'd been the one who betrayed their love and given herself to Bachmann. He wasn't sure in his soul how he felt toward her. There was affection. There was dismay. But he'd made a decision. She was his wife.

Lucille looked at her husband. He'd not rejected her. She held the thought in her mind. He'd not forgiven her.

They sat in silence.

When after a time they did speak she told him she wouldn't be lonely. She'd work in widows' and children's relief and make and maintain contact with the families of the Baraboo Guards. She'd write to him every week. She'd use the banker he recommended for any further advice on their investments. She didn't mention Nathaniel Bachmann.

He'd be careful, he promised her. He'd dress warm and stay dry. He'd drink less and stay close to the Baraboo Guards.

The clock struck nine. It was time for him to go.

She helped him put on his gear, handing him the haversack filled with good things to eat on the journey. Strapped to the haversack was the brightly burnished tin cup.

James held her by the elbows, slightly away from him, memorizing her face.

"I want you to come back to me," she whispered.

"I will."

"I won't walk to the depot with you."

"No. It's late."

"I won't say good-bye."

He drew her close and kissed her, holding her, driving away the thoughts of her in Bachmann's arms. He turned and took his black hat from the table.

Lucille watched him go. She shuddered when the door closed, then fell to the sofa, crying. She'd managed to keep him in her life. She felt that Nathaniel Bachmann was gone from both their lives. All she had to worry about now, she realized, were tens of thousands of Confederate soldiers who were intent on killing the man she loved.

54

VIRGINIA—Winter, 1862-1863.

George McClellan was replaced at army command by Ambrose Burnside. The Baraboo Guards wondered whether Burnside was going to fight all winter.

The Army of the Potomac marched south from Sharpsburg to its old camps at Falmouth across the Rappahannock River from Fredericksburg. Robert E. Lee and his ragged Army of Northern Virginia veterans dug in on the high hills behind Fredericksburg.

Burnside sent the Federals across the Rappahannock on December 13, 1862, and hurled the brigades, corps by corps, into slaughter at the base of those fortified hills.

The Baraboo Guards crossed the Rappahannock downstream from the blood bath at Fredericksburg and went in with the Iron Brigade against their old enemy, Stonewall Jackson. While the fight downstream from Fredericksburg wasn't as bloody as the fight for the hills beyond the town, it was battle enough for the men of the Twenty-fourth Michigan to prove to the Westerners that bounty men could fight. The Michiganders earned their black hats.

Burnside next sent the Army of the Potomac on a sweep up the Rappahannock to try to turn Lee's left flank. That march bogged down in bottomless mud.

The Baraboo Guards straggled back to Falmouth and went into camp at Belle Plain for what remained of the winter of 1862-63.

Late in January, with the regularity that followed each Federal defeat, Ambrose Burnside was replaced by Joseph Hooker. When the Baraboo Guards heard of the change in command they barely paused in their work of daubing mud on the sides of their winter hovels. As they'd done the previous winter, the men from Sauk County spent their time trying to stay warm, dry, and busy with drilling, wood cutting, and picket duty along the north bank of the Rappahannock.

In mid-January, James received the letter from Lucille telling him of her pregnancy. Their child would be born, as best she and Doctor Yeager could figure it, early in July.

On a morning in February, Ethan and Gus manned a picket post on the Rappahannock. They stood several yards back from the bank in a thicket, well hidden from sharpshooters on the far side. Ethan leaned against the trunk of a large tree, his Springfield in the crook of his left arm. Gus rummaged in his haversack and found two hardtack crackers and a piece of cooked pork that needed some work. He used his pocket knife to scrape away the spoil and made a sandwich. He bit and chewed slowly, sipping cold tea and whiskey from his canteen.

Ethan rubbed his abdomen. He'd give anything for a good dump. The merchant worked on the thought. One didn't foul a picket post. He'd move several yards away, where dead berry bushes gave good cover. His bowels hadn't moved in three days and he had the headache. Even the thought of taking a good dump comforted him. Maybe, he wondered, he could worry the thought into the act. There was nothing to keep him occupied watching the river. Nothing happened during the winter days and the Confederate pickets on the other side were quiet, out of sight. It wouldn't take long. Gus could watch their piece of river for the short time he'd be gone.

Ethan hadn't had this problem back in Baraboo. He'd been as regular as the sun, up in the morning and out to the privy for a full job. Even on those

Wisconsin winter mornings when the wooden seat was coated with ice crystals he'd had no problem. He'd wiggle around once or twice to warm the frozen boards and then relax and let go. He considered himself a gentleman. He'd go out before Lily to warm the seat for her. He knew men in Baraboo who drew the line at that, sending their wives and all their children out first on the coldest mornings to warm the seat for them. That wasn't Ethan's way. It seemed to be working. "Gus!" he whispered.

The blond looked at him, his jaws working on pork and hardtack.

"Be back in a minute!"

Gus nodded.

Ethan picked his way cautiously through the undergrowth, watching where he placed his feet. A rustled leaf or a snapped twig could bring a deadly minie ball from across the river.

The merchant studied what he could see of the far bank. He'd be out of sight where he stood. He rested his Springfield on the earth pointing toward the Confederate bank of the Rappahannock. He unbuttoned his galluses and dropped his trousers, squatting, making himself comfortable. Oh, Lord, he sighed, that did feel good. It'd been a long time. Ethan's headache left him. He reached to his right for a handful of leaves.

"Keep your hand close, Yank!" a voice called from across the river. Ethan froze.

"Keep squatting and keep your hands in sight!"

The merchant searched frantically through the bushes and undergrowth of the far bank, wondering where the rebel could be. He raised his eyes. In the fork of a large tree, thirty yards away and barely visible in his butternut rags, a Confederate sharpshooter grinned down at Ethan over the barrel of a musket that was pointed at his head. Without thinking Ethan let his right hand slide across the earth toward his own musket.

"Let that Springfield lay, Yank!"

Ethan started to tremble. He wanted to pull up his trousers. He wondered if he could dive for the bushes on his left and pray the rebel's shot would miss. That was a fool's hope, he decided.

"What do you think, Huey?" the ragged rebel called to someone. "Ought we let this Yank crap all over Virginia like he's doing?"

"Hell, no!" a voice giggled. "Calvin, you go on and wipe that Yank's ass with a minie ball!"

Ethan started to sweat.

"My front sight is resting on that scar over your left eye, Reb!" Gus' gravelly voice called.

The man in the fork of the tree paled and squirmed. Ethan could clearly make out the scar on his tanned face.

"Now, you Yanks!" the rebel cautioned. "We're just funning!"

"I've got him covered, Ethan," Gus said. "Get your galluses hauled up."

Ethan scrambled to pull himself together. He threw himself to the ground and grabbed his musket, cocking the hammer.

"Easy now, Yanks!" the man in the fork of the tree called. "No sense starting the war up here and now!"

"You'd best get the hell out of that tree, Reb!" Gus shouted.

The rebel dropped from sight like a falling stone.

Ethan heard him hit the ground and roll into the underbrush. The merchant decided not to try to make it back to the picket post. He could cover the river from where he lay.

"Hey, Yanks!" one of the rebels called after a while.

"What?" Gus answered.

"Y'all them fucking Black Hats?"

"We sure as hell are!"

"Hey! Black Hats! Want some tobacco?"

"We've got tobacco."

"This is good stuff. Virginia leaf."

"What do you want for it, Reb?" Ethan asked.

"Whiskey. Coffee. Sugar. Hell, Yank, it don't matter. You got it, we be needing it. We ain't been out raiding your supply depots for a while."

"I don't have anything on me, Reb," Ethan admitted.

"Y'all be on picket duty here about midnight?"

"Probably."

"Bring coffee and sugar with you. We'll trade tobacco and some Richmond newspapers. How's that?"

"We'll think on it," Gus responded.

"Hey, Yank! Tell that friend of yours who was taking a crap to slip that Springfield to half-cock, will you?"

Ethan held the hammer and eased the trigger back. He let the hammer slide forward to the safe position. "Half-cock!" he confirmed.

"No sense wasting a bullet when you're going to need all you got next time you try to cross the Rappahannock."

"Plenty more where these came from, Reb," Gus advised.

"Hey, Half-cock!"

"What?" Ethan answered, not caring for the sobriquet.

"You bring some coffee and sugar with you tonight, too? Hear?"

"Psst! Calvin!" the other rebel hissed. "Officers coming! Keep out of sight, Yanks! Whistle a couple bars of some song along about midnight. We'll be here."

Ethan and Gus sought out Murphy after they were relieved. "Rebs across the river want to trade with us," Gus told the Irishman, pouring coffee from the pot. "What do you think?"

"We'll want to make sure they aren't contemplating trading you a minie ball for your immortal souls, that's what I think!"

"One of them had the drop on me this morning," Ethan told the little man. "He could have shot me if that's what they're after. I think they're all right."

The Irishman scratched his chin. "There's trading going on, one side with the other," he considered. "So I've been hearing. What could they have that we'd want?"

"They said they'd trade some tobacco and some Richmond newspapers."

"Aye. That's about all they'll be having. That and some trousers out at the knees. Well, let me be thinking on this. Tobacco, now, I could be bartering off to the suttlers if it's good leaf. Richmond newspapers, I could be offering them as souvenirs. We'll see what comes of the first night's commerce. I'll be making up a small box of some coffee and sugar, some preserves from the suttler, a small bottle of spirits. We'll be seeing."

"How are we going to get it over to them and their stuff back to us?" Gus wanted to know. "I'm not swimming the Rappahannock in February, for Christ's sake!"

"We won't be having you swim the river, lad, and we won't be trusting your new Rebel friends too far, too soon. I'll find a box that's good and tight. We'll launch it well up-stream from where they'll be expecting, working it down and across on the current at the end of a line. The one at our end of the line will be out of their sight, should there be treachery in their minds. We'll be retrieving it the same way. And, just to make certain, we'll have Olaf and Wayne and Peter in the bushes with their Springfields."

"Sounds good to me," Gus judged.

Ethan nodded.

The first night's trade went well. Calvin and his pal Huey sent over ten pounds of good Virginia leaf, six recent Richmond newspapers and a handful of Confederate uniform buttons.

Murphy found a ready market in the camps for the tobacco and the newspapers. There were promises of a continuing market if he could provide quality souvenirs.

The little man talked with Ethan and Gus. Confederate infantry seldom had more than their fierce courage and the butternut rags they wore. The three pondered what they could get Calvin and Huey to furnish them from the other side of the Rappahannock.

Ethan worked on the problem for several hours. He took this as a personal challenge, for he was the merchant among them. He came up with an answer. "Bowie knives."

"Bowie knives!" Gus scorned.

"Bowie knives. Every Confederate I've seen had a bowie knife the size of a cavalry saber hanging from his belt. We'll trade Calvin and Huey for bowie knives."

"Oh, shit, Ethan!" Gus objected. "Every man in the Army of the Potomac has a better knife! What would any of them want with an old Reb knife that's probably made from two pieces of board and a ground-down chunk of wagon spring?"

"I was thinking of bowie knives with CSA carved into the grip on one side and maybe the number of one of the Stonewall Brigade regiments on the other. I think those would trade."

Gus shook his head.

The Irishman considered the blond. "Now, the lad might be onto something."

"I think I am," Ethan insisted. "We'll say they were taken from live Rebs."

"Taken in trade?" Gus argued.

"We won't say that. We'll just say they are genuine Reb bowie knives taken from live Rebs. Every staff officer and headquarters clerk in the Army of the Potomac will want to have one. Maybe two, so they can send one back to the folks at home. People want things like that."

"Shit!" Gus snorted. "If we do this, half of Lee's army is going to be busy making genuine Reb bowie knives in the coming weeks! There's going to be one hell of a shortage of wagon spring leaves on their side of the river."

"It doesn't matter if they make them up to trade with us," Ethan insisted. "I tell you, there can be profit in this. What else do they have to offer?"

"Not much," Gus agreed.

"We'll talk with Calvin and Huey tonight."

"Hee!" the Irishman cackled. "Ah, the simple beauty of it! It's the staff officers and the headquarters clerks who're having access to the pressed tongue, the canned oysters, the peaches in brandy and the lobster paste our poor larder has been missing." The little man gave Ethan an elbow in the ribs. "Don't you have the most devious mind, you rascal!"

Calvin and Huey thought the idea excellent. The following night they sent over in the box twenty-four crude, brand-new genuine Reb bowie knives with CSA carved into one side of the rough wooden grips. Half the load had 5TH VA INF carved into the other side. Half had 27 VIR VOLS. Murphy traded well and the members of the mess traded for delicacies that they shared with their partners across the river.

No one in the Army of the Potomac questioned the right of the men from the Iron Brigade to have available for trade genuine bowie knives taken from live rebels. In the following weeks there were more knives traded in the Federal camps along the Rappahannock than ever there were rebel prisoners taken by the Iron Brigade, with or without bowie knives on their belts.

James brought Lieutenant Colonel Ford to the mess for supper one evening. The three Federal partners of the trading consortium had all they could do to keep straight faces while they complimented Lieutenant Colonel Ford on the fierce knife he wore on his revolver belt. One grip was carved CSA. The other was carved 33RD VA INF.

A month after Ethan's idea was put into practice Calvin and Huey and their regiment were replaced by a Louisiana battalion that shot first. The bowie knife enterprise ended, as did the supply of good food for the men of Murphy's mess.

55

In the spring of 1863, as his predecessors had done, "Fighting Joe" Hooker went after the Confederate army that protected Richmond and kept the rebellion alive. Hooker put together a series of complicated plans that involved triple movements across the Rappahannock River. His plans were perfectly executed. Once over the river, the three Federal columns plunged into an area of second-growth woodland known as the Wilderness. Hooker successfully brought his three columns together at a clearing in the Wilderness called Chancellorsville. That was as far as Hooker's perfectly executed plans held together.

Robert E. Lee took the initiative by throwing his rebel divisions against Hooker's larger force. The Confederates fought the Federals to a standstill. In the dusk and darkness of the second day at Chancellorsville Stonewall Jackson's corps came screaming out of the trees and brush on Hooker's far left flank and rolled up the Federal line like a carpet. Only darkness and the most desperate fighting prevented the rout and slaughter of the Federal army.

The Baraboo Guards missed the heavy fighting of the five days of Chancellorsville, coming onto the field on the fourth day to hold a line of rifle pits while the rest of the Federal army began its retreat across the fords of the Rappahannock.

Hooker's Chancellorsville campaign cost the Federals seventeen thousand casualties. It accomplished nothing.

On the field at Chancellorsville the Confederates buried the dead and tended the wounded of both sides, twelve thousand of their own in addition to the thousands of Federal wounded left behind in the retreat.

The Southerners were stunned by the cost of Chancellorsville, for among the dead was Thomas Jonathan "Stonewall" Jackson, gunned down by a volley of musketry fired in error by some of his own men.

Rain fell on the retreating Federal columns. Ethan pulled one foot clear of the deep mud while carefully settling the other foot into the muck ahead. His black hat was soaked through and water ran from its high crown to his collar. His blanket roll hung wet and heavy on one shoulder and his Springfield weighed down the other. Ethan had the solids again.

Lightning flared ahead, flashing over the road, illuminating the long column of men trudging in the rain, heads down, shoulders bent, musket barrels aslant.

"Why the hell'd we leave Belle Plain?" Gus mumbled. "We're just going back there a hell of a lot wetter than when we left!"

"We left Belle Plain to fight Lee," John said, walking at the side of the column, his officer's sword tucked up under his arm. The carpenter was wet and chilled.

"We didn't give him much of a fight," Gus lamented. "We seldom do. Damn! I lost my shoe!"

"Find it?" Ethan asked, taking Gus's musket.

"Yeah. Damned mud!"

James walked behind Colonel Bache and Lieutenant Colonel Ford at the head of the Second Wisconsin's column. Even with a rubber poncho around his shoulders, rain worked into his collar and made its way down his back. The chill didn't matter. James had a letter from Lucille describing her pregnancy and expressing her love for him. He dreamed of being in Madison in the summer when their child would be born.

He didn't think of Nathaniel Bachmann.

56

PENNSYLVANIA—June and July, 1863.

Robert E. Lee did not give the Army of the Potomac time to rest and recover from the defeat at Chancellorsville.

Early in June the Confederate commander pulled his forces back across the Rappahannock. The Baraboo Guards concluded that the death of their old enemy Stonewall Jackson had shaken the Confederate command and

that Lee was taking his gray and butternut legions back to the entrenchments of Richmond. That would shorten Lee's supply lines and give him
a fixed base from which to maneuver and fight. McClellan had thrown
the Army of the Potomac against the Richmond entrenchments to no avail
in 1862. To the Baraboo Guards, Richmond seemed the safest place for
Lee to go.

But rather than giving over the offensive and falling back to Richmond,
Lee marched his army north. On Lee's last raid the Army of the Potomac
had barely stopped his Army of Northern Virginia at Antietam. The men
from Sauk County figured there'd be hard fighting before the summer of
1863 was done.

Toward the middle of June the Federal camps on the Rappahannock
came to life. As McClellan had done in 1862 when Lee went north, Hooker
led the Army of the Potomac in pursuit of Lee's hard-marching veterans.

The first day on the road the Baraboo Guards marched twenty miles in
heat and dust. The men from Sauk County tramped footsore and weary
through stations and villages they'd visited a year before—Warrenton,
Catlett's Station, Bristoe Station, Centreville. They bivouacked that night in
sight of Henry Hill, where they'd first gone into battle.

Gus dropped to the ground when the company broke ranks. "Oh, God,
Ethan," the blond prayed. "I hurt. I need a drink. I need a woman."

Murphy lay face down in the weeds, panting and wheezing.

Ethan sat heavily, his head on his knees, his blue uniform covered with
a silting of road dust, his perspiring face splotched and red. He looked at
the Irishman. "Are you all right, Murphy?"

The little man nodded, his pointed face creased with dust and sweat.
"Aye," he coughed. "You're seeing the symptoms of a man dying for his
country. 'Tis nothing to be concerning yourself about."

"Damned Irish!" Olaf panted from where he lay in the weeds. "We'll
bury you in a whiskey keg!"

"You're all heart," Murphy sighed, rolling onto his back, "you bastard
Viking!"

The marching continued. The fifth day, the Baraboo Guards splashed
across the fords of the Potomac River at Edwards Ferry and climbed the far
bank into Maryland. The last day in June they crossed the Pennsylvania line
and went into camp at Marsh Creek with the rest of the First Corps.

James sat with them after supper. If Lucille were correct in her figuring
she would be a mother and he a father in the coming days. With the army
on the march the news James awaited would have to come by mail. It could
be weeks before he learned how she'd come through the ordeal of delivery
and whether they were the parents of a son or a daughter.

James sat a little away from Murphy's fire, sipping coffee and whiskey from his tin cup and listening to the twenty Baraboo Guards who had survived their two years with the army.

They were hardened, these survivors, by ten battles and thousands of miles of dirt roads. They were leaner and tougher than they ever had been. Their enthusiasm was long gone, replaced by a dogged persistence. Their pleasures were simple—a night's sleep, a dry blanket, a cup of hot coffee, a plate of beans and the time to eat them.

They'd stripped down to the basics of the soldier on campaign. Gone were the heavy knapsacks. Anything worth carrying got tucked into the ends of the rolled blanket. The little shelter tents had long since been thrown into a roadside ditch. They'd proved handy in camp but heavy on the march. The black hat, a short infantry jacket that had replaced the long frock coat, worn trousers with deep pockets, shoes, haversack and canteen and the precious tin cup, musket and bayonet and cartridge box, these made up the equipage of the soldier who marched on dirt roads and fought in open fields.

The Baraboo Guards were on their feet at three o'clock on the morning of July 1, 1863. Murphy had hardtack and coffee for them and Carl had them in ranks when Colonel Bache called the regiment to attention. They were on the road from Marsh Creek by three-thirty.

The Second Brigade had the head of the corps column on this day's march, Indiana and New York men under the command of the Sixth Wisconsin's former colonel, Lysander Cutler. A Maine battery followed the Second Brigade. The Iron Brigade marched in the dust of the Maine gunners.

Robert E. Lee and seventy thousand Confederate veterans were off and about somewhere to the north and west in Pennsylvania. George Meade, who had replaced Joseph Hooker on the march, led a hundred thousand Federals, organized into seven corps, through western Maryland and central Pennsylvania, searching for Lee.

The First Corps, led by fifers and drummers, marched confidently into the beautiful new day. The hills and fields of central Pennsylvania were green and ripe with grain and fruit.

The road crossed a creek and the Baraboo Guards splashed through the ford. Battery B was drawn up on the far side waiting for the infantry to pass and clear the road. The regular gunners lounged beside their pieces.

"Hey! Red-leg!" Gus shouted. "What is that big thing?"

"It's a cannon," the unsuspecting artilleryman answered.

"That's what your girl friend said when she saw mine!" Gus cried, to cheers from the marching infantry.

James strode at the head of the regiment with Colonel Bache and Lieutenant Colonel Ford. He thought of Lucille constantly. James couldn't imagine her as she described herself in her letters, heavy, bloated. The law clerk knew little of the mystery of birth but he knew its dangers and he feared for her.

Four abreast, the Baraboo Guards marched easily, following Company I. Murphy took his briar pipe from his mouth and raised his left hand. The fifes and drums had ceased. Over the sounds of shoes on the road and equipment striking equipment Murphy heard something.

"What is it?" John asked from the side of the column.

"Sounds," the Irishman told him.

"What kind of sounds?" Ethan asked.

"Be still!" the little man commanded.

"What do you hear, Murphy?" Wayne asked.

"Popping!"

"Popping?" Gus laughed. "Like popcorn?"

"Popping!" Murphy said. "Like carbines!"

"Carbines? Well, hell, Murphy," Gus drawled. "Carbines means cavalry. Some bunch of yellow-legs got themselves into a scrap. The hell with them! Ever seen a dead cavalryman?"

"Shut up, Gus," John ordered. The carpenter was trying to listen over the sounds of marching men.

"What do you think?" Ethan asked.

The Irishman looked at the merchant, his pinched face serious. "Who would yon cavalry be popping away at with their wee carbines?"

"Rebs!" John stated.

"Aye."

"That might be some Reb foraging party out looking for supplies," the carpenter suggested.

"Would one Reb be wandering far from the rest this distance into the state of Pennsylvania?" Murphy asked him.

"Christ!" the carpenter swore. "Our army is scattered to hell and gone through Maryland and Pennsylvania looking for Lee!"

"Aye, Johnny Barks," the little man agreed. "If that firing means they've found the man, it'll be the First Corps going in against his tens of thousands and trying to hang on as best we can until the rest of the army can be getting up."

"That'll take a day," John said.

"Look to your priming, lads," Murphy suggested. "I'm thinking we'll be asked to buy the army that one day."

A cavalry officer galloped a frothing horse over the gentle ridge to the left of the road and charged toward the column on the road, shouting and waving his arms. Officers from the marching infantry rode to meet him. The cavalryman drew rein in the field and pointed excitedly to the west, the direction from which he'd ridden. General Reynolds, First Corps commander, cantered out with his staff to talk to the anxious rider. Reynolds gave terse orders. His staff officers turned their mounts and galloped toward the infantry column, shouting to the brigade commanders. Reynolds and an orderly spoke with the cavalryman for a moment then spurred behind him up the ridge.

The pop and snap of carbine and revolver fire was clear now, and closer.

The First Corps halted on the road. Steeples and roof tops of a town showed over the trees ahead to the north. Colonel Bache knew the place. The town was the seat of Adams County, Pennsylvania, he told James. A college town. A market center. A crossroads called Gettysburg.

Men in the column loaded muskets and twisted bayonets onto the muzzles. They pulled cartridge boxes around to the front of their belts and took quick pulls on canteens, firmly setting the cork stoppers.

The Second Brigade faced left and moved off, forming into battle lines, following its officers and color bearers into the fields beside the road. Half-companies of skirmishers trotted forward and began to work up the slope of the ridge toward a line of trees. With a cheer and a shout the Second Brigade marched for the crest of the ridge.

More cavalry officers rode from the trees and waved frantically to the lines of infantry, pointing over their shoulders to the west. The sound of revolvers and carbines was louder now. Over the sounds of firing Ethan heard the high warbling tenor of the rebel yell.

"That'll confirm any doubt, the yell," Murphy told the merchant. "That'll be them."

The Iron Brigade formed battle lines. James drew his sword and ran to his place at the left front of the Second Wisconsin. The color sergeants moved to the center, stripping away canvas cases from the flags and shaking the silk fabrics loose to the bright July sunlight. The Second Wisconsin started up the ridge.

James heard, above the firing and the distant rebel yells, over the swish and crackle of hundreds of pairs of legs moving through bracken and high grass, the clear chirp and whistle of birds. Their singing reminded him of Lucille, of the thicket on the shore of Lake Mendota. He'd always think of her when he heard the songs of birds. He worried about her. He brought his thoughts back to the work at hand. He'd best keep his mind on his own well-being for the next several hours.

The Baraboo Guards topped the ridge, passing a red brick seminary building and moving steadily through lines of cavalry troopers, John Buford's men. The troopers rose from their cover behind logs and boulders to cheer the infantrymen forward as they moved past and down the ridge. This was, after all, infantry work.

The Baraboo Guards came into line with the other companies of the Second Wisconsin at the bottom of the slope of the ridge, facing west a few yards from a small stream. The undergrowth across the stream was clouded with powder smoke. Butternut and gray bodies lay on the far bank and in the water, left behind where Buford's troopers had felled them in their last charge.

Carl walked the rear of the line. "When they come, fire low," he told the men from Sauk County. They knew what was about to happen but Carl's voice was familiar and reassuring to them. "Load carefully. Take your time. Fire slow. You know what to do."

"Damned Rebs!" Olaf cursed.

"Hush, now, you terrible Viking!" Murphy told the farmhand. "Keep your hatred in check and your voice down. If Johnny Reb finds it's your own self waiting for him, he'll be changing his mind and not coming."

The Irishman sucked on his pipe. He could feel the cold touch of the haunt on the sides of his soul. They'd be coming, running through the trees and undergrowth on the far side of the stream with all their fierce fury and the wailing of their banshee yell. They'd be across the stream and in among the lads from Sauk County in but a few seconds. Their first rush would have to be stopped as soon as it began and that would be a job of work. Ah, the Irishman admitted, there'd be good days in a man's life and there'd be bad. The man had no say in the matter. Tum-tum-tiddley-tum-tee-day, he crooned. Tum-tiddley-tum-tee-day.

James stopped to help a wounded cavalry captain to his feet. Blood coursed down the officer's yellow-striped breeches. "Who are they, Captain?" he asked, helping the officer straighten up.

"Some are Archer's Tennessee men, from the few prisoners I got to talk to. Whoever the rest of them are, they're Reb infantry, Major, and they're good at it. You're welcome to them."

"How large a force?"

"Large, Major. I figured a couple of divisions when I saw them on the road this morning. I made them at fifteen, seventeen thousand with some batteries. We've only had some heavy skirmishing with them so far. They've been quiet here for a while, maybe three-quarters of an hour, but they've sure been raising hell north of the road. Across the creek, here, they're getting ready for a charge. They'll be mean as stirred hornets when they come. Take care, Major."

"Why don't you head up the hill and get that wound taken care of?" James suggested.

The cavalryman looked at the distance he'd have to walk to the crest of the ridge, where a dressing station had been set up. "You're the Black Hats, aren't you?"

"Yes. The Iron Brigade. First Corps. We're the Second Wisconsin."

"You're the best we can put in front of them, Major. I couldn't help counting you as you passed through our lines. I wish there were more of you."

"So do I," James told the officer. He watched the cavalryman limp up the ridge, one hand holding his bleeding thigh. James was startled by shouts and calls from the trees across the stream and then the wailing scream of Southern voices. It rose in wave after wave of sound, its frightening harmony carrying threat and danger, fury and fear, confidence and blood-lust. James shivered. He wished they'd come and be done with it. Along the lines of the Second Wisconsin musket barrels lowered and leveled to point across the stream, a bristling hedge of bayonets before the muzzles. James heard the clunk-tunk of hammers being cocked. His throat was tight and dry. He tried to swallow.

They came.

The undergrowth across the stream shook and erupted as line after line of howling Confederates leaped down the far bank of the stream into the shallow water. Wild men in butternut and gray with slouched hats and bearded faces, with muskets and bayonets and bare feet, ragged, furious and screaming, splashed toward the near bank.

"Second Wisconsin!" Colonel Bache shouted.

The line of musket barrels pointed into the oncoming rush.

"Fire!"

The volley roared with flame and smoke. Confederates shrieked and fell, stumbled, jumped, collapsed into the water. Wounded men and dead men were pushed aside and run over by the compact mass of surging men coming from behind. The rebel line swept to the near bank of the stream.

The second rank of men from Wisconsin stepped forward and volleyed into the faces of the charging mob.

Ethan reloaded. He concentrated on the movements—bite, tear, insert, ram, withdraw, cock, cap, aim, fire—crack!

The rebel line steadied, some men standing knee-deep in the water. The Confederate volley exploded. Men in the ranks of the Iron Brigade fell, dropped to the earth, tumbled backwards, shrieked with agony and pain, grabbed bleeding chests, arms, faces, stomachs.

Ethan aimed and fired again, feeling the buck of his Springfield's wooden stock against his shoulder. A man behind him grabbed the merchant's arm as Ethan started to reload. He handed Ethan a loaded and capped musket, taking Ethan's empty one. The men in the rear rank began loading and passing forward muskets to the front rank, where they could be used to better advantage.

Ethan worked steadily, not thinking, cocking, aiming, firing. Cocking, aiming, firing. Cocking, aiming, firing.

The butternut and gray line wavered, rippled, then turned and ran for the far bank of the stream, for the shelter of the trees and undergrowth there.

Ethan paused and breathed deeply, shuddering. He looked across the shallow valley. They were gone, back into the woods. They'd come again. The banks of both sides of the stream and the water itself were covered and filled with gray and butternut shapes, some lying still, some crawling or trying to rise. Thick clouds of powder smoke drifted in the valley of the stream.

"Get our wounded back from the line!" Carl shouted.

Ethan pulled his canteen to his mouth and sucked water, gagging on the first swallow. His mouth was filled with powder granules from biting into the paper cartridge wrapping. He corked his canteen and peered into the slowly rising cloud of smoke. He recalled, too clearly, the face of one Southerner. The man had been looking into Ethan's eyes when a minie ball from the merchant's Springfield blew the man's head into a pink mist.

"Yo!" a voice called out across the stream. "Jack Henry! Them ain't Pennsylvania militia like the man told us! Them's those fucking Black Hats!"

"Black Hats!" a man in Company I shouted.

"Black Hats!" The companies to the right and left took up the cry. "Black Hats! Black Hats! Black Hats!"

"Whenever you're ready, Johnny Reb!" Gus roared, shaking his Springfield.

The gray and butternut waves came again, rushing from the woods and underbrush of the far bank of the stream with the same wild abandon and uncontrolled fury of the first charge, running over the bodies of their own men, screaming and firing and stumbling and falling, splashing through the water and running up the near bank. Where the lines closed men fought with bayonets, musket butts, swords, revolvers, knives and bare fists.

Ethan fired. His throat was tight and his temples pounded. Minie balls whizzed near his head and thumped into the bodies of men to his right and left. He passed the fired Springfield back and groped for a loaded musket. There was no one in the rear rank to hand him a musket. The rear rank had moved forward to take the places of men fallen from the front rank. Ethan reloaded for himself.

Castle Newton neatly tapped aside a Confederate bayonet and thrust his officer's sword into the rebel's throat. The tanner's son jerked his blade free and collapsed, a pistol bullet through the tintype picture of his mother that he carried in the pocket of his shirt over his heart. Stepan Fedkenheuer aimed carefully at the buckle of a charging Confederate officer in gray but a minie ball through his chest knocked him to the earth, blood and gore and gristle coating the front of his infantry jacket. Wayne Roohr loaded as quickly as he could move cartridge from box to muzzle. A rebel sergeant stepped in front of the stage clerk and grimaced, almost apologetically, as he fired his musket into Wayne's face. Hollis Oostendorp rammed a cartridge home and withdrew his ram rod. He dropped, a ball through his skull at the temple. Peter Everett fired and reversed his musket. He swung its wooden stock and battered one screeching rebel on the chin, seeing blood and bone fly. A bayonet speared the farmhand from Sauk City in the stomach. Peter screeched and dropped his musket, grabbing the hot barrel of the Confederate's. The rebel pulled the trigger and blew Peter off the blade, a broken figure that ran several steps backward before crumpling to the earth.

Officers ran through the thinned ranks, grabbing men and pulling them bodily up the slope of the hill. "Fall back!" they shouted. "Fall back and form at the seminary!"

"Stay!" Olaf shouted, aiming and firing. "Fight!"

"Fall back, Olaf!" James shouted.

"Stay! We can fight!"

"God damn you, Olaf!" James screamed. "Come on! We're falling back!"

The farmhand fired into the swarming mob before him. He looked at Ethan, at Gus. They nodded. He'd go. He didn't want to.

Firing and reloading, trudging up the hill and stopping to fire and reload again, the Baraboo Guards fell back to the brick seminary building atop the ridge. A breastwork of wagons and boxes had been thrown together in the yard. The men from Sauk County found places behind it, grabbing cartridges from cases that were broken open on the ground.

Carl reloaded. He ran down the roll in his head. He'd seen the Irishman up and firing a few minutes before the company fell back from the stream. Olaf and Gus were standing beside him. He could hear John Barks off to his left shouting for the Baraboo Guards to form on him. Ethan stood near his brother-in-law. Carl didn't know where the rest of the men from Sauk County were. He'd seen Wayne go down, and Hollis. Carl moved toward

John. He counted eight men standing with the carpenter in the yard of the seminary.

The tavern keeper wiped his face on the sleeve of his infantry jacket and looked up into the clear blue sky. This would be a beautiful day back in Baraboo. Carl's bayonet was bent outward from the muzzle of his Springfield. He unfastened it and threw it away. He stopped a wounded man from the Nineteenth Indiana and took the man's bayonet, twisting it onto the muzzle of his Springfield.

James reloaded his revolver. He thought of Lucille. He wanted nothing more than to be able to turn from this obscene place and walk until he came to a railroad that would carry him to Madison, to her.

"Major Peck!" a lieutenant from Company B called out.

"Here," James answered, abruptly bringing his thoughts back to the hill on which the Second Wisconsin had formed.

"Sir, Colonel Bache has been taken from the field, seriously wounded. Lieutenant Colonel Ford is dead. You command the regiment, Major Peck."

"Thank you, Lieutenant," James said calmly.

"God help you, Major Peck," the lieutenant whispered.

"I pray He will. Are there officers with the companies, Lieutenant?"

"Not many, sir."

"On your way back up the line, Lieutenant, I want you to see that someone is in command of each company. Officer, sergeant, corporal, private, anyone. See that the men in the companies know who that is and that person knows where I am."

"Yes, sir."

"Regimental headquarters will be here by the road. Send me any of the color guards who are alive and have them bring the flags with them."

The lieutenant saluted and left.

James listened. Through all the blast of battle, the birds still sang.

The rebels came again, screaming their savage yell. On command, the companies in the yard of the seminary fired, volleys by sections, blowing men backwards, sideways, dropping them in heaps. Battery B on the road fired double-shotted barrels of canister into the Confederate ranks and swaths of ragged, barefoot men were swept away, only to be immediately replaced from what seemed to be an endless source of screeching, deadly men in gray and butternut.

The First Corps held. The Confederate charge slackened, then fell back. A carpet of writhing, moaning forms covered the slope of the seminary ridge in front of the breastworks. Blue-uniformed bodies lay at the feet of the men behind the overturned wagons and piled crates. Gentle hands helped the Federal wounded who could stand to their feet and sent them on their way eastward toward the town of Gettysburg. Those staying at the breastworks reloaded.

James wiped his face with his left hand. He listened. The birds were no longer singing.

They came again, their yell rising as they ran, firing and surging forward. They closed briefly on the Federal breastwork. Bayonets stabbed and slashed. Musket butts crushed muscle and bone. Frederick Auerbach, the cobbler from Merrimac, looked up from capping his Springfield in time to see the long bowie knife that cut his throat.

James stood in the center of the line of the Second Wisconsin with the men from Company E, aiming each revolver shot as the sheriff of Sauk County had taught him. He heard the crash of a volley from his left. He stepped back from the line to look through the dense cloud of powder smoke. A force of Confederates was working around the flank of the regiment. The rebels there fired again, their bullets cutting into the Federal formations at the breastwork on an angle from the rear. Other rebels ran to join the flanking force. Confederate officers waved and gestured, calling for more.

James shouted at the companies on the left of the line of the Second Wisconsin, pointing at the flanking rebel formations. He wanted two or three companies to turn and face the Confederates. A minie ball smashed into James' left arm above the elbow and sent him spinning, his revolver flying out of his right hand. He fell hard on his face.

"They've flanked us!" a captain from the Nineteenth Indiana shouted as he ran along the rear of the lines at the breastwork. "Fall back in formation! Keep your alignment! Fall back firing!"

"Come on, Gus," Ethan told his brother-in-law. "Let's get the hell out of here. Where's Murphy?"

"I'm with you!" the little man chirped, aiming and firing. "We'll be keeping ourselves together and joining up with some bunch that's still in formation. Come on, Olaf, you bloodthirsty Viking!"

The remnant of the First Corps fell back along the road to Gettysburg, turning by companies to volley into the pursuing Confederate battalions, then resuming the march eastward into the streets of the town. South and east of Gettysburg a large Federal force was taking position and throwing up breastworks on a long ridge that ran north and south. The retreating men of the First Corps headed there.

Carl joined Ethan and Gus, Olaf and Murphy, as the straggling units marched through the streets of Gettysburg.

"Have any of you seen Captain Barks?" the tavern keeper asked.

Ethan shook his head.

"Major Peck?"

Gus shrugged.

"We should look for them," Carl said.

"There's naught we can be doing for either of them, First Sergeant, whilst we're here in the streets of the town," Murphy told the tavern keeper. "If they're with this mob, we'll be finding them when we get to where we're going."

In the narrow streets of Gettysburg men of the First Corps mixed with men of the Eleventh Corps who had come up and gone onto action north and west of the town. The Federal battalions crowded into Gettysburg. Men too badly wounded to continue were left on porches of the homes of Gettysburg. Some of the citizens of the town took the men in to nurse and to hide from the oncoming rebel divisions. Others locked their doors and bolted their shutters against the bleeding wretches on their doorsteps.

Federal batteries on the ridge southeast of the town began shelling the advancing Confederate columns. The survivors of the First Corps and the Eleventh Corps marched toward the protection of the guns.

Carl led his small group up the side of the ridge.

Thousands of men in blue were digging earthworks, placing cannons, forming into their regiments and brigades and divisions on what was known locally as Cemetery Ridge. The Army of the Potomac was coming up, corps after corps, preparing for battle, using the hours won for them by the First Corps and the Eleventh Corps.

The price of those hours had been high. The Iron Brigade, John Gibbon's proud Black Hats of the First Corps, eighteen hundred strong that morning, straggled into line late in the afternoon a mere five hundred tired, forlorn men.

Ethan, Gus, and Carl leaned heavily on the muzzles of their muskets. Murphy joined the three, bringing their canteens. Olaf sat on the ground, wrapping a sweat-soaked neckerchief around a bullet crease in his ankle.

John found them. His sword was gone. His black hat was missing. He staggered. Carl reached and took the carpenter by the arm. "Are you all right, Captain?" he asked. Murphy handed the carpenter his canteen. John drank and handed it back. "I'm so tired," he sighed. "I've never been this tired. Where are the rest of the men?"

Carl stared back toward the valley and the ridge where the tower of the seminary could be seen above the trees.

John wiped his face. "This isn't all of us!"

"I think so," Carl told him.

"There can't be just six of us!"

Carl wouldn't argue. He reloaded his Springfield.

"What do you want us to do?" Ethan asked.

John blinked. He didn't know.

"Murphy?" the merchant asked.

"We'll be finding us a hidey-hole," the little man said, wiping his pointed face. "Captain Barks, you'd best be finding brigade command and discovering what they've got in store for us next."

John nodded. That made sense.

"We'll be keeping our eyes peeled for any of the Baraboo Guards who'll be wandering about," Murphy said. "I'm thinking we'll not be finding more. I'm thinking, my Captain, the Baraboo Guards went out of service on the far slope of yon ridge, lad."

"Want one of us to go with you?" Ethan asked.

John shook his head. "I'll be all right. Find a safe place. I'll see where brigade is and get back to you." He turned and walked unsteadily away.

"Murphy," Carl said, capping his musket. "Find us that hole to hide in. We need cartridges, food. And, Murphy, we need all the whiskey you can get your hands on."

The little man spat and shouldered his Springfield. He was tired in his soul. He felt the cold touch of the haunt. He'd not time for that. He led the men eastward, looking for a place with rocks that would give shelter from Confederate artillery fire. He'd just as soon have the lads sit the rest of this one out.

57

James breathed hard and fast. His left arm was numb. He realized something was very wrong. He sensed movement, men running and shouting. Then he remembered being hit.

He opened his eyes. He was lying on his chest, his face turned to his right. He couldn't see his left arm and, for the moment, he was content not to see it.

He recalled the Confederate force that had worked its way around the left flank of the regiment. Even the veteran Second Wisconsin wouldn't stand long with fire coming in from its flank and rear.

James called out to the men who ran past him, shouting that he was alive, that he was wounded, that he wanted them to take him with them when they fell back from the lines at the seminary. He tried to move, sending fierce slivers of pain up his left arm into his shoulder and neck.

Fighting unconsciousness, he concentrated on what he could see—feet and legs running by, shod feet, bare feet, ragged gray and butternut trousers. He listened to the shouting and the trailing edge of a victorious rebel yell.

James closed his eyes and breathed calmly. He realized he'd been unconscious and the regiment had fallen back from the barricade in the yard of the seminary without him. He tried not to think what being wounded and left behind the Confederate lines could mean.

A wild-eyed Confederate soldier in a ragged homespun jacket dropped to the earth beside him. The man, dirty and bearded, stared into James' eyes.

"Shit!" the rebel cried. "Cap'n, I got me a live one here!"

"Stick him if he shows fight, Cassius!" a voice responded. "I ain't got the time to never-mind. Barfus' Battalion! Gather on me! Hunker down! Rest up! Reload!"

The Confederate soldier looked intently at James. He jerked his musket back for a bayonet thrust. "Y'all going to show fight, Yank?" he asked, hesitating, suspicious.

"No," James told him, watching the point of the man's bayonet.

"Whoo!" the rebel exhaled, wiping his perspiring face. "No need to stick you then. Whoo! I been running my ass off! Y'all wounded, Yank?"

"My arm," James replied, relieved he wasn't going to die on the rebel's bayonet.

"Shit! Be grateful! Could be your head!"

The rebel busied himself loading his musket. James watched, feeling detached from the frantic activity. He noticed the rebel's cartridge box hung from a rope belt on two strands of twisted rags. The Confederate capped his musket and placed it on the ground. He looked at James. "You're one of them fucking Black Hats!"

"Yes," James admitted. "The Second Wisconsin."

"Put up a good scrap when y'all set your minds to it!"

"We try," James agreed.

"Try! Shit! Hell, man, they told us y'all were Pennsylvania militia backing up that Yankee cavalry! Hunh! Pennsylvania militia y'all sure as hell weren't!"

James wanted to keep talking to the man. The numbness in his left arm was waning and pain was starting to sear and settle in. He couldn't turn himself over. "How is it going?" he asked. "For our side?"

"Shit! We run you off this ridge. Clean back through the town. Y'all forming on another ridge about a mile from here. We're going to play hell trying to run y'all off that ridge, Yank."

"You seem to have had little trouble running us off this one," James offered.

"Shit! Tell that to the boys laying back there in the trees and in the creek!"

"We gave you a fight?"

"Some! Going to be one hell of a fight from here on out."

"I gather I'll miss it."

"Sure as hell! Hey, man, you're out of this shit with that shot you took in the arm! You're home free if you live through what the surgeons are going to do to you!"

"Barfus' Battalion!" a voice called. "Form up!"

"Got to go, Yank," the rebel said, taking up his musket. "Got to chase your boys some before General Lee'll let us rest for the night. Don't worry about that arm. One whack from the saw-bones and you'll be good as new. You'll have a list to starboard but you'll be all right."

"Reb!" James called as the Confederate rose to his feet. "Who are you?"

"Me? Hell, man, I'm Cassius Jepson out of Pamlico County, North Carolina."

"Barfus' Battalion!" the voice ordered. "Forward!"

"Got to go, Yank!"

"Good-bye, Jepson!" James called from the ground. "And, Jepson!" he added. "Good luck!"

The man from Pamlico County ran to join the infantry forming around Major Barfus. Rebels dumped cartridges from the boxes of Federal dead and stuffed them into the pockets of their trousers. A few threw away flint-lock muskets and took Springfields from the hands of dead Black Hats.

Following Major Barfus, the battalion shouted and surged forward.

James raised his head to watch them clear the top of Seminary Ridge. The movement pushed splintered bone into torn muscle. James screamed, grimaced, fainted.

58

John found the Baraboo Guards in the hidey-hole Murphy had selected on the reverse slope of Cemetery Ridge.

The carpenter had been reassured by his visit to brigade headquarters, where order and regulation still existed. John was in control of himself when he stood over the hole and looked down at its exhausted, dirt-covered occupants.

"Well?" the Irishman demanded.

"This is all of us," John confirmed. "Major Peck is missing. He hasn't been seen since the fight at the seminary."

"The regiment?" Carl asked.

"Fifty, maybe sixty, left."

"And that out of our once proud thousand," Murphy sobbed, almost weeping.

"At headquarters," John told them, "they say we bought the day the army needed to come up. We lost three men out of four doing it."

"What's done," the Irishman sighed, "is done." He took a long pull on a bottle of whiskey.

John realized the five men in the hole were drunk. He wanted to be drunk with them. "What's left of the Iron Brigade is on the line, facing north," he told them. "There're some breastworks. We're to hold them."

"Do we have to go?" Ethan asked.

The carpenter looked into the sad eyes of the merchant. "Yes."

Ethan got slowly to his feet. He blinked. He found his Springfield and climbed out of the hole. The merchant shouldered his musket and walked, stiff, unsteady.

Gus stood and cleared his throat, spitting mucus and powder granules. He climbed out of the hole and followed his brother-in-law, trailing his Springfield's butt in the dirt.

Olaf put out a hand and pulled Carl to his feet. The two staggered and helped each other along as they walked slowly north behind the brothers-in-law.

John stepped down into the hole and sat by the little man, who was curled on his unrolled blanket, the bottle in his hands.

"There was a time," John said, "when you'd have been the first one up and out of here."

"Aye," the Irishman sighed heavily. "There was that time."

"What is it?" John asked, taking the bottle and drinking from it.

"Ah, my Captain," the little man said slowly. "I could be sitting here and telling you my back is paining me so that I must be begging off the duty for the day. I could be telling you that."

John said nothing.

"I could be telling you that I'm an old man with too many miles of marching already behind me for to be going out into what the rest of this day has to offer. I could be telling you that."

"You could," John agreed.

"I could be telling you I'm a convicted man and not fit to be serving in the ranks with the likes of them."

"Yes."

"Ah, Johnny Barks!" Murphy cried. "I should be telling you I'm the coward I am and you should be shooting me for it as I'm sitting here!"

"No."

"I don't want to go back out there!" the little man sobbed. "There's naught I can be doing now for the lads! They're gone, the most of them! I fear it out there! God help me for the miserable coward that I am, man, but I fear it out there!"

"You're no coward, Murphy," John said softly. "You taught us most of what we know."

"Aye!" the Irishman sobbed, wiping his pointed nose on the filthy sleeve of his blue infantry jacket. "Weren't the lot of you learning it well! I was teaching the hundred of you! There's not a handful left!"

John sat and studied the Irishman. "Look, Murphy, Major Peck told me about you," he said. "You never volunteered for this like the rest of us did. You don't have to be here. If you want to go, go. Get out of here. You've earned that."

"You're telling me I can be running?"

"I'm telling you I won't stop you from doing what you've earned the right to do."

The little man looked up into the carpenter's face. "You'd be letting me go?"

"There's not a man left alive in this company that would stop you."

Murphy thought for a moment. He struggled to stand, using his Springfield as a staff. He reached for the bottle of whiskey. The carpenter handed it to him. Murphy took a long pull. "Aah!" he exhaled, wiping again his pointed nose. "I'll be on my way."

"California?" the carpenter asked.

"The north breastworks. The lads'll be needing someone to be working up a stew, what with the things this day has brought onto them and with what the morrow might have in store."

"You don't have to go back there!" John shouted.

Murphy broke and sobbed, leaning heavily on his Springfield to keep from falling. Tears rolled from his eyes onto his pinched face and cheeks, cutting channels through the grime and the dust and the residue of powder smoke. "Aaagh!" he cried. "Aaagh! Ain't that just the fucking hell of it?" he pleaded. "Ain't that just the fucking hell of the whole thing? Free, you're saying I am to be going! Free, for once in my miserable life as never I've been free! Free to be going and me not having one place on God's green earth to be going to! Aaagh! You're offering me the warm breezes and the rolling surf of the California coasts and all I got to go to is hell-fire and damnation at the north breastworks alongside my mates! Aaagh! Ain't that the fucking hell of it!"

"Murphy!" the carpenter started to respond.

"Stuff your yap!" the little man cried. "I do as I do. Would you have me otherwise?"

"I guess not."

"You're a fine man, Johnny Barks, to have made the offer."

"You're a good man, too, Murphy."

"That's been said," the Irishman sobbed, wiping his eyes on the sleeve of his blue jacket.

John stood and put his hand on the little man's shoulder. Together, the carpenter and the horse thief walked up Cemetery Ridge through the gathering divisions of the Army of the Potomac to where the survivors of John Gibbon's Iron Brigade were deepening some hastily dug rifle pits.

In three hours Murphy had a thick stew going in an iron pot that a squad of Vermont infantry spent the rest of the day searching for.

59

James felt something tugging at him. He opened his eyes. Someone tugged at his haversack, pulling its strap over his head. The tugging and pulling caused bone to scrape on bone in his left arm and the pain brought James back to consciousness.

"Sorry for dragging you home from the dead, Yank," a tanned Confederate soldier said, spitting tobacco juice. "Got orders to take haversacks and cartridge boxes from you Yanks. Y'all won't need them and our trains ain't got up."

"Take them and be damned!" James cursed, his arm throbbing.

"Intend to, Yank."

James rolled onto his back. That eased the pain. "Soldier," he said civilly, "I'd like to keep the tin cup. On my haversack strap, there. It means something to me."

"No shortage of tin cups in the Confederacy, Yank," the rebel said. "It's what goes into them we lack. I'll tuck it into the front of your coat. One of those thieving provosts'll most likely steal it if they see it out. They yours?" the rebel asked, digging hardtack from James' haversack and chewing it.

"They?"

"Them," the soldier said, nodding at the line of blue bodies that lay behind the breastworks.

"They were my men."

"They're dead men now. Here, stretcher bearers! Take this Black Hat. He's worth saving if any of them are. You're going to lose that arm, Yank."

"So I gather. How's the battle going?"

"We come up here looking for a fight. We found one. Load him easy on that stretcher!"

Two rebel soldiers lifted James onto the window shutter that doubled as a stretcher and carried him through the woods where the Iron Brigade had fought and died. His mind was clear. He listened to the sounds of the aftermath of battle, the shrieks of wounded men, the shrill voices of excited men. The stretcher-bearers carried James to a field surgery set up in a shallow valley protected from Federal artillery fire.

A surgeon wearing a bloody leather apron walked to the litter. "Are you in pain, Major?" he asked. The surgeon was an elderly man, tall and thin, dignified in spite of his bloody garb.

"I am," James admitted.

"Can you tell me your name and organization, sir?"

"Peck. James Peck. Second Wisconsin."

"Major Peck, I have little time," the surgeon said, gently moving the fabric of the law clerk's left sleeve to examine the wound. "I have many to care for, ours as well as yours. That bone is shattered. Your arm is beyond saving. It has to come off. I can leave a few inches below the shoulder. You may recover from the trauma of amputation or you may not. I'll do what I can for you or I'll tell these men to carry you to that field and place you with those for whom there is no hope. Those are the only choices I can offer. I must warn you I have no chloroform and little whiskey. What do you wish me to do, Major Peck?"

"I have a wife and child," James said. "I have to live."

"I can't assure you life, Major. Only certain death from infection or a poor chance at living. I'm sorry."

"I'll ask you to do your best, Doctor."

"I shall, sir. Orderly, have these men carry Major Peck to the next table. I'll give you some whiskey for the pain. I promise to work as quickly as I can. I hope you're a strong man."

He wasn't a strong man. An orderly tied a wooden dowel between his teeth to prevent him chewing his tongue. He bit into it until he could no longer stand the agony of the slicing of his flesh, then he tried to spit out the dowel so he could scream. When he struggled under the knife two orderlies sat on his shoulders. He vomited and choked on his own fluids when the saw started to cut into the bone of his upper arm. When he fainted the surgeon nodded and finished his work, throwing James' left arm into a wooden tub that was nearly filled with limbs and bloody bandages.

60

July 3, 1863, was a fine, clear day.

Orderlies carried James to the yard of the seminary and put him with wounded and dying Federal prisoners. The orderlies placed him in a sitting position with his back to the shattered trunk of a large tree. One orderly wrapped his coat around him and buttoned the front to protect his throbbing shoulder.

James watched Confederate batteries lining up on Seminary Ridge. He counted more than a hundred guns parked wheel to wheel as far down the ridge as he could see. By noon he understood that some grand plan was under way. He watched. He'd nothing else to do to take his mind from the pain where his left arm had been.

"Major Peck?" a refined voice asked.

James looked up. The surgeon stood over him. "Doctor . . ."

"Milstadt," the surgeon introduced himself. "How do you feel, Major Peck?"

"I feel like someone just sawed my arm off," James responded weakly.

"That was day before yesterday," the surgeon said. "Have you been able to sleep?"

"Some."

"Have you been able to keep down food and water?"

James shook his head.

"Give me your tin cup, Major."

"I'd like to keep it."

"I'm a butcher, sir, not a plunderer. Please give me your cup."

With his right hand, James worked his cup from the pocket of his coat. The surgeon poured brandy from a bottle and added a little water from a wooden pail. "Sip this slowly," he said. "It may stay down. It's good brandy. Our cavalry took it from one of your supply trains last night."

James sipped. "I've been watching your guns come into battery along the ridge, Doctor," he said. "Do you expect us to attack you?"

"We'll do the attacking, I fear. General Lee has ordered a full assault on the center of your line. General Pickett's division will lead the attack."

"The Army of the Potomac is on that far ridge, Doctor Milstadt. There are a hundred thousand men over there."

"Yes. Entrenched and covered by your excellent artillery."

"General Pickett's division will be slaughtered, Doctor Milstadt."

"Yes, it will. Your gallant stand at Willoughby Run the other day won this battle for your army, Major Peck. The fighting isn't over, but our army now faces the full seven corps of yours. Had your men not stood and fought, and given your army the time it needed to concentrate, we'd have defeated you, one corps at a time as your army came up, and we'd be in Harrisburg, Philadelphia, Baltimore, and even approaching the gates of Washington this very moment."

James looked up at the surgeon, who stared across the shallow valley between the Confederate lines on Seminary Ridge and the Federal lines on Cemetery Ridge.

"Why will they do it, Doctor Milstadt?" James asked. "The men of Pickett's Division?'

"They've been ordered to do it, Major Peck. This is war. Why did your Black Hats stand and fight and die at Willoughby Run the other day?"

"We stood and fought, Doctor Milstadt, because we were there. We had no choice."

"A gallant, brave fight, Major Peck."

"I can't find consolation in that," James said. "Too many good men died."

"Such is war, Major Peck. I'll order you to be left behind when we retreat. We'll fail in our grand assault on your center and we'll have to retreat. I expect that to happen tomorrow evening. I can do nothing more for you. Your people will find you and they'll be better able to care for you."

"Thank you."

The surgeon stooped and tucked the brandy bottle into the front of James' coat. As the old man stood up, one gun in the line of Confederate batteries fired, then a second.

"The signal guns, Major Peck. The battle opens. I must go and, I fear, prepare for hard work."

James remained sitting against the trunk of the shattered tree during the hours of the Confederate bombardment of the Federal lines on Cemetery Ridge. The Southern guns hurled tons of iron across the shallow valley. He watched sixteen thousand men in gray and butternut form behind the guns and move forward through the intervals, aligning, shaking out crimson battle flags. He watched them march into the valley, across and up the far ridge into smoke and flame and destruction. He watched the shattered remnants of the assaulting columns straggle back.

The assault failed.

It accomplished nothing.

61

Thunder rolled over the ravaged ridges of Adams County, Pennsylvania. A violent rainfall washed open shallow graves of hastily buried men and pounded the exposed corpses of those who lay where they had fallen.

Two hours after midnight, in the early hours of July 4, John Barks led a patrol into Gettysburg. The carpenter and his five Baraboo Guards moved cautiously. John didn't know whether the Confederates had pulled out of the town. With the rain and thunder he couldn't see, couldn't hear.

Ethan, the point man of the patrol, preceded the others by half a block. At each intersection, the merchant swept the dark streets with his Springfield before waving the others along. He peered around the corners of houses and probed into dark corners with his bayonet. The streets were littered with dead men and dead horses, broken wagons and gun carriages, abandoned muskets and equipment, discarded plunder from the houses.

Ethan stepped into a street. The porch of a house before him was illuminated briefly in a flash of lightning. Ethan saw forms on the porch—bodies or wounded men. He stepped up to the porch, careful not to tread on a hand or leg. One man was propped against the wall of the house, bare shoulders shining in the rain that blew onto the porch. A piece of carpet sheltered his hips. He was alert, looking up into the merchant's face over the point of Ethan's bayonet.

"Are you Yank or Reb?" Ethan whispered.

"Yank," the man answered weakly.

"Have the Rebs pulled out?" Ethan asked, looking over the other forms on the boards of the porch.

"They're gone."

Ethan recognized the voice. He knelt beside the man. "Gus!" he hissed back down the street. "Get up here with some light!"

Gus ran to join his brother-in-law on the porch, bringing a lantern from under his rubber poncho. He struck a match on the post of the porch and held the flame to the wick.

"John! Murphy! Carl! Olaf!" Ethan shouted, forgetting caution. "Get up here!"

The men clattered onto the porch, crowding into the glow of Gus' lantern.

"God damn them!" John cursed, looking down at James' gaunt face and at the fouled bandage that hung loosely from his left shoulder.

"Hello, John," James whispered harshly.

"Major . . ." the carpenter started to say. He couldn't finish.

"They took all I have," James sobbed. "My clothes. My shoes. My arm. They took my tin cup, John. Everything."

The Irishman shoved his way to the center of the group. "Sweet Jesus, Son of the Virgin!" he whispered. "Ah, now, poor lad, don't be fretting. You're back with them that loves you, Major, darling. We'll be caring for you from now on."

The Irishman handed his Springfield to Carl and knelt beside the law clerk. He touched a wrist to James' forehead. "You're burning with fever. You're needing a warm, dry bed. What's inside here, lad?" he asked, nodding at the house.

"Family," James whispered. "Locked their door when the Rebs put us here. I think the rest of these men have died since then."

"Gus," the little man said.

Gus reversed his musket and battered open the door.

The family, father and mother and two daughters, cowered at the far side of the room. "Sir!" the father protested. "This is a private home!"

Gus snarled.

The father became silent.

"Carry the lad in," Murphy told Ethan and Carl. "Ever so gently now! Where's there a bed?"

The owner of the home gulped. Gus raised the point of his bayonet. The man pointed to the rear of the house down a hallway.

Ethan and Carl carried James to the bedroom and set him on a soft mattress. Murphy pulled quilts over him. James had been naked under the piece of carpet. He shook, his teeth chattering.

"Water!" Murphy ordered. The owner of the home blinked, nodded, fled. "Lots of boiling water!" the Irishman shouted after him. "Captain Barks, you'd best be taking Carl and Olaf and finishing your patrol. Gus and Ethan and I will be staying here with the lad and giving him what care we can."

The carpenter nodded. He had no problem taking orders from the little man. The three men left.

"Gus," Murphy said. "You'll be standing guard at the door of this house. No one comes in. Not even General Meade."

Gus hefted his Springfield and walked outside, closing the battered door.

Ethan stood at the foot of the bed and stared at the stump of the law clerk's arm.

"Come, now," Murphy told the merchant. "We've our work to get to. Find the kitchen of this place and get a piece of meat into a pot. Start a thin broth with plenty of butter and salt in it. We'll want to get something warm into the young major. And, Ethan, find if the man of the house is a drinking man. I've not a drop of the spirits on me."

"Will whiskey help him?" Ethan asked, nodding toward the law clerk. "In his condition?"

"Damned if I know, lad," the little man said. "It's me we're needing the whiskey for."

62

James, weakened by loss of blood, shock, and exposure, was hospital-ized at Harrisburg.

The five remaining Baraboo Guards called on him the day the Army of the Potomac began its cautious pursuit of Lee and his battered but still deadly Army of Northern Virginia. Murphy tucked a bottle of good whiskey under James' pillow. James wept when they were gone, drank the whole bottle, and was sick to his stomach for three days.

He received Lucille's letter with the news of the birth of their daughter. When the mails caught up, there were regular letters from her.

He tried to write to her, sitting for hours with a board across his lap and a pencil in his good hand. He couldn't think of anything to say. A nursing nun took to writing a few lines of docile greeting for him to sign.

When the surgeons let him get out of bed after ten days, he strolled daily through the city of Harrisburg, exercising to regain his strength, trying to avoid thinking about the loss of his arm.

He began to frequent saloons and to drink heavily. He bought a civilian suit and put away his uniform. He wanted nothing to do with soldiers. He wished he'd died at Gettysburg. He carried a deep sense of guilt that he didn't understand and couldn't overcome.

He received in the mail his commission as colonel of the Second Wis-consin. He put the document away with his uniform.

In mid-August, five weeks after the battle, James left a railroad worker's saloon with a bottle of whiskey in his right hand.

On the street, a battalion of home guards surrounded several hundred Confederate prisoners. The rebels, ragged and forlorn, sat in rows in the dirt near the railroad switch yard.

A few local boys taunted the rebels and threw horse droppings into the lines of seated men. The guards laughed and pointed when a turd splat-tered on one of the Confederates.

James made his way past the guards and the onlookers on the board walk.

"Get back where you belong, you old bastard!" one of the guards shouted as the law clerk stepped away from the crowd. James glanced up. He thought the guard was shouting at him.

One of the prisoners, an officer, an old man, knelt beside a man in but-ternut rags who lay in the dirt.

"This man is bleeding, soldier," the kneeling officer said. "I'm a surgeon."

"You're going to be a dead surgeon if you don't get your old ass back on the street!" the guard shouted. He swung his bayonet toward the kneeling officer's head.

"Soldier!" James ordered.

The guard turned to face the one-armed civilian.

"Let the surgeon attend to that wounded man," James told the guard.

"I don't take orders from you!" the guard snarled.

"I advise you to," James told him, stepping into the street.

The kneeling surgeon looked up.

"Doctor Milstadt," James said, "you removed my arm the first day at Gettysburg. May I offer assistance?"

"Yes," the surgeon said, remembering the young officer. He nodded toward the threatening guard. "Please hold back your Yankee there while I tighten this dressing. I promise not to organize an escape."

Several guards, attracted by the commotion, gathered around their comrade. A sergeant hurried across the street and glared at James. "What the hell's going on here, Strauss?" he asked the guard.

"I told this old bastard to sit down like he's supposed to," Strauss explained. "Then this one came along and started interfering," he said, pointing at James.

"Who the hell are you?" the sergeant demanded.

"I'm Colonel Peck, Second Wisconsin Infantry, Sergeant. Have your men return to their posts. Make those boys stop throwing horse droppings."

"Blausch, Trostle, get back where I put you!" the sergeant ordered. "Strauss, keep these two Rebs covered. Keep this fellow here. I'm going to get the major."

"Thank you, Colonel Peck," the surgeon said, finishing with the filthy dressing. "Would it be asking too much of your generosity to let me stand for a few minutes? My bones aren't fit for much. Sitting in the dirt of this street does tax them."

James helped the surgeon to his feet.

"I'm sorry you didn't get away with General Lee and the rest of your army, Doctor. I apologize for the treatment you and these men are receiving. Your keepers are home guards. They can be cruel."

"No more than war is cruel, Colonel Peck. How is your arm?"

"It's healing."

"Yes. And, Colonel Peck, how are you? Are you healing?"

James glanced into the surgeon's eyes then looked away.

"May I offer you a prescription, Colonel Peck?"

James looked at the surgeon.

"Put the blame for what has been done to you where it properly belongs. On the war. Be grateful you're alive. Didn't you tell me you've a wife and child? Think of them, Colonel. Why don't you go back to Gettysburg? See the place. You may find something there you won't find in a Harrisburg saloon."

"What the hell is going on here?" the home guard major demanded, running from the entrance of a nearby saloon. The sergeant followed him.

"This man here," the guard, Strauss, said pointing at James. "He told me he was a Federal colonel."

"Federal colonel, my ass!" the major snarled.

"Go, Colonel Peck," Doctor Milstadt said. "You've been a great help."

"Sit your old ass back down, Reb!" the major shouted, grabbing the surgeon and throwing him to the ground. "You stay there until I tell you to get up and get on the cars or I'll have one of my men put a bullet into you!"

"I want your name, Major!" James demanded, stepping forward.

"Strauss! Trostle! Get this one-armed son of a bitch out of my sight! If he gives you trouble, bayonet him!"

Doctor Milstadt shook his head at James. Nothing would be gained by a confrontation.

The following morning James rented a mare and rig and drove the thirty miles to Gettysburg.

New grass grew over slashed turf where the fighting had taken place. He rested the mare and sat for an hour on Seminary Ridge overlooking Willoughby Run where the Baraboo Guards had fought and died.

The next morning James put on his uniform and took the cars for Madison.

63

MADISON, WISCONSIN—June, 1864.

James sat at Judge Faircloth's desk, penciling revisions to a legal brief, frowning, scratching at the stump of his left arm with the end of his pencil. The arm itched and cramped as if the elbow, wrist and hand were still there.

Lucille came down the stairs and into the library.

"Is our daughter sleeping?" James asked, placing the pencil on the desk.

"Like a tired little soldier in the field," Lucille replied, crossing the room to stand behind him. She massaged his neck and shoulders. James stretched, enjoying the feel of her fingers. When little Ellen napped in the afternoon, that was their private time together.

"Can I get you a glass of sherry?" James asked.

"In a while," Lucille whispered, bending and touching her brow to the dark hair of her husband's head.

"Yes, Mary?" James asked, looking up at the serving girl who tapped at the door. "What is it?"

Mary was upset. She had strict orders to give the colonel and Mrs. Peck their time alone when the little one napped. "Men, sir!" she blurted. "There are men!"

"Here?" James asked.

"Here, sir! Men, sir!"

"Did they ask to see me?"

"Aye, sir! They asked directly to see the Colonel!"

"Tell them to come back, Mary," Lucille said. "Tell them the colonel will see them in an hour."

"I did tell them, ma'am! They won't go!"

"Perhaps I should see them, "Cille," James suggested. "They may be clients."

"These won't be clients, sir!" Mary objected. "Not these! They're soldiers, sir! All ragged and hairy and smelling so! They've mud on their shoes!"

"Are they wearing black hats?" James asked, taking Lucille's hand.

"Aye, sir! Big, busted, battered black hats such as the Colonel had on when he came back from the fighting!"

"Show these men right in, Mary," James said.

"Aye, sir," the serving girl said, thinking of the mud on their shoes and her carefully brushed carpets.

"Do you want to see these men alone?" Lucille asked.

"Stay, 'Cille. If they're who I think they are, I want you to meet them."

Mary appeared at the entrance to the library and pressed herself against the wall, pointing weakly into the room.

The four men crowded in, standing self-consciously, uncomfortably, black hats in their hands, uneasy among fine furnishings. Mary was right. They were ragged and hairy and they smelled of perspiration, smoke, old clothing. They did have mud on their shoes.

James released Lucille's hand and walked around the desk, his throat tight with emotion. He couldn't speak. With his one arm he embraced the tavern keeper, the merchant, the farmhand, the big blond.

He stepped back and looked at them. " 'Cille," he said, taking her hand, "these are the Baraboo Guards. Let me present First Sergeant Elsasser, Private Evans, Private Larson, Private Gaard. Gentlemen, this is my wife. 'Cille, these are the men with whom I went to war."

The four stiffened.

"Gentlemen," Lucille bowed, smiling. "Please stand at ease. Colonel Peck, I'll leave you with your comrades in arms. I'll send Mary in with a tray. Gentlemen, I insist your colonel order you to stay with us for dinner." She touched James on the arm. "I can never repay the debt I owe you for caring for my husband. Now, please throw those blanket rolls and haversacks out into the hallway and take a seat. I'll help Mary with dinner. Twice as much as for any other four guests and no beans, no pork, no hardtack. Is that correct, Sergeant Elsasser?"

"Yes, ma'am," Carl answered.

Lucille excused herself. As she left the library, she breathed deeply. The library had taken on the smell of the marching infantry. She gave the necessary orders to Mary and returned to the hall. As she'd done as a girl when banished from her father's confidential conversations in his library, she took a chair and sat out of sight where she could listen.

"You look fit," James told the Baraboo Guards, sitting on the front of the judge's desk. "Thank God you've come through it alive. I take it you've been mustered out, discharged?"

"We're out of it, Colonel," Carl spoke for the rest. "Some of the boys in the other companies reenlisted for the duration of the war. We didn't. Our time was up. We came home."

"You've done more than your share, Carl. All of you. You were the Iron Brigade. Have you been to Sauk County?"

"We came right here, Colonel. We've got to talk to you."

James nodded. "This is all of you?"

The men looked at each other. "This is the Baraboo Guards, Colonel," Carl said. "Us and you. Captain Barks, we buried him just before we left the army. That would be Thursday, last. He got all shot to hell at Cold Harbor."

"John Barks was a good man," James said. "I saw his wife in Baraboo three weeks ago. She prays for him. She won't have heard. They haven't published the casualty lists from Cold Harbor."

"I'll see her when I get to Baraboo in the morning," Ethan said. "I'll tell her."

"He tried not to die," Carl said bitterly. "He tried so hard to hang on to life but he was just all shot to hell."

Mary came into the library carrying a tray of bottles, a pitcher of water, crystal glasses.

"Thank you," James said. "Put that on the desk, Mary. I'll pour for my friends."

James took a bottle in his right hand and pulled its cork with his teeth, smiling an apology and nodding at this missing left arm. He poured into the grimy tin cups the men held out to him. Each raised his cup to James and drank.

James refilled. "Now," he said, settling into the judge's leather chair behind the large desk. "Tell me."

Carl glanced at the others.

Ethan nodded.

"Murphy's dead, Colonel Peck," the tavern keeper said.

James shook his head slowly. "I find that so hard to believe," he said, remembering the tough little man. "I guess I didn't think the rebel had been born or the bullet molded that could take Murphy from us."

"No Johnny Reb shot Murphy!" Olaf blurted. "Our own men did it!"

James stared in disbelief at the farmhand.

"Firing squad," Carl confirmed.

"My God! What happened?"

The tavern keeper wiped his face with a dirty hand, shaking his bald head. "It was June Third. That was twelve days ago. We were in the lines in front of Cold Harbor. That's where Captain Barks got shot. We'd been trying to take the rebel earthworks for days. We'd been marching and fighting for a month. Colonel, that General Grant is a butcher! He threw us against them day after day after day. We had losses that made Antietam and Gettysburg look pale. Outfits were all disorganized and confused. We were made part of the Fifth Corps under General Warren. They did away with the old First Corps. There weren't enough men left to call it a corps. We didn't know the men we were fighting with. The Second Wisconsin was just a handful mixed in with others. We went in before dawn that day. Murphy was with us when we set off. You know how we used to stick together like he taught us? To take care of each other?"

James nodded.

"We lost him, Colonel," Carl confessed. "It was mixed up and confused. We went looking for him when the fighting died down. Like we did after Antietam, remember? We couldn't find him. Some fucking . . . oh, hell, Colonel, I shouldn't talk like that in your home!"

"It's all right, Carl," James said. "Go on."

"Well, like I was saying, some fucking Pennsylvania Bucktail officer came along and found Murphy wandering around on the field. He sent him back to the provosts under guard. The provost ran charges of cowardice against Murphy. They put him in the stockade at Belle Plain. They court martialed him. They shot him."

"Like that?" James asked, aghast.

"We talked to the provosts," Carl went on. "Those new regiments, Colonel, they're all conscripts and bounty jumpers and shirkers. All of them.

There were desertions like we never saw before. Skulkers. New men were sent into battle on the points of the bayonets of veteran regiments marching behind them. The provosts told us General Grant had drawn a line and wanted deserters and skulkers shot to set an example for the new men. They told us Murphy was as good as dead when those Bucktails turned him over to them on the field at Cold Harbor."

"My God," James groaned, wiping his face with his one hand. "Couldn't you have gotten word to me? I might have been able to do something. I promised Murphy I'd come if he needed me."

"You couldn't have done anything, Colonel," Ethan told him. "It happened fast. Just a matter of days. We tried to break him out of the stockade at Belle Plain."

"And damned near got yourselves killed doing it!" Carl accused.

The merchant shrugged. "He'd have tried for one of us."

"Ethan talked to that Bucktail officer who sent Murphy in," Carl went on. "The officer testified at Murphy's court martial that he never arrested Murphy," the merchant explained. "He said he sent him back to get him out of the way of a Confederate counter-attack. He wasn't a bad man, that Bucktail. It didn't do any good. They wanted men shot."

James covered his face with his hand.

"There was an awful lot of skulking and deserting going on," Gus added.

James rubbed the stump of his left arm. It itched severely.

"Tell him the rest of it," Ethan said.

The tavern keeper hesitated.

"Carl?" James asked.

"There were desertions and skulking in the Wisconsin regiments, Colonel Peck. Even in the veteran regiments. The governor of Wisconsin sent an officer from Madison to prosecute the state boys. I guess the governor wanted the state to look good, going after its own."

"I find it hard to imagine Wisconsin prosecuting its own men," James objected.

"Like I told you, Colonel, it was pretty bad toward the end of our time."

"The officer the governor sent to prosecute Wisconsin men," Ethan interjected, "was Nathaniel Bachmann."

"Bachmann!" James cried. "He deserted himself! He ran away from us at Bull Run!"

"He prosecuted Murphy and got him shot by a Federal firing squad," the merchant stated.

James sat back in the judge's leather chair. He'd heard in Madison that Bachmann had been sent to the Army of the Potomac as an emissary for the governor. He hadn't bothered to find out what Bachmann's specific orders were. He thought he'd seen the last of Bachmann when he and Lucille married. "Did any of you see Murphy before . . ."

"I did," Carl spoke.

"How was he?"

"He was strange, Colonel. Something was missing from inside. Do you know what I mean? It was like something had gone out of him. He smiled when he saw me but he didn't say anything. He just shook my hand. That was all. He hummed that doodle-dum-dee-day stuff. They made us form and watch it. We tried not to but they made us. He sat on his coffin puffing his old pipe with the firing squad standing so close they had to aim down at him. He didn't seem to understand they were going to kill him. It was over quick."

James shuddered.

"He wasn't a strong man," Ethan said. "We always thought he was but he wasn't. He was just like us. Remember, Gus, that night on the Potomac when it rained so hard? We came in from picket duty on the river and the fire was out. His cookery was all blown away by the wind. He talked about the war going on and on. He wept that night. I never knew him to weep any other time."

"John Barks told me about the first day at Gettysburg," the tavern keeper added. "John told him he could go, he could run away from it. Murphy told John he'd no place to go but back with his mates on the line. We were all he had."

"One week and he'd have been out of it," Olaf said. "One damned week!"

"Gentlemen," Lucille said, opening the library door, timing her entrance. "Dinner is ready. I'll have two Baraboo Guards escort me to the dining room. First Sergeant Elsasser, my right arm. Private Evans, my left. Shall we?"

64

James insisted the four veterans stay the night. They'd take the Madison-Baraboo stage in the morning. Ethan asked James for some firewood and the men built a fire in the garden. They'd be comfortable around a fire on the ground. They were uncomfortable in the house, unused to chairs, to walls, to carpets, to china place settings. They hadn't slept in a house or been in a decent bed since mustering in Baraboo three years before.

James brought whiskey and joined them, sitting on a wooden lawn chair.

"Murphy," Gus toasted with his tin cup. "He was a man."

"Weren't they all?" James asked, standing to give Lucille his chair as she joined them.

"Murphy was different," Ethan said softly.

"He never volunteered, like us," Carl added. "He rode to war chained to the brace of a wagon box."

Olaf's thoughts were only partially on Murphy. Hans too had been killed by Nathaniel Bachmann.

James thought of the sheriff of Sauk County who'd brought the little man along with the Baraboo Guards.

"Murphy was murdered," Carl insisted.

"No, Carl," James said, shaking his head. "He was killed by the war. He died no differently than those men who fell to gunfire or fever or accident. War is killing, he once told me, nothing more, nothing less. War and the men who make war killed Murphy. Just as war and the men who make war killed the Baraboo Guards."

"Let's not get into a dirge," Ethan suggested. "Like he'd say, it'll bring on a haunt."

James raised his glass in a silent toast.

The four raised their tin cups.

They drank in silence, the five survivors of the hundred volunteers who had mustered in Baraboo in May, 1861.

James stood beside Lucille's chair and watched them shake out their blankets and curl up on the earth. In minutes, the four veterans slept.

James gazed into the fire. He felt close to the men at his feet, to the men from Sauk County who lay buried at Bull Run, at Groveton, at South Mountain and Antietam, at Fredericksburg and Chancellorsville and Gettysburg, at Cold Harbor. He could almost see their faces in the flames of the fire. Two faces especially, that of the harsh sheriff and that of the wily Irishman, seemed to gaze back at him.

Why, he wondered, had they gone to war? Why, once they learned what war was, had they stayed? Why had they marched and suffered and fought and sickened and died as they had?

Why had he?

They'd believed in their cause, the preservation of the Federal Union, but more, they'd believed in themselves and in their comrades, in the Baraboo Guards. The Confederates had believed in their cause or had been carried forward in its name but they, too, had believed in themselves and in their comrades—Attwater's Battalion, Barfus' Battalion, the fierce Stonewall Brigade.

Events had carried them along to places where they found themselves involved in the daily living of the life of the soldier, be that marching in the rain or sleeping on the ground or burying rotting corpses or standing together on the line and fighting for their lives. They'd signed on for their own reasons whether they understood them at the time or not. They'd paid the price of being where events took them when the cost came due. He recalled his answer when the Confederate surgeon at Gettysburg asked him why he stood and fought and gave his arm at Gettysburg. James had answered he'd done it because he was there. The war had taken him there.

Even as James watched the men sleeping at his feet in the quiet and safety of his garden in Madison, far to the south armies still battled and men still died.

The war would end some day. As Murphy said, the living would go on for those who remained.

Lucille touched his right arm. He finished his drink and handed the glass to his wife.

He drew himself to attention and raised his right hand to his eyebrow. "Men of the Baraboo Guards," he whispered, "I salute you."

The End

THE BARABOO GUARDS—AFTERWARDS.

NATHANIEL BACHMANN continued on the staff of Wisconsin's gover-nor. On May 1, 1866, five years to the day after he mustered the Baraboo Guards, he was shot to death with a .58 caliber Springfield army musket. His killer was never found. Madison police determined from the powder burns that his assailant had stood in front of Nathaniel Bachmann, close enough for the former army officer to recognize whom it was that killed him.

AMOS AUGUSTUS GAARD, JR. returned to Baraboo, changed little by the war. On July 23, 1867, Gus was shot and killed by Angeline Asbaugh's brother in the woods north of the farm Gus called Asbaugh's Ash Pit. Angeline was with Gus at the time but did not testify against her brother.

ETHAN EVANS found himself a wealthy man on his return to Baraboo. Herman Priecz had been a faithful steward. Lily had not changed. Less than a year after his homecoming, Ethan left Baraboo quietly one night. He died as Private John Burns with Custer and the Seventh Cavalry on the Little Big Horn River in Montana Territory on June 25, 1876.

OLAF LARSON left Wisconsin and moved to Kansas shortly after Nathaniel Bachmann's death. He bought land there, farmed, married and sired thirteen children. He named his first son Hans after his brother who was killed at Bull Run. He named his second son Orland after the father of the good woman he took to wife. Olaf died, prosperous and fat, on Christmas Eve, 1893.

CARL ELSASSER went into business when the railroad came to Baraboo and by 1870 had thirty-one restaurants and taverns, known as the Diamond Houses, all along the line. The name came from the diamond emblem in the center of his old first sergeant's chevrons. Carl died in 1899, a wealthy and respected man.

JAMES PECK developed a prosperous law practice in Madison. He and Lucille travelled the world and, when not away, hosted weekly evenings at home until her death in 1886. James took an active role in the Grand Army of the Republic, the national organization of Federal veterans of the war. He developed an extensive correspondence with former officers from both sides, and eventually published his memoirs. He died on May 23, 1906, the last of the Baraboo Guards.

HISTORICAL NOTE.

There was no company of volunteers from Sauk County in the Second Wisconsin Regiment, although Sauk County did furnish Company A, the Sauk County Riflemen, to the Sixth Wisconsin Regiment. There were two separate Company K's in the Second Wisconsin during the course of the American Civil War, but neither of these companies was recruited in Sauk County.

The Baraboo Guards is based on the written records of the units and the men who served in the Second, Sixth, and Seventh Wisconsin, the Nineteenth Indiana, and the Twenty-fourth Michigan, the Black Hats of the Iron Brigade of the Federal Army of the Potomac.

ABOUT THE AUTHOR

John K. Driscoll, a U.S. Marine Corps veteran and a student of the Civil War since 1961, has marched and camped with the First Virginia (reenactment) Regiment and has fired the Springfield .58 caliber musket in competition. He lectures widely on Civil War topics. His latest book, a biography of Civil War General Justus McKinstry, was published in 2006.

www.ingramcontent.com/pod-product-compliance
Lightning Source LLC
Chambersburg PA
CBHW051141030726
47504CB00004B/982